I0599964

LILLIAN LYLE

AUTHOR

ISBN: 979-8-9926193-0-0, 979-8-9926193-1-7

AN OFF THE BENCH NOVEL

The False Start

LILLIAN LYLE

THE FALSE START

OFF THE BENCH
BOOK 1

LILLIAN LYLE

For DFW
I wouldn't be where I am today without the existence and support of this group. Cheers to quidditch sprints and ROD and the #ClawComeback.
Xoxo

PLAYLIST

Chapter One

LILA

K atie owes me big time.

I hop off the train, weaving through the crowd, dodging puddles on the crowded brown-line platform. I only agreed to go out after my best friend had begged, literally on her knees with big puppy dog eyes, to show me how important tonight was to her. She wouldn't say *why* it was so important that we go out; we're not even going anywhere special.

She asked to meet at our regular bar. We've been going there since grad school as a joke to meet guys, because nothing screams desperate like going to a sports bar and waiting for a man to hit on you. Somewhere along the way it became *our* spot, boys watching sports be damned.

Maybe she finally clinched that commercial job she was excited about. That would certainly be worth celebrating on a dreary Thursday night. I plaster a smile on my face as I round the corner that brings Cornside, my favorite bar, into view.

I spot Ray working the door and give him a small wave. He meets my smile with a wink, jerking his head at the door behind him.

"Thanks Ray," I say, the tension in my jaw loosening. Ray

always makes sure I get in an Uber on my way home and that I have a bottle of water for the ride. Beneath that black t-shirt and pounds of scary, tattoo-covered muscle, he's a big softie.

I step inside the bar, glancing around the dim interior, the bright TVs on the walls providing just enough light to see by, until I spot a familiar black bob sitting at the bar. As I weave my way over to Katie between the busy tables, my watch buzzes. My heart sinks as I read the message preview.

DENNIS

Babe, I'm sorry. . .

I sigh, the sour taste of disappointment crawling up my throat as I sit at the bar beside Katie and open the full message on my phone.

DENNIS

Babe, I'm sorry. You know how crazy this client is, I think I just need some space to focus on work right now. I think we should take some time apart. Just for a little while.

I roll my eyes. What kind of idiot do I have to be to think it would actually work out this time around?

"What's up?" Katie asks, slurping her already half-empty martini and throwing a pointed look to the phone clutched in my hand.

"Dennis said he needs *space* to focus on work," I spit out. "As if I don't know what it's like to have a stressful job."

"What're you drinking?" asks the bartender—a new guy I don't recognize—giving my pissed expression a wary look.

Katie jumps in. "G&T, Bombay, make it a double." I grimace at her. "On my tab, please." She ignores my objection, giving the bartender a grin as he sets the drink down onto the bar. She swivels in her stool to face me. "I don't get why you're still with him. You guys have been off and on since he moved to New York.

It's not like he's making any effort to move back. Do *you* want to leave Chicago?"

"Well definitely not to move there, ew." I hate New York. It's covered in trash with rats crawling in every subway station. No amount of Broadway shows or celebrity run-ins could make me want to leave Chicago. It doesn't matter how good the pizza is. "Besides if I ever left you, you'd probably drag me back."

Katie laughs before giving a sigh. "At least we could go to fashion week." She sets down her empty glass. "Well, since you clearly need cheering up, I have plans for us tonight."

A battle starts raging in my head, the angel and devil on my shoulders shouting at each other over the noise of the bar. On the one hand, there is absolutely nothing I'd rather do than forget that my boyfriend—*ex*-boyfriend—couldn't balance our relationship and his job, but it's Thursday, and being hungover at work is only getting harder as I get older.

"What kind of plans, Katie? It's a school night."

"The kind I knew you wouldn't agree to if I had told you ahead of time."

I groan, running through my current outfit situation, how I might turn it from corporate to club appropriate, which is clearly where we're headed if Katie's Cheshire grin is anything to go by.

"Katie, I'm not dressed—"

She shoves a bag at my chest. "Go change and drink this," she says, putting my mostly full gin and tonic into my hands. "I'll get you a refill."

I sigh. If I'm already here, I might as well have fun. I down my drink, shuddering slightly. The bartender is heavy handed tonight. I glare at Katie who smirks, popping the stuffed olive from her drink into her mouth. Giving up, I turn and stalk through the crowded bar toward the ladies' room at the back.

She can't possibly be serious.

I'm standing in the large stall, gaping at the outfit Katie picked. I'm no prude, but I'm also not twenty-one anymore, not by a long shot. Dresses like this are usually reserved for that short stretch of time when your adult metabolism hasn't yet caught up with your college drinking habits. I pull on the black bandage dress with a sigh, shaking my head at the four-inch red-bottoms she chose and trade out my mules. Walking up toward the mirror at the sink, I grab the small pink pouch from Katie's bag, finding everything needed to refresh my face after a long day. I quickly touch up my makeup in the mirror, giving my hair one last fluff before tossing my work clothes into the bag and marching out of the washroom, both more and less confident in my appearance than I was twenty minutes ago.

I carefully make my way back through the bar, stumbling only once in the clearly brand-new shoes. Katie's on the phone when I finally get back to the bar, but as promised, a fresh drink sits on the counter in front of my empty seat. I drop the bag onto Katie's lap and take a sip.

"Right, see you soon." She giggles. My eyebrows shoot up, understanding why I've been left in the dark about this evening's plans. Katie isn't one to giggle on the phone. She hangs up, and I stare at her until she relents.

"They're going to meet us there," she explains, answering my unspoken question as she opens her Uber app.

"Who is meeting us where?" I take an extra-large gulp of the fresh G&T, only barely suppressing another shudder. I silently apologize for judging thirty-year-olds so harshly at Carrie Underwood karaoke nights in middle school. It's not even whiskey, and I'm still struggling.

"I finally finished Theo's condo, so he invited us out to celebrate." Right, Theo McClane, star wide receiver for the Chicago Avalanche and childhood classmate of the one and only Katie Chen. "I accepted on both our behalves."

Katie went to an elite prep school in New York and graduated knowing several current household names, many of whom are all too happy to support her budding career as an interior designer.

She branched off from her mother's Los Angeles-based firm once we finished graduate school, wanting to focus on a different level of clientele. Theo is just the latest of many sports stars, B-list celebrities, and C-Suite executives Katie has persuaded into being a client.

It helps that she's actually good at her job. She specializes in luxury high rises, and with her background, she has access to many professional athletes and corporate executives who don't want to put down too many roots. She's constantly attending galas and games courtesy of her clients, sometimes bringing me along for the ride. I used to always jump at the chance, because who doesn't love free food and drinks with the excuse to dress up or enjoy a free game, but it turns out some of her clients are absolute assholes. Theo's one of the exceptions though. We've been out before a couple times with their other classmates from school, and he and Katie have stayed close, which means, by association, he's been brought into my own circle. Thankfully he's funny.

He's been on my mind a bit more than usual with our workplace fantasy football league, as he keeps putting up double digits every week. If only I'd actually managed to snag him in the draft.

"Uber's two minutes away." She hops down off her stool. "Finish that," she says, pointing at the half-full drink in my hand, "and let's go." She snatches up her bag, now full of my clothes, and leaves me to follow her out to the street after chugging a second drink in less than an hour.

The black Escalade pulls up in front of the bar, and Katie double checks the license plate before sliding in. I climb in after her as she pulls out her compact and lipstick to touch up her pout and clip a few pieces of hair back out of her face.

I lean my head back against the seat and stare out at the city as we creep through the traffic. The bustle of people moving between work and home brings the city to life amongst the lights sparkling from the skyscrapers downtown. My cheeks are buzzing, and I press my forehead against the cool window. I managed a late lunch at the office, but it's not holding up well against the gin. At least the idea of Dennis isn't quite so painful anymore. Though it hurts less and less each time we break up. I wish I could figure out if it's because I'm more confident we'll get back together or if I'm not letting myself care quite as deeply each time we inevitably make up.

She closes the compact with a snap that jolts me from my melancholy. Katie turns toward me, inspecting my face for the first time since using her makeup in the bathroom.

"Well don't you clean up nicely," Katie praises, making me roll my eyes. "No, I'm serious you came straight from work, and even just the change of clothes and some new lip color makes such a difference."

"Katie, it was your makeup. You put it in the bag."

"So? I didn't force you to use it."

I laugh, I may put up a fight, but she's never been wrong about fashion, and I've learned to trust her opinion. Once, in grad school, I wore a hot pink blazer against her advice to a networking event in an attempt to embody the goddess that is Elle Woods only to get the wrong kind of attention. Since then, I've listened to her suggestions, and they've yet to steer me wrong.

I grin at her. "Thanks, Katie."

"Anytime." She smirks, her mouth pulling into a true smile as the car slows. "Oh, look we're here," she squeals.

I peer out the tinted windows and groan. It's one of the new clubs in West Loop. I can hear the pulsing music from outside and try not to imagine the headache-inducing beat once you're inside. The line is wrapped around the building, disappearing down the block, and I blanche.

"Katie, I'm not waiting in line for a club, I'm not twenty-two anymore."

"Babes"—I roll my eyes. Katie's clearly been watching too

much *Love Island* again—"we don't have to wait in line." She flashes a gold pass on her phone. "I've got a golden ticket."

"This isn't the Wonka Factory," I mutter, fighting back a laugh. Katie ignores me, and I open the door of the Escalade. "Thank you," I call back to the driver and hop out.

I straighten my dress, trying to pull it down an extra inch or two. Katie is quite a bit shorter than me, and while I have an inkling she bought this dress for me and didn't find it randomly in her closet like she implied, Katie usually forgets to consider that I'm five-eight, the heels putting me at an even six feet tall.

Katie likes to joke that whenever she's meeting up with a guy, she'll make him stand next to me to see if he's lying about his height. Not that it actually matters when she's only five-foot-three, but according to Katie, "If a man can't be honest about his height, what else is he willing to lie about?" Words to live by for any woman honestly.

I walk past the line of early-twentysomethings, all dressed uncomfortably similar to my own club-wear and feel the frat boys eyeing my legs as Katie follows close behind me to the front door.

I stop awkwardly at the bouncer, and he stares at me, a question in his eyes. I clear my throat; I hate skipping the line. I grimace and turn to Katie expectantly.

She flashes the gold pass, and the bouncer raises his eyebrow. "ID?"

I laugh, the drinks I chugged at the bar starting to course through me. I haven't been ID'd in ages. The bouncer just looks at me, and I realize that he needs our names more than he needs our birth dates. Blushing, I quickly dig through my purse and pass over my license. He says something very quickly into his radio and hands our IDs back.

"One moment, ladies." He smiles at us as another man pulls back the curtain over the door.

"Right this way. I'll be taking you to our VIP suite," he says, turning and setting off into the dark club.

The "suite" is a large roped-off area set on a raised platform at the very back of the packed dance floor. One black couch surrounds a low table on three sides, but I can't make out the faces of those sitting on it.

Katie darts ahead toward the hunk of muscle standing at the bottom of the stairs. "Theo, darling! Thank you for having us!" she coos.

Theo McClane is good looking, and he knows it. He's tall, six-foot-three at least, but lithe. He was built to be quick but has large hands and broad shoulders. His wavy, dark-chestnut hair and the playful spark in his hazel-green eyes give his entire demeanor a "frat boy" look that makes me constantly question my own age. He's exactly what my type would've been a decade ago, before I learned what guys like that usually brought with those charming, good looks. Now I date for stability and a future. Consistency and dependability, because even if Dennis isn't Prince Charming, I at least know where I stand with him, and that's more important than the butterflies. It's something Katie doesn't understand. She's all about the passion. Attraction and magnetism, that's how Katie Chen will fall in love.

I finally reach the steps to the VIP area, when suddenly, a burly-looking middle-aged man knocks into me from where he's dancing with gusto. I can't catch my balance fast enough in the new shoes, and I'm going down. In a club. On a dancefloor.

This is where I die.

A pair of large hands catches my waist, steadying me and pulling me back up.

"Are you okay?" a deep, gravelly voice asks from behind me. How that idiot managed to knock me over and then catch me I'll never know. He should really watch where he's spastically dancing honestly.

I turn, ready to tell him as much when I realize his hands are still on my waist. My mind sharpens as my irritation grows. This creep can fuck right off and get his grubby hands off me, thank you very much. The words die in my throat as I'm met with not the gross old man, but a strong, clean-shaven jawline, my eyes traveling up and up—*God, how tall is this guy?*—until I meet a pair of grey eyes so piercing I can feel my soul cleave apart. The breath rushes out of me along with every single coherent thought I've ever possessed.

"Are you okay?" he repeats, finally letting go of my waist. I'm suddenly missing the weight of his hands when all I'm left with is the humid club air and my own balance. He's looking at me with concern and maybe a touch of alarm.

"Oh." I clear my throat, finding it extremely dry all of a sudden. "Yes, thank you." I smile at him.

"Well, shall we?"

"Shall we what?" I ask, confused.

"You were headed into the back? For McClane's party?" Now it's his turn to look confused.

"Oh, right, yeah, I didn't realize you were going too." I'm floundering. What is it about eyes that always throw me off my game? So what if he's hot? I see hot guys all the time, though normally not so close, and normally not grabbing my waist, but still. Maybe I just need to get laid. It's been, what, almost three months since Dennis and I actually spent the night together? I should really go visit. I make a mental note to ask him about scheduling a trip on our next call, before I remember that we just broke up.

The stranger, oblivious to the train wreck happening in my head, unhooks the velvet rope and gestures me forward.

"Lila! There you are," Katie calls from her seat on a leather sofa at the edge of the platform, a drink already half empty in her hand. "Oh and I see you've met Cal." I turn to the man, who nods back. A synapse fires somewhere in the recesses of my mind, and it connects. Cal, Theo's best friend from his and Katie's circle of friends from prep school. Katie's invited me along a few times when he was in town, but it always coincided with something at work. He's another football player, but for one of the New York football teams. The Upstate Cosmos, I think.

"Well at least I know the name of my savior now." I smirk at him regaining some semblance of cool. He shoots me a grin before making his way over to one of the small tables and pouring himself a whiskey.

"Come sit," Katie squeals, patting the seat next to her.

"I think I need to catch up," I say with a laugh, settling down in the empty seat. I pour myself a tequila shot from the bottle on the table and grab a lime. "Cheers." I down the liquor, savoring the burn this time and pop the lime into my mouth. I drop it, now juiceless, in the empty shot glass and laugh as Katie pours herself a drink.

"Theo, show Lila the photos of your place," Katie orders, as he sits down on her other side.

I wave her off, leaning across her to talk to Theo directly. "How've you been? I haven't seen much of you since the season started."

"Better now that I have my condo redone. I started showering exclusively in the locker room toward the end there. Of course, without an offer from my favorite blonde, I had no choice." He shoots me a wink.

I roll my eyes, but can't help the way my face heats, though it might be more the tequila than the man.

"Oh, don't bother, Theo, we're trying to cheer Lila up tonight and you'll only end up annoying her somehow." Katie smacks his arm.

Theo gives her a mock pout he's able to hold for all of three seconds before bursting into laughter. "Fair point. But why are we trying to cheer you up tonight?"

Katie jumps in before I have the chance to respond. "She and Mr. Finance Vest just broke up."

"We'll probably get back together, Katie just doesn't like Dennis much. It's not a big deal," I say with a shrug.

"Aww, Kathy, why don't you like him? I'm sure if Princess here likes him, he can't be all bad." Theo lets out a bark of a laugh, drawing Cal's gaze.

"First of all," Katie starts, "don't call me Kathy. Second, your *princess* over there has terrible taste in men, so yes, he one hundred percent can be that bad. Third, Dennis lives in New York and frequently finds reasons to not be around or available. Fourth, they break up every other month—"

"It is *not* every other month." I ignore the tugging memory of an eerily similar conversation earlier this summer at Theo's rooftop pool. Theo's even met Dennis once, demanding to know what I saw in him the moment Dennis excused himself to the restroom. At this point, each time we hit a rough patch, it's a hot topic of conversation for the first ten minutes before something new and shiny comes along.

"—Lila pretends she's fine with it because it's easier than admitting she's alone and likes it that way." She continues like I haven't spoken.

"I do not—" I break off as Cal joins our group, leaning against the wall next to me.

"What's this now? It must be interesting if you're screaming across the club." He smirks down at me. God, he's hot. It's not cheating to think that right? No, definitely not cheating. And even if it was, we're broken up. I'm just appreciating art, in a way. Cal is art. He's dressed casually, in dark jeans tailored perfectly to his broad thighs, hugging his hips as he leans against the wall. The grey of the shirt brings out the silver of his eyes, making them flash in the pulsing lights of the club.

Theo and Cal are momentarily distracted by a commotion at the DJ table, and I take the time to continue admiring his physique.

"Ow!" I yelp, Katie's elbow leaving a bruise against my ribs.

"You're drooling," she whispers, smirking. I narrow my eyes at her.

Cal refocuses his attention back to me, and I answer his original question. "Nothing, Katie's just on a mission to get me to appreciate my own happiness as much as her life coach thinks I should."

Katie cackles, "Sharon hasn't been wrong yet, you'd do well to follow her advice."

Theo scoffs, but Cal just raises an eyebrow, "Well, by all means, what's first on the list?"

I let out a dignified sniff. "I'd rather not waste my time on advice from someone who doesn't even have a PhD, I'd rather just get another drink." I stand, brushing by him with a touch more contact than strictly necessary. I pour another shot, looking up at Cal to find his intense gaze locked on me. I smirk at him, holding his gaze while I take the shot, sucking the lime and letting my cheeks hollow. He swallows visibly, his eyes a swirling dark storm, and I sever the eye contact, allowing myself a small bit of satisfaction.

I turn to my best friend. "Let's dance."

Chapter Two

CAL

She walks away, disappearing into the crowded dance floor, Katie trailing after her. My body burns where she brushed past me. Theo looks at me with one eyebrow raised, a shit-eating grin splitting his face. I don't smile at him. She's hot, sure, and clearly likes to play, but there's something else I can't put my finger on.

Maybe it's that she's exactly my type, with her long, honey blonde hair and big brown eyes, or it's the way she drew and kept my attention the entire time I've been in the same room with her. It was like she was the sun and I, a mere mortal, couldn't help but be drawn into her orbit. If Theo would've told me all of that about his new friend Lila Summers, I might have made more of an effort to visit over the last few years.

And she walked away. Something in my chest hums in approval, both excited for the challenge and relieved she isn't just another jersey chaser.

"Hey, Basset. Good game last weekend," a sandy-haired man says to me, punching me lightly in the arm.

"Thanks, man," I say with a nod.

"I know how tough it can be getting traded mid-season, but

you kept up, which is more than I can say for myself." He laughs wistfully, shaking his head.

Who is this guy? Not a teammate, I can tell that much. He's a good bit shorter than I am and has a build like Theo. His eyes give me pause though. I could swear I've seen them before, an electric blue like that would be hard to forget.

"Aaron Byron. I'm not sure we've officially met." The name clicks into place in my mind as I shake his outstretched hand. Aaron Byron, third baseman for the Hail, Chicago's professional baseball team, traded mid-season last year from New York for a couple draft picks.

"I'm surprised we've never crossed paths in New York," I say. He shrugs, unbothered, and pours himself a drink from the bottles on the table, holding it up in offering.

I take the whiskey bottle and pour a healthy measure into a fresh glass for myself. "So, how have you been adjusting to the city so far?"

"It's not bad," he says. "I had a bit of a rough season last year, so I didn't go out much, but this one's been looking up, so it's been good. You know how it goes."

I did at that. When you were winning, when you had good stats, the city was your oyster. When you weren't, well, it was better to be almost anywhere else.

I open my mouth to agree, when a hurricane of a person bursts into the VIP area once more.

Katie Chen walks right up to the table, pouring herself a drink from the bottle of vodka before adding a splash of soda water.

"Having fun out there?" Theo asks her with a wink. She gives him a sly smile in return.

"Lila needs a drink. Cal, why don't you bring it to her? I want to sit down for a minute."

"Uh." I pause. "Okay, what does she want?"

"She's easy. Just surprise her," Katie responds. I narrow my eyes at her. Lila may be a lot of things, but easy didn't strike me as being at the top of that list.

She meets my gaze with a bored expression, and I sigh, mixing together vodka and cranberry juice, because what girl doesn't like a vodka cran? Barney Stinson was right on that at least.

Hands full with both drinks, I look out at the dance floor. "Where is she?" I ask Katie.

She points to a lone woman dancing in a red spotlight in the center of the club. My mouth goes slightly dry as her body moves to the beat of the song.

"Get out there, big boy. She's waiting." Theo gives me a small shove, and Aaron laughs. I shoot him a glare but follow his irritating instructions, weaving through the dance floor toward her, moving slowly with the crowd of drunk dancers.

She comes into view, and I almost turn back. She's found a partner to dance with. He's tall, almost as tall as I am, and holding her close, his hands exploring her body in a way that should be considered indecent in public. I watch for a moment longer, just to convince myself she's alright when I see her pull away, creating some distance between their bodies.

The man pulls her back toward him as his hands move up to brush her breasts, his face smug knowing he has the upper hand and she's alone, and I'm contemplating which drink to drop so I can hit him right in his smug face.

Mine obviously.

I'm almost there, when she wrenches out of his grasp and lurches forward straight into my chest.

My hands are still full, so I can't reach out and catch her, but my body, conditioned to take hits from people bigger and moving faster than she is, weathers the blow, even as it knocks the breath from my lungs.

I grunt at the impact as she tangles her hands in my shirt to pull herself up and find her footing. My chest warms where she touches me, her fingers lingering over my pectorals. I try to not be too obvious and flex slightly, telling myself it will help stabilize us both, even as I note she's clearly fine and standing on her own two feet. I glance around, looking for the man, but he's slipped into the throng of people around us.

I grasp for something to say as I stare down at her. Remembering the extra drink in my hand, I hold it up. "Katie asked me to bring you this."

She looks at the drink with suspicion. "What is it?"

"Vodka cran." I shrug. "Seemed like a safe bet."

She hesitates, and I wonder if she doesn't like cranberry juice. Her eyes flit around the floor, and I realize with horror why she's nervous.

"Here," I say and take a sip of the drink, "not drugged, I promise." I wink, trying to dissolve the strange tension that's formed.

She laughs and takes the drink. "Thanks."

"Are you okay? That looked uhm—"

"Oh, yeah. I'm fine. Just another washed up wannabe who thinks he's God's gift to women." She shrugs, and I'm at a complete loss of what to say to that absolute blasé response.

We stand somewhat awkwardly in the middle of the crowd, people dancing around us as we sip our drinks in silence. I have a hard time not watching her mouth as it closes around the lip of the glass.

I'm just about to suggest we head back to the table with the others when an old school song starts, and Lila's face lights up with the power of a thousand suns.

"I *love* this song," she shouts over the music. I'm still trying to figure out what song this could possibly be when she giggles, tossing back the rest of her drink, handing the empty glass back to me and starts to sway with renewed vigor.

It clicks when the crowd starts chanting along. *Sweet Caroline*.

"So good! So good! So good!" Lila shouts with the crowd

around us. I'm standing there like an idiot watching her dance, but she looks so happy I can't stop staring.

The music shifts back into a more electronic beat, and Lila grabs my shoulder. "Dance with me."

Her intense gaze is locked on my face, her hand still on my shoulder as I survey her, but one look in her eyes and I'm draining the last drops of whiskey left in my glass. Setting both empty cups on a nearby high-top, I give her one last moment to take it back. She doesn't lower her gaze, and I have my answer. I grab her hips, spinning her back against me just as she was minutes ago with another man. The competitive drive in me pushing me to make it good enough so that she forgets she was dancing with anyone else tonight.

We dance for hours or only minutes. Time is meaningless when her body is pressed against mine like this. I hold her to me, one hand wrapped around her waist, and I can feel every roll of her hips from both sides.

She rests her head back against my shoulder, and I slide my free hand up her side wanting to cup her face, but it's a mistake. My thumb scrapes against her pulse point and she shudders against me, her hand reaching up to run through my hair, pulling my face toward her neck. I can't help but groan, my hand coming to rest along her collarbone, much too close to where I want it to be as my body heats. My blood rushes south, and I quickly step around her as the song transitions, bringing us face to face so she doesn't feel what she just did to me.

I can't help but touch her as we dance, her eyes closed in ecstasy as I run my hands over the sides of her torso, skimming close to her tits but no further. She allows it, and I take no additional liberties but make small circles over her ribs with my thumbs as I grip her waist.

She finally opens her eyes and meets my gaze, and it takes my breath away. Her eyes are heady, pupils dark with want, her breath sharp as her eyes flit down to my mouth and back up. Fuck, does she want me to kiss her?

Do I want to kiss her?

I think I want to do a lot more than kiss her.

The song changes again and *Get Low* comes on. Great, exactly what I need, a song about grinding while I'm trying not to come in my pants.

Lila doesn't care about my self-control, the heady look disappearing from her eyes and a smirk playing upon her lips as she drops into a crouch in front of me, her face level with my dick.

Fuck.

She looks up at me, and all I can picture is that mouth doing something else and frantically try to think of something else.

She drags her hands up my thighs, so close to where I need her to touch, her nails scraping against my torso as she rises back up to standing. She's closer than before, her arms coming up to my shoulders and her hands tugging on the hair on the back of my neck.

I can't help it. I grasp her hips, pulling her flush against me as I slide my leg between hers. Some part of me knows I can't take her right now, even if we find a bathroom or a hallway. But she can ride my thigh as we dance. She can know how good I could make her feel if she'll let me.

She grinds down, and I press my forehead to hers as the song ends.

She's staring at my mouth, and I lean in.

The lights flicker on, and we break apart, both breathing heavily. She glances at her watch and blanches. I check my own. 1:45 am. We're closing down the club. Thank God we don't have morning practice tomorrow.

"Come on, let's get you home," I say, taking her hand and guiding her through the throngs of people headed toward the door. We're swimming upstream back to VIP, and it takes a few minutes, but she doesn't let go of my hand.

Theo looks pointedly at our entwined fingers as we approach, and I drop it once we're clear of the masses and roll my eyes at him.

"Cal, why don't you and Lila share an Uber? You only live a few blocks from each other," Katie coos from her perch on the leather couch. Lila shoots her a glare.

"Err, sure," I mutter. "If you're okay with that?"

She shrugs, which I take as a good sign.

"Right then." I stand there awkwardly with my phone. "What's your address?"

She yawns spectacularly but takes my phone, putting it in the app before handing it back. "Oh, Katie's right. You're only just down the street from me." I hold out my hand, an offer, and she takes it with a mere second of hesitation and lets me lead her back through the crowd to the street to wait for the car.

After only a few minutes, passed in silence, the black Lexus pulls up. I check the plates quickly before opening the door for her. I've only just slid in beside her and shut the door when her head rolls forward onto my shoulder.

"Are you okay?"

She nods. "Just tired," she says with a yawn.

"You both good?" asks the driver, a sharp look in his eyes.

"Yeah, we're fine. She's good." I meet his gaze with one of my own and lift my arm along the back of the seat, letting Lila tuck herself into my side.

She falls asleep within seconds, and I'm left with the rest of the drive to watch her as she sleeps, to count the small breaths she takes and the little noises she makes.

The driver pulls over, and I shake her gently awake.

"Lila, I think this is you." Her eyes snap open, but she blinks slowly as if she can't focus. "Do you need help getting up to your apartment?"

"No, I'm fine." She is most definitely not fine, but I'm not going to force my way into her building.

She must read the hesitation on my face, because she opens the door and hops out onto the street.

"Really, I'm fine. Thanks for the ride, and good to meet you, Cal." She gives a small wave and shuts the door, walking up to her building, her hips swaying enticingly and entirely at odds with her assurances that she didn't need me to accompany her to her apartment.

She walks into her building, disappearing around a corner in the lobby, and will myself to relax. I haven't danced like that with someone in years, since before I was drafted.

A throat clears from the front seat. "Where to next, sir?" the driver asks expectantly.

"Corner of Randolph is fine. Thanks."

The car drives a few blocks down the road and stops outside of my new home. A buddy in Boston recommended it when I got traded. The security is tight and the amenities top notch with the well-equipped gym, lap pool, and on-site grocery store. I could've done a lot worse. I fish out a twenty from my wallet and drop it on the passenger seat as I get out of the car.

"Thanks for the ride." The driver nods, and I head inside.

Charles is stationed at the front desk and nods to me. I like Charles. He's quiet, never prying into my life or even the team, but always pleasant to the residents. To outsiders, he never takes any shit. No one's gotten past Charles unless I invited them personally. I wave to him before scanning my key fob at the double doors and heading through to the elevators. I punch the top button.

I bought the apartment three days after being traded. I couldn't stand the hotel any longer, and even if it took a decent chunk out of my inheritance, it was worth it for the peace and quiet. Chicago is already so much better than the East Coast, quiet in more ways than one. Away from my father's thumb and the stuffy relatives who visited for a chance at the "American Experience" in New York City.

It always surprises people when they find out I'm from England since I've lost most of my accent, but the majority of my family still lives there. My father brought me to the States with him when I was in primary school, and he opened a US branch of his consulting firm in New York, which is where I'd undoubtedly be working if I hadn't gotten drafted by the Cosmos.

Ding!

The elevator slides open to reveal my home. I drop my keys and wallet into the bowl on the side table in the hall and head straight toward my master bath. The shower set to scalding, I step in, hissing at the sting of the water against my skin as it turns from pale to pink in the steam.

The water flows over my head and shoulders, and I take a few deep breaths, doing everything I can to avoid thinking of Lila Summers, how she slid up my body as we danced at the club. My breathing turns ragged, and I grip the marble shower wall with my left hand as my right fists around my cock.

I groan, rock hard already, and give into the fantasies running wild in my head. How she felt pressed against my thigh, how she'd look riding it into oblivion, her body pressed against mine, my hand closing around her throat. I quicken the thrusts into my hand, my breathing hard, even as my mind wanders to that Uber ride and how she felt tucked into me, how she leaned in and slept on my shoulder, trusting me to make sure she got home safe.

I cry out as I finish and rinse off, turning the water to cold. God, did I really just finish to the thought of half-cuddling with a girl I just met? Why does it matter so much that she got home safe? It's more than I feel when I get Katie home safely, just a chivalrous good deed. What is wrong with me? Maybe it's just been a while. Tori hasn't been over for at least a week, maybe two.

I step out of the now frigid shower and wrap a towel around my waist, heading to my bedroom. I pull on a pair of grey joggers and grab my phone from the pocket of the jeans I tossed to the ground earlier. It must be some new record. I haven't checked it once since I got to the club, well since *she* got to the club, except to order our ride home. I scroll through the notifications, disregarding the CNN updates and other notices, and see one missed call from my mother—I'll call her in the morning—and three texts from Tori.

TORI

Hey, how've you been?

I have a show coming up next week. You game?

U up?

I checked the time stamp. The last text was only sent 15 minutes ago. I sigh and ignore it. I don't need her tonight, even if it'd be more fulfilling than just my own hand. I like Tori, and we have an arrangement that works well for both of us: a relationship only in the most basic sense but nothing serious and nothing even remotely official. Just casual, mutually beneficial sex and a date to any events we need to attend. It doesn't hurt to have a popular model on my arm, and she certainly never complains about how I look in a suit.

Staring at my phone, I realize I don't have *her* number. I never asked for it, or even implied I'd wanted it. She'd definitely mentioned a guy though. A boyfriend? An ex? Someone. I snort, tossing my phone onto the charger by the bed and lay back. If that girl—no, *woman*—was mine, there's no way in hell she'd be grinding on other men the way she'd danced with me tonight. If she wanted to dance, I'd make myself available to dance with her, but she wouldn't be grinding on strangers.

I roll over, trying not to dwell on that line of thought and pull the comforter over myself, falling asleep quickly, only to be plagued with dreams of challenging brown eyes and high heels wrapped around my head.

I wake with a start to the blaring of my alarm, my head already pounding to the beat of the incessant beeping. I groan. I'm never drinking on a weeknight again. No more Thursday drinks, no more happy hours, I swear. I scroll through my phone, checking my Outlook calendar, and my breathing eases slightly. At least I don't have any client meetings today.

I make my way on shaky legs to the bathroom and stare at myself in the mirror, my eyeliner smudged down my cheek, hair limp and matted, and wince. I forgot to take my makeup off last night. My mom keeps warning me about wrinkles now that I'm in my thirties, and here I am, sleeping in a full face of makeup. I grab a cotton round with a sigh and dump micellar water on it, scrubbing at my eyes and savoring how the pressure offsets the pounding inside my head.

Face now clean, or at least makeup free, I turn on the shower, running it colder than usual, and step in, hoping the temperature will sooth my hangover and wake me up. I wash quickly, the cold water doing nothing to alleviate my oncoming migraine, and exit the shower without washing my hair. Dry shampoo is going to have to do today. I'm already dreaming about coming home and getting back into bed.

Thankfully, it's Friday, and with no big meetings, I can dress a bit more casual. I throw on dark jeans and a blouse, adding a blazer since the fall weather calls for a second layer.

Shit, I'm already almost twenty minutes late and have no makeup on and no plan for caffeine.

I text Sadie, my coworker-turned-friend.

> Hey, running late, cover for me pls!

SADIE
> You got it!

I swipe on some mascara then grab a clip for my hair before running to the elevator. I open my Starbucks app, adding an extra shot to my iced latte and grab one for Sadie as a thank you, clipping my hair up as I walk through the lobby.

The walk to Starbucks is thankfully on the way to the office and only down the block, but I open my email anyway, scrolling through as a pit of dread settles into my stomach. Email after email, all urgent, pop up. Last night around eight, an oil rig off the Texas coast exploded—well, a small part of it. One of my bigger clients, C&C Gaming, sent twelve emails complaining about lead times and price increases on the oil needed for their plastics. So much for a quiet Friday to recover.

I'm typing out a quick ping to my assistant when I reach Starbucks. I scan the coffee bar for my order, but my eyes catch on a shock of blonde hair.

My mind is assaulted with memories from the previous night, of running my hands through hair like that, molten grey eyes filling my field of vision as they drew closer.

Oh God.

I'd forgotten the dancing.

I danced on him like he was a pole. And I just broke up with my fucking boyfriend, better yet he just broke up with me. What the hell is wrong with me?

I'd used the excuse before that the best way to get over a man was to get under another one, and it never once helped me feel better or get over anyone.

I think back to the text from Dennis last night. He dumped me. There's no other way to spin it. And because he was stressed at work. I never even responded to his message. Honestly, as far as he knows, I could be in prison, or dead. Not even a follow-up text this morning. My stomach twists uncomfortably as I remember the fights we'd have following a breakup. The radio silence is a nice change even as I feel the reality of the situation sink in, our breakup feeling more like a breakup and less like a break. I can't help but feel like it's because I didn't call him to talk afterwards. A tiny voice that sounds suspiciously like Katie scolds me for my line of thinking.

I have absolutely nothing to be ashamed about. I can dance with whoever I want. I think there's a song about that somewhere. I can dance if I want to? I make a mental note to look it up later as that line plays through my head on repeat.

"Ma'am?" A voice jolts me from my mental ramblings, and I realize with horror it's the blonde barista staring at me, a concerned look on his face.

"Sorry, yes?"

"Did you have an order?"

"Oh yes, please, for Lila."

He hands me the drinks with slight hesitation.

"Thanks," I call, a bit to brightly as I nearly run for the door, desperate to get out of whatever emotional spiral I've fallen into.

I shake my head to clear it as I walk through the tall, skyscraper lobby where the consulting company I work for houses its Midwest division. Mentally I start making my daily to-do list.

"Lila!" Sadie shoots me a smile, and waves as soon as I step out of the elevator bank.

I grin at her, setting the extra coffee on her desk before heading into my office.

Kevin pokes his head in the moment I sit down. He's a good assistant, if a bit overeager at times.

"Lila, James wants you in his office before the staff meeting," he announces, and I groan. James, one of the senior executives, only requests me if something is about to ruin my day.

"Alright, I'll be there." He nods, pulling away before he pops his head back in.

"By the way," he grimaces, and I brace myself. "Colton will also be there." He closes the door behind him as if scared of the explosion.

"Fuck."

Colton Varga is the world's biggest idiot. Even I can't claim that title after last night, it's that secure in his name. His daddy owns some hockey team in Toronto, and for whatever reason, that gives him the right to walk around Chicago like he owns it. I can't understand where he gets the balls, but boy, I'd love to kick them some day.

I glance at the wall clock. Definitely not enough time to get grounded before walking into that meeting.

◉ ◉ ◉

The explosion was bad. That's the first thing made clear once I walk into James's office. While no casualties, the rig is out of commission for at least six months, which means a delay for the entire supply chain, driving up cost across the board.

James drones on and on about the client and their retainer being crucial for my portfolio. As if I don't know that. As if I didn't spend every minute at my desk this morning researching other suppliers and sending follow-up emails to reassure their

Chief Operating Officer that we had it under control. That *I* had it under control.

"So that's why I brought in Colton," James says, and I blink at him.

"I'm sorry?"

"He works with a few clients in oil and gas. It's a perfect fit for him to join you and tackle this issue."

Colton is smirking at me from his chair next to mine.

"C&C Gaming is my client, I have it under control. They trust me." I try not to plead, to keep up the tough girl act and ignore my pounding head and the inadequacy that washes over me as an incompetent man-child gets assigned to save my client.

"No one is disputing that Lila," James starts.

"I don't want your clients. James brought me in to help fix the supply shortage," Colton says, speaking for the first time. I fight the urge to scowl at him.

"If you both work together, I'm confident you can come up with an agreement between your clients that is mutually beneficial to both of them and to us." James gives us both a pointed look. Right, got it. Don't lose the clients and get a double cut of the agreement.

"Fine, yes, I appreciate any help you can offer," I grind out.

The grin on Colton's face makes my blood heat.

"Great!" James claps his hands together. "I'll leave you to it, but I'd like a weekly status update." I nod and gather my things, when he clears his throat. "I'm sure you've both heard the rumors, but we're launching a new division of the firm, focused solely on smaller companies and start-ups. The managing partners haven't identified someone to lead it yet, but you both would be eligible to make partner if your work stays consistent."

I fight to keep a straight face even though I'm dancing around the office in my mind. I've wanted to make partner since I started working in consulting. "I won't let you down, James."

He nods and waves toward the door, a silent dismissal.

I'm heading back to my own office when I feel a presence behind me.

"What?" I hiss, whirling to face him.

"Oh nothing," Colton says innocently. "I just thought you'd want to talk strategy, but if you're in too much of a hurry with something else, I won't bother."

"You know I could've handled it. Why? Do you want my clients? Or just to make me look bad?"

I know I should watch what I say, but my filter is gone today. I need to go home and eat something with carbs and take a nap. In that order. The loss of the Hathaway account last week still stings, and knowing that Colton plucked them from my competent hands with sweet promises and free hockey tickets is salt in the wound. At least if he won the account off of his own merit, I could find a way to forgive him, but—

He lets out a low whistle. "Damn, Summers, you're in a mood today. Was Target out of ill-fitting blazers or something?"

He turns away, strutting toward his own office as I'm left gaping after him. There's no fucking way he just said that. What an ass!

I stalk back to my office, slamming the door shut behind me and seethe behind my desk. My computer pings with a DM from Sadie.

SADIE

You okay?

Just Colton. I'm fine.

🙂 They have donuts upstairs if you want one.

I lock my computer and grab my phone. Yes, carbs would be good right now, especially sugary carbs. I stop by Sadie's desk on the way up.

"You wanna come?" She nods and joins me on the elevator ride.

"Do you want to hear the new demo we put together this weekend?" she asks.

"Of course." I nod enthusiastically. She plays the song until the elevator doors open.

"Sadie, that's so good," I gush. "I love your drum solo in the middle. It really shows off the work you've been putting in."

"Thanks." She blushes. "We actually booked a slot at Lollapalooza next summer."

"Sadie, that's amazing! I didn't realize they book so far out."

"All our networking must have worked out. I volunteered this year just to get a feel for the behind the scenes of it all, but on Sunday, I finally saw one of the producers, and he asked for the link to our demos." I grin, happy for her and so happy to be thinking about something positive for the first time today. "I guess he liked it because he called me last weekend and offered us a daytime slot on Friday!"

"That's seriously so cool. I'll start playing your songs on repeat so your streams increase."

"You're the best," she says, as we reach the break room. It's scattered with several half-empty boxes of Mighty Fine donuts.

I grab a powdered sugar one, not caring if it makes a huge mess on my dark jeans. I need comfort food. We head back down to our floor, making small talk about her current portfolio.

"Back to work I guess, but at least a sugar high will help." I grimace.

"You said it." She turns back to her desk, leaving me in my office.

● ● ●

The rest of the morning is uneventful, turning to afternoon sluggishly as only a Friday can. By the time 3:00 p.m. rolls around, I'm checked out and ready to be done. With only three more things on my to-do list, that's looking like a possibility sooner rather than later.

I check my phone out of habit and see several message notifications.

KATIE

How was the rest of your night ;)

That good?

Come on, they were fun though right? Would you want to hang out again? Theo finally gave in and promised to teach me about Hockey!

Okay if you don't respond by 2:30 I'm assuming you're down to hang out again 😄

Perfect I'm adding you to a group text.

I glance at the clock, 3:05 p.m. Damn, Kris Jenner might work hard, but she hasn't met Katie yet.

KATIE

Lila's down! Theo, when can you explain Hockey to me?

I snort. Katie decided a few weeks ago she was going to date a hockey player and has enlisted Theo who spent much of his childhood in the Upper Peninsula of Michigan surrounded by backyard ice rinks, where the kids are born with skates on their feet.

KATIE

Don't forget you promised.

THEO

We have practice today and a lift session, and a game Sunday, but Monday we just have film in the morning.

I look at the calendar. Miami is playing on Monday, and while I might have to let Colton help out with my client, I can damn well make sure I beat him at fantasy football this week.

I have a thing Monday, I'm out.

KATIE

No you don't. You're just going to be watching the game.

THEO

Game? As in football?

Yes Theo, girls can like football too.

I roll my eyes.

THEO

Perfect we can all watch it then.

Fine.

I switch my phone to silent and slip it in my bag. Whatever, I was going to watch the game anyway, Katie's right. Maybe watching with a pro player will help my points this week; I need all the good juju I can get right now.

I finish up my to-do list, grateful it hasn't spontaneously multiplied in the last hour, and by four, I'm walking home thinking only of how soft my bed will be in approximately twenty minutes.

Chapter Four

CAL

Today is not my day. Film this morning was a disaster. We lost Sunday and the offensive coordinator had it out for me, specifically. How I was supposed to simultaneously catch the ball and block the linebacker from sacking Blaze I'll never know, but that's what happens when you're the new guy. The expectations are high, and the respect is low. Another thing my father was wrong about.

Respect is earned, especially as a professional athlete. It's one of the things I love about the game. It's hard to earn and easy to lose, the stakes are high but only for yourself.

My only comfort is the rest of the team is getting reamed out right along with me, even if not to the same extent. I mean, I get it, but even as hard as I've been working to learn the plays, I can't plug my brain into the iPad and download the information.

If he's going to call wildcard plays, I'm gonna fuck up, simple as that.

But now, after I finally sat down to relax—maybe with a nice whale documentary—someone is pounding on my door. I groan. Only four people have access to my condo through the building. My mother, my agent, Tori, and Theo.

With a pretty solid idea of who's incessant knocking is setting my teeth on edge, I stalk to the door and fling it open to reveal Theo's grinning face.

"What do you want?" I say, not entirely unkindly.

"Let's go out. I wanna watch the game."

"I really have no interest in watching more football tonight, especially if it's accompanied by someone yelling. Even if it's not at me."

"Oh stop whining." He smirks, shoving his foot in the door as I try to slam it in his face. Whining my ass.

"I thought it'd be fun, and I already made plans for us to meet there."

"Us?"

"Aw, Callahan, are you embarrassed to be seen with me?" He makes a sad puppy dog face at me, blinking his eyes exaggeratedly.

"If you stop looking at me like that, I'll go," I agree, really just anything to get that look off his face. It's disturbing. I won't be able to sleep for at least a week. "No grown man should be able to make your eyes look that pathetic."

"That's the spirit!" He drops the face and steps into my home, looking me up and down. "Go change. I'll wait."

"Are you serious?" I look down at my clothes, a plain black t-shirt and grey joggers. "What's wrong with this?"

"You're kidding, right?"

I blink at him.

"Just go change. I'll call an Uber."

I grunt, stomping off to my room to put on jeans and a flannel.

Theo gives me yet another once over as I emerge from my room. "Great, let's go." Seriously, how many times is this guy gonna check me out today? I follow him through my building silently, secretly hoping he runs into a wall or a glass door the way his nose is buried in his phone.

The Uber drops us off in Wrigleyville, frat party central of the city, at a sports bar just divey enough that I'm hesitant to eat anything that comes from the kitchen. Awesome. This is exactly the relaxing environment I was craving. I scowl at Theo.

"Really? This is where we just had to go?" I ask incredulously.

He ignores me, walking straight into the bar and sitting himself at a table toward the back of the room with a view of the giant screen showing the pregame show for Monday Night Football. I sigh, walking up to the bar, and order a whiskey. With a wince, I down it immediately before signaling for another and handing over my black card. "Keep it open."

The bartender nods, and I head over to the table Theo's picked out, settling in for a painful game featuring my former team playing their biggest divisional rivals. We watch the pregame in silence as the bar starts to fill.

People will really watch anything for a drink special.

"You think the Cosmos are gonna pull it off tonight?" Theo asks as the starting lineup pops up on the screen.

I shrug. "A few weeks ago I would've said yes on principle, but realistically? The Miami coach is changing the game, not to mention that while Jackson might be good, he's not me." Kenny Jackson is the rookie tight end who, thanks to my trade a few weeks ago, has been starting for the team, and his showing is about what you'd expect from a big-ten rookie.

"Theo!" a female voice calls over the ever-increasing noise in the bar, and we both turn to see a tiny woman hustling toward us, her black hair swinging about her face.

"Katie, glad you made it." Theo gives her a one arm hug as she sits next to him.

"Callahan." She pins me with a look and I'm back in sixth grade being scolded for taking her favorite pen.

"Katherine."

She rolls her eyes. "Lila's not here yet?"

I choke on my drink, and they both look at me as I splutter between coughs. "You didn't tell me she was coming."

"I didn't realize it'd be a problem." His face is the picture of innocence, even as Katie looks smug.

"It's not," I say dismissively, waving it off and turning my attention back to the game. "Just didn't realize you girls liked football."

"Well I don't, but Lila does. She even has this fantasy thing she's super into."

I gape at her. Lila plays fantasy football? I shove down the immediate need to check her lineup.

"Ah, there she is!" Katie squeals, pointing to the door, where Lila Summers is standing, glancing around the crowd. She spots us, a look I can't place flitting across her face when she sees me sitting here. I try to tamp down the little match of hope that ignites that it might be joy.

I drink her in as she walks toward us, too focused on the people around her to notice me watching her. She's wearing tight dark jeans that hug her curves perfectly and a leather jacket giving her just a touch of an edge I wouldn't mind cutting myself on. Her blonde hair flows down her back and to her waist, held back by a pair of black sunglasses.

"Hey." She nods at me as she gets to the table and takes a seat facing the screen. She turns to Katie, giving her a quick hug.

"You came," Katie says.

Lila rolls her eyes. "Of course I came. You know I'd be watching the game anyway. It's a big fantasy week, and you said you're buying."

"Theo's buying." Katie tosses a smirk at him.

He gives an exaggerated sigh and ushers them to the bar to buy a round, though I have a sneaking suspicion it'll somehow end up on my tab when I check it at the end of the night.

"So, a big fantasy week, huh?" Katie asks once they're settled with drinks.

"I'm playing Colton."

Katie's face twists in disgust. I'm about to ask who Colton is when Theo butts in.

"I didn't know you played fantasy. Is it a work league?" he asks, eyebrows raised.

"Yup."

"Can I see your lineup?"

She eyes him warily but opens her phone, "Don't touch it," she warns passing the phone to him, the ESPN app open to her current players.

"You don't have me," he says with a pout. She rolls her eyes, and I can't help but be curious if she has me on her lineup, if she was disappointed this week like everyone else.

"Sorry, Theo, bad draft pick." She shrugs.

"Travis Kelce as your tight end?" he asks, and I sit up straighter. Of course she'd have Kelce. It couldn't be someone I'd actually have a chance against.

"I mean, would you have chosen differently?" She laughs. Ouch. The blow hits like a lead hammer.

"Take a look at her bench," Theo says indifferently as he passes me the phone, but there's an edge in his eyes I don't like. I scroll down, and there it is—John Basset (TE).

I clench my jaw, eyes glued to the screen as something in my gut twists uncomfortably. I can't look away from my name on her roster. It dawns on me that she might have no idea that it's me. She knows I play football, but without my given first name, I'm not sure she'd really make the connection. My tiny unflattering photo on ESPN still shows me in my blue Cosmos uniform since I haven't had an updated media session yet.

Her voice breaks me from my pity party.

"You know, I'm undefeated so far this season," she says with a huff, "and I need to win this week. I'm playing this extremely irritating guy at work, so it matters. At least to me." She holds out her hand for her phone back, but I can't make myself give it back.

I can't stop the words that tumble out of my mouth.

"Why is Basset on your bench?" I ask quietly. Theo gives me a look, pity in his eyes, and my stomach roils. I'm a tight end in the NFL. I don't need pity because some girl didn't start me in her lineup.

"Well," she starts, with the air of explaining something simple to a child, "Kelce has a better record and better stats this season, so, he starts." My stomach sinks further, but she's not wrong. Although they play him like an extra receiver more often than not, so it's not a fair comparison, but if it's about points, she's right.

"Basset is definitely the better player. He just might not put up the same points as Kelce," Theo points out, ever the wingman. She snorts in response, sipping from the seltzer in her hand.

Her eyes zone into the game as we watch the first three quarters, even as mine can't seem to leave her face. She cheers at all the right moments, nearly upending the table when the Miami wide receiver scores.

"I won!" she shouts, jumping up.

"Congrats, babe," says Katie, with barely a flicker of emotion.

Lila's staring at her phone scrolling when I decide I can't not tell her. If I wait much longer it'll be a thing, and I don't want it to be a thing. If she's that into football, she'll figure it out in about a week. Unless she never sees me again, but for some reason that doesn't feel like an option.

"Hey so I think I should just set the record straight—" I start, but she gives me an apologetic look and answers a call.

"Hey," she says. "I'm just out with Katie, we're watching the game." There's a pause and mumbling on the other end of the line. "Well, I do. And besides, Theo's here and his friend Cal." I hear an angry voice on the end of the line and stiffen. "Oh my god, can you calm down please?" she hisses, glancing around. She flushes when she catches my eye and looks down at the table with a frown. Even only hearing her half of the conversation, it doesn't seem to be going well.

"Hang on," she says to the phone, before turning to us. "I'm sorry I need to take this, but I'll be back." With that she heads back through the bar and outside to the street.

"Ugh, it must be Dennis." Katie grimaces.

"Dennis?" I can't help but ask.

"Her ex—well, for now at least." She rolls her eyes. "He doesn't really like Theo, and I'm sure he wouldn't like you either if he met you."

I bristle. "He doesn't even know me."

"No, but you look like that"—she waves a hand in my general direction—"so it doesn't actually matter if he knows you or not."

I roll my eyes and glance out the window. I can make out Lila talking quickly into the phone, hunched into herself and face crumpling. I know right then that I never want to be the reason she looks like that.

Chapter Five

LILA

"I'm sorry. I can talk now," I say, once I'm outside free of both the noise and pitying eyes.

"Oh, but you couldn't talk in front of your friends?"

"It was just loud, okay? The bar is packed and everyone's yelling, so if you wanted to talk, I just needed to come outside. It's also rude to talk on the phone at a table full of people, not to mention that I assumed this would be a private conversation. Everyone at that table knows who I'm talking to right now. It's not like I'm hiding it."

"Oh so there are more people?"

"No, that's not what I said." Why was it so hard to get my words out? He always twists them to make it sound worse than it is. "It's just the four of us: me, Katie, Theo, and Theo's friend Cal."

"Tell me more about Cal."

Shit, how did he zero in on that.

"I don't really know him. I've only met him once before, in passing at a club." That's basically the truth. "He's one of Theo and Katie's friends from prep school." I sound exhausted even to my own ears.

"Whatever, Lila. If you're going to cheat on me, can you just be honest about it?"

Jesus Christ, not this again. Six months after he moved to New York, the cheating accusations started, and every time I think we've moved past them, there's someone new that he's worried about. My circle has gotten smaller and smaller over the years as I remove people Dennis didn't like or saw as a threat. My eyes sting, even as I try to level my voice.

"I've never cheated on you, Dennis, I swear. Nothing's ever happened between me and anyone else. But we broke up on Thursday, so whoever—"

He cuts me off before I can get the words out. "Just your slutty dancing."

"You've been to the club too. I don't hold it against you that you might dance with your friends."

There's silence and for a brief moment, I think I've won, even if it's only the battle of today.

"So, they're your friends now?"

I cringe. "You know what I mean, they're not just random strangers." Cal's thigh between mine flashes in my mind, and I shut down the very un-friendly feelings that course through me.

"At least when I go out, I don't dress like a twenty-one-year-old whore in clothes I'm busting out of just to get attention. You'd think the attention from your boyfriend would be enough, but no. You have to have strangers panting over you in public, as if they're not just staring in disgust at a grown woman pretending to be in college still." The words land, blow after blow raining down on me as I stand rooted to the pavement. That's his big card to play, and it hits every time.

"You don't mean that." The spot behind my eyes starts to sting, and I try to keep the shakiness out of my voice.

"Whatever you say, Lila." I hate how he says my name like that. The emphasis on the 'la' like I'm some dumb girl with a fake valley accent. "And here I was thinking we'd get back together and could finally be happy." He sighs, like he's actually upset that we're not a perfect happy couple.

"You broke up with me, remember?" I feel like I'm caught in some never-ending time loop. It's Dennis and Lila, it's always been Dennis and Lila, but it's never 'look how happy they are.' He's called it off at least six times over the last couple years, and I always take him back. I don't even know why really, only that I do, and, in a way, I can't imagine a life with someone else. What we have is at least consistent. He loves me in his own way, even if Katie and our other friends don't see it. He wasn't always this way. He used to be sweet and caring and take me on fancy dates and make me laugh. One day, I'll get that person back. We just need to get through the rough patch.

"Why would I break up with you? I just was stressed out at work and needed some space. Of course, I don't want to break up with you, baby. I'm sorry I just love you so much, the idea of someone taking advantage of you like that makes me crazy. Theo's always given me a bad vibe, you know that. I can't imagine his friends are any better." He says the last line with a scoff.

"Nothing happened with Cal. Why can't you ever just believe me?" I ask, the tears finally spilling over as my voice breaks. "It's so exhausting fighting like this, and I love you. You know I love you. I wouldn't cheat on you, okay? Why do you have to do this?"

"Do you really love me?"

"Yes!" I scream, causing several people walking by to stare at me in alarm.

"That's all that matters. I won't let anyone rip us apart, Lila." I wish that my heart fluttered at the declaration instead of the lead weight dropping into my stomach. "I have to go. We'll talk soon."

Click.

I stare at the phone screen. He hung up. Are you fucking kidding me? I look back at the bar, the crowd of people cheering and know I can't go back.

I open my Uber app and set my pickup location. Three minutes away, thank God.

A hand brushes my shoulder. "Hey, you okay?"

I whirl around, finding Cal standing there, his arm still outstretched.

"Yeah, I'm fine."

"You don't look fine."

"Wow, thanks." I deadpan, trying to force some levity into the situation. How much had he heard?

One minute away.

"Seriously, are you okay?"

"I'm fine. I just needed to deal with something, and I didn't realize how tired I was, so I'm just gonna go home. I already know I won anyway, so really there's no point in staying." I try to grin at him, but my mouth doesn't work properly.

"You're not going to say bye to Katie?"

"I can text her, or since you're here, you can tell her I went home. She knows where to find me."

I realize with a start he also knows where to find me.

"You weren't going to say goodbye to me?"

"Goodbye." I can't quite meet his burning gaze.

I see my car and wave.

"There is a point."

"What?"

He clears his throat, staring at his high-end Nike sneakers. "There is a point."

"A point to what?"

"Staying for the rest of the game." He looks up, and I can feel the intensity in his eyes boring a hole into the side of my head.

"Oh, yeah?" The car pulls up, and I open the door, meeting his gaze finally. His silver eyes are like molten steel, nearly melting my own resolve.

"I thought we were having fun."

I give him a sad smile. "We were."

I slide into the seat and shut the door behind me, refusing to look back up at him.

I make it halfway down the block before I start crying again.

● ● ●

The second I walk in the door, I turn my phone off. There's not a single person I want to talk to right now, and I know Dennis won't actually speak to me for at least twenty-four hours. I eye the open bottle of wine on my counter and grab my emotional support water bottle instead. This thing has been through hell and back and honestly seen more shit than a Lollapalooza port-a-potty, so it can get me through tonight.

I'm slightly dazed as I sink into my large sectional and turn on the TV, flipping to an old season of *Love Island* on autopilot and settling back against the throw pillows. Nothing can make you feel better about your own love life than hot twenty-year-olds dancing around in bikinis and talking shit about the washboard abs they have as partners for days on end, and I firmly believe that.

A door slamming down the hallway startles me awake, and the show is now four episodes ahead from where I left it. I glance out the windows and see the inky blackness oozing around my building, interrupted by the skyscrapers lit up against the night in varying colors.

I glance at my phone, finding only a black screen, and then switch it on.

It starts to buzz.

And buzz.

And buzz.

I drop it on the couch, getting up to wash my face of the salt tracks left behind from my earlier sobbing. At least I had sucked down enough water before my nap to keep the swelling of my cheeks to a minimum. I pop a melatonin because, at this point, I might as well just go back to bed. It's already nearly one in the morning.

I walk back to the living room to check my thankfully now silent phone and scroll through dozens of notifications.

My eyes catch on one from the front desk to my building. A delivery, around 11 p.m. I frown, trying to think if I'd ordered takeout before I passed out.

I throw on an old hoodie and my Uggs and go check it out, knowing I'll just think about it all night otherwise.

I step out of the elevator and see Maureen's braided head peeking out from behind the tall front counter.

"Hey, Maureen."

"Miss Lila, these came for you!" the older woman says, pointing toward a large vase full of pink and white roses clustered around three bright sunflowers.

I blink in shock.

"I think you have the wrong person. There's no way those are for me." Never once in all our years together had Dennis ever sent me flowers like this. He must feel absolutely horrible about earlier. I hadn't bothered to read the three messages waiting from him before I came downstairs.

It's impressive honestly, to have gotten them here this quickly after our fight. And they are beautiful.

"I checked the card, they're definitely for you—Lila Summers."

"There's a card?"

"Well, of course, how else is your beau supposed to court you?" she asks with a wink.

"It's not really courting if they're apology flowers and we've been together for a few years now."

"Wells if my husband looked like that, I wouldn't be working the night shift, I'll tell you that much."

I start. "What do you mean? You saw him? Not just a delivery man?"

"Oh no, honey, he wanted to deliver them personally, but your phone went straight to voicemail, so he left them here for you."

My mind is whirling. How did Dennis get here so quickly? Common sense says he didn't. That the flowers are from someone else.

"What did he look like?" I ask cautiously, even as I take a step toward the flowers, reaching for the card I see sticking out of the top.

"Oh, girl, in a word? Gorgeous." She laughs. "Tall, so tall my neck got tired just from looking at him, and blond hair most girls would kill for, but his eyes, Lord his eyes. I thought they'd just about swallow me up."

My hands are shaking as I pull the card off the bouquet, seeing my name, Lila Summers scrawled in an elegant hand across the front. I turn it over and my breath catches.

Lila,
You deserve to be happy.
Cal

My eyes are burning once more as I scan the note a second time.

"Well?" asks Maureen.

"Well, what?"

"Are you going to forgive him?"

I can't help but smile. "He never needed to be forgiven."

I wake surprisingly refreshed considering the night I had. I pad into the kitchen, seeing the large floral bouquet sitting atop my counter, and my heart skips a beat. I stare at them for what might have been fifteen seconds or an hour until my alarm blares from where I left my phone on my nightstand.

I jump to attention, running to switch it off, and hop in the shower to get ready for work, my mind constantly wandering to a dangerous corner. Is he thinking about me this morning? I order my coffee, sending a manifestation to the universe that he might have the same idea I have. And if I spend a little more time than usual on my makeup and choose my favorite shirt for work, that's my own business. Even in a city as large as Chicago, our apartments are close enough that a casual run-in is possible.

The Starbucks, while by no means empty, is bare of Cal or any look-alike baristas. I try to ignore the way my heart falls just a little bit. The same way I've been ignoring the five text messages from Dennis.

Look good, feel good. That advice has never led me astray, and it won't start today.

I walk into the office with my head held high and my shoulders back. I am the main character today, even as I'm greeted immediately out of the elevator by Kevin, his expression full of false cheer.

"What's wrong?" I ask.

"How do you know something's wrong?"

I level him with a stare.

"Right, uhm, Colton's in your office."

"So that's why you're out here?"

He nods.

"Right. So, why exactly is Colton Varga in *my* office?" I panic about our close fantasy score last night, but I came out on top in the end so he wouldn't be here to brag.

"He said he had urgent news on the rig situation."

Of course, and he needed to get in early to sit in my office and wait for me, just to prove he could.

I take a deep breath. "Okay, thanks for the heads-up Kevin. If you hear shouting just ignore it, 'kay?" I plaster a smile on my face.

Kevin grimaces as he takes my jacket from my arm. I march to my office and push open the door.

I fight the urge to start yelling when I see him lounging in my chair, his feet on my desk as he fiddles with his phone, probably playing some stupid game.

"Colton, can I ask what you're doing at my desk?"

He glances up and smirks at me. "Lila, how good of you to finally get here."

"Please take your feet off my desk," I say, a hint of danger in my voice. "Now."

He looks back down at his phone. "You know I've been waiting for twenty minutes to give you information for *your* client."

I cross my arms and glare at his over-shined dress shoes still resting on my desktop. "It's barely 8:30, and we both know you've maybe been here for five minutes."

"I'm wounded you'd think I'm not being honest." He closes his eyes, one hand placed over his heart as if in agony. I roll my eyes.

"What do you want, Colton? Seriously."

He drops his feet but stays seated. "I found you a supplier for C&C."

"What?" Part of me is convinced this is some elaborate prank.

"I found a supplier, one of my clients."

"Are you serious?" My brain kicks on, and my focus is suddenly razor sharp. He wouldn't risk his clients for a joke. "And they're in? Like all in?"

"Yes." A weight lifts off my shoulders. "But they'll want to meet you before they sign."

"That shouldn't be a problem."

"Great, we leave next week. That should give legal time to draw up the paperwork and get the travel booked." I nearly groan.

"You're coming too?" I can't entirely keep the whine from my voice. As grateful as I am to have this on its way to being solved, I'd rather handle it alone.

"Obviously. They're *my* client, after all." He stands, grabbing three mints from the bowl on my desk before pausing at the door. "You're welcome, *Lila*."

"Thanks, Colton. I appreciate it." The words taste sour leaving my mouth, even as my sarcastic tone provides the spoonful of sugar. I do kind of mean it though. It's a huge help.

"I'll send over their file so you can take a look."

I nod. "Great, thanks, copy Kevin also."

"Sure thing." He leaves, and I fall back into my recently vacated chair.

At least that's one thing in my life starting to clear up. Now I only have the shit show of my personal life to deal with. I scoot forward, only to realize the idiot messed up my chair settings, and I have to spend the next several minutes fixing it, cursing him under my breath the entire time.

The rest of the morning is spent reading through the file Colton sent over. Dover Industries is a readily able supplier that falls perfectly in C&C's price range. They honestly couldn't be more perfect.

I'm pulled out of my research by an unknown text.

UNKNOWN

Hey, I just wanted to make sure you got the flowers.

Cal?

How'd you guess?

I did get them, they're beautiful. But you didn't have to do that.

CAL

I know, but I wanted to.

Something in in my heart clenches.

CAL

And the shop was on my way home, and my mother has always had a rule about flowers and women who are upset.

I wasn't upset.

Ok fine. I was obviously upset, but it wasn't your fault.

I'm very much aware.

But that doesn't mean I couldn't be the reason to make you smile again.

Well, thank you, they are lovely. And they did help. 😊

I'm glad.

Who handed over my number anyway?

You already know the answer

Theo obviously

I should've known. No respect for anyone's privacy.

I can always delete it if you'd prefer?

No, keep it.

I'm curious about your mother's rule though?

Just know it involves tea or flowers, and the occasional sweet.

I'm holding you to that, you know.

I'm counting on it.

I swipe out of the conversation and see three other messages that need attention, one from Katie that I click on first.

KATIE

Hey, you know what I think would help?

I can only imagine.

What?

If you got back in the studio!

I really haven't had the time. You know I'd love to, but it takes so much time and I just don't seem to have a lot of that right now.

Right... I booked you the studio tonight, just in case you want to go.

> You're kidding, why would you do that?

You need a break. And nothing gets you out of your head like pottery.

> Thanks, Katie. I'll try to get out early and go.

Just take care of yourself okay? It makes the rest of us nervous.

I check my work calendar, grateful to see no urgent meetings after 4:00 p.m. With Colton having found a supplier, I should be able to make it to the studio, and my heart soars. It's been nearly a year since I sat at the wheel, felt the clay in my hands. I love making pottery, turning an ugly plain lump of clay into something beautiful that people want to display in their homes. It's refreshing to take time to see the beauty in the world, and pottery lets me do that. It makes my mind go quiet when nothing else will.

I open the last text from my younger sister and suppress a groan.

KAYLA

Hey, Mom said to ask you about the shower next month. You're coming right?

> Yes of course, I wouldn't miss it.

Are you bringing anyone? Or anything?

> No, I'm not bringing anyone.

> Do you need me to bring anything?

> Also shouldn't you not be planning your own baby shower?

Yeah, I think she has a list somewhere of the food we still need. I'll tell her to send it so you can pick something.

Well, maybe but you know how she is.

Okay, well I'll bring whatever you need.

How are you feeling by the way?

Some days are better than others. Alex is trying to help, but the morning sickness still hasn't stopped.

Is that normal? You're almost at six months right?

No, not normal. But the Dr says it can happen, so just to keep taking my vitamins and eating when I do have an appetite.

Okay, well I'll talk to Mom about food, but let me know if you need anything, okay?

Thanks. Love you.

love you too

My little sister, almost six months pregnant with her first kid. Our mother's disappointment was bad when Kayla beat me down the aisle, two years ago, but now giving my mother her first grandchild? I can hear the disapproving sighs from the suburbs thirty miles away.

I can't blame Kayla though. She's always wanted to be a mom, and the pregnancy hasn't been easy on her. But I'm excited to spoil my soon-to-be nephew.

Hey, just talked to Kayla, what do you need me to bring to the shower?

MOM

Oh good, can you make deviled eggs?

Yeah, that's fine.

And you can come early to help set up right?

Sure

You know she'd do the same for you.

I said sure

Are you bringing anyone?

No

Dennis isn't flying in?

I didn't ask him. I thought baby showers were supposed to be for women.

I leave out the part where we're not even together right now. I made the mistake of telling her once that we had broken up, and she nagged me nonstop for a week. Apparently, I need someone to take care of me, and Dennis's family pedigree should be enough. I swear if I have to hear "You can't let a good man like that get away, Lila" one more time I'm going to lose it.

MOM

Alex and your father will be there. I thought maybe you'd want to celebrate as a family.

Well, I don't think he can come. He's been really busy with work lately.

Right, well since work is so important to you both no wonder you're not prioritizing your family.

We're not ready to get married. It's not like I'm alone in this, Mom. A lot of women are getting married later in life now.

> You're thirty-three, Lila, and not getting any younger. At this rate I'll probably be dead before you even have children.

I roll my eyes.

> You can't be serious.

MOM

> I'm just saying. Take your sister for example. She found a nice young man and settled down and now has a lovely home and is going to be a wonderful mother.

> Don't you want that?

> I don't know, Mom, but I'm done with this conversation.

> I'll bring the deviled eggs, and I'll be there early to set up.

> Don't be so dramatic, Lila, I only have your best interests at heart.

I stare at the screen, fuming. All the benefits of my feel-good flowers from last night wiped away in one conversation. My eyes are burning, and I wipe at them harshly, likely ruining the makeup I spent extra time doing this morning.

"Kevin," I call, and he's there in an instant.

"Is there anything I can push until tomorrow?"

"Everything but your one-on-one with James at two."

"Great."

"Do you want me to move something?"

I sigh. "No never mind. Just don't schedule anything after four please. I have an appointment to get to."

"There's nothing on your personal calendar. Did I miss something?"

"No, I just added it. But I need to be out by five thirty tonight."

"Got it, nothing after four."

I smile at him. "Thanks, Kevin."

"Anything else I can get you?"

"No, I'm okay, did you have a chance to look at the file Colton sent over?"

He nods. "They seem like a good fit."

"It seems that way. He wants to go out next week to the site. Can you get the travel booked?"

"Yep, sure thing. Do you want me to get you separated on the flight?"

I laugh. "As long as I'm not in a middle seat, it doesn't matter." The thought of Colton squished into a middle seat is too funny to contemplate.

"Will do." He leaves as quickly as he popped in. Sometimes, I swear he can teleport.

●●●

The rest of the day passes quickly, and I'm able to leave on time for the first day in weeks. Smiling, I head into the studio. It's empty except for the assistant currently organizing the glazes along the far wall.

"Hey, Denise."

"Lila, it's been a minute since we've seen you around here!"

"I know. Work's been crazy lately. I haven't been able to get away."

She nods sympathetically, pushing her big, round glasses back up her nose from where they'd slid down to the tip.

"Well, you know where to find everything, but let me know if you need an assist. You have the studio until closing."

I grin, dropping my bag next to the wheel near the window. I'll have to find a way to thank Katie. She booked the entire studio for me. I normally don't mind coming for open workshop when there's a few others quietly working, but I do my best creating when I'm alone.

I cut a large block of porcelain clay and wedge in a few powdered colors—pinks and oranges today, something fun and bright—and get to work.

It grounds me, the clay between my hands, the water and slip sliding over my fingers as I guide it into center, even as my manicure suffers. Gradually, the lump of clay takes shape, and I begin to pull the walls. I shape the piece as the sun sets and the city darkens, as Denise sweeps the backroom and shuts off the kiln.

I sit back and admire the vase, the swirls of color just coming through, and breathe.

"Well, that's lovely," Denise says from over my shoulder. I jump, almost forgetting she was here.

"Thanks, I got some flowers yesterday that needed something just like this."

"I'll let it dry out and then, if you want, we can glaze and fire it for you. You'll need to trim it though."

"Thanks," I say, wiping off my hands on the apron and stretching my back out. "I'll come check on it later this week and see what I want to do with it. I'm hoping the colors come through a bit stronger after the bisque firing."

"I hope this means we'll be seeing you around more?"

I nod, grinning "I hope so."

◉ ◉ ◉

Set Your Roster!

. . .

The alarm goes off at noon, and I jump. I normally finalize it Wednesday night and then turn off the alarm, but I spent the past two nights at the studio and came home too drained to look at stats.

I finish lunch with Sadie and plop down behind my desk, opening my ESPN app. My thumb hovers over John Basset on my bench, and sigh, opening my texts from last night.

CAL

Hey, I need to tell you something.

What's up?

You remember when Theo and I were looking at your fantasy roster?

Yeah...

There's a reason he was so protective of his teammate.

I mean sure, if they don't all believe in each other how are they supposed to play well enough as a team to win?

No, it's more than that. You know I used to play for the Cosmos right?

Yeah.

Well, I requested a trade earlier this year, and they finally made it happen. I'm new to the Chicago Avalanche.

What?

Callahan is my middle name and I've used it since I was a kid since my dad is Johnathan Basset. But on the official paperwork and in football I still use John. The John Basset on your roster is me.

> Oh, why didn't you just tell me?

I kinda thought you already knew when we met at the club. I assumed Theo or Katie would've mentioned the trade, it was why we all met up that night.

> Oh, that makes so much more sense now. Why are you telling me now then?

You'd figure it out soon enough, and I didn't want it to be weird when you did.

I didn't want to feel like I was lying to you about who I am.

> Does this mean I have to start you this week?

Only if you think I deserve it.

> I guess we'll have to see then, won't we?

Just do me a favor and don't tell me if you don't.

Let me pretend you picked me.

I flip back to my fantasy roster. Sure, it was a bit of a shock to learn the guy I'd been thinking about nearly non-stop for the last few days is currently sitting on my bench, but it's not like it's a real game.

I'd immediately run to the internet to validate his story, and after two hours of digging that would make the most thorough CIA agent proud, I can confirm that Johnathan Callahan Basset, age thirty-four, did indeed get traded to the Chicago Avalanche from the Upstate Cosmos only a few weeks ago, mid-season. He also drastically overpaid for his condo according to Zillow, but I guess if you're on a timeline, there's not a lot of time for negotiation.

I feel slightly guilty as I leave John Basset on the bench for the week and lock the roster. Even after the flowers and the consistent daydreams, I can't make myself start him, not when having Kelce is a guaranteed twenty points. They play tonight in Dallas though, and if I can't support him through fantasy, I'll definitely be watching the game.

> Hey, do you want to watch the game tonight?

KATIE
What game?

> Cal and Theo's. It's at 7 tonight.

Fine, if I have to.

First round is on you though.

I roll my eyes. Of course it is, but I can't stop the grin that spreads across my face. It's always fun to cheer on my fantasy players, but I don't *know them* know them. This is different. I *know* Cal, maybe more intimately than I care to think about right now, but he and Theo are my friends. It makes it more personal, and I want them to win for them, not just for the benefit it brings me.

I swear I don't breathe through the whole first quarter. May I never have a son that wants to play football because I don't think I could watch them get hit play after play. But Katie chatters nonstop about the hockey rules she's learning from Theo and the players he's promised to introduce her to, and after a couple drinks I'm able to relax and enjoy the game more.

"You really think you'll be into a hockey player?"

"Have you seen them? They're *hot*," she says, waggling her eyebrows suggestively.

"They're not the only ones," I mutter under my breath,

grateful when she doesn't hear, and turn my attention back to the game.

We both scream when Theo catches a touchdown in the middle of the third quarter, half of the bar erupting with us as the Avalanche pulls ahead, putting them in a good position to win.

The last two minutes are tense, Dallas with the ball on our forty-yard line, almost to field goal range, but the defense holds them there, and we win! I pull out my phone, a text to Cal already composing in my mind.

"Who are you texting?" Katie asks slyly.

"Uh no one, never mind." I slide my phone back in my jeans pocket.

"You should you know. He'd want to hear from you."

"You really think so?"

"Definitely." She winks at me. "How's Dennis these days?"

My stomach drops. "I'm sure he's fine."

"You haven't talked?"

"Not since he called me at the bar."

"Do you miss him?"

I inhale sharply, then let out a slow breath thinking. *Do* I miss Dennis?

"I don't know."

Katie purses her lips. "Well regardless, your *friends* deserve a 'congratulations.' Theo just caught the game winning touchdown, and Cal helped block for him, so really, it's a shared victory." She sips on her martini delicately.

I gape at her. "Since when do you know what blocking is?"

"You're not the only one who can understand football, you know. And I never said Theo was *only* teaching me hockey rules."

I shake my head. "Fine, you're right." I huff. "It's not weird to just say 'good job.'"

I pull my phone out but hesitate.

"Should I text them in a group?"

Katie just looks at me with pity.

"You know what? Never mind, I'm a big girl, I can do this." She pointedly ignores the pep talk I'm giving myself.

> Great catch tonight, and congrats on the win!

THEO
Thanks! We'll celebrate when we're back!

I open a second message.

> Congrats on the win! It was a great game.

CAL
Thanks.

You watched the whole thing?

> Of course! It was so much more exciting when I had people to cheer for on the field

Well as long as you're rooting for me, I'll make sure I stay on the field.

My heart does that little flutter thing, and I put my phone away quickly.

"I think it's time to go," I say, flagging down the server with my credit card.

"Okay, I'll call a car."

By the time we've paid, our Uber is waiting outside, and we jump into it, trying to dodge the chilly fall weather.

The driver drops me off first, and I step out.

"Thanks for watching with me!"

"Yep, see you this weekend?"

"Yeah. Text me." I shut the door, and head inside, waving to Maureen on the way up.

Once I'm in my apartment, I sigh and open my phone to Dennis's messages, finally ready to bite the bullet.

DENNIS

I'm sorry, I shouldn't have said that.

I know you didn't cheat on me it just makes me sick to think of someone taking advantage of you.

Come on, Lila, don't be like this, you know I love you.

Lila, baby. You can't ignore me forever.

Let me know when you're done punishing me, for something I've already apologized for.

Sorry, I know I should've answered sooner. Work just got really busy.

A message pings a few minutes later as I'm getting ready for bed.

DENNIS

I'm sure.

I think I should come visit. We can talk this through

I think you're right. When are you thinking?

I bought a ticket for this weekend. I land Saturday.

Okay.

Don't sound so excited.

Sorry I am. I'll see you Saturday!

I close my phone, trying to summon the happiness I once felt at the thought of seeing my long-term, long-distance boyfriend.

It doesn't come.

I can't believe I'm doing this.

After Theo caught his touchdown, I made the mistake of saying, "We'll celebrate this one," and somehow, I'm now hosting a party in my condo. Charles had a field day with the guest list when I handed it to him earlier.

Apparently, there's a protocol with the noise ordinance in the building to protect the other residents from parties. Since my unit is insulated from the rest of the building however, I don't *need to worry*. To be honest, it would've been nice to have a reason to *not* have people over. Ever.

But here we are, me sitting on the couch, sulking as I scroll through Instagram and all my tags from the game and Theo directing caterers around my living room.

"You can set up the bar over here. We'll want easy access to the roof," he shouts at the director from across the room, pointing toward the large balcony doors.

"Where do you want the taco station?" she asks, reading from a menu.

"Cal, what do you think?"

I slouch down further into the couch and say nothing.

Theo rolls his eyes. "Just set it up on the kitchen island."

He strolls over, popping a tab on the IPA he's holding.

"Are you really not going to help?"

"This is *your* party. It's just being held in my apartment."

He sighs. "I was hoping you'd be a little more excited since Lila's coming."

"Why would I be excited about that?" I ask, trying to keep my face neutral as my stomach churns at the idea of her in my home.

"Oh, no reason, I guess. You seem to be getting close, and you can never have too many friends." He smirks.

"We are friends. It's fine she's coming."

"You're not just a teeny, tiny bit excited to see her?"

I roll my eyes. "Don't you have a party to plan? Leave me alone."

"If you're here you should at least help."

"Sounds like a great reason to not be here then." I push myself up and grab my keys. "I think I'll go for a run."

"Are you serious? The party is in three hours."

"And I'll be back in one." I grab my AirPods and pop them in. "Have fun with your caterers, Theo!" I call as I let the door slam behind me.

The sun is out, and it's the perfect weather for a long run. Unfortunately, that means the entire city of Chicago is somehow along the lakefront, but the pounding of my feet against the pavement is soothing nonetheless even as I dodge strollers and rollerbladers.

After three miles, my muscles are burning enough to wipe the thoughts of dancing with Lila from my mind, and I push myself faster. Theo's already hinted twice that he's got a great DJ for tonight and a "down and dirty" playlist, whatever that means.

I'm breathing hard, my shirt soaked in sweat, when I pause along a stretch of the path right on the water and look out over Lake Michigan. It really is peaceful.

I look down the path, and let out a long breath, before turning and heading back home.

●●●

"Took you long enough," Theo says the minute I've stepped through the door. I grunt at him in acknowledgment, still breathing heavily. He points toward my bedroom. "Just go shower, okay? The food will be here soon."

I blink in acknowledgment.

"And that was more than an hour!" he sing-songs at my back. I slam my bedroom door at him.

I take a long, scalding shower and when I emerge, I feel almost like a person again. I take a bit of extra time shaving and shaping my hair into a perfectly tousled, effortless look that takes significantly more effort than anything else when the pounding on the door comes.

"Are you ready yet? You take longer to primp than my sister!" Theo shouts from the hall.

I wrap a towel around my waist and stride through my room to yank the door open.

"What more could you possibly want?" I snap. It's not often I'm annoyed with Theo, my best friend of over two decades, but it's quickly approaching.

"You were in the shower for almost thirty minutes. People are going to be here soon, and you can't greet them like that." He waves at my towel.

"Can't I?" I smirk, flexing my abdominals.

He rolls his eyes. "Get dressed, John."

I glower at the use of my given name and shut the door on him once more.

"A button-down please," he calls from the other side.

"I know how to dress."

I stare at the shirts in my closet, begging for an appropriate option that isn't a button-down. But I have a pretty consolidated wardrobe, so with a sigh, I pull out one in navy and slide it on before adding just a spritz of cologne. It's only seven thirty when I check my watch, a gold Rolex passed down from my grandfather. I really shouldn't stall anymore.

I head out to the living room, taking care to shut my door behind me. We may not be in college anymore, but people never seem to grow out of the urge to get drunk and fuck in other people's beds.

"Finally," Theo groans when I emerge from the hallway. "It's like you were trying to take as long as possible."

I roll my eyes. "Do you need help with anything else?"

"No, it's basically done." He nods toward the bar set up by the patio doors. "Get yourself a drink and try not to make a mess of anything."

I ignore the jab and stride over to the bar. The server hands me my G&T when the front door opens, and Theo greets the first people of the night.

I ignore the newcomers and focus on the sunset over the city.

"Hey, man"—a hand claps my shoulder—"nice place." I turn to see Aaron, the baseball player from the club, and grin before clasping his now outstretched hand.

"Thanks, glad you could make it."

"Well, McClane did promise a great time, and a special once-in-a-lifetime look at your penthouse." He laughs.

"I've been meaning to get a muzzle for him." I glance over at the man in question, animatedly talking to two women near the taco bar.

"How's the season going?"

We chat about football as more and more people squeeze into my condo. It's spacious, but usually it's only me, so with the addition of several food stations, a bar, and about fifty additional people, I'm just a little overwhelmed. Theo must have invited every professional team in the city because they're all here. I even see a couple of Flurries players—one I recognize from a recent interview on their dominating World Cup performance last year —eyeing up the shrimp cocktail from a corner.

The party's in full swing when a tinkling laugh gets my attention, if only because I've been half listening for it since Aaron showed up.

I turn to look at the door and see Lila walking through, glancing around as Katie gives Theo a hug. He leans down to whisper something in her ear, and she giggles, Lila looking on with an amused expression on her face. Her eyes sweep the room, meeting mine for a moment, and she smiles, offering a small wave before looking away quickly, her face falling. I frown, what could I have possibly done?

Theo leads them over to a group of Storm players, and Lila doesn't look back at me once. It stings more than I care to admit.

I turn to grab another drink at the bar and find Aaron has struck up a conversation with a few of the Avalanche cheerleaders. They make space for me in their circle quickly. The woman next to me, a pretty girl with dark, curly hair and deep eyes smiles at me, the bright white of her teeth contrasting nicely against her dark skin.

"So, Cal, how has the transition to Chicago been?" she asks.

I shrug, and she smacks my arm with the back of her hand playfully.

"It's really fine. The team is solid, and the guys have all been decent to me. Not much to complain about."

"Well, if you ever need anyone to show you around the city, get a more personal tour, I'd be happy to show you." She looks up at me, her big brown eyes full of promise. A couple weeks ago I'd have been all too happy to take her up on it, but there's no twinge of intrigue now.

I can't help but glance up at Lila, and I find her eyes locked onto the girl's hand wrapped around my arm. I shake it off, stepping back to put some space between us. If there's one person I'm interested in here tonight, it's not the girl standing next to me. I need that to be abundantly clear.

"Uhm," I clear my throat. "Excuse me, hosting duties."

I grab another drink from the makeshift bar and survey the groups of people clustered around my home. My eyes find her before I can stop them.

Lila's chatting animatedly with Katie and a couple girls I don't recognize. Seeing her happy in my space does something to my chest I can't examine right now. I barely know this girl. Sure, we've been texting, and the physical attraction is there—I only think about dancing with her every night before bed—but great chemistry and flirty banter don't make a relationship. I should be focused on my new team and getting settled in Chicago.

She laughs, and I can't help the smile that spreads across my face.

"Hey, pass me one of those, would you?"

I turn to see a guy I can't place gesturing to the fridge I just pulled my beer from. I grab another and hold it out for him.

"I'm Cal, Avalanche tight end," I say.

"Brayden, defenseman on the Storm." He cracks his beer and takes a long sip.

I should've guessed hockey. The guy is around my build, but if he played on the Avalanche, I'd know him. I haven't met most of Chicago's hockey team yet. Theo's big on inter-sport friendships, hence tonight's guest list, but personally, I don't quite understand the appeal of the missing teeth and legal fights on the ice.

"Thanks for coming."

He nods, and I can't decide if I'm grateful he's not a talker or annoyed that he's making me carry the conversation.

We enjoy our beers for a few minutes before he breaks the silence.

"Your game last weekend was solid, I caught the end after practice. Dallas isn't an easy team."

It's my turn to nod as I sip my own drink and Katie drags Lila by the arm toward a group of loud men, though she doesn't seem overly upset about the movement.

My disgust must show on my face because Brayden speaks up.

"My teammates." The derision in his voice is surprising.

I snort. "Not a fan?"

He raises one eyebrow. "Nah, not of that group."

Katie has glued herself to the loudest of the bunch, a guy with dark hair who loops his arm around her waist.

"Are they your friends?" he asks, indicating the manic pixie that is Katie Chen and Lila next to her, looking slightly lost amongst the new group.

I nod.

"Watch out for them then." With that cryptic message, he pushes off the bar and walks over to a small knot of people near the window, leaving me to determine why I'm keeping an eye on my friends.

I make the rounds for the next twenty minutes, playing the good host and thanking people for coming—mother would be proud—until I can't take the small talk anymore and find Theo.

"How much longer do you expect this to go on for?" I ask, pulling him away from the giggling blonde latched onto his arm.

He waves me off. "Until people leave, I guess. The caterers are here for another hour."

I groan, glancing around the room, my eyes landing on something that makes me see red.

Lila is nearly pressed up against one of those ice skating morons—the ones I was just warned against—his hand low on her back as she giggles into her cup.

Oh *hell* no.

Before I can register what I'm doing, I'm stomping over to their group. Her eyes widen in shock all traces of the giggly, sultry girl a moment ago gone. She pushes herself away, but the asshole she's talking to pulls her back in with a tug on her arm, and she ends up flat against him. I'm not watching where I'm going, and a basketball player knocks into me, the extra six inches he has on me enough to send me into the glass coffee table in front of the couch. I fall through it with a crash, and it shatters around me.

"Oh my God, Cal are you okay?" She pushes away from the hockey player and kneels next to me, careful to avoid the broken glass. Bright red streams of blood are running down my arm, dripping onto my hardwood floor. I can barely feel the stinging through the green haze clouding my mind.

"Oof bro, that looks bad," the hockey player tells me.

"You don't say," I mutter, piercing him with a glare.

His grin falters. "Can I, uh, get you anything?"

"It's my house," I bite out.

"Sweet, man, you've got a nice place." The grin is back.

"Yeah, I know."

"Cal—" Lila starts.

"You didn't hit your head, right?" someone asks. I shake my head.

"You need to make sure you get the glass out," Katie chirps from her perch on the lap of the loud player from earlier. I narrow my eyes at her.

"Here, I can help you." Lila offers her hand to help me up, and I take it, ignoring the twinge in my elbow.

I stare at my bleeding arm as my breathing returns to normal and a stampede of people move toward my door, muttering. I ignore them, focusing on a drop of blood running down my pinky.

"Theo," I call out over the music, and he strides over. "Parties over."

"Seriously?" Theo asks. I hold up my arm, a piece of glass visible in my forearm. "Yeah okay."

"We'll clean the cuts," Lila says, pulling my good arm as she leads me toward my bathroom.

I gesture toward my bedroom door, further down the hall where she follows me through it and into my ensuite. I'm suddenly grateful I keep my room neat as I track her eyeing my belongings all nicely put away.

"Can you take your shirt off?" she asks, once we're in my bathroom. Her eyes take in my chest as I undo the buttons and pull it free, flexing slightly more than necessary. She motions for me to sit on the toilet seat. I do, lifting my arm to try and stanch the blood flow as she wets a washcloth under the tap, her hands shaking slightly.

She gently washes away the blood, removing the bigger pieces of glass with ease. She works in silence, and I watch her. I should probably feel guilty for stomping over to claim her like a cave man, but given that it led us here I can't bring myself to regret it. Coach will be pissed since I'll have to take it easy until the cuts all heal, but none of them feel deep enough to warrant stitches. I tell her that there's gauze under the sink, which she wraps around the wounds. When she's finally done, I speak.

"Thanks, you didn't have to do this."

"I know, I wanted to." She meets my gaze and smiles. "Are you okay?"

"Yeah." I swallow. "Can you do me a favor though?"

"What?"

"Stay away from those hockey players?"

She laughs, but there's no humor in it though. "What is this, some kind of weird competition?"

"No." I don't elaborate.

"That's not your place." I meet her eyes, and they're blazing.

I stare at her, unflinching. I've already overplayed my hand.

"You're not my boyfriend."

"Oh, do you have one of those again?" I snap, regretting the words immediately as she sucks in a sharp breath, her gaze dropping from mine.

"I don't know," she says quietly. "But we were just talking."

"Talking wasn't all he had in mind. I mean, *come on,* Lila, he was practically on top of you."

"Right, because that's so much worse than what you and I did on that dance floor."

I inhale sharply. We haven't discussed that night once, it's been taboo. Even as it floods my memories during every shower.

"That was different."

She laughs darkly. "How so?"

Because it was me. I stand and step toward her. "You know it was."

She glances down. "You need to keep it elevated." I didn't realize she was holding a towel, but as she wraps it gingerly around my elbow, her eyes soften.

"Thanks," I say thickly, the pain throbbing more intently now.

"I might have missed some of the smaller pieces of glass."

"It's fine." I straighten my arm and flex, and though there's a dull throbbing, I don't have any sharp pains.

"Lila—" I start, but her eyes fly up to meet mine, full of panic.

"I need to go, Katie's waiting." She leaves my room at a near run. My place is nearly clear of guests; the caterers are cleaning up their own spaces, and Theo, Katie, and a few others linger in the living room.

"Lila, wait," I call after her, catching her as she pulls Katie toward my front door. "Please, we need to talk."

"No, we don't, Cal. We really, really don't." The pleading look is what gets me, my heart nearly cracks open at the vulnerability there. I know I'll give her whatever she wants, because she's not asking for much. She's not chasing after me for my money or status like girls did in prep school, or latching on to me knowing an NFL contract is in my future like they did in college or throwing themselves at me now for a chance at a slice of fame. If all she wants right now is my friendship, she can have it.

"Okay, Lila. Whatever you need," I say softly. She gives me what could almost be a smile and turns to leave.

She disappears down the hall before I close the door and survey the mess in my living room.

Chapter Eight

LILA

I ignore the sinking in my gut, the idea that there was a possibility he would cancel up until this moment.

DENNIS

Just touched down, be there soon.

But no luck. Dennis's here. It's stupid really.

I should be excited to see him.

I *am* excited to see him.

The little voice in my head says otherwise.

I wipe down the counters once more and survey my living room. There's nothing he can complain about. I've basically deep cleaned the entire place, even fluffed the throw pillows— Katie showed me the appropriate way to "chop" them, since I've apparently been doing it wrong for years. I'm as ready as I'll ever be.

I grab a book off my shelf, trying and failing to focus on the words when all I can think about is how Cal looked at me last night, what might have been said if I hadn't run away. I can be a big girl and admit that's what I was doing. I flip through the cowboy romance book catatonically, eyes glossing over the pages without taking in a word of the ranch hand's dirty talk until my phone rings.

I jump, grabbing it from the table in front of me and see Cal's photo covering the screen.

"Hello?" I ask quietly, chewing on my bottom lip.

"Lila, are you okay?" Cal asks. "You've been ignoring my texts." I had ignored all three of his messages apologizing and asking to talk about last night.

"Why wouldn't I be?" I pace around my living room, exercising some of my nervous energy.

"That's not an answer."

"I'm fine, Cal. I'm just busy."

He sighs on the other end of the line. "Anything I can help with?"

I shudder, thinking of him being anywhere near Dennis right now.

"No, it's fine. I'm almost done anyway."

"Done with what?"

"Nothing. I'm just cleaning." I put the pillow I just picked up back in its spot.

"Oh, nice." He pauses. "Listen, Lila, I think we really need to talk –"

A knock sounds at my door.

"Cal, I have to go. He's here. Can we please talk later?"

"Who's there?"

"I have to go, I'm sorry." I hang up and open the door to find Dennis already typing away on his phone. His grey vest ever present over a pressed white button-up and dark jeans.

"Hey babe." He looks up at me, sliding his phone into his front pocket.

"Who was that?"

"Who was what?" I ask, my smile brittle.

"I heard you talking to someone." He glances around like he expects someone else to be in the kitchen.

I shrug and throw my arms around him instead.

He pulls me in close, and I squeeze my eyes shut, ignoring how wrong it now feels. He lets go and starts meandering through my apartment. "Are you still using that housekeeping service I sent you?"

I grind my teeth together. "Yes, she comes on Sunday."

"That explains it then."

"I did try to straighten up this morning," I mumble.

"Aw, sweetie, I know. You just aren't made for domestic life." He laughs, but there's nothing warm about it.

Here we go again. "There's nothing wrong with wanting to work," I snap.

He holds up both hands in surrender. "I never said there was. Why are you so defensive?"

I take a deep breath and slowly let it out. "No reason. It's just been a long couple weeks."

He strides through my living room, dropping his suitcase on my white comforter, and I flinch. Something about luggage is so dirty, and to put it on a bed? No thank you.

"Can you put your bag on the floor? I just washed the comforter."

He rolls his eyes but moves it to the floor at the foot of the bed.

I sit down gingerly on the bedspread as he unzips the bag.

"So what did you want to do this weekend?" I ask.

He shrugs, pulling out his phone again. "Is there anything happening?"

"Like what?"

Another shrug as he taps away on his phone, clearly only half listening.

"We could always do one of the museums or Chinatown?"

"That's fine."

"Okay, why don't we do Chinatown tonight then? I could invite Katie—"

"No."

"What do you mean 'no'?"

He slides his phone into his back pocket and stands up, taking my hands in his.

"Let's do something just the two of us."

"Okay, like what?"

"Why don't I take you out? You have something nice to wear, right?"

I glance at my closet, the various blouses hung up by color. "How nice?"

He grins, and my stomach flutters. This is the Dennis that made me fall in love all those years ago.

●●●

I stare at myself in front of the floor length mirror, the ice-blue satin setting off my olive skin nicely. The mock-neck halter meets at the back of my neck, and the fabric drapes down the sides of my torso, leaving my back mostly bare. A slit up to the thigh, paired with strappy heels, shows off my legs.

The door opens to my bedroom, and Dennis pokes his head in.

"You look gorgeous, babe," he says, eyes drinking me as he strides toward me and presses a kiss to my temple. He's wearing a tailored navy suit sans tie with a crisp white button-down. In other words, he looks fantastic. Every man looks good in a suit.

I smile at him—we stand almost eye to eye with my heels—and press a kiss to his lips. It feels almost like we're back to being us.

"Are you going to tell me where we're going yet?"

"Nope. It's a surprise."

I mentally scroll through the nicer restaurants in town, contemplating which ones have dress codes.

"The car will be here in two minutes," he says before heading toward the living room.

I grab my Chanel bag, a gift to myself with my bonus last year, and follow him out into the living room.

The car ride is tense as Dennis takes not one but three work calls, each progressively more frantic until we pull up outside RPM Italian.

My heart sinks as I stare at the restaurant. The food may be good, but this is where we were when Dennis told me he was moving to New York, and I haven't been back since.

He gets out first, heading to the door without waiting for me, still talking to his client on the phone. I sigh, thanking the driver before stepping out onto the crowded street and heading into the low lighting of the restaurant.

We're seated right away, he's still on the phone when the server comes for our drink orders.

"I'll have a—"

Dennis holds up a finger, cutting me off. "Simmons," he says, "I know. I'll handle it tonight, I promise, but I'm just sitting down to dinner and my girl is giving me the death stare." He winks at me and laughs. "Yes, I know how they are. Right, well I'll call you first thing tomorrow with an update." He hangs up and sets his phone face down on the table, and I ignore the instinct to grind my teeth at his comments.

"Sorry about that. You know how annoying clients are."

"Can I get you something to drink, sir?" the waitress asks, the smallest bit of impatience showing through.

"We'll get a bottle of the '99 Merlot."

I smile at her. It's fine with me, though not what I originally intended to order. Dennis's a bit of a wine snob, and honestly, if it's wine I'll probably drink it, so whatever he wants is fine.

Once she's left the table, I ask, "Is everything going okay with work?"

"Why wouldn't it be?" he snaps.

I stare at him, taken slightly aback by the harsh tone.

"Sorry," he says, running a hand through his hair. "This one client has been on my ass for weeks now, and it's getting to me."

"I'm sorry, anything I can do to help?"

The corners of his mouth pull up in the smile that used to sweep me off my feet, and his voice drops an octave as he leans in close. "I can think of one or two things." I shiver at his breath caressing the shell of my ear as his hand comes to grip my exposed knee under the table.

My face heats, and I can feel his eyes on me.

"Would you like to try it, sir?" The server is back with the bottle of wine, two glasses in hand.

"Please." Dennis sits up, pulling his hand back to his own lap and leaving my leg feeling cold without his touch. Some part of me sings at his interest, remembering how hungrily he touched me in those early months. The part I'm doing my best to ignore is squirming at the wrongness.

He okays the wine, and the server pours it into my glass and then his, leaving the half-empty bottle on the table. I quickly gulp down half of it, even as he eyes me disapprovingly across the table.

The wine is good. I can tell that much, and I feel a teeny tiny bit bad for chugging it, but the social lubricant is what I need right now, independent of flavor.

"Do you want oysters?" he asks with a smirk.

My answering grin is all he needs. On our first date, we got drunk on champagne and ate our way through several dozen oysters. We made it our mission in the first few years of dating to always get oysters when we went out, even if we were someplace that you really shouldn't order raw seafood from. But after only two bouts of food poisoning in all those tastings, the tradition lives on tonight.

He places our order and refills my wine, holding his glass up in salute.

"To us."

I clink my glass to his and can't help the smile that spreads across my face. This is what I wish Katie saw.

Dinner goes well, all things considered. Dennis only took one work call, and it wasn't until dessert. A black car pulls up out front, and he waves me toward it, holding the door as I slide across the backseat, my dress catching on the seatbelt buckles.

His phone rings again, and he answers it, shooting me an apologetic glance, his hand coming to rest on my knee to placate me. I'm pleasantly full after a filet and half a dozen oysters—not to mention slightly tipsy after slightly more than half a bottle of wine. His fingers draw small circles against my inner thigh, and I fight the urge to shiver, the combination of wine and shellfish aphrodisiacs heating my core.

He pulls on my leg, inching his hand higher as he spreads my thighs. The smirk on his face says he knows what he's doing, even as his words are focused on his phone call. I fight back a moan as his pinky skims the lace of my thong, and he withdraws his hand, leaving me near panting in the seat next to him. He's still on the call as we pull up outside my apartment, part of me assuming he'll hang up once we're there, but he doesn't. He merely opens the door after I scan in, palming my ass as I pass by him.

The minute we step inside my apartment he ends the call, shutting the door behind him.

"Come here," he growls at me, pulling me toward him as his mouth slants over mine.

He kisses me hungrily, swallowing every sound that escapes me. It's been months since we've been together, and the toys don't always cut it. His body around mine is what I've been craving. *Needing.*

He kneads my ass as he backs us toward my bedroom.

Chapter Nine

CAL

The club is hot. Sweat drips down my back, but the feel of her body pressed close to mine is all that I care about right now. I slide one knee in between hers, and she slides her hips forward, her eyes burning as they meet mine. She presses herself down on my leg, and I stifle a groan and dip my head into her collarbone, allowing myself a taste of her skin. It's salty, and I flick my tongue out along her pulse point.

RING.

RING.

RING.

I jolt awake, my phone screaming at me from the nightstand.

I grab it, the throbbing in my hand from the shattered glass acute as I answer the FaceTime.

"What, Theo?"

"Good morning to you too." He's outside somewhere, but I can't place where.

"Good morning. What do you want?" I groan, sliding out from between my silk sheets. I need ibuprofen. My elbow is on fire. I click off the TV, still showing the Earth Channel video featuring orca whale migration patterns that I fell asleep to last night.

"We're getting brunch with the girls this morning. Get ready."

"What time is it?" I ask, finding the bottle of pills in my medicine cabinet.

"Almost eleven, sleeping beauty. Late night?" He waggles his eyebrows suggestively.

"Yeah, something like that," I mutter. Knowing today was free, I overindulged and drank nearly half a bottle of whiskey after our team workout, unable to get Lila and our conversation in the bathroom out of my head.

"Well, drink some water, eat a Big Mac, whatever you have to do, because we're meeting them at noon."

"I don't know if that's a good idea, Theo." I pop two Advil and dry swallow them, doing my best to will the hangover away.

"Why not?"

"I don't think Lila really wants to see me right now."

"She'll be fine." I can picture his shrug from here.

"I thought her ex was visiting. Or maybe not ex anymore," I mutter.

"No idea, but Katie made a res, so I told her you'd be there."

"Fine," I bite out. "Where are we going?"

"I'll pick you up in twenty."

"Theo," I protest, but he's already ended the call. I groan, stomping to the kitchen to grab a water from the fridge before downing half of it.

It's fine. I can do this. I flex my arm, feeling each individual cut. Most of them opened up at practice yesterday, and I got an earful from coach about taking care of my body during season, especially the parts of it necessary to catch a football.

My phone pings.

THEO

19 minutes

I dress quickly, throwing on jeans and a long-sleeve henley.

He's outside in his Range Rover exactly nineteen minutes post text, an extra coffee in hand.

"Thanks," I grunt, taking it. I savor the first sip, not having had time to make my own.

He nods and lets us ride in silence until we pull up in front of a hotel.

"I thought we were doing brunch?"

"It's on the rooftop."

"Theo, it's like 50 degrees."

He rolls his eyes. "It's covered. Don't worry your little sensitive behind."

I shoot him a glare, but he's already out of the SUV handing his keys to the valet. With a sigh, I follow him through the revolving door, through the lobby, and into an elevator that takes us to a covered rooftop.

It's a pleasant sort of place, with bright light coming in through the glass ceiling and a little outdoor terrace for when the weather is nice.

"Ah, there they are." I follow his pointing finger to a blonde head at the far corner, leaning in close to Katie in their half booth. As we walk closer, it's obvious the two are having a heated conversation, trying to keep their voices low.

I grab Theo's arm—this doesn't seem like something we should intrude on—but can't help overhearing Katie's next words.

"What do you mean he asked you to finish yourself?" Katie whisper yells, clearly horrified. *What?*

"*Shhhhh!* Exactly what I said." Lila crosses her arms, "He literally rolled over, and then by the time, I was out of the shower he was asleep."

I freeze, remembering the labored breathing Lila made during my dream only an hour ago. My cock twitches with interest. I can't be listening to this.

"That *asshat*! I can't believe he did that. Isn't this the first time you've slept together in months?"

"Yeah, the last time I went up there we had a fight and didn't. So, I don't know, after a nice date like that I just expected more?"

"Wait but are you back together then?"

Lila shrugs, but Katie's eyes flick up to us, still paused a table away.

She shakes her head, raising her eyebrows to indicate the audience.

Lila turns, eyes wide, and her face heats as she looks at me. I'm not sure if she knows we heard their conversation or not, but she's definitely imagining it now. I hope she knows I'd never let her go unsatisfied in my bed. If she ever let me into her bed, she'd have to beg to stop coming.

"Ladies," Theo greets them, swiftly giving each a kiss on the cheek before plopping himself next to Katie and leaving one seat next to him and one next to Lila. I hesitate for a moment before following Theo on his side.

Lila looks slightly relieved, and I find it hard to be happy that she's grateful I didn't sit next to her, our last conversation ringing through my mind. Where is her boyfriend anyway? Isn't he here this weekend?

"Hey, I didn't know you guys were joining us," Lila says, throwing Katie a glare.

"You know I couldn't pass up an opportunity to rile up Dennis at least once," Theo says, grinning wolfishly as she grimaces.

So, he is coming. Awesome. My arm stings, and I shake loose the fist I made subconsciously.

"Where is he anyway?" I ask, feigning nonchalance.

"He needed to check in with work, but he's meeting us here." She glances at her watch. "He should be here any minute now."

I glance toward the empty door. At least that explained the seating arrangement.

"Ah, anything for work." Theo nods sarcastically. Lila scowls at him, and I fight the twitch of my lips.

"Let's at least order some drinks," chimes in Katie with a wave to the server.

We order a round of mimosas, Katie and Theo falling into easy conversation I can't bring myself to pay attention to while Lila just stares down at her water glass. I can't tear my eyes away from the bubbly woman I met a few weeks ago, suddenly withdrawn into herself. I puzzle at the sudden change when the obvious answer makes himself known.

"Babe, sorry I'm late, but you know what they say, the client's always right." The voice grates on me immediately, and I turn to see a moderately goodlooking dude approaching the table. He's seriously overdressed for brunch in khakis and a button-down, a vest thrown over it making him look like an overgrown toddler. He has a slight build, similar to Theo, but without the obvious six-day workout schedule we keep, and while tall for the average guy, he still falls a few inches short of both my best friend and me. My chest warms slightly at the comparison.

He slides in next to Lila, glancing around at all of us. "Lila, why don't you introduce me to your friends." His gaze is ice cold as it locks onto me across the table.

"Uhm, yeah, well you know Katie and Theo, but this is Cal," she mutters, gesturing to me without looking at me. "Cal, this is Dennis, my uh . . ." She trails off, glancing at his face and then shrugging. He gives her an affronted look before turning his attention back to me.

I nod at him, making an attempt to rearrange my face into something resembling a pleasant look. By the way his eyes only ice over, I'm guessing it didn't work.

I should say something nice, but I'm not sure I can manage anything more polite knowing this is the asshole who made Lila cry outside a bar after just a phone call.

"Any friend of Lila's," he says, with a smile that doesn't reach his eyes, and it doesn't escape me that he didn't actually finish the saying.

"Good to see you again Dennis. I was just saying how boring everything has been lately." Theo smirks.

"I guess that does tend to happen when your team can't manage to win more than a few games a season." Dennis sneers at him. "Although, at least you seem to have picked up a new player who can actually catch the ball."

"Hmmm, you wouldn't be talking about Basset, would you?" Theo asks, openly grinning now as Lila glares at him from across the table. If only looks could kill.

"Is that his name? The new tight end?"

"So nice of you to give your regards in person." He nods to me, and I still as Dennis slowly turns to look at me, fully taking me in.

"You're John Basset?"

"I go by Cal actually."

I can almost see the steam coming out of his ears.

"Does anyone need another mimosa?" Lila asks loudly, though she's the only one who's drained their glass.

He turns to her with a look so withering, I'd do almost anything to pull his attention back on me to spare her.

"What do you do, Dennis? Since you're so familiar with my own career it seems."

He scoffs. "I work in finance managing high net worth individuals. Not all of us can just play games all day for a living." The way he says it, like *fin-aunce,* reminds me so much of my father I can barely take him seriously. I raise one eyebrow, not quite sure his insult really landed the way he intended it to.

"Since I quite enjoy *playing games*, as you put it, I can't say I'm complaining. But that sure does sound fascinating. High net worth individuals, I'm sure they're very grateful for your help." I hear a snicker to my left, as Theo hides his face in his champagne flute.

The server comes by just then, saving us from what I'm sure would've been a well-reasoned retort, though I can't make myself care. "What can I get you all to eat this morning?"

We place our orders, and I can't help but notice an awful lot of whispering coming from the other side of the table.

"—knew you'd be angry."

"So, you lied?"

"I never lied."

"Was it him on the phone yesterday?" Dennis demanded, his voice rising slightly.

Lila's eyes flit to me briefly and that seems to be all the confirmation he needs. His face hardens, but he seems to notice they've garnered the attention of the table.

"We'll talk about this later."

She nods, looking back down at her now full glass of champagne and OJ.

I open my mouth to diffuse the tension but promptly close it when I have absolutely nothing to say. We sit in silence for a few minutes, the tension on the other end of the table palpable.

"Are you going to the Morgan charity event next weekend?" Theo asks. I look at him perplexed. Why wouldn't I be going? Our families have been linked for years, if I *didn't* go my mother would flay me alive.

"Of course."

"You bringing anyone?" He takes a swig of his mimosa as I gape at him. This is definitely not the time for this conversation.

I shrug.

"Are you seeing anyone?" Dennis asks abruptly.

I shrug again, and Theo coughs. I don't owe him anything, and my private life is private. He doesn't need to know that I spent this morning in a wet dream with his girlfriend.

"How's work Lila?" I ask, "That guy still giving you trouble? The one you beat in fantasy?"

She snorts. "He's really turned over a new leaf since I killed him that week. One of Colton's other clients is able to cover the supply gap with the explosion in the gulf, and since they both work with our team, it's relatively easy to get the contract approved." A sparkle I haven't seen since that first night appears as she's talking, and I'll be damned if watching her passion about her work doesn't do it for me. "We're going down to Houston to meet with their M&A team to walk through it before bringing it back to my client."

"That's great," Katie coos, cheers-ing Lila with her nearly drained glass.

"You're going to Houston?" Dennis demands.

"Yes, later this week."

"When were you going to tell me?"

"I thought I already had," Lila defends herself. "Besides it's just a work trip. You take them all the time."

"You're going *with* Colton?"

"He's insisting on coming since it's his client in the first place." She shrugs. "Can't say I blame him. I'd feel the same way if it was reversed."

His retort is cut off by the arrival of our food, and for a few blissful minutes, everyone seems content.

Obviously, it couldn't last.

"So, let me get this straight," Dennis says, setting his napkin onto his now empty plate, "you're going to Houston *alone* with this guy I thought you couldn't stand, and you neglected to mention it even once?"

She rolls her eyes but doesn't respond, remaining focused on her avocado toast.

"For how long?"

"I don't know Dennis. Probably a few days?"

"So, it's an overnight."

"Jesus, what the fuck is your problem? It's just a client trip." The table falls silent as she snaps.

"A client trip involving travel and a hotel with one other *male* coworker." His eyes narrow on her.

"Can we not do this right now?" she pleads, shooting a pointed look at the rest of us trying to appear interested in our meals.

I can barely focus on getting my fork to my mouth though, so it might not be as much acting as I want to believe. I can't believe he's talking to her like that, and in public. I shovel the rest of my potatoes down my throat at record speed, needing to get some space from the situation as I my temper rises, my mind playing his words over and over. The crestfallen look on Lila's face pushes me over the edge, and I throw my napkin on the table. Pushing up from the booth, I stalk toward the restroom at the back of the restaurant.

I'm staring at myself in the mirror over the sink for several moments before the door pushes open behind me.

"You good, buddy?"

My jaw clenches. "I'm not your buddy." I turn to face Dennis.

He smirks. "Well, that's clear."

"What do you want?" I bite out.

"Stay away from Lila."

"Or what?" I let out a laugh, closing the distance between us.

"She's mine."

"I thought you broke up?" I sneer at him.

He just snorts.

I blink at him. "She's her own person, you insolent prick. And if you're too bloody blind to see that, you'll lose her sooner than you think."

"So, that's your game, tell her she deserves so much better, and she'll turn to you when I'm done with her?"

I grimace. "If she could hear how you're talking about her now, she'd be done already."

"Oh yeah?" he snarls, leaning toward me.

I shrug, sliding a cold mask over myself. This isn't the place to do this. If he wants me to kick his ass, I need a witness that he started it. I push past him. "She does deserve better, and if she needs help realizing it, I'd be happy to oblige."

He grabs my arm.

"Take your hand off me," I snarl, using every inch of my height to my advantage and leveling him with the look that causes most defensive linemen to clam up. He lets go, and I push open the swinging door with enough force that it slams into the wall with a crash.

I pull my wallet from my pocket on the way back to the table and drop a few twenties in front of my plate. "Your boyfriend is a real tosser."

Lila flinches as Theo lets out a low whistle at my accent coming through.

"Are you okay?" she asks, quietly.

I snort. "Yeah, fine."

"What happened?"

"Nothing." I look pointedly at Theo. "But I'm leaving."

"Cal, wait—" Lila's voice cuts through the current of emotion inside me.

"No, I can't right now. I'm sorry." She grabs my wrist, her touch so different than her asshole of a boyfriend—or not boyfriend, whatever he is right now.

"Cal, I'm sorry."

My eyes soften as I take in her soft expression, and I want nothing more than to take her in my arms.

"I can't." I shake my head and pull my wrist from her grasp. "I'll call you tomorrow," I toss over my shoulder, not even knowing who I'm really saying it toward at this point, and head for the door.

Chapter Ten

LILA

I watch the Uber drive away Sunday afternoon with palpable relief, the words he'd yelled in my face still ringing through my mind. This trip was a mistake on so many levels, only serving to confirm both my worst fears and insecurities. I need the definition more than ever now. Something I'm able to manage and control while the rest of the world spins away from my tight grasp.

My phone buzzes, pulling me from my melancholy, and I check my Teams app.

COLTON

Flights are booked for Wednesday

I sigh, turning back into my building, ready to purge the weekend from my apartment. I put on Sadie's new music and turn the volume all the way up as I deep clean the bedroom, going so far as to rearrange the furniture to better increase the feng shui— or at least that's what the minimalist podcast said. Katie would probably disagree since she designed the room to begin with.

Once I'm sweaty from pushing furniture around and covered in dust that shouldn't even exist with Dennis's cleaning service, I collapse and let myself cry for the first time this weekend. The sobs wrack through me as my chest shudders. It's a good cry though. Therapeutic in a way. All my frustration and resentment and fear and pain exiting through my tear ducts. I've nearly soaked my shirt sleeve through when I finally come to a stop, my breathing leveling out. My room is a disaster, everything from my dresser piled together on the floor, but that's easily remedied. My relationship with Dennis, my friendship with Cal, my own self-worth? Not so much.

I can't do this anymore. I'd told Dennis as much, and he'd laughed in my face, telling me to call him when I was done throwing a tantrum. I don't even think I have the energy to scream at him if I wanted to, though. I'm being held together with what feels like chewing gum and paperclips, slowly falling apart at the seams as each new weight tests the strength.

I need to find my sparkle again. It's been dull for so long, constantly muffled by the everyday stress of life and everyone's expectations. That night dancing with Cal was the first time in a long time it came back—until the weight of what that meant crashed down on me, that is. Now it's just another reason I feel like I'm drowning.

⬤ ⬤ ⬤

On Wednesday morning, my carry-on suitcase is packed, and my entire apartment is spotless thanks to the deep clean I gave it over the last couple days. I eye my phone, silent on my kitchen island. It's been that way since I put it on Do Not Disturb immediately after emerging from my crying coma. I sigh and shove it in my bag, letting it fall all the way to the bottom.

I double check the lock and head downstairs to the waiting car.

"Took you long enough," Colton says as I slide in beside him in the back seat. His hair is gelled to perfection, which only stands to annoy me further. "We've been here for ten minutes."

"It's just eight now," I point out.

"I texted you we were on our way twenty minutes ago when we left my place." He raises one eyebrow at me.

"Oops, sorry about that." I glance at my phone sheepishly. At his questioning look I sigh. "I have my texts muted. Well, my whole phone really."

He snorts. "God, why?"

I shrug. "Needed a break, I guess."

"Well break's over princess," he mocks. "This meeting *needs* to go well."

"I know." I bristle.

"Hey," he holds both hands up in surrender, "I normally wouldn't say anything." I glare at him, "Okay, fine, maybe I would, *but* you just said you're having a rough time, and we really need you're A-game here, Summers. If anyone can close this deal, it's you."

"That's not exactly what I said," I point out. He just stares at me, and I sigh, deflating a bit. "I know. I've got it, I promise." Wait, I think there might have been a compliment somewhere in there.

"Alright, well I sent you an email a few minutes ago with the docs to review."

"I'll download them in the airport and look them over on the way."

He nods and we fall into a relatively companionable silence as we ride to the terminal.

I've barely finished reading the information Colton's compiled when we land in Houston hours later, home of Dover Industries. If all goes well, we'll be here for two days and then head up to Austin with their legal team to finalize the deal with C&C.

Colton stretches in the seat beside me as we taxi in, crowding me into the window. I huff, but he took the middle seat for the three hour flight, so I don't complain.

"You caught up?" he asks, glancing at my open laptop.

"Almost." He raises his eyebrows at my tone.

"Who are we meeting with?" I ask. "There are two different people named throughout the contract, but they're doing the same thing."

"Oh right, Shahir and Selena, they're co-CEOs."

"Excuse me?"

He laughs, and I realize I've never heard him laugh genuinely before. "Yeah, it's a bit unconventional." He stands and grabs our bags from the overhead bin before waving me ahead of him off the plane. "Their father left them the company with the caveat that they run it together. If one of them sells or leaves, the whole thing gets sold to this really toxic private equity firm with the proceeds going to the local parks' foundation."

"Wow, and they actually function working together like that?"

A shrug. "They're still making it work after five years of running it together. And they've doubled the growth each of the last two of those years, so I'd say they function pretty well, yeah." He smirks. "That's not to say that they don't snap at each other in every meeting I've had with them though."

"I can't imagine running a company with my sister." I shudder. I love Kayla, but there is no way we'd both come out of that one alive.

"I didn't know you had a sister."

"Oh, uhm, yeah she's a few years younger than me."

"I always wanted a little brother, or sister, I guess. But wasn't in the cards."

I snort. "That totally tracks."

"What?"

"That you're an only child."

"I'm going to pretend that's a compliment since we're supposed to be wooing my client."

We step outside, and it's an effort not to groan in the hot, humid air. How is it still so gross here? It's solid jacket weather in Chicago. But moreover, what is with Colton? Why is he being so nice, and is it a trick?

"Are we going straight there?"

He shakes his head, "We'll check in first and meet them for dinner."

"Great, I could use a shower." God, how am I already sweating?

"Uber will be here in two," he says flashing his phone.

"I see it, over there," I exclaim, pointing over the sea of cars to a white Ford Escape pulling in.

I slide into the seat grateful for the blasting AC, and pull out my phone, deciding that being across the country is an appropriate time to finally deal with the messages I've ignored over the last few days. With a sinking heart, I note the absence of one message thread but focus in on Kayla's.

KAYLA

Can you help paint the nursery this weekend?

Or not.

Seriously Lila?

You don't need to be rude, you could just say you're busy.

"Fuck," I breathe. Maybe the total technology silence was a mistake. I ignore the questioning look from the seat next to me.

I'm sorry, I had my phone on Do Not Disturb for a few days while I was dealing with some things. I can help on Saturday.

She responds after only a few minutes.

KAYLA

Saturday's fine. I think Alex is getting the paint at 9:00 so anytime after that you can swing by.

Ok, see you then

After five minutes of no response, I close my phone without checking the other messages. She has a lot going on, sure. Growing a human is hard, but is it really so difficult to just say, "Hey you're my big sister and I love you, what's going on with you?" I shouldn't expect much, she's never been very touchy-feely, but it just sucks when I try to be there for her and get nothing in return.

"Everything okay?" Colton asks.

I shrug, and surprisingly he drops it.

I lean my head back against the seat and close my eyes until we pull up to the hotel, rushing through check-in before collapsing on the fluffy, king-size bed in my room. I need a reset. A full-body reset, if possible, in the next twenty minutes. I pull my hair back and turn on the shower, turning the water temperature all the way up before stepping in. I hiss as the water burns my skin but grit my teeth and let it wash over me. I don't bother actually showering, I just stand in the hot water, turning slowly to get both sides of my body.

Once my body is numb and my mind clear, I step out of the tub and check the time. I have a little less than an hour to get myself presentable, and since I currently look like I just bathed in red wine, there's quite a bit of work I need to do.

I pull on a navy blue silk midi dress and pair it with my light grey blazer. I think I look pretty smart with my hair tucked back in a clip, a few pieces left out to frame my face, and with five minutes until our designated meeting time—and my skin looking much more like my classic olive—I head toward the lobby.

I immediately like Selena; with ease and quick wit she puts her brother in his place, and Shahir, his caramel brown eyes a shade slightly warmer than his twin's, has a quiet intelligence that permeates the space around him as he and Colton banter about one of the recent lobbying bills.

We're enjoying our second bottle of wine, and the dinner plates have been cleared away when the talk turns to business. Colton straightens in his seat next to me, turning slightly as if to give me the floor.

"We're just not really sure a gaming company is right for us. Oil is a finite resource, and everyone needs it," Shahir says, swirling his glass and glancing to his sister.

Selena agrees with a nod. "I don't know anything about the industry, and it's not really recession proof, is it? I mean CPG goods are a guarantee." The plastic packaging for laundry detergent and Lunchables might be recession proof, but I'm determined to make them see gaming is just as stable.

"I assume you're familiar with the lipstick theory?" I ask. Nods come from all around the table, so I continue.

"The gaming industry has become that for, not just men, but an entire generation. Think about it, if you can't afford to travel the world, you can build your own with the Civilization game. The online capability allows these games to provide human interaction in a way they couldn't before, and the capabilities are only growing." I glance around and see Colton smirking at me. A beat passes but he simply inclines his head towards me, his eyes flicking towards Selena, who's staring unblinking at me, hanging on every word.

"They have real-time workout games that may replace gym memberships, immersive worlds built after popular fantasy books you can spend weeks getting lost in as you live like your favorite character, and games designed to encourage teamwork. Video games *are* the future and completely recession proof, if that's a concern. Building up that partnership now is mutually beneficial to both sides and especially to Dover Industries." I conclude my speech and glance to Colton. He's grinning which tells me, once again, I've secured the deal. I smile to myself, knowing this could be the one that clinches the promotion to partner.

Shahir sighs. "We'll draw up the paperwork in the morning." Selena nods in agreement and we toast to a new partnership.

● ● ●

I'm in my Austin hotel room after getting the sign-off from Dover Industries the night before we fly home, exhausted. The deal is a go, and the clients are getting along spectacularly. I collapse on my bed staring at my phone.

I'd started several messages to Cal over the last couple days but deleted every single one of them.

I take a leap of faith that my grandmother would applaud me for and call him.

He answers after two rings.

"Lila?"

"Hey."

"Everything okay?" It's loud wherever he is, and I hesitate before answering.

"Yeah, just getting ready to fly home tomorrow." *And I hadn't heard from you.* But that sounds needy, even in my own head. Let alone to a man who isn't even mine.

"Oh, right. How was the trip?"

"It was good, they both signed the deal."

"That's great."

There are a few beats of awkward silence before he breaks it.

"So, what's up?"

"I—nothing I just thought I'd check in."

"Oh." It's not just in my head that he sounds disappointed. "Well thanks, I think?"

"No . . . sorry, I just, I think we should talk. I don't like how we left brunch."

"Are you still with him, Lila?"

I pause. "Yes," I whisper. "I mean I think so, I don't know. I'm not sure, we didn't really talk about what we are now."

"Then there really isn't anything to talk about. It's fine. I'm your friend, but not his, he made that clear." He breathes a laugh. "Not that I'd want to be."

"Right," I clear my throat. "So, we're good?"

"We're good."

"I'm beat, and need to be up early, so I'm going to head to bed, but I'll see you around?"

"Yep, talk to you later."

I hang up and should feel better, but then, why do I have a mountain-sized lump in my throat?

● ● ●

I'm finally back in the office on Monday, my feet still sore from painting Kayla's nursery all day on Saturday. And now I can't stop staring at the article Sadie shoved under my nose. Her band had been hired to play for some big event, and they were featured in the article, but it's the first page that has my full attention. The accompanying photo worth significantly more than the typical thousand words, at least to me.

MORGAN EVENT RAISES RECORD HIGH DONATION FOR LAURIE CHILDREN'S HOSPITAL

The photo beneath shows several beautiful people, all dressed to the nines in black tuxes and silk dresses, but my eyes are drawn to a couple in the front right. Cal is holding a tumbler of amber liquid and smiling down at a gorgeous brunette draped on his arm.

She has a sappy look plastered on her face as she looks up at him, and I have the sudden urge to throw the phone across the office. The closeness with which they're touching, that's not two strangers who just met. They know each other, probably well, intimately even.

She looks somewhat familiar, though I can't place her face. My thumbs hover over my text thread with Katie. If anyone would know—other than Cal, obviously, but I'm not dumb enough to ask him—it's my gold-mine-of-information best friend. I hesitate before hitting send, thinking through the conversations following for once in my life.

I text myself the link to the article online and screenshot her face before running it through a reverse image search on Google.

Several photos come up almost immediately, and I feel slightly dizzy.

Victoria Winston.

Of course I recognize her. She's a model approaching Heidi Klum-level fame. My skin is hot despite the cool weather outside blowing in from my open windows. My watch buzzes, drawing my attention away from the article and reminding me that I have about ten minutes before our weekly update meeting with James. I seriously regret not stopping for coffee this morning when I could really use a mood booster in the form of a pumpkin cold brew right about now.

With my biggest client now reassured that they are a priority, and their supply chain locked down after our trip last week, my inbox stays manageable and the rest of the day going smoothly. It works out well considering I can't stop thinking about the article in the Tribune.

There's only one thing to do when you can't stop thinking about someone you shouldn't think about at all and his clearly hotter-than-you girlfriend.

Drinks tonight?

KATIE

Say less

Meet you at 6?

See you then!

I smile to myself as I slide my phone back into my bag for the last hour of work. No one is there for you like your best friend.

● ● ●

"So, how was work today?" Katie asks once we're settled in a booth with our martinis in front of us.

"Work was fine." I shrug, taking a sip of my cosmo.

"Drinks on a Monday? I was sure Colton must have been acting up again."

"He's actually been on his best behavior since we've been working together." She looks at me like she doesn't believe me. "That's not why I needed a drink."

Katie sits up straighter in the cushy booth. "Spill."

I laugh. "Did you know he had a girlfriend?"

"Colton? Why would I know that?"

I shake my head. "Not Colton, Cal."

"He doesn't have a girlfriend," she says automatically.

"I thought you might say that." I pull out my phone, the article already loaded and hand it to her.

Her mouth drops open as she stares. "That's Victoria Winston."

"No shit."

"Sorry, it's just, I didn't even realize she was in Chicago. I assumed she still lived in New York."

"To be honest, I've never actually thought about her, but

sure." Something about Katie's response was strange. "Do you *know* her?"

"You don't actually think they're together, right? And she was a few years behind us, but her family would be at events for our school."

"Look at how they're standing." I clear my throat and point. "He's touching her so casually and she's looking up at him like that."

"Yeah, that does seem more than friendly," she says. "If their families are friendly though . . ."

"She's like ten years younger."

Katie shrugs. "He's never mentioned a girl. And we're not that old, she's max like six years younger. Maybe seven."

"Never?" I shake my head. "He's never even on his phone much when we're all together, but athletes don't exactly have the best reputation."

"You'd think he would have brought her around at some point. Was she at his party last week?"

"No." He definitely wouldn't have acted like he had if his girl-friend was there. There's a strange slimy feeling that creeps into my gut.

"Hmmm . . ." Katie trails off, sipping her dirty martini.

I down the rest of my drink, trying to keep that weird feeling at bay.

"So, anyway, I just needed to dish, but I should really get going, I have an early client call in the morning."

"The one from last week?"

"No, it's actually a new exploratory call with a tech start-up out of Denver," I say pulling on my jacket as I stand from the table.

She gulps the rest of her drink. "Well good luck, hang on one sec we can walk out together."

I fiddle with my phone for the minute it takes her to get her coat on and her bag and we walk out of the bar.

"You sure you're doing okay?" she asks, a serious look in her eye.

I pause. "Of course. Why wouldn't I be?"

"You know you're allowed to be not okay even if you don't have a reason, right?"

I'm actually floored for a moment. I can't think of a single thing to say as a lump forms in the back of my throat.

"What?" she asks, tossing her hair. "I can be philosophical every so often. That minor in college wasn't for nothing."

I laugh, forgetting her temper tantrums over those couple graduate-level philosophy courses she'd taken and a weight lifts off my shoulders.

"You're right. And Katie?"

"Yeah?"

"Thanks." I smile, pulling her in for a hug.

"Anytime babe. Text me when you're home, 'kay?"

"I will." I turn heading toward my apartment. The walk is nice this time of night, the city alive enough that I'll never feel alone but quiet after the frenzied, crowded streets of rush hour commuting. It clears my head.

It's good that Cal has a girlfriend, or whatever she is to him. It makes it less messy. Just one night between friends that almost got out of control thanks to outside influence and too much alcohol. No, this is better. I can—and should—focus on Dennis, or at least on myself. The last few months might have been rocky, but we can get through it, right?

We always do.

Chapter Eleven

CAL

My phone dings loudly, pulling me from a dream that slips from my mind like water in a strainer. I scowl at the offending device. Why I never remember to put it on silent I'll never know. It's like the universe has decided to make this small inconvenience my penance for being alive.

The little bubble of hope that ballooned in my chest at the text notification is promptly stabbed with a pin when I see the message.

DAD

Great photo this morning.

What fucking photo?

A quick google of my own name pulls up a photo from the Morgan fundraiser on Friday. I scan it quickly and roll my eyes. Tori and I are barely in it, the focal point being the Morgan family themselves, all smiling bright into the camera.

I toss my phone to the side and groan. Dear old Dad's always liked when I'm out with Tori, especially when I'm seen at fancy events with her. Quite frankly, it's one of my least favorite things about being with her. We grew up in similar circles, our parents frequenting the same charity events and fundraisers. The small group of us who found it all rather dry would sneak off to get drunk in whatever side room we could find. We reconnected after she started modeling in New York. After a few too many nights out closing down the city that never sleeps together, occasionally joined by Theo or one of our other old friends, we fell into bed together.

The following morning, while I was stumbling over myself about how I wasn't looking for anything serious and apologizing for my less-than-gentlemanly behavior, she laughed in my face and told me in no uncertain terms that, if she wanted to marry me, she'd have a ring already. With a pat to my cheek, she made it clear that this was strictly to be a casual relationship. She said if I could escort her to events, it'd be helpful to both of us and our careers.

I can't fault her for her logic. Since I started being seen with her, I've gotten twice the sponsorship deals, and I know she's been able to get all kinds of additional brand sponsorships in the outfits she wears out with me. We're always photographed together, even if we would have flown under the radar separately.

We're each other's default date and the occasional physical release, though the latter hasn't happened for several weeks now despite her bringing it up in her not-so-subtle late-night texts and even hinting at it after the Morgan event.

It's not her fault, but the idea of fucking her makes a part of me want to shrivel inside. I hadn't seen her in person since meeting Lila, and the stark difference in the chemistry might have short-circuited my brain. I feel alive when I'm with Lila, and with Tori, I just feel like I'm existing. I normally feel like I'm existing, so I hadn't noticed how wrong it was until the electricity sparked that night on the dance floor, and now some primal urge in me craves it.

That alive feeling? It's the best thing in the world.

That craving follows me around every *fucking* day.

The blaring of my alarm pulls me from my morose thoughts. I need to get up. We have practice in an hour, and I *need* to start showing up on the field if I want to keep playing. As coach constantly reminds us, "There are hundreds of men who would kill to be in our shoes, so if you don't want it bad enough, they do." It's very inspiring, if what you want to inspire is fear of job insecurity.

I roll out of bed and throw on a pair of sweats before heading to the kitchen to make my daily morning protein shake. I shudder as the chalky mixture runs down my throat. I've never been one for the fake powdered shit, but since I'm trying to bulk extra muscle this season, without it I'd be eating about four chickens a day, and that's a tad overkill.

⬤ ⬤ ⬤

A drop of sweat winds its way down my forehead as I hold my plank, threatening to partially blind me as it edges closer to my eye.

Thirty seconds left. I close my eyes, starting to mentally count.

Thirty.

Twenty-nine.

Twenty-eight.

Twenty-seven.

I feel someone pass above me but keep counting.

Twenty-five.

Twenty-four.

Twenty-three.

A sharp kick to my obliques drops me to the floor.

"What the *fuck*?" I curl in on myself and groan, wiping the sweat out of my eyes and blinking against the sting. I peer up and see Katie standing above me, arms crossed and one high heel tapping on the floor of the training room. She stares down at me, her eyes hard and lip curled.

"Can I help you?" I ask, gritting my teeth as my side throbs with what I know will be a bruise in the morning.

"Where's Theo? He told me to meet him here."

"Why would you meet here?"

She frowns. "I was in the area."

"Try the squat racks." I point to the section in question and see Theo's brown curls poking out from behind a rack.

"Thanks." Katie heads off.

"Hey," I call after her and she turns her head. "What was that for?" I indicate my ribs, where the blossom of color is already present. She narrows her eyes and turns back toward the squat rack but barely goes more than a few steps before tossing a casual "congratulations on your hard launch" over her shoulder.

"What?"

"Your new girlfriend?" She turns to face me. "Victoria Winston?"

"What?" I repeat, seriously confused now.

"Your photo in the paper. It's all over social media."

"She's not my girlfriend," I say rather dumbly, pushing myself up to sitting.

"It sure looks like it in that photo." Her lips press into a thin line as she assesses me.

"She's not my girlfriend. We're just friends and we attend events together sometimes." I shrug.

"Well, I'm just telling you now, it *looks* like she's your girlfriend from the way you're standing with her. And I'm not the only one who reads the paper or looks at Instagram." She stares at me pointedly.

Fuck.

"She saw it?"

"Obviously."

"What did she say?"

Katie scoffs. "Good luck, Cal."

Double fuck.

I get back into plank position and start the last thirty-count over, mind whirring.

Thirty.

Twenty-nine

Twenty-eight.

● ● ●

It's a media day today, which means that after practice the team spends a little extra time primping in the locker room before being rolled out before a variety of reporters. Most of the sound bites never see the light of day, but if it catches someone's ear you could be on ESPN's prime-time segment tomorrow.

I'm waiting for Blaze to finish up his questions when I finally spot my favorite reporter, Gavin, sneaking in the back, notepad clutched in his hand. I push off the wall I'd been leaning against and stride quickly over to him.

"Hey, man," I whisper, and he jumps.

"Oh, hey, Cal, did I miss much? The wife was sick, and the sitter was late, so I needed to stay with the boys until she got there."

"Nah, man, Meadows is almost done, and you know he never has much to say anyway."

Blaze is a great quarterback, but he has a tendency to ramble on in interviews. The only bonus is that none of it ever means anything. Right now, he's on a tangent about his grandmother's meatball recipe and how nothing in the city truly compares to the authentic-Italian grandma meatballs. He's probably right, but the only thing that will come from it, if anything, is several top Italian restaurants offering him a taste test of their meatballs. If we're lucky, they'll send a couple pans to the training facility for lunch one day.

Gavin chuckles, tuning in to the meatball tangent. He starts off toward the reporters gathered at the front of the room, but I grab his arm.

"I actually have a favor for today if you don't mind."

Chapter Twelve

LILA

I sigh and wipe the sweat from my brow as I set the piping bag down on the counter, four dozen deviled eggs officially done. I finish packing them up in the tins I bought for the baby shower when I catch sight of my ratty hair in the mirror next to the door. I glance at my watch.

If I shower right now, I'll still make it twenty minutes early. Not quite the hour I committed to, but there's no way I can show up to my little sister's baby shower with greasy hair and last night's smudged mascara.

After a quick shower, I'm feeling slightly better, even if my hair is going to be naturally beachy with frizzy uneven curls rather than the artfully beachy I'd prefer, but with the top half pulled back in a clip, maybe no one will notice.

I jump in my Uber, the fruits of my labor—my deviled eggs— buckled in beside me and try to slow my breathing as we drive down the highway and out into the suburbs. It's a strange feeling, to be both happy with your life and entirely inadequate when your younger sibling surpasses your own timeline. The very last thing I need right now is to spiral out of control and give my family one more reason to think I'm falling behind.

My childhood home is decorated in light blue and white, with balloons tied to the mailbox out front and streamers twirled around the porch railing. I sigh, pasting a smile on my face as I push open the front door.

It's absolute chaos inside.

Blue hydrangeas have exploded over the dining room, flowers covering the table with a pile of diapers in the middle of the living room floor.

"I'm here," I call out. "Sorry I'm late."

"*Finally,* Lila. You said you'd be here an hour ago," my mother laments, popping out from behind the corner.

"I brought deviled eggs." I hold up the tins of goodness and step carefully through the loose flower petals over to the kitchen. "Uhm, aren't people coming in half an hour?"

"Wow, I hadn't noticed," she snaps. "You could make yourself useful and actually help you know."

I close my eyes and count to three. This is for Kayla. "What can I do?"

She points to the dining room table turned flower garden. "Those need to go in vases and pinned up in the streamers."

"Sounds great."

I make quick work of the flowers, and within fifteen minutes, I have the three vases complete with bunches of the blue and white flowers. I can't help but notice that not one of the vases is one that I've made for my parents over the years and place them strategically on tables throughout the two rooms, brightening up the space.

With the rest of the hydrangeas, I pin one in the center of each knot in the streamers around the ceiling, adding some much needed depth. Gathering up the leftover stems and loose petals, I dump them in the outdoor compost bin, just as Kayla and Alex walk up the driveway.

"You might want to give it a minute," I say as I hug her.

She groans. "How's mom?"

"A tad stressed."

She winces.

"Is there anything we can help with?"

"*You* should sit and put your feet up. Alex, I could use."

He gives me a salute. "Put me to work."

They follow me into the living room, and Alex and I get to work on a diaper pyramid display while Kayla eases herself into the rocking chair. He places the last two on top right as the doorbell rings.

"Perfect timing," he says, smiling at his wife. She really is glowing.

I open the door to my three aunts—Becky, Brenda, and Sally —each holding a giant pack of diapers.

"The presents are in the car, dear. Can you grab them?" Sally asks, before they shove past me into the house.

"Sure," I mutter, more to myself since no one can hear anything over the cooing that has started in the living room.

I grab the three large gift bags from her SUV and set them next to Kayla in her rocker before falling into my own folding chair across the room.

Over the next twenty minutes, the house fills to an uncomfortable level. Aunts, cousins, Kayla's friends from over the years, and the occasional male relative crowd nearly every inch of standing space throughout the living room, the pile of presents next to the mom-to-be growing with every ring of the doorbell.

I try to make myself inconspicuous, sipping my blue mimosa in the doorway to the kitchen.

"I would have thought you'd be having one of these soon," a nasally voice says from behind me. I turn slowly to face Alex's mother, Felicity.

"It just isn't in the cards for me right now," I force through my teeth.

She clucks her tongue. "You, poor dear, you'll find someone

eventually." I stiffen as she pats my arm, condescension oozing from every word.

"You know I'm still seeing Dennis, Felicity." It might be a bit of a stretch of the truth, but she doesn't need to know that. "You met him a few Christmases ago."

"Oh, is that still going on? I thought he moved to New York."

Our conversation has unfortunately drawn the attention of the people nearest us, and it's not me that's first to respond.

"They're just doing long-distance now," Aunt Sally responds snidely.

"I never understood long-distance dating," Aunt Becky chimes in. I clench my jaw, reminding myself once again that today is not about me.

Aunt Brenda has to add her two cents in. "It just seems a little backward at this point, sweetie."

"Well, good thing it's not your relationship then," I snap, finishing off my drink.

"Oh, honey," Aunt Brenda chides. "We didn't mean to upset you."

"I'm not upset."

"Hmm." Aunt Becky purses her lips together.

"Well, he'll need to move back if you want to start a family, you know," Aunt Sally points out.

"I know," I bite out.

"And it would be ever so nice to have baby Gregory grow up with cousins around his age," Felicity chimes in.

I blink at her, pressing my lips together, because thinking of Gregory as the name of an infant makes me want to do nothing but laugh. "Right. Well, if you'll excuse me, I think I should freshen up Kayla's juice." I step quickly away from them, feeling significantly worse than I did fifteen minutes ago, and grab the orange juice from the kitchen to fill my sister's half-empty glass.

I shamelessly fill the rest of the two-hour party sulking in the corner behind Kayla's chair where thankfully there is only space for one person, pausing my personal pity party to take notes on who gifted what. And finally—*finally*—it's time to leave.

I'm gathering my empty trays when I spot something that gives me pause on the muted TV in the kitchen: a replay of an interview with the Chicago Avalanche from earlier today, a bold headline scrolling across the screen.

CHICAGO'S MOST ELIGIBLE BACHELOR CONFIRMED SINGLE

My breath hitches when the photo of Cal pops up, and I turn up the volume on the TV just as the interview starts playing.

"You've been notoriously single for years but have been photographed with one Victoria Winston, can we put the rumors to rest?"

Cal smirks at the reporter, and my stomach does a weird sort of flop.

"Tori and I are old family friends. She's definitely not my girl-friend . . ." The interview continues, but I turn the TV off, the roaring in my ears too loud to handle the additional noise.

"Ooh who is that? He's cute," Aunt Becky coos from behind me.

"Just a friend." *Shit*. I should definitely not have said that.

"Lila, don't be silly, that's an NFL player," Aunt Brenda scolds, popping in beside her sister.

"Yes, he is. He's also friends with Katie. You know I'm actually friends with Theo McClane too, right?"

They snicker.

"Well, confirmed single or not, that man can have me ten ways to Sunday," Aunt Sally jokes, and disgust roils through me at that wonderful mental image. Her sisters cackle in agreement, and I flee the kitchen before I'm forced to hear anything more.

"Sorry, mom, I have a work thing, so I can't stay to help clean up," I call over my shoulder trying not to break into a dead sprint toward the Uber waiting at the curb. I sink into the backseat of the Toyota Corolla that has just become my lifeline as it takes me back to civilization.

The ride back feels like it takes both five minutes and five hours, but when I'm finally home, I close the door behind me and slide down to the floor, my face in my hands taking deep breaths to keep the tears at bay. Something about spending a few hours with my family always causes the need for an immediate release of pent-up emotion. Maybe it has something to do with the absolute train wreck of emotional stability coupled with the fun competitive edge my parents always drove into us. At least Dad has always meant well.

After a few minutes I shakily get to my feet and gather my thoughts, the interview playing over in my head.

They aren't together then. He really is single.

He wouldn't lie about something like that in an interview, right? There was no room for ambiguity in his answer. Definitely not, his girlfriend.

Definitely not.

I can't help the small smile that breaks over my face.

My fingers hover over my messages app, and I steel myself.

> Hey, how've you been?

I mentally kick myself. That's the best I could come up with? Even so, he replies almost instantly.

> CAL
>
> Hey Lila
>
> I've been alright, busy I guess.

> That's good, staying busy I mean.

> Yeah, we're looking pretty good this year so everyone's pushing extra hard in practice to prep for the next few games.

We really want to claim that playoff spot.

Oooh yeah, makes sense. I believe in you guys though, the last couple games you've looked really good.

Oh really?

I flush, grateful he isn't here to watch me fluster.

You know what I meant

But I won't pretend that I don't pay special attention whenever you're on the field.

CAL

Everyone needs someone to play for.

And who do you play for?

Ask me again when you're ready for the answer

I smile, a warmth blossoming in my chest that feels like coming home after a long day and fall into a blissfully comfortable sleep.

Chapter Thirteen

LILA

The rest of the week flies by. Cal and I are able to resume our easy friendship, even if it's a bit more tentative than before, and thanks to Colton's client, work has been going smoothly.

I should've known karma would send me a curveball.

DENNIS

Hey babe, we have a company party next Tuesday.

Okay

This is really the first thing he says after we haven't spoken since he was here? I should be surprised, but I'm not. Just disappointed, once again. How do I get out of going? The last thing I want to do is be paraded out in front of his colleagues. Especially with how he spoke to me this past weekend.

DENNIS

I have a plus one if you can come up for a few days.

> I don't know if I can.

Please babe, I'm sorry for what I said, you know I didn't mean it. But I really need you here.

You've always been the one I can count on.

Thanks for that guilt trip. But he's not wrong. His parents aren't in the picture anymore, and it has always been the two of us against the world. I can do this one thing for him. And maybe we can work it out while I'm there. I hastily check my calendar.

> I think I can make it.

DENNIS

It's formal, I'll get you a dress. Go ahead and use my points for the flight.

> Thanks.

Looking forward to it.

Love you babe.

I close my eyes and breathe, willing myself to be excited. It's not anything I haven't done before, and sometimes the events are even fun. Not quite as fun as those I've gone to with Katie, but it's close.

I pull up my United app and scan through the flights. I hesitate before booking the Monday morning flight. Sunday is suddenly off limits according to some small part of my mind, and I don't want to have to share it with Dennis. Not when they belong to someone else.

> Just booked a Monday morning flight, I'll fwd you the email confirmation.

DENNIS

Sounds good, I'll see you then.

It's only a few moments before my phone pings again.

KATIE

Hey, are you busy Sunday?

No, but the guys are playing if you want to watch

Cool

???

Twenty minutes later, another text appears.

CAL

Hey, do you want to come to the game on Sunday?

Like in person?

Yeah

Definitely!

Great, I have a ticket for you.

How much do I owe you for it?

Don't worry about it, I had an extra.

You don't have to do that!

I have one for Katie too.

Okay cool, thanks!

I'll send them over now.

THE FALSE START

An email notification pops up on my phone screen. I click in, looking at the tickets he just sent over, and my jaw drops.

> Cal!

> These are in a suite.

CAL
> Yep! There'll be food so come hungry and have fun!

> I can't accept these, it's too much!

> I told you I had extra tickets. It'll make me happy to see them go to someone who will enjoy the game and not just the bar.

> Alright, if you're sure . . .

> I'm sure.

I switch back to my messages with Katie.

> Did you know Cal got us box seats?

KATIE
> 🫠 WHAT?

> Yeah, I know! He said they were extra?

> Yeah okay.

> Open bar!

> Yeah, and think of the field view!

> 😊 🎉

> It'll be fun!

> 🎉

I've never been in a box at Soldier Field, and to say I'm excited would be an understatement. This game is a big one, a divisional rivalry against Green Bay, and occasionally a game like this draws various celebrities who grew up in the Midwest, not to mention the famous WAGs of the players of both teams.

I scroll through outfit inspo on Pinterest for the rest of the evening, each photo contradicting the one prior, and fall asleep with my phone clutched in my hand.

● ● ●

On Sunday morning, I'm wide awake before my alarm has a chance to go off and hop out of bed, my excitement rivaling a small child on Christmas morning. I lay out my outfit over the covers, wanting to see it all together, and smile. The vintage Avalanche sweatshirt is the perfect choice for today's game.

I'm stepping out of the shower when my phone pings across the room. It's a delivery notification. Odd since I didn't order anything and it's a Sunday, but I throw on an old pair of sweats and run down to check.

"Miss Lila, *another* special delivery for you this mornin'," calls Maureen from her spot at the front desk.

"What is it?"

She holds up a silver Avalanche jersey, a navy '85' emblazoned across the back .

"That handsome man dropped it off just a few minutes ago," she says with a smug smile.

"The same one from the flowers?"

"So, you *do* know him."

"Of course, I know him." I laugh. "We're just friends."

"Oh, honey, that man is not *just friends* material."

I shrug noncommittally and take the jersey from her outstretched hands.

"Have fun today," she calls to me with a wink as I head back to my apartment. I let her see the eye roll that follows.

"Thanks, Maureen!"

Well, a jersey certainly changes things. Things being my outfit. I can't not wear it if he brought it over here. Katie will probably be wearing a jersey too, along with hundreds of other people at the stadium. It's not like a statement or anything if I wear it. And I'd much rather wear a jersey anyway; I just didn't have one before now. I head straight to my closet, flipping through hangers like I'm in a reality show. It's chilly but not cold, so I pull out a long-sleeved white bodysuit and pair it with jeans, tucking the over-sized jersey in at the waist and picking out my favorite pair of heeled booties.

I'm bouncing around my apartment, hair and makeup done, just waiting until ten when I can meet Katie and head over to the stadium. We're meeting up with Maggie, Theo's younger sister, at the game. I've only met her once, but she's very similar to Theo, just less flirty, at least with me.

I'm staring at my reflection and second guessing the jersey. It's almost too . . . intimate. I know hundreds of people have worn Cal's jersey, but they all bought their own. He *gave* this one to me. It's his. What does it say about us if I wear it in public? Is it a sign we're something more than friends, or can friends wear each other's jerseys if they're professional athletes?

I groan. It'll be fine. Dennis isn't coming, and he's really the only one who would make a fuss. And with other actual famous people in the crowd, any reporters will assume I'm just a random guest, maybe someone's sister. After my small mental breakdown, Katie's name pops up on my phone.

KATIE

3 min away

I take one last look in the mirror, fluffing my hair out for good measure. There's no time to change now even if I wanted to. I grab my smallest purse, praying the security guards will be nice today—too many of my friends in grad school have lost bags to the Soldier Field security team—and head to meet the Uber.

Katie gives me an appraising look as we leave the car and walk to the stadium.

"What?" I ask, self-conscious.

"The jersey looks good on you."

I roll my eyes, since she's wearing a vintage jacket. "He dropped it off this morning."

"He'll be happy you're wearing it."

I don't have time to contemplate what that means as we're whisked through security and up to the box.

Maggie greets us with hugs and vodka seltzers when we finally get up to the suite. Seeing that she's also wearing a jersey puts me at ease about my own outfit decision.

"I'm so glad you guys made it," she squeals. "Black cherry or peach?" Katie claims the peach.

"Thanks." We all toast our drinks. "This is so cool," I say after a sip. I step further into the box and try to keep my cool. There are tureens of Italian beef, Chicago hotdog fixings, and mac 'n' cheese piled high, a full bar stocked along the side, and a large platter of cookies and brownies.

Maggie shrugs.

"So, Maggie, what have you been up to? It's been, what, two years?" The last time I saw Maggie was at a hip-hop concert Katie brought me to. She'd been fresh out of college at UCLA and figuring out what was next in her life, which at the time, consisted of traveling and partying a little too hard, according to Theo.

"I landed a job with Chanel! I'm on their web design team."

"That's great. Congratulations." Katie hugs her.

"No, what's really awesome is the discount," Maggie says with a sly grin. "Forty percent if you can believe it." I gasp.

"I love silver hardware," mentions Katie seriously. "Gold for Lila over here."

Maggie nods. "You got it, ladies."

Just then the "Star Spangled Banner" starts, and the stadium goes silent as a local winner of a recent talent show sings his heart out. Cheers and applause erupt as he holds out the last note, and then we all turn to grab our seats as the game starts.

Today's game is packed, and the crowd is divided and wild. Each play is met with screams of celebration and jeers from the fans of both teams. I cheer with the best of them, screaming with delight alongside Maggie and Katie as Theo makes catch after catch carrying the team down the field. I can't help as my eyes are drawn during each offensive play to number eighty-five, the one that matches the one on my own back. Cal's number.

I can't help but peer into the boxes around us, the two to our right belonging to other players on the team. In our neighboring box, three gorgeous women sit side by side in the front row. They're the kind of pretty you don't think exists in real life because the only way to look that perfect is through Photoshop and Facetune filters. This is proof that some people really are God's favorite. The girl nearest me has a rock on her left hand that would blind the International Space Station.

"Who is that?" I ask Maggie, trying to point nonchalantly.

"Bridget Evers, she's engaged to the other wide receiver. She played division-one volleyball at UCLA and landed on the cover of Sports Illustrated last year, and then he popped the question at the opening game of the season."

A model *and* a division-one athlete.

"The other two next to her are also dating players, but I can't remember their names." Maggie shrugs. "I've found that until they get the ring, most of the girlfriends are only around for a season."

I look past the trio into the next box and see a heavily pregnant women doing her best to corral two more young children with the help of an older woman. Each of them wearing the same jersey of one of the linemen.

Is this what it means to date a player? Are you either a perfectly manicured Barbie or a mom of three? I shove the thought to the back of my mind and refocus my attention on the game playing out in front of me.

Cal is having a pretty good game, making several impressive blocks and once even being the sole reason Theo made it down the field. His lack of receiving yards makes me guiltily glad he's still riding the bench on my own fantasy team. Tight ends in fantasy aren't just about who's the best player after all, it's all about the points.

With twenty seconds left in the fourth quarter, the Avalanche take their last timeout. We're down by four at the twenty-yard line, and my anxiety is at an all-time high as I watch my friends down on the field. The crowd is eerily silent as everyone waits with bated breath the two teams huddled on opposite sides of the field. Cal says something to Blaze Meadows, their quarterback, one of the coaches listening intently. The coach shakes his head and Cal points down the field his eyes blazing, though his mouth is covered as the camera zeros in on their conversation. With a quick word from the QB, the coach relents, giving a small nod to Cal, and the two players share a grim look before heading back to the field.

I hold my breath as Meadows drops into the pocket with the ball, scanning the field to find Theo occupied with two defenders.

I see it at the same time the Jumbotron does—Cal doesn't block. I gasp as Cal side-steps his own lineman, turns to snag the ball out of the air at the ten-yard line, and easily outstrips the linebacker to his right. As he nears the end zone, he's facing the wrong way to see the fullback lunge for him.

"Cal!" I scream, but it's futile.

I'm too far, and with the roar of the stadium, it's unlikely he'd hear me if I was standing ten feet from him.

The defender hits him hard, knocking him backwards, and they both crash to the ground. The scream of the crowd goes up as the replay on the Jumbotron shows Cal's arm, still holding the ball, cross the goal line before his knee touches down.

"*TOUCHDOWN!*"

I'm jumping up and down with Maggie, screaming at the top of my lungs with delight at our win, at *Cal's* win. People better at math than me do the calculations, and thanks to Cal's catch, we've officially secured a place in the playoffs for the first time in a decade. The news echoes around the stadium, and everyone is cheering even more loudly, me right along with them, until I realize he hasn't gotten up. I sober up immediately, staring at the place he lays on the ground, hand still clutching the ball, surrounded by teammates.

The medic runs onto the field, calling for the golf cart moments later and helping Cal onto it. He's still holding the ball, if it's glued to his glove. His face turns up, eyes landing on our box and as the Jumbotron focuses on the close-up, he smiles slightly before being carted off the field and into the bowels of the stadium.

The last few seconds count down, and we secure the extra point and the win, but all I can focus on is the sudden nausea that's churning in my stomach. Katie and Maggie pull me into the small kitchenette of the suite.

"Come on, Lila, celebrate!" Maggie whines, "He'll be okay. We can go see him if you want."

I brighten at that. "Really?" Then cringe. "I mean, he might not want to see me, but he's my friend who just got hurt, so of course, I'm concerned. I would be for Theo too, of course, or really anyone on the team . . ." I trail off and realize I've been rambling, as Katie stands smirking at me.

Maggie rolls her eyes. "Let's go. Just follow me and keep your passes out," she says, indicating the family and friends passes we were issued when we entered the building.

We follow her down through the stadium and into a network

of tunnels before popping out into a large room with several dozen people milling about.

"This is where some of the family members come after the games," Maggie explains as the three of us stand off to the side, eyes on the large double doors to the players' locker room area. Theo pushes through them first, clearly drunk on victory with a giant smile on his face as he shakes his freshly washed hair over his sister, making her squeal. He gives Katie a hug and pauses when his eyes meet mine, reading the concern that must be etched into them.

"He'll be out soon. He just got cleared by the trainer. No concussion, just a bad hit," he explains quietly. I nod, grateful for the update, though my shoulders don't relax quite yet. We wait around another quarter of an hour as Maggie and Theo catch up before Cal finally makes his way out of the doors toward us, moving slightly slower than his normal speed, and only then do I release the tension in my muscles. He looks okay.

He meets my gaze, and I could swear his features brighten a fraction.

"Hey," he says, eyes never leaving mine.

"How're you doing? Are you okay?" I ask, needing to make absolutely sure.

He chuckles, eyes crinkling. "I'm fine. I was cleared by three different doctors. I didn't get a CT, but no one seemed to think it was necessary right now."

"I can take you!" I blurt out.

"Lila, I'm okay," he insists. "Really."

I throw my arms around him and hug him tightly. He freezes under my touch, and I step away quickly.

"Sorry, I was just so worried when I saw you go down."

He flushes, mumbling something I don't catch.

"But you won! That was such an amazing catch!"

I glance at his hands, and he's still holding the ball. I raise an eyebrow at him, and he looks down at it sheepishly.

"Thanks. They, um, they said I could keep the ball, since it was my first touchdown on the team."

"You deserve it, Cal."

He smiles, but doesn't respond, and we're left in a slightly awkward silence until Theo loudly calls from a few feet over. "I'm absolutely starved. Dinner anyone?"

I giggle, but Cal waves a hand, and we all head out, intent on finding something that will curb his never-ending appetite.

Chapter Fourteen

CAL

"So, party at my place tonight," Theo announces when we've finished dinner. I stifle a groan, half from the pain throbbing throughout my left side and half out of exasperation.

"A party? Are you sure?" Katie asks.

He laughs and waggles his eyebrows. "I need to show off the new decor at some point, don't I?"

Lila gives me a once over, and I straighten automatically. "I don't know if that's such a good idea, Theo."

I frown at her words, but Maggie jumps in before I have the chance to. "Cal needs to rest."

"I'm fine. My head barely hurts." Not a complete lie, since the pain is mostly in my shoulder.

Lila's eyes focus in on me. "I really don't think you should drink if they were worried about a concussion."

"I was cleared," I remind her, her eyes narrowing until I'm left squirming in my seat. "Fine, I won't drink . . . a lot."

She crosses her arms with a huff but lets it go. I sigh. Getting properly tipsy would dull the pain better than the ibuprofen I was recommended by the trainer.

Maggie stands, dragging Katie to her feet right behind her. "We'll go get drinks and meet you in thirty?"

Theo waves them off, and the two of us head over to his condo a few blocks away with Lila.

"How are you feeling, really?" she asks quietly from behind Theo, whistling while he walks like he's out of a fucking Disney cartoon.

I glance down at her, the preliminary annoyance fading at the concern in her big brown eyes. "I'm *really* feeling fine. I'll be sore tomorrow, but no worse than after taking a couple hard hits at practice."

"What about your head?"

"Secrets don't make friends," Theo singsongs back at us, and I chuckle.

"Someone's just overly concerned for my well-being."

"I am not." She pouts, and it's adorable. "I'm the right amount of concerned. You just seem to be under-concerned."

I roll my eyes, draping one arm across her shoulders and pulling her body flush with mine. Before I know what I'm doing, I drop a kiss to the top of her head. She looks up at me in surprise and rather than see the horror in her face, I drop my arm and stride forward to catch up to Theo.

🏈 🏈 🏈

"Damn, McClane, Katie did a number on your place." I take in the front room, completely unrecognizable from the last time I was here. It resembles my mother's guesthouse more than my own bachelor pad now. Splashes of color brighten up the previously monochrome apartment. Throw pillows dotting the couch and a cushy red chair sits near one window.

Lila smacks my arm. "It really looks great, Theo."

He grins at her. "Katie did the hard work, I just gave her my credit card." He turns to me. "She'll be on you soon, now that you've bought a place here." I shudder. I love Katie like a sister, but that woman will touch my apartment over my dead body.

"You're lucky she didn't max it out," Lila snickers.

"Don't tell her," Theo whispers conspiratorially, "but I had the bank put a temporary limit on it."

We laugh just as the door opens.

"What's so funny?" Maggie asks, carrying three large paper bags as she follows an equally heavy-laden Katie into the apartment.

"Nothing. Cal just said something funny."

"Wow, good to see he's found his sense of humor. I thought it had gone to die with the rest of his personality," Katie quips, deadpanning.

"Miss Chen, have I personally insulted you somehow?" I offer as graciously as my sarcasm will allow.

"She's just pissed you interrupted her flirting with the hockey player at the last party," Lila fills in.

Heat creeps up my neck as everyone but Maggie remembers what a fool I made of myself that night.

"Well, if I promise not to repeat the experience will you forgive me?"

She shrugs, pulling out a tequila bottle. "Ugh fine, it's not like I could stay mad at you anyway. Now who wants shots?"

I reach to take an offered shot glass when Lila loudly clears her throat. I look up and see her glaring at me and drop my hand.

"I'll pass tonight," I tell Katie. She tips it into her own mouth, chasing it with a lime wedge. I grab a beer from the fridge instead, ignoring Lila's narrowed eyes, but the lack of verbal admonishment must mean it's at least an acceptable choice, and slump down on Theo's new and rather uncomfortable couch.

It doesn't take long until we're joined by several other players and friends. They all laugh, filling their cups as Katie pours out shot after shot. My head is starting to pound. Lila sways to the music filling the apartment, giggling at something Maggie said, and I can't be here anymore. I want nothing more than to be in my own bed, the new documentary on grey whales calling my name, but I grit my teeth, not wanting to cause a scene.

I slip onto the balcony and find it blissfully quiet, the cold air a welcome relief on my sore body. Who needs ice when you have Chicago winter?

Theo still has his patio furniture out, and I sink onto the small couch, grateful Katie chose something practical when it molds to my body. I rest my hands on my thighs, and take in the city below us, spread out and glittering for miles.

I sit like this until my face grows numb, and then I'm too cold to leave. Just as I'm contemplating making an excuse to head home early, the balcony door opens and Lila steps out holding two drinks.

"Hey." She offers one of the cans to me.

I smile up at her. "Thanks. I'm surprised you're letting me drink."

"It's non-alcoholic." I grin as she takes the empty seat next to me. It takes nearly every ounce of self-control to keep from leaning into her warmth. "Cheers." She cracks the top of her seltzer, and I do the same, clinking cans before I take a sip of the drink she brought me.

After several minutes, she breaks the silence.

"It was a great game today. Thanks for the tickets." Then almost as an afterthought, she adds, "And the jersey." She blushes, and I'm much less cold now.

"No one's ever worn a jersey for me, you know." I can't keep the smirk out of my voice, and I know she hears it by the way she shifts.

"There were hundreds of people who had your jersey on just today."

"But only one of them was there for me. The rest are fans of the team. They might be carry-over fans from the Cosmos, but to most I'm just the shiny new player. Next year they'll be the first to buy whoever the new big trade is. The new rookie." I scoff. Seeing the royalty checks come through from jersey sales is always a cool feeling, until I start to line up the timing.

"Oh," she says, falling silent, and I mentally kick myself for shutting her down after she not only sought me out but tried to start a conversation.

"Yeah, so thanks for wearing it." I turn to her smiling.

"Of course, Cal." Her throat bobs as she swallows. "How's your head?"

Safer territory. Friend territory. That's fine.

Her words bring my attention back to the pounding I had nearly dissociated from, and I let out a long breath. "I have a pretty rough headache, honestly. It's why I came out here in the first place."

"Oh," she says again.

"The music's just a little loud, and I'm not really in the mood to make small talk. But as much as he drives me up a wall, I'd rather Theo not actually hate me, which he might if I ruined another party." I let out a dry laugh.

"If you want to be alone in the quiet, I can go." She stands, but I reach up and grab her wrist, halting her movement.

"No, stay. It's different with you."

She laughs nervously but sits back down. "If you're sure."

I make a low sound of approval in my throat.

"Tell me something that's not small talk. Tell me something real."

"Like what?" she asks, another nervous laugh bubbling up through her lips.

I shrug. "Doesn't matter. My head hurts less listening to you." That and I want nothing more than to peel her shell back and learn every single thing about Lila Summers. To know what makes her tick, to know what gets her off, to know what she dreams about.

"Why do I feel like you're making that up?"

I grin at her, a look I've perfected over the years with a ninety-nine percent success rate on women. "What's worse, me making it up or you not doing it because you think I *might* be making it up and then I'm not and you miss your opportunity to help?"

She groans. "I've only had, like three drinks, and I still can't follow that."

"Something real," I prompt.

She looks back across the city, quiet for a moment, and I think she's ignoring me.

"I secretly hate that my sister is having a baby."

I'm floored. I hoped she'd answer, hoped she'd give me something real, but this is deep. The kind of deep you hesitate to tell your therapist just in case she somehow gets you committed. But hang on, what? I knew she had a sister, but as I try to find the box in my brain for Lila's family, I don't remember her being pregnant. Aren't most people excited to be aunts? What happened to make her so upset over it? I want to ask all these questions, but my mouth isn't working properly.

"It's not that I don't want her to have a baby or be a mother. I think she and Alex will actually be great parents, but I just wanted to be first, you know?" She pauses for breath before launching into an explanation I desperately want but don't feel I deserve. "She's younger, and she's always been the golden child. I did it all first, and I even did some of it better, but none of that matters. I got the big fancy job in the city and the great new apartment, but she got the husband and the four-bedroom house in the suburbs, and that's always been the measure. So, because she did all *that* first, she wins, and now I'm just the sad, old maid who can't find a husband and is married to my job because it's the only thing I'm good at."

She takes a shuddering breath, and I have the urge to wrap her in my arms.

"So, yeah," she continues with a shrug as she stares off into the distance, "I just sometimes wish they had decided to wait a few more years. Maybe even given me a chance to get a bit more settled, maybe find my own husband, I don't know. And I feel horrible for feeling that way, because I should be happy for them —I *am* happy for them—I just don't really know how to experience this specific happiness without feeling like I'm watching my life pass by, and I forgot to get on the train."

That gives me pause.

"Is Dennis not going to be your husband?" I ask quietly. I think they're back together, but it's not really a *friend* thing to ask about. Not in our friendship.

She shrugs. "I don't know. It's so hard to know with the distance. It doesn't feel the way it used to. *I* don't feel the way I used to, and I don't really know what to do about it, but I wouldn't marry him if he asked right now. He knows I won't go to New York, and I don't think he's ready to come back to Chicago." She slumps, and I wrap an arm around her shoulders before I can think better of it and pull her to me.

"I'm a terrible person."

"You're not a terrible person," I tell her, rubbing circles on her upper arm with my thumb.

"I just told you I don't want my sister to have a baby, and I don't want to marry my long-term boyfriend."

"Hey." I wait for her to meet my gaze, her face partially lit by the adjoining room. "You're not a bad person. And that's not what you said. Almost everything was about you, how you wanted to be recognized for the great things you're doing in your own life. You shouldn't be held to someone else's standards or definition of success. That's not a crazy concept."

"Not gonna touch the other one, huh?" She laughs, blinking as a tear falls down her cheek.

I wipe it away with my thumb, my palm lingering as it cups her jaw. It would be so easy to lean down and close the space between our mouths. Her eyes flit down to my lips and back up. I could, I realize. I could kiss her, and she would kiss me back tonight. But she didn't say he wasn't her boyfriend. And the idea that she'd be thinking of him is out of the question.

I hear a familiar upbeat tune start to play through the glass window into the apartment.

"Here," I say, standing and pulling her up with me. "It's not 'Sweet Caroline,' but I happen to love *this* song."

She laughs, recognizing the popular Journey hit as everyone starts to sing the first chorus. "I didn't have you pegged as a soft rock guy."

"I'm really more of a podcaster if I'm honest."

"Even before games?"

"We can't have our phones for ninety minutes before games or even at halftime, so I got used to going without or just settling for whatever's playing in the locker room," I say, remembering what a tough transition that was. She stares at me dumbfounded.

"I always assumed players had their curated pre-game playlists." I laugh, it's a common misconception.

"Dance with me, Lila." I hold out my hand and wait for her to take it before pulling her in toward me and placing my free hand on her waist. We sway slowly and offbeat as the music fades into a slower country song. The guitar strums a contemplative background noise for the moment as Lila steps nearer and lays her head on my chest, the hand not tucked into mine wrapping around my neck.

"Tell me something about your family," she whispers against my shirt.

I take a deep breath, thinking for a moment before I say, "My dad doesn't approve of me playing American football. Well, any sport professionally really. He wants me to take over for him at his company in a few years."

"You still could, right? When you retire from the NFL?"

"I don't want to."

She doesn't push, and it gives me the space to open up on my own. "I don't want anything to do with him."

"Why not?"

"My childhood wasn't the best." She tenses, but I can't handle another question. "Tonight's not the night to get into it, but if I never saw him again, it would be too soon."

She doesn't respond but continues to dance with me until the end of this song and the next.

And the next.

This feels different. I should really tell her now, tell her how my feelings are anything but friendly. How I want her to give us a chance.

"Lila—" A wave of cheers inside cuts me off and ends whatever bubble we've been in for the past twenty minutes or so. We break apart, and Lila checks her phone gasping.

"It's already after eleven. I should get home."

"Yeah, I'm feeling the hit from earlier." My body hurts, but more than anything, I just want an excuse to be near her for a few more minutes.

"Do you want to split an Uber"

I nod. "We should say goodnight first."

We step back into the living room, a group of hockey players surrounding Katie as she explains something, one of them paying entirely too much attention to her ass, and I roll my eyes. I get Theo's attention and point to the door, then to Lila. "I'll make sure she gets home," I call to him over the noise. He waggles his eyebrows back at me, and I glance over to see Lila narrowing her eyes at him.

We ride the short distance in silence, our earlier conversation stretching to fill the distance.

"I'll see you later?" I ask as she steps out of the car.

"I'm actually headed for New York tomorrow." A lead weight

drops into my gut. She's going to New York. For him. But it can't be my imagination that she seems disappointed in her plans. "But I'll be cheering you on next Sunday if we don't all do something before then."

"Have a safe trip."

She's going to New York. And I almost told her—

No.

She's going to New York.

I'm throwing toiletries into my open bag and getting more stressed by the second. I should've left for the airport ten minutes ago, and I'm still not packed. It's not like me, but I woke up late after a nearly sleepless night of tossing and turning, replaying my conversation with Cal on the balcony over and over. And here I am, not packed and late to the airport for the first time in my life. I've been all over the place lately, and I can't fix it.

I shove the zipper closed on my overflowing suitcase, leaning my weight into it to try and compress the half-folded clothing inside. I grab a hoodie and drag a brush threw my hair as I call an Uber.

My heart thunders as I see the arrival time, approximately fifty minutes before my plane takes off. I grit my teeth and head downstairs to wait for the car. I open and close my message app about five different times, debating on whether or not to text Dennis before the black Toyota Corolla rolls up in front of me.

A minute later, we're off and I'm doing my absolute best to focus on answering work emails instead of backseat driving as we crawl along I-90. I make note of the time as we pull up to the terminal.

T-minus nineteen minutes until take off.

I powerwalk to the pre-check line. While it's not long, it's longer than the ten minutes I have until boarding closes. I start drafting the message and cancel it once again.

When I'm through TSA, I'll get rebooked then call him.

The line moves pretty fast, and I'm on the other side, bags in hand at T-minus seven minutes until takeoff. I take a deep breath and start running toward A14, my rolling suitcase dragging alongside of me.

I'm panting when I reach the gate. The door is securely shut, and the gate agent looks at me with disdain.

"Any chance I can still get on?" I gasp between breaths.

"The door is shut," he says matter-of-factly. "I can get you rebooked if you'd like."

I nod.

"Name?"

"Lila Summers."

"Final destination is New York?" He types on the keyboard, peering at me over the screen, and I can feel the silent scolding.

"Yes."

"I can get you on a flight to JFK, in at 3 p.m."

"Great, I'll take it."

I settle into a seat at what will be my new gate and take a deep breath before I start the call.

"Hey, is your flight delayed or something?" Dennis asks the second he picks up.

I cringe. "I missed my flight actually." I pause. "Traffic was absolutely terrible getting here, and then the TSA line was crazy. I'm sorry."

He sighs, long and hard. "I was really counting on you to be here Lila."

"I know. I'm coming, I promise. They rebooked me in a couple hours. I'll still be there for the party tomorrow."

"I made dinner reservations with some of my colleagues for us."

"I know, but I still have a key. I can get changed and then meet you there?"

I hear his long exhale on the other end of the line. "Yeah, that's fine, I guess."

"I didn't mean to miss my flight, I'm sorry."

"I just can't believe you. You've never been late to the airport in your life, and you knew this event was important to me. I mean, what was so important you couldn't get here on time?"

I don't say anything, and he's silent for a moment.

"I'll text you the details for dinner."

"Thanks, Dennis."

"Text me when you land." The line goes dead before I can respond.

Well, that could've gone worse.

● ● ●

The rest of the flight goes without a hitch, and as the sun sets over the skyline of New York City I climb into a taxi and head to Dennis's midtown apartment. I let myself in, taking in the space. I haven't been to visit in months, but the place looks nothing like it used to. It was always sterile—minimalistic furniture chosen for aesthetic rather than comfort, all black and white with the occasional wood tone. No color, no warmth. It would've been a perfect set for a Hugo Boss commercial. But now, there's a rug.

A blue rug in the entryway.

I step through the doorway and glance around. There are throw pillows on the couch, and a soft-looking blanket thrown over the back of it. It still looks like a living room you'd find straight out of *Vogue* rather than *Good Housekeeping*, but it is definitely different.

I roll my suitcase into his master bedroom, and I'm greeted by a clean, white comforter, a quilt thrown at the end of the bed. I idly wonder when he updated all his decor, a nagging feeling pulling at my gut.

I find the dark red dress I packed for dinner tonight and pull it on. With the help of dry shampoo, eyeliner, and some bronzer, I'm ready in about fifteen minutes and headed out the door.

Dinner is surprisingly painless. They've already ordered and while Dennis did get me a salad, he at least ordered truffle fries, and right now I'm taking the wins where I can get them. None of his colleagues talk to me aside from a perfunctory "hello" when I sit down. Flying always drains me so, while usually being ignored would sting, tonight I don't mind and simply enjoy my fries and the expensive red wine they've ordered for the table.

"Would it have killed you to make a good impression tonight?" Dennis asks angrily once we're in a cab headed back to his apartment.

"What do you mean?"

"You didn't speak to anyone. Not once."

"No one bothered to talk to me either. I laughed at jokes and waited for an opening or for someone to even look at me, but as soon as I sat down, I was invisible."

"Yeah," he mutters, staring out the window at the passing city streets.

"What did you want me to do?"

"I don't know, but not that."

We stew in silence for a few minutes.

"Why can't you just make me look good?" he bursts out.

"What?"

"All the partners at work, most of the associates even, have girlfriends or wives that *help* their career. And all you did was sit there and eat."

My face flushes, shame twinging the edge of my anger. "I didn't even ask to go to this. I wasn't expecting dinner tonight out with your work buddies until a few hours ago. If you had plans, I could have just ordered out and relaxed or we could've just gone out the two of us." My chest is heaving.

"Fine," he snaps. "Next time I'll go by myself then."

The words sting, even if I suggested them.

We're silent for the rest of the ride, barely speaking once we're back. I turn in early, exhausted from traveling and the argument, and I'm asleep before he comes to bed.

● ● ●

The following morning is tense, but since we're both working, the actual interaction we have is limited until around three. I'm working from his home office while he's at his actual office in the financial district downtown. The sudden slam of the door makes me jump, and then he's yelling.

"What the fuck, Lila?" He yells as he comes into view of the office doorway, and I flinch at the noise.

"What?" I ask, confused.

"You know what you did. You told me not to worry about him."

"What are you talking about?" I'm annoyed now, and he thrusts his phone in my face.

My stomach flutters at the photo on the Barstool Instagram page of me at the Avalanche game, wearing Cal's jersey.

"What?" I ask again.

"You're in his jersey! And the article says you went home together," he spits out. "I can't believe you."

I'm piecing it all together now, my annoyance growing.

"Okay, so first of all, Katie and Theo's sister are literally in the photo behind me. Maggie's wearing a jersey too. Cal offered his, and I didn't have one to wear, what was I going to say? No?"

"Yes exactly. No!"

"Second of all," I continue as if I didn't hear him, my voice growing louder to compensate, "the *five* of us left the game together to go get dinner nearby, we didn't 'go home' together." I stand from the desk and cross my arms, readying myself for battle.

"You're such a fucking whore. We both know you're fucking him." My blood turns to ice in my veins, and a calm washes over me.

"I'm not. I told you that when you were in Chicago a couple weeks ago. We're *friends*," I say, much more calmly than I feel. "And *don't* call me a whore."

"Then don't act like one."

I laugh, and he looks almost scared at the sound. "I'm not." I look him over and realize as if a lightbulb has exploded in my head, I don't have to do this. This isn't the person I fell in love with. I'm not even the person who fell in love with him anymore. I've become this mess of a human being, being a bad friend, showing up late to work, drinking more than usual. I don't like it, and I don't have to stand for it.

"I can't do this anymore Dennis. I'm not cheating on you, and I never have."

He sneers at me stepping closer into my space. "Then why is there an inside source saying you left the after party together?"

"Oh my god, we split an Uber." I throw my hands up in exasperation. "We live two blocks away from each other, and we were both ready to leave so it made sense." He slams his hands on the desk on either side of me, and I can't help but jump.

"Show me the ride."

"What?"

"The ride. Your history will show two stops if you really *just split an Uber*." He mocks the last part in a high pitched voice that I'm sure is supposed to be me.

"Cal ordered it. You can check the app, but that ride won't even be on my account."

He shakes his head. "Get out, I can't even look at you right now."

I grab my laptop from his desk and put it back into my work bag. Making quick work of packing up the stuff I used last night. I repack my suitcase and roll it through the living room, opening my United app.

"Where the hell do you think you're going?" he asks from the where he stands in the office doorway.

"Home, obviously."

"We have the gala tonight. You have to go."

"Actually, I don't think I have to do anything. And right now? I really don't want to go."

"Are you fucking serious? You cheat on me, and now after one fight you're just leaving?" He steps toward me, and I roll my suitcase to create a barrier between us.

"I didn't cheat on you! But yeah, I guess I am."

"If you leave, we're done." I almost laugh.

"Yeah, I think we're done either way, at this point." I sigh, opening the door to the hallway.

"Excuse me?"

"Dennis, we should break up, for real. Neither of us even want to be in this relationship anymore."

"You know you can't actually do any better than me right? You're not twenty-two anymore. Your football player won't want you, and neither will anyone else. Not for anything more than a quick fuck." The words hit like poison arrows, exactly as he means them too.

"I think I'll take my chances." And I close the door before he can respond.

A single tear tracks down my cheek as I sit in the back of the taxi on my way to JFK. My relief is palpable but tinged with fear of the unknown, the insecurities Dennis hit on coloring every thought.

I'm able to change my flight once I promise United my kidney, and I board my flight home before I was even supposed to be at the stupid gala. I'm squeezed into the tight middle seat and text Katie before we take off.

> I'm coming home.

Then, I turn my phone off and ask the flight attendant for a double vodka on the rocks. Her eyebrows raise, but she must see my expression and take pity on me, even as the lady in the aisle seat next to me watches with thinly veiled disgust.

I toast her and knock half of it back. "My boyfriend and I just broke up."

She purses her lips and turns her attention to her airport romance novel.

I log into the Wi-Fi plan and find the article Dennis shoved in my face. There was clearly a source who was at Theo's as it references us looking "cozy" and then leaving together. I'm irrationally annoyed, not even that it may have just ruined my relationship, but it was a private party in someone's home. The athletes there deserve some semblance of privacy. I'm typing a comment out to tell the article author so, when the vodka starts to kick in, quicker than usual with a combination of high altitude and low carb intake. While justice is important, a nap right now feels more urgent, and I slide my phone in my sweatshirt pocket and lean my head back against the headrest, closing my eyes.

I jolt awake when the plane touches down ignoring the disapproving glance from aisle lady. I turn my phone back on with a sinking feeling.

But as my notifications come in, there's nothing from Katie.

She hasn't even seen the text.

As soon as I'm in baggage claim, I call her. The idea of going home to my empty apartment tonight is killing me.

The phone rings and rings, then goes to voicemail.

What the fuck? It's not like her to not be on her phone.

I check her location, and she's in Los Angeles.

Strange. She's at her mom's house, more specifically. At least she's not dead in a ditch somewhere.

I get in a taxi, telling him to head to the loop and try calling once more.

"I'm going to need a specific address pretty soon," the driver calls from the front.

"Sorry, give me one second," I fumble, as tears burn my eyes. I rattle off the first address I can think of.

Chapter Sixteen

CAL

I'm playing GTA, when there's a knock on my door. I grumble, glancing at the clock hanging in the kitchen. It's not exactly late, but it's later than is socially acceptable for randomly dropping by.

I don't have the energy for real people tonight, thanks to the three missed calls and one unanswered voicemail from my father after the photo of Lila in my jersey surfaced this morning.

I pull the lock and open the door, "Theo, what do you possibly . . ." and trail off, stunned. Because it's not Theo standing at my door but Lila.

Lila with a suitcase.

"What—are you okay?" One question trumps the other as I take in her swollen, red eyes.

She shrugs.

"Erm, do you want to come in?" I stand back, opening the door wider, as she walks past me leaving her suitcase at the door before heading straight to the couch and sitting as if in a trance. I shut the door and pick up the gaming headset.

"Hey, guys, I gotta go." I disconnect from the call and shut off the console before gingerly sitting on the other end of the couch from her.

"Can I get you anything?"

She shakes her head.

"Lila, what's wrong?" I ask more urgently, a slight panic beginning in my chest.

"I didn't know where else to go." A small tear escapes down her cheek, and I hate myself for asking.

"Hey, it's okay. You can be here, it's fine. You just seem, uhm, not yourself, so if you need something, please tell me."

"Katie didn't answer, and I didn't want to be alone."

Pride blooms in my chest as I realize she considers me that close of a friend, before again reminding myself that I'd be happier if she wasn't upset like this to begin with.

She curls herself into a ball on her end of the sectional, and I cringe, glancing around in a panic for literally anything that could comfort her. I settle on a blanket draped artfully over the chair in the corner. It's fluffy and soft, nothing I would've chosen for myself, but my mother gave it to me as a housewarming gift when I moved into my New York condo. It made the move to Chicago with me, and if I'm honest with myself, it is awfully nice for those chilly fall days when you don't want to turn the heat on yet.

I drape it over her shoulders, and after a second thought, I grab her a bottle of water from the kitchen and the entire box of tissues. I set them gingerly on the table in front of her before sinking onto the cushion next to her. I run my hands over my thighs nervously, trying not to stare at her.

"You can play your game." She sniffs. "I didn't mean to interrupt your night."

"How about we watch something?" I offer.

She shrugs.

"What are you in the mood for?" I turn on Netflix, flipping through some options, trying to gauge any level of reaction, but she stares blankly at the screen. "A rom-com, maybe?"

"No," she says sharply.

"Right, no rom-coms." I scroll past that section.

"How about *Lion King*?"

She snorts. "I was thinking more *Star Wars*."

I gape at her. "*Star Wars*?"

"Yeah, preferably the original trilogy."

I snort. "Coming right up."

I press play on *A New Hope* and settle in.

"Popcorn?"

Another shrug. Popcorn sounds good to me though now that I've put it in the universe, so I throw a bag in the microwave. I wait for it to finish popping before dumping the whole bag into a big bowl and setting it down in front of us on the table.

"It's over, for real this time," Lila bursts out suddenly about thirty minutes in, and I actually jump, so invested in the movie already. The originals are some of my favorites.

"You and Dennis?"

"Yeah."

"What happened?"

She swallows, pushing herself up to sit properly on the cushions. "He saw the photo of me at the game. In your jersey."

"Fuck. I'm sorry, I didn't really think about it." It's a lie. I definitely thought about it, but the guilt creeps up my throat as I see the pain I caused her, all for the brief vindication of seeing her in my name and number.

"It's not your fault, Cal. And it's been coming for a while I think."

"Maybe so, but it can still suck." She gives me a small smile.

"Yeah, it does."

She turns back to the movie, and a moment later, I mirror her.

"What am I even *doing*?"

I startle at her tone. "What do you mean?"

"I'm just starting from scratch at thirty-three. I don't have time to fuck around anymore, you know? My sister's having a baby, and all I can do is fight with my boyfriend, *ex-boyfriend*, and work and jump around at football games. What am I doing with my life, Cal?" She looks so sad I can't resist wrapping an arm around her and pulling her into my chest. She shudders, and I almost release her until she sinks into me and starts sobbing.

I rub soothing circles on her back as she cries, her tears soaking my t-shirt.

"It's okay, it's okay," I repeat quietly as Luke and Obi Wan watch Leia's request for help on the screen behind her.

Lila eventually quiets, but she doesn't pull away. Instead, she turns her body slightly to watch the movie and snuggles into me her hand clutching the fabric of my shirt and my arm still draped across her shoulder.

I can't keep my eyes off her, and before I know it, the credits start rolling, and she speaks again.

"I don't think I can do another action movie."

"Alright," I say cautiously. "What are you feeling?"

"I don't know," she nearly wails.

"What do you normally watch to decompress?"

"True Crime. I'm really into the podcasts on cold cases." I blink at her, because what the fuck?

"Okay, well that might not be ideal right now."

"Yeah, I know." She laughs. "What about you? What do you watch to relax?"

I shrug. "Uhm, whale documentaries usually."

"Seriously?"

"Yeah." I try to keep my expression neutral, but I know it's a bit quirky. But what can I say? I like the big swimmers.

"They have that many?"

"There are a lot of different kinds of whales, Lila."

"Well, far be it from me to judge right now. I'll try it."

"Seriously?" I echo her earlier words.

"Show me the whales."

I chuckle and put one on featuring belugas, one of my favorites, even if they're not technically whales.

She leans back into me, her grip on my shirt easier. It's a short film, but after only a few minutes I realize her breathing has slowed into a deep, even cadence.

I ease her off me and back onto the couch and stare down at her for a moment. Should I wake her up? I decide against it and pick her up carefully, trying not to jostle her too much and carry her down the hall to my guest room. Setting her gently on the bed, I drape the blanket over her and plug in her phone, setting an alarm for the morning in case she's going into work. After a moment's hesitation, I grab an extra t-shirt from my closet and put it on the nightstand next to a bottle of water.

"Goodnight, Lila," I say softly, leaning over her to press a kiss to her forehead.

I close the door to my own room quietly and fall into my own bed, my emotions warring with themselves, even as I drift off into sleep with a smile on my face.

I didn't think I'd be this upset. We've broken up before, and after the first few times I mostly stopped caring, but this feels different. A part of me knows it's final in a way none of the others have been.

We want different things, and that's not going to change.

The words I've told myself every thirty minutes this morning echo in my head, and even though I know they're the truth, it doesn't hurt any less.

I woke up in Cal's guest room yesterday, and from the moment I opened my eyes, I've been a mess. I made some bullshit excuse he probably saw right through and hightailed it out of there. I can't believe I chose him over being alone.

Who am I kidding? Of course I believe it, because I'd probably do it again, but I haven't yet. I've found comfort in Indian takeout and reruns of *Grey's Anatomy* and don't plan on leaving my couch for the foreseeable future. Well, until that future includes a meeting I can't take from my living room, but so far, Kevin's been able to arrange everything to be virtual. And with McSteamy on the screen, it's much easier to read through contracts.

At least the Thanksgiving holidays are coming up, so I can

hunker down and think about nothing other than my own existential despair at the fact that I'll probably just die alone. Maybe I should adopt a cat. Or six cats. If Taylor Swift can have three, I need at least six to be a cat lady, right?

I'm just closing my laptop for the day, all crises averted for now, when there's a knock at my door.

I'm not entirely surprised to see Katie standing there, holding a Pequod's pizza box and a bottle of wine under one arm.

"I brought sustenance."

"You know I normally *can* manage to feed myself."

"Yes, but there's no reason that you shouldn't be able to lean on your friends."

"How do you even know? It's not like we've talked about it," I grouse, but open the door wider to let her into the room.

"I'm really sorry about that. I tried calling you back yesterday."

"I turned my phone off." I turned it off as soon as I got home from Cal's. I didn't, and still don't, need his pity or anything Dennis might say.

"Do you want me to go?" Katie asks, and I know if I told her yes, she'd go, leaving me the pizza and all my feelings to sort through on my own.

"No," I almost whisper, the tears threatening to spill over.

"Oh honey." She wraps me in a hug, and I let myself cry into my best friend's shoulder. "It'll be okay."

We stand there until my sobs reach a soft sniffle, and I pull away.

"Thanks, I needed that."

"No thanks needed. What are best friends for?"

"I thought they were for tequila shots," I say with a laugh.

"Well, I did bring wine." She grins.

"How did you know I needed this?" I ask, opening the pizza box.

"It's what makes me so awesome obviously."

I roll my eyes and grab two plates from the cupboard, sliding two pieces of the veggie pizza onto one of them.

Katie's already emptied the bottle of wine into two wine-glasses and pushes one toward me.

"Cal told me I should check on you."

"He did?"

"Well not exactly, but he told me what happened the other night and mentioned you hadn't returned any of his texts since. But then, when you didn't answer any of *my* texts, I knew it was a Pequod's level emergency."

"Emergency might be a stretch." I cut into the slice and groan as I take the first bite, I almost never order deep dish, but it's so good.

"Really? What show are you bingeing?"

"*Grey's*," I say sheepishly.

"Right." She rolls her eyes, biting into her own slice. "Not an emergency."

"Hey, it's a good show."

"I never said it wasn't, but you only watch it when you're upset. It's like the opposite of a comfort show."

"Shonda is a master. She makes you *feel* things."

"Yes, yes, I know. But maybe focus on your own feelings instead?"

"Fine, what do *you* want to watch?"

"*Love Island UK* just dropped their new season on Hulu."

"Oh, hell yes." We leap onto the couch, and I start the new season. By the second episode we're both laughing and speaking in bad British accents about the absurd number of scaffolders— what even is a scaffolder? —and how great it'd be to be twenty-three with no responsibilities again.

As the third episode ends, Katie finally asks what I've been dreading.

"So, do you want to talk about it?"

I sigh. "Not yet. I probably should. I just can't really process it yet. We've broken up before, but this feels different, you know? I'm not really sure what to do."

"You know where to find me when you do."

I start the fourth episode and smile at her.

"Thanks Katie." I pause. "Do you want to talk about why you went home to LA?"

"Not yet." She gives me a sad smile.

I nod, settling back into the couch. She'll talk when she's ready, but Katie's one to process everything in her own mind first.

◖ ◖ ◖

Katie coming over kicked my ass in gear. No more wallowing, I am going to process my feelings like an adult.

Step one is admitting a problem, right?

After another day of working from home, I'm ready to get out of my apartment for more than the elevator ride downstairs to meet the delivery guy from Bhoomi. There aren't many places I can go where my day-four hair will be socially acceptable, and I don't have the face for a slicked back bun. There's one place, though, that I can always go no matter what I look like. A judgement-free zone where I can be myself.

As I step into the pottery studio, peace settles into my gut. The stress and sadness melting away as I wedge out my clay and choose a wheel. Denise waves at me from where she's loading the kiln, and I grin at her.

I'm elbows deep in clay when a commotion at the front door pulls me from the vase I'm working on, a Christmas gift for Kayla.

"No, she's definitely here, I tracked her location," a familiar voice says. My head snaps up to find not only Katie but Cal and Theo too standing in the small entryway of the studio. I can't look at Cal, the embarrassment from weeping all over him the other night too fresh.

"Wow." Theo gives a low whistle. "That's really good Lila."

I look at the vase and shrug. It's slightly uneven at the belly, but overall, I'm not embarrassed by it. Handmade art is always a bit unique.

"What are you guys doing here?"

"We came to see you, obviously," Katie answers.

"Uh, okay. But why?"

"We're taking you out," announced Theo, a proud grin spread across his face.

"Right now?"

"You could change first." Katie looks pointedly at my clay splattered t-shirt, and I realize with horror that I resemble a homeless child in my oversized, mud-smeared shirt and cut-off jeans, glaze painting one side of my calf from where the electric mixer was a bit too intense.

"Or not. Who knows if they'll let you through the door though." Cal laughs, and I flush. He's moved closer to me, taking a closer look at my vase, and I suddenly feel the urge to squish it back into a ball. "I mean, I'd let you in, but it's not always up to me." The corner of his mouth quirks up in a smirk, and my mouth is suddenly drier than it had been a minute ago.

"Well, I'll let you guys have fun then." I return my attention to the wheel in front of me.

"Lila." Cal leans over the wheel, taking care not to disturb the almost-finished vase. "You're coming with us. We'll wait for you."

I glance up and meet his gaze. The grey so light it's almost silver today.

I swallow and nod. "Okay." My voice is breathy, and I clear my throat. "Yeah okay. I need to finish this piece and then clean up. And *then*, I need to shower and change." I turn back toward my vase. It really does look pretty good. I just need to add some texture and compress the rim before I can call it done for the day.

I'm choosing a metal rib tool when I notice that my three friends are standing there staring at me.

"What?"

"Nothing." Theo shakes his head. "That just looks so cool. I kind of want to try it."

"They have lessons you know. That's how I got started."

"Here?" His face lights up like a damn Christmas Tree, and I can't help but laugh.

"Yes, Denise can get you signed up if you're serious." I nod toward the woman in question.

"Oh, *hell* yes." I roll my eyes as he sets off to sign up for a beginner pottery class.

"He's going to be insufferable now, you know." Cal smiles.

I shrug. "That's different how?"

"Come on, now. More potter-ing, less talking," Katie teases.

"Yes ma'am," I say, saluting her with my metal rib.

I finish adding a swirl pattern along the belly of the vase, taking one final look before removing it to a wooden block to dry.

"Alright, let me just clean up, and we can go."

When we make it out of the studio, the sky is dark, a sure sign of winter in the north, though it's an unseasonably warm night. Lila can barely meet my eyes, but she flushed as I spoke to her at the wheel. She somehow looked incredible even covered in clay, her jean shorts and oversized t-shirt leaving plenty to the imagination, and even more so now that she's covered up in a mismatched sweat suit.

"You can shower at my place, it's the closest," Katie says, leading us toward her apartment.

"I can just shower at my *own* place. I'd need to change anyway, I don't have extra clothes with me," argues Lila.

"I have stuff you can borrow."

"But—"

"You know you're not gonna win this one," Theo says with a laugh.

She rolls her eyes, and I chuckle, laughing harder when she shoots me a glare. There's a smirk playing across her lips though, almost as if she can't help not smiling with the rest of us.

Katie's home isn't very far, and after only a few blocks, we're traipsing through her black-and-white-tiled lobby and into the gilded elevator. While my building might be nice, Katie's screams old money in a way only Gold Coast can.

"We'll just hang out on the balcony while you freshen up." Katie waves Theo and I out toward the large double doors off the living room. "I'll set out the clothes on the bed, and you can use my master bath," she says, leading Lila through a door that must be her bedroom.

"It's all set up, right?" Theo asks the second we're inside.

I nod. "I confirmed with the guy while we were at the studio."

"She's gonna love it."

"I hope so." I shrug. "I just hope it helps. I can't see her like that again." I shudder remembering how broken Lila looked when she fell asleep against me in my apartment after the breakup. Like her very soul had been shattered.

"It's weird, I never really got the sense they were that serious."

"I don't know, mate. She seemed really upset over it, though. They were still together a long time."

"And you're okay with that? Being a rebound?"

I scowl at him. "First of all, we're not together. We're just friends." He snorts and I pointedly ignore him. "And second, I'm not a rebound. There's something about her. I don't know. If we're doing it, we're doing it for real."

"Damn, so it's like that?"

"Yeah." I sigh. "It is." Lila has woven herself into my life in a way I wouldn't have thought possible until now. I want to show up for her. I want to be there next to her and protect her from pain.

Katie slips out onto the balcony and grins. "Is everything ready?"

"Yup, I was just telling Theo, I confirmed at the studio and we're good to go."

"Excellent. She's going to be blown away."

"Literally," mutters Theo as he adjusts the hair that's blown down into his eyes.

"They don't call it the Windy City for nothing," Katie teases.

"We both know that's not why they call it the Windy City," grouses Theo.

"Whatever." She shrugs.

I pass the next few minutes in silence, mulling over the conversation with Theo while the man in question whispers to Katie. I have a suspicious feeling that they're talking about me but realize I don't actually care. If Katie's on board, I'll have even fewer obstacles.

Lila joins us not long after, with her long hair still damp and curling softly around her face. I've never seen her without makeup before, and my eyes are drawn to a freckle just above the corner of her mouth. I didn't even know she had freckles.

"This is really what you want me to wear?" She gestures to her outfit, a pair of dark blue skinny jeans hugging her legs, a soft-looking grey hoodie hanging off her. "I thought we were going out."

"You're perfect," I say dumbly. She looks at me, meeting my gaze finally and blushes. That damn freckle winking at me as the corner of her mouth lifts.

"No, he's right. It's fine for where we're going," Katie confirms.

"Should I at least dry my hair?"

"Only if you think you'll catch cold. But it's pretty warm out tonight, so you'll probably be fine."

Lila shrugs. "If you say so."

We head back out into the city, down to Oak Street Beach and find Manuel at the tunnel entrance leading out to the beach, standing with crossed arms.

"Hey man," I say. "Thanks for setting it up."

"No problem. Everything should be good to go. Just call me if you need anything. My team is nearby." I shake his outstretched hand and nod.

"What's going on?" Lila asks.

"It's a surprise," whispers Theo. She scowls at him. "Oh, come on, everyone loves surprises."

"No, Theo, they really don't."

"Well, you'll love this one. I promise," I say, jumping in.

As we cross onto the beach, we all remove our shoes, carrying them as we step onto the sand. The wind is whipping around us, blowing Lila's hair around her face like a small hurricane.

"There!" I call out, pointing toward the setup down the beach a hundred feet or so. There's a large blanket laid out with a few pillows on it, a mini wooden table in the center, and a big basket full of what I know to be food and wine. There are small paper lanterns set up around the edges, bathing the area in a soft glow, and blankets to protect against the wind if it picks up again.

Lila gasps, and my stomach does a little flutter. "It's beautiful," she whispers.

"Come on." I gesture forward, and she leads us to the blanket, sinking down onto one of the pillows. I lower myself down between her and the basket, leaving Theo and Katie to find spots on the other half of the picnic blanket.

I take wine glasses from the basket and set them on the table, handing Theo the wine to open and pour. I reach in again to find the wrapped charcuterie board and fruit tray and place them on the center of the small table.

"What is this?" Lila asks quietly.

"What do you mean?" I pause in rummaging in the basket and look up at her.

"Why'd you do all of this?"

"I just thought you deserved something to remind you of how much you matter to the people who care about you," I murmur, not really needing Theo or Katie to be part of this conversation.

"You didn't have to do that." I can see her flush by the light of the lanterns.

"I wanted to, though. You deserve to be shown how important you are."

"Come on, you guys," interrupts Katie. "Stop whispering, and let's eat."

"Alright, alright, calm down." Lila flashes me a quick grin, before taking the full glass of wine Theo's handing her.

"What're we eating then?" she asks, looking over the trays of food.

"We also have some little sandwiches and some sausage rolls," I say, pulling them out of the basket.

"How very British of you, Johnathan," Theo teases in a very bad imitation of a British accent.

"Oh, shut it, or you won't get any of them." He salutes me with a grin.

"This all looks so good," Katie squeals, grabbing a cucumber sandwich from the top of the small basket they're tucked into.

"Manuel and his team did a great job."

We all dig into the food in front of us, the wind catching every once in a while, at the blanket, but the air is cool, winter still held at bay by one last warm spell this week.

When the sandwiches are cleared and we're all picking at the charcuterie, Theo dives headfirst into the deep end.

"So, Lila. Any plans for Thanksgiving weekend?"

"Not really, I'm sure I could go back to my parents, but I might just hang out in the city. There are a couple places that do a pretty nice Thanksgiving meal, even for one, though I guess any of you are welcome to join me. Maybe I'll see if any of the food pantries need help or something."

"Well, since Cal and I have to be back on Sunday, we were thinking of heading up to my parents' lake house, if you wanted to come? We won't really be doing the whole celebration thing since Cal is British and I can't cook, but a weekend away is still a weekend away."

"Where is it?"

"Up in the UP—the Upper Peninsula of Michigan. It's a bit of a drive, but worth it."

"That does sound kind of nice," Lila says, hesitation in her voice. "When are you leaving?"

"We're leaving on Tuesday," Katie says. "You'll love it, Lila. It's so peaceful."

"I won't be able to then." She frowns. "I need to work Wednesday, I have a couple meetings I need to be in-person for before the long weekend, but thanks for the invite."

"Are you sure? You can work from the house. They have pretty good Wi-Fi." Katie says.

"Yeah, I'll need to be in-person with the rest of the team." Katie pouts as Lila continues, "It's fine, I'll be fine here. I'll probably just get some extra studio time in and watch an entire season of *Love Island*."

"I could drive you," I blurt out. Lila stares at me.

"I don't want to keep you here."

"No, I was planning to leave Wednesday afternoon anyway. It'll only be a couple more hours if I pick you up after work."

"Are you sure?"

I swallow. Am I sure? Five hours alone in a car with Lila? "Yes, of course. It'll be nice to have company on the drive." I smirk. "Just don't make me listen to one of those murder podcasts you made me listen to."

"Hey!" she scolds, smacking my arm. "I didn't *make* you do anything. You wanted to see what they were about. It's not my fault that you couldn't sleep." She shrugs, and I laugh. "I'm not listening to an ocean documentary either, so don't get any ideas."

"Maybe let's just stick to music on this trip." I grin at her. We finish the snacks in comfortable conversation joking about TV and podcasts.

"Alright, I have shit to do, so I'm gonna head out," Theo says, standing and grabbing his shoes.

"I'll see you all up at the lake house next week." He turns to me. "See you at practice tomorrow."

I nod.

"I think I'm gonna head out too. Do you need help cleaning up?" Katie asks.

"Nah, Manuel'll be back to get everything."

"Okay, I'll see you around, Cal. Text me later, Lila."

And suddenly, it's just the two of us, alone on the beach. We could be the last two people in the world, and it wouldn't feel any different.

"Are you feeling any better?"

"Sure, I mean I was pretty hungry." She laughs.

"I meant from the other night." I turn to face her.

"Oh," she says quietly. Not quite meeting my gaze. I reach over and tilt her face to look up at me.

"Lila." I can see her breath hitch as I say her name. "Are you okay?"

"Yes," she breathes. "I just can't believe you put all of this together."

"You deserve to be happy. You deserve the world laid out at your feet."

"Cal, don't," she whispers.

"Don't what?"

"I don't know if I can . . . I can't . . ."

"I'm not asking for anything, love."

"But—"

"Shh, it's okay," I say leaning in. "It's really fine."

She tilts her face up to meet mine, and I'm a hair's breadth away from my mouth being on hers, when someone calls out my name.

"Sir, Mr. Basset?"

I lift my head and straighten with a groan. "Yes, Manuel?"

"Do you want me to clean up? I saw the other two leaving."

Well, I would've preferred you wait until I'd called you, and we were also leaving. But since you're already here. "That'd be great, thanks." I stand, offering a hand to help Lila which she takes.

"Come on, you up for a walk along the beach?" She smiles at

me, offering her hand. I take it, intertwining our fingers, and grab our shoes in the other. It turns out big hands are good for more than catching footballs.

We walk in silence for a few minutes, before she breaks it.

"I'm not ready for another relationship."

"I'm not asking for one."

"Isn't that what you want?"

I shrug. It's not *not* what I want. But I want her, and it's not what she wants. I'll wait if that's what she wants. I meant what I said to Theo—if we're doing it, we're doing it. If that's tomorrow or next year, what does it matter?

"I can't have you just waiting for me. You could have any girl in the city, and I'm not even fully over my ex. It's not fair to you."

"Hey, only I get to decide what's fair to me. But I'm fine with whatever this is right now. I'm not asking for anything else."

"What if I'm not ready for a long time?" she whispers, and I almost don't catch it over the sound of the waves crashing against the beach.

"We don't have to decide anything right now."

"Cal, I just don't—"

"Do you enjoy being with me? Just like this? Hanging out together, talking?"

She nods.

"Then that's really all that matters right now. We don't need to put pressure on it or make it anything else. We can still just be friends."

"Are you sure?"

"I'm sure." We've walked to a little raised area, and I drop down into the sand, pulling her down next to me.

"You and your ocean sounds," she teases.

"Technically, it's a lake," I point out. "Fresh water and everything."

"It's basically a freshwater sea. There are literally tides. Normal lakes don't have tides."

I roll my eyes. She shivers next to me.

"Are you cold?"

"A bit. I think the wind is getting to me."

"Do you want me to call an Uber?" I ask, my heart sinking. I never want this night to end. Once we leave this beach, we're back to real life. But here, on the sand, looking up at the stars in the sky, it's just us.

"No, it's okay." She grins at me, and I drape my arm over her shoulders, tucking her into my body warmth.

"Better?"

"Much, actually." She rests her head against my shoulder, and I'm momentarily back in that moment we first met. But this isn't the club. It's quiet here, and more innocent that it was then.

I rest my cheek on top of her hair and stare out at Lake Michigan, the lull of the water like waves of peace washing over us.

Chapter Nineteen

LILA

The next few days fly by, and whether it's because work is so busy that I don't have a second to breathe or because I'm still reeling from my conversation with Cal on the beach, I'm not sure.

He made it clear he has no real expectations, and I enjoy spending time with him, but I'm not ready for anything serious again. I was so sure about Dennis in those first few years. And even when we started breaking up, there was always the thought we would end up together in the end. But this time feels real.

It's easy with Cal, easier than breathing, and I have to catch myself from falling over and over again. Because it'd be so easy to jump, to leap, off that cliff. But I can't, not yet. What if he doesn't catch me? What if he decides afterwards that it's not worth it, that *I'm* not worth it? Or that he'd rather have one of the perfect models that are always surrounding professional athletes.

But he makes me feel so safe and taken care of. Like he genuinely cares for my happiness, and if I asked for the moon, would find some way to get it for me, wrapped up in Gucci gift paper.

It's fucking scary.

We're driving up to Theo's parents' lake house tonight together, and the idea of sitting in a car next to him for hours uninterrupted makes my heart race. I wish I had a car so I could drive, but he already offered and given that it's a known fact that I *don't* own a car, it'd be a bit ridiculous to rent one.

I took a half day just to give myself plenty of time to pack and get ready, but I'm regretting it now. I'm packed and ready to go—have been for over an hour—and I still have another ninety minutes until when he said he'd pick me up. It'll just be me and my anxiety sitting here, waiting. It dawns on me that I could go on a coffee run and have one for him ready to go.

> Hey, I'm gonna grab a coffee before we leave, do you want anything?

CAL

> That'd be great.

> Black coffee with 4 sugars.

>> Wait are you serious?

> . . . ?

>> FOUR sugars?

> Never mind

>> No, I got it. I'm just making sure it wasn't a typo or something. I know how touchy those autocorrects can be.

> 🙁

>> Black coffee 4 sugars. Got it.

I smile to myself. Who would've thought that Callahan Basset likes his coffee sweet enough to rot your teeth. I pace my apartment and contemplate calling Katie just for something to do, but she's already up at the house likely getting drunk on cherry wine with Theo.

I eye my suitcase. I'm sure I packed for any situation, but one last check can't hurt. I unzip it, taking in the contents that are half folded, and immediately pull everything out and dump it in a pile on my bed.

God forbid anyone sees the inside of my suitcase, because I've yet to master the art of folding. I repack more carefully, taking my time with each item.

I grab my keys, and head out the door to grab our coffees, ordering them on the app on the elevator down. I'm just picking them up when my phone buzzes.

CAL

Leaving in 10

I'll be ready out front!

I grab a few extra sugars, just in case, and hustle home. The last thing I want is to be late.

I'm dragging my overly full suitcase through the lobby, taking care not to spill the two coffees balanced in the other hand, when I see a black Mercedes coupe pull up out front. I blink back the surprise at the choice of car. I always pictured him driving something a little more practical. But every boy likes his toys, so I shouldn't be that thrown off.

He gets out of the car, coming around the back to take my suitcase from me, lifting it easily and sliding it into place next to a leather duffle bag in the trunk of his car.

"Thanks," I say, flushing slightly as he smirks over the roof of the car at me.

"Don't mention it."

He walks toward me, and I'm momentarily stunned. Is he going to kiss me? But he passes me, opening my door and gesturing for me to get in.

"Here," he says, taking the coffees from me as I climb into the low-seated car. He hands them back to me once I'm settled and closes the door before walking back to the driver side and sliding in much smoother than I did. I hand him his coffee.

"Four sugars, as promised," I deadpan.

He rolls his eyes. "I never make fun of your drink choices."

"Yeah, because they're reasonable drinks. You have, like, an entire day's worth of sugar in that cup."

He shrugs, taking a sip and savoring it.

"What did you get? Some over-priced pumpkin latte?"

I hug my vanilla sweet cream cold brew to my chest.

"No," I say, defensively.

He snorts. "Sure, whatever you say."

The radio is on, and we pass through the city and onto the highway in amiable silence, zipping along at speeds that would make me nauseous with less pricey suspension.

"Did you have anything you wanted to listen to?" Cal asks as we're passing the Wisconsin border. "We'll lose the signal here in a bit."

"I can start a queue," I say brightly. "Anything on the veto list?"

"Uhh . . ." He pauses. "Maybe just nothing too slow. I wouldn't want to fall asleep at the wheel."

"Nothing too slow, got it."

"And no true crime."

The first couple hours pass easily. We chat every so often about the song or what we imagine Katie and Theo are getting into unsupervised, but the silence is comfortable between conversation bursts and doesn't need filling.

His elbow rests on the center console between us, his long fingers tapping on the gear shift, almost restlessly. I'm torn between watching the road and admiring his hand.

He has short, clean nails—he probably gets manicures for his nails to be shaped so perfectly. A few times each hour, his hand will twitch slightly toward me, like he wants to rest his hand on my thigh but pulls back at the last minute.

I part my legs, letting my left leg lean against the edge of the seat, that much closer to his waiting fingers, giving him the option if he wants it. I know I do.

The first raindrop hits the windshield and jolts me out of my hand fantasies. It's quickly followed by several more, and soon we're in the middle of a downpour.

"Do you maybe want to slow down a bit?" I ask, a hint of a joke in my voice as I clutch the seatbelt across my chest.

He spares a glance at me and frowns but pulls the car back to a reasonable speed. "Are you okay?"

"Thanks." I smile gratefully at him. "Yeah, I just don't really like driving in bad weather. I had a bad accident in college where I hydroplaned and crashed my mom's car." His face softens and his hand comes down and squeezes my knee reassuringly. My heart skips a beat, and as if he can feel the odd stall in my cardiovascular system, he releases it and takes the wheel with both hands.

It's easy to see why after a few moments.

The rain has turned into sleet as we've continued north. Many of the cars around us have slowed to a veritable crawl by highway standards, most with their hazards on.

"Wow, it's really coming down out there," I say.

He grunts, focused on the road, his knuckles turning white from gripping the steering wheel so hard.

"Do you want to pull over and just wait it out a bit?" I ask.

"No, it's fine. Just let's maybe turn the music down? I'm not used to driving in weather like this."

"Oh, of course." I reach toward the knob on the console just as he does the same. He must sense my tension because he lets me manage the radio and keeps both hands firmly on the wheel.

It's another twenty minutes or so, and this time the silence is anything but comfortable. Cal is clearly stressed driving through the storm, but there's nothing I can do except try to not be distracting.

We seem to be through the worst of the storm, the sleet coming down lighter and lighter and Cal eases up on the wheel.

"Just be careful. The road is probably really slick."

"Yeah, but at least I can see now." He chuckles.

"Do you want the music back?"

"Oh right, yeah sure." We're coming up to a bend in the road, and just as I reach for the knob to turn back on the playlist, we hit a patch of ice made slick by the rain and spin out. The colors spiral around me—the black of the car, the green of the pine trees outside, the grey of the road, the white of the snow all blurring together. My pulse is racing, and I'm not ready to die. I'm not ready to let Cal die either. I blindly reach toward him as the car skids off the road into a small ditch.

We come to a stop and look at each other, my hand clutching his arm.

"Are you okay?" He asks frantically, cupping my face and turning it as if to check my neck isn't broken.

"Cal, I'm fine, I'm *fine*." I grip his hands, still on my face but no longer tilting my face back and forth.

"Are *you* okay?"

"Yeah. I can't believe we spun out like that."

"Yeah, the roads can be really dangerous when it's in between rain and snow like this." I gesture out the window to the loose flurries now floating by. "We're both okay though, right? That's what matters." My hands are shaking slightly, and I shove them under my legs to hide them from sight.

He nods. "You didn't hit your head or anything right?"

"No, if anything I'll just have a bit of a bruise from the seat-belt," I joke, trying to lighten his mood. He only frowns. "I'm *really* okay, Cal. We can try to get out of here, or I can call AAA."

"Here, I'll try first." He revs the engine, but eases into gear. The car doesn't move, and he gives it more gas.

"I think the wheels are just spinning." He groans. "I can try pushing it if you want to take over?"

"Oh yeah, I can help push if you want?"

"I got it, just try to steer."

He opens the door, and a flurry of snowflakes drift in with the gust of cold air, and I clamber over the center console into the driver's seat. I roll down the window a bit so I can hear Cal outside and signal I'm ready.

"Go!" he calls out, and the car shifts slightly as he pushes from the back. I hit the gas but the tires only spin mud.

"Hello," a disembodied voice says. "It appears you may be in need of assistance."

"Uhm, Cal?" I call out. "Is your car talking to me?"

"If you do not need assistance, please respond now by pressing the *No Assistance Needed* button on the center screen. Otherwise, we will connect you with our on-call professionals."

"Cal!" I yell. "Your car is asking if we need help."

He appears at the window, breathing heavy and cheeks pink with cold.

"I don't think we're moving any time soon, so yeah might as well."

He rounds the front of the car and slides into the passenger seat.

"Weird, I've never been in this seat before," he mutters, and shrugs just as a ringing sound fills the car.

"Hello, this is the Mercedes on-call hotline. Do you need immediate assistance?" A male voice asks from the other end of the line.

"We spun out and are stuck in a ditch," Cal responds.

"Understood, sir. Let me check your location and see how far the nearest tow truck is to you. Can I put you on a brief hold?"

"Sure."

Cal looks over at me, "I'm sorry about this."

"It's not your fault. It could literally happen to anyone." It's happened to me twice now.

"I should've just driven slower."

"Cal, it's okay. We're both okay."

He opens his mouth to respond, but the man on the other end of the phone comes back at that moment.

"Mr. Basset?"

"Yes?"

"I've located you off of I-43 near Haven, Wisconsin, is that correct?"

I check the map and nod.

"Yes, that's correct," he affirms.

"Unfortunately, there are no tow trucks available in your area available within the next three hours. We recommend finding a place to wait indoors until we can confirm a tow truck."

I sigh, and it's only covered up by Cal's groan.

"We're in the middle of nowhere. Where are we supposed to wait?"

"One moment, sir."

I pull out my phone and see a bed-and-breakfast only about half a mile away near the lake. I show him the screen. The look in his gaze is questioning, and I nod.

"We may have found somewhere to wait. How do I contact you to tell you where to bring the car?"

"I can provide you with a phone number now."

He takes his phone out. "Great. I'm ready."

After giving him the number, the on-call agent says, "Please call that number and have your information as well as the new address available. Please also take your keys with you and lock your vehicle behind you when you leave."

"Thank you."

"Is there anything else I can assist you with today, sir?"

"No, thanks."

"If you'd like to take a survey rating the service you received today, please stay on the line. If not, you may disconnect by pressing the *Dis*—"

Cal hits the *Disconnect* button on the display, cutting off the call.

"You could've at least taken the survey," I tease.

He levels me with a look.

"Okay okay, too soon." I force a laugh, and he tries to join me, but it comes out sort of strangled.

"How far is this place you found?"

"The Lake Lodge is about half a mile and should be just off the next exit."

"Is there anything in your suitcase you absolutely need for the next few hours?"

I think through my meticulously packed extra underwear. "I'm probably okay. I just wish I'd brought a warmer coat." I zip my North Face fleece up to my chin.

"Hold onto that thought."

He gets out of the car and pops the trunk, rummaging around until he pops back in with a blue-and-grey winter hat and a sweatshirt. He hands both to me.

"Put those on, and they should help."

"Are you sure? You're not dressed much warmer than I am."

"I'll be fine. We play in weather thirty degrees colder than it is right now."

"It's not that far. You should at least take the hat."

"Lila, I'd rather be a bit cold and know you're warm than us both be a bit cold. Just put them on."

"Yes, sir." His eyes darken slightly and there's a swopping sensation low in my gut.

"Ready?" I ask, once I'm dressed for the elements.

He nods and opens his door, coming around to shut mine behind me. He holds his hand out for the keys. I drop them into his waiting palm, and he locks the car twice before slipping them into his front pocket.

"Just promise me you won't text Katie about it yet?"

"You just don't want Theo to know."

"I'm man enough to admit you're 100% correct. But still, please?"

"I'll wait to tell her until we at least know how long it's going to be."

"Deal." He sighs. "Let's go then. Hopefully they have a kitchen and maybe a hot shower we can use."

We start off down the side of the highway, and I'm grateful I had the foresight to wear my bulkiest shoes on the drive. I couldn't have picked a better pair of shoes to wear on this fun little hike through the icy roads than my L.L.Bean boots, though I might have gone with slightly thicker leggings.

As we're nearing the exit, I slip, nearly falling flat on my ass, but Cal catches my arm, pulling me up easily.

"Here, let me take that." He takes my purse off my shoulder and loops it over his neck, seeming completely unbothered that he now has a cross-body purse slung around him.

"You don't need to," I argue.

"I should've offered earlier, I honestly didn't notice you had it."

"I just figured having my charger might be good."

"Yeah, that's smart."

"Okay, it should just be up here to the right off the exit." I point toward a heavily forested area with one road winding through it.

In the dark, away from the streetlights of the interstate, I'm feeling less brave about my plan to walk to a strange place.

Cal takes my hand in his and trudges forward. The warmth from his fingers flows into me, and I know, without saying anything, that he knows I'm not feeling great about our little adventure anymore, but he won't let anything happen to me.

A small sign appears out of the darkness, lit by a single small spotlight.

THE LAKE LODGE

"Well, this is it. Serial killers or no," I joke.

Cal gives me a wan smile. "Come on, let's face our fate."

The Lake Lodge comes into full view. A large log cabin, with bright windows, red shutters, and what would be a charming garden in the summer but is now just a lot of leafless bushes poking out from underneath a fresh layer of snow. We walk up the stone-lined pathway and hesitate at the front door. Cal glances at me for a split second before he gives a one-armed shrug and pushes it open.

Chapter Twenty

CAL

The entryway is bright and cheerful, festive holiday decorations filling the small space occupied with a front desk and a cushioned two-seated bench. A doorway revealing what looks like the main living room fills the entire righthand wall opposite the bench.

"Well, hello," a short, curvy woman says from behind the desk. "What can we do ya for?"

"We, uhm." I clear my throat, unsure exactly how to phrase it without sounding like an idiot.

"We had some car troubles just up the road and needed somewhere to wait until the tow truck can come. Is it all right if we stay here for a few hours?" Lila answers, giving my hand a small squeeze, and I realize it's still intertwined in hers.

"Of course." The woman smiles at us. "Will you be needing a room for the night?"

"I don't think so. They said they should have a truck out to us in a few hours," I answer.

"No problem at all. They're still serving dinner in the dining room, if you want to get a bite to eat.

"Thanks, and sorry one more thing," I say. "What's the

address? I need it for the tow company." She rattles off the address, and I type it into my phone. "Thank you so much."

"The dining room is just through there." She points through the open doorway, and Lila and I both smile our thanks before heading through into the living area.

"I'm going to call back with the address. See if we can get an update," I tell Lila, nodding for her to find a table. I call the phone number, and after only a few minutes on hold, I'm able to give them our new location.

"It doesn't look like we'll be able to get anyone out this evening," the woman on the other end of the line says.

"Seriously? I thought it would only be a few hours."

"I apologize, sir. With the storm, all our trucks are either unable to get out or too far to get to you tonight. I can guarantee delivery of your vehicle by eight tomorrow morning if that's acceptable?"

I groan. At least this place has beds and showers. "Fine, it's not like I have a lot of choice," I mutter.

"I apologize again, sir. Is there anything else I can assist you with today?"

"No, that'll be all." After a second thought, I add a gruff, "Thanks."

I hang up and hesitate before going into the dining room, eyeing the front desk. Should I just book a room now? I should probably get two rooms. Is Lila the kind of woman to be annoyed if I don't update her first, though? She's at least the kind who deserves to have all the information up front. She also deserves to have everything taken care of, so she doesn't have to worry.

"Did you need help finding the dining room, dear?" the cheery woman asks, pulling me from my spiraling thoughts.

"Uhm, no, I can manage. Thank you." I nod quickly to her and stride through the living room, into what was probably once an ornate family dining room, and now is comprised of several smaller tables, all shoved much too close together for any real privacy or conversation.

Lila is sitting alone at a table for two in the very back of the room, chatting with an elderly couple at a table a mere six inches from ours. I sigh and make my way over to her, dodging the scattered tables and chairs. It's not that I don't enjoy talking to strangers—though I definitely don't—I'm just exhausted and knowing that we're in for a long night without any of our stuff unless we trek back out to the car isn't really improving my mood.

"You didn't tell me he was so handsome," the elderly woman coos as I pull out my chair to sit down. I glance between her and Lila and raise one eyebrow at the latter.

"Handsome, huh?" I ask, smirking.

She flushes, eyes darting up to me before she fixates on a knot in the wood of the table surface.

"Oh, son, enjoy it while it lasts. Lord knows it's the first thing to go," the older man grumbles. His wife smiles at him.

"I think you're still as handsome as when we were married."

He scoffs but meets her smile with one of his own. His face melts into softness as he gazes at his wife. They look to be lost in a moment of their own, so I take the interruption to turn back to Lila.

"So, I talked to the tow company. They're not able to get out here this evening."

"Seriously?" she asks, a note of panic coloring her voice.

"I can see if there are any rooms available tonight here or I can call Theo and have him come get us, but if he's been drinking it might be a bit until he's sober enough to drive the couple hours left."

She shakes her head. "No, we can just stay here. I just wish I had thought to bring more than just my phone charger in from the car."

"I can go grab something if you need it," I offer.

"Absolutely not, it's freezing out there, and it's only one night.

I think I can survive." She rolls her eyes. "You didn't think I was that high maintenance, did you?"

I raise one eyebrow at her. "Love, you can't be more high maintenance than what I'm used to." The words land all wrong, the creases in between her eyes to pull together before I add, "Theo needs at least three different kinds of hair products before he'll even step foot on the field for practice, and he wears a helmet." She laughs. "So, no, and even if you were, it wouldn't scare me off." I laugh uneasily, trying desperately to add in some levity to the words that just left my mouth.

She stares at me, the ghost of her last laugh still etched on her face. I rack my brain for something to say when the waitress stops by for our dinner orders.

I point at something on the small menu without reading it and don't hear what Lila orders over the roar in my ears.

"Wine," I blurt out as the waitress turns to leave.

"I'm sorry?" she asks, turning back to me.

I clear my throat. "Do you have a wine menu?"

"Red or white?"

"Er," I glance at Lila and can't remember what she prefers. "Can I see both please?"

"No, I mean, we only have one kind of red and one kind of white. Which would you like?" she clarifies a bit impatiently.

"I'll have a glass of white, please," Lila requests quietly.

"Make it a bottle of the white." I tell the waitress. She nods and heads back to the kitchen.

The wine comes quickly, and even though it's horribly sweet, it at least gives my hands something to do in the stilted silence that has descended on the table since my confession.

"So how long have you two been together?" the woman at the next table asks, jolting us both out of our bubble.

"Oh, uhm we're not—" Lila starts.

"Young love, there's nothing quite like it," the woman continues as if Lila hadn't spoken at all.

"Ma'am, I don't think you under—" I start.

"Don't call me, ma'am. That's my mother-in-law. Call me Cindy." She indicates her husband. "And this is Ed. We're here for our thirty-seventh wedding anniversary, aren't we, Ed?"

The man nods. "Best thirty-seven years of my life." The deadpan he gives me has me cracking a grin.

"Oh, stop," she says, smacking his arm affectionately.

"Thirty-seven years? That's impressive," Lila says.

"You want to know the secret?" Cindy leans in conspiratorially. "Three orgasms a week, and not ones you give yourself." I splutter into my wine glass, and Cindy winks at me.

"Are you getting the job done?" she asks me, one eyebrow raised.

"Uhm, excuse me?" I cough, pretty sure I have bad white wine as a part of my sinus membrane now.

"If he's not, you can tell me. Ed can give him some pointers," she whispers to Lila. "But looking like that it'd be disappointing if he's not good in the sack."

Lila giggles, and I glare at her, but before I can defend myself, the waitress is back setting down a pot pie of some sort in front of me and lumps of off-white clay covered in gravy in front of Lila.

She digs in happily as I watch with horror.

"What are you eating?" I ask, trying to keep the disgust out of my voice as she's clearly enjoying it.

"Chicken and dumplings."

"Like soup dumplings?"

"No." She laughs. "It's a southern dish, I think, but it's sort of a cross between a noodle and like the bottom crust of a pot pie." She gestures for my own untouched dinner. "It's a dough, but it's rolled really thin, at least that's one way to make it, and then they're cooked in the gravy. It's kind of a mix between soup and gravy really. My grandmother used to make it for us when we'd visit her in the summer, and when Kayla and I got old enough we'd help." She smiles at me for the first time since I've sat down.

A full real smile. "It's delicious, do you want to try?" She holds her fork up, one of the so-called dumplings stabbed by the prongs.

"Uhm, sure," I say, hesitantly. I reach for the fork, but she just moves it toward my mouth, and I open it on instinct, letting her feed me the dumpling. It *is* delicious.

"Damn, that *is* good."

"Told you," she says, smugness coloring the words.

I look down at my own pot pie, suddenly wishing I had paid more attention to the menu, and cut into it. The steam breaks the surface of the golden brown crust, a thick brown gravy sliding out.

It smells heavenly.

I dig in, and the tender beef and vegetables rival the flavor of Lila's meal.

"Is the food really good, or am I just so hungry that anything would taste this good?" I ask in between bites.

"No, it's *really* good. Like, we might have to stop on the way back for dinner just to eat here again."

I laugh. "We could work it in the schedule, I'm sure."

"The chocolate fudge cake is divine," Ed adds in, cutting into a slice of his own cake.

"Very powerful aphrodisiacs, chocolate." Cindy winks at me, as she steals a bite of Ed's cake. "Unless of course you have a different dessert planned for the evening."

Lila blushes bright red. If only I could be so lucky.

"Cake sounds great," I say brightly. "So how did you two meet?"

Cindy launches into a story involving a life raft and emergency smoke signals that I have trouble following, but for a few minutes of peace and Lila's small smile across the table, I try to pay attention and laugh in the right places.

When the waitress comes to clear our plates, I order chocolate cake for both of us.

"Well, I think we'll head up to bed," Cindy says, pushing up from the table. "I brought our good earplugs just in case noise travels though, so don't worry." She shoots one last wink at Lila before taking her husband's arm and leaving the dining room.

"Well, that's a relief, since mother says I snore." I joke, and Lila laughs, though her eyes grow wide at the solitary large slice of chocolate cake the waitress just set down between us on the table. Two forks on the plate next to it.

"Sorry that's the last one, but I brought two forks in case you want to share," she says. "Anything else I can get you? Coffee? More wine?"

"I'm okay for now." Lila looks up.

"Thanks."

I watch with admiration as Lila's mouth closes around her fork with her first bite of cake. And whether it's from the way her eyes close in ecstasy or from the nearly half a bottle of wine I've already had, I can feel myself get hot.

I grab my wineglass tightly, draining the last remaining sips.

"This cake really is amazing," Lila says. "Want a bite?"

"I thought we were sharing it?" I lift an eyebrow at her.

"Well, since I've already eaten a third of it, I just assumed you wanted me to have it." She smirks at me.

"I'll take a bite." I lean forward over the table and eagerly take the bite she offers me from her fork.

"That is good. Wow." I blink, letting the sugary smooth frosting wake up my tastebuds from the painful gulp of wine I swallowed. "Okay we are definitely stopping on our way back."

She laughs, eating another bite of cake. I pick up the second fork, not quite content to only have the one bite anymore.

We finish the cake, the silence much more comfortable than when we sat down.

"Well should we go see about rooms for the night?" I ask when the plate is scraped clean.

"Yeah, I could use a hot shower, too."

We make our way through the emptying dining room and

back to the front desk to find the same woman seated behind it with a warm smile.

"Did you two enjoy dinner?" she asks brightly.

"It was delicious," Lila gushes.

"Our cook is one of the best there is. Now will you two be needing a room tonight or did you get your car situation figured out?"

"I think we'll need rooms for the night," I emphasize the plural in the word.

"Oh, I'm sorry dear, we only have the one left tonight. With the storm, more people stayed an extra day. It's a miracle we have one at all actually."

I glance at Lila, and she doesn't meet my gaze.

"Right, well I guess that's better than nothing."

"It's our honeymoon suite, very romantic." She smiles and makes a note on the ancient-looking computer.

Didn't this lady just hear me say we wanted two rooms? Why would she think we would want a romantic room? The absolute last thing I need right now is to get this night all wrapped up in something it's not or make Lila uncomfortable.

She slides a key across the desk, a key that has little hearts all over it. Excellent.

"Top of the stairs on the third floor. It's labeled."

"Thanks." I do my best to keep my tone neutral, but the knowledge that I'll be spending the night with Lila after two glasses of wine has my nerves jumping like they're trying to qualify in the Olympic trials.

I gesture toward the stairs for Lila to go first and follow her up to the third landing with three doors leading off of it. One is labeled simply Room 7, the other Maintenance, and the final door, directly across from us, is painted white with bright pink roses and labeled Honeymoon Suite.

I sigh, fitting the key into the lock, and push the door open.

We're greeted by a large open room, a small sitting area to the left with two cushy-looking armchairs in front of a fireplace, an end table between them with a bucket of ice holding a champagne bottle, two flutes sitting ready next to it. In the middle of the room, against the far wall, is an enormous bed. I have a California king at home, and this must be at least a foot bigger than that. The white comforter is covered in red rose petals, and I stifle a groan. How did they prepare this? Did it sit ready for a couple to awkwardly stumble upon, or did they set it up when we went to dinner, anticipating our use of it tonight.

Lila walks through the doorway, giving the room no more than a cursory glance before dropping her purse onto the bench at the foot of the bed, and strides toward the door that must lead to the washroom.

She pushes open the door and gasps.

"What is it?" I ask, stepping into the room finally and shutting the door behind me.

"Come look at this shower." Her voice sounds oddly breathy, but I step up behind her to peer into the bathroom.

The shower is enormous, with two shower heads facing each other and a large glass door separating it from the rest of the room.

"I bet the water pressure is great." She nearly moans.

I laugh. "Go on. Take a shower. I'll clean up the flowers."

I step out of the shower feeling refreshed. The lodge itself might be rustic chic, but there's absolutely nothing rustic about this shower. I pat myself dry using one of the fluffy white towels and realize the issue as I look around at my clothes scattered over the tiled floor.

I don't have any other clothes.

A white bathrobe hangs on the back of the door to the main room, and I slip it on. I fold my clothes neatly, tucking my panties under my shirt and carrying them out with me into the bedroom.

Cal has cleared the comforter of roses, though a few escaped petals dot the rug under the bed.

"The water pressure is amazing," I say as his head snaps up sweeping over my figure, his gaze lingering on the skin exposed by the neckline of the robe. I resist the urge to either untie the entire thing or run back into the bathroom to put on my clothes from earlier.

"Do you feel better?" he asks, getting to his feet.

"Much."

"Good." His eyes linger on mine, his gaze intense, the silver of his eyes a swirling pool that could suck me right in if I'm not careful.

"I think I'll try it out for myself." He steps around me and into the en suite, the door shutting with a click behind him.

I steady my breathing and wipe my suddenly sweaty hands on the robe. I'm glancing around the room for something to do until I can conceivably pretend to sleep and avoid the tension of spending the night together, when I spot the champagne on the end table.

I grin. Liquid courage. Perfect.

I make quick work of the cork and pour a healthy measure into one of the glasses, taking a long draw. I refill the glass, and fill the second one as well, before sitting to wait for Cal.

I've gone through about two-and-a-half scenarios of how tonight can go—each dirtier than the last—when the bathroom door opens, revealing Cal dressed in nothing but a single towel wrapped around his waist.

His muscular, trim waist. The muscles pointing right to where —no. I can't think of his dick. Unfortunately, now that's all I can think about. My cheeks burn, and I force my eyes up the rest of his body. If only that helped, because with row after row of hard abdominal muscles and his chiseled chest, my body temperature has risen at least five degrees, and I need a cold shower. I finally bring my eyes meet his, and he smirks. Busted.

"There was only one robe." His hands grip the towel knot, and I swallow. "Who has a honeymoon suite with only one bathrobe?"

"I don't know," I say, my voice quite a bit huskier than I intended. I could swear his eyes darken a fraction. I clear my throat. "Champagne?"

"You couldn't wait for me?" He winks, but strides forward, taking the glass from my outstretched hand.

"It was just waiting there, begging to be drunk." I force a laugh. Why am I the only one affected by our proximity given that we're naked under these two pieces of cloth?

"Cheers," I say, clinking his glass with mine. He drinks half of it in one go, and I know now I'm not the only one affected. He's just better at hiding it than I am.

We sip our drinks in silence, not meeting each other's eyes.

"So, uh, I can sleep on the floor tonight," Cal finally says. My eyes fly to his face.

"No, you have a game on Sunday. Won't that ruin your back or something?"

"I think I can manage one night, Lila."

"It's fine, really. I could sleep on the floor, or even in this chair really." I squish myself further into the cushion as if to demonstrate how comfortable I can be here.

"Absolutely not."

"We could just share the bed?" I suggest hesitantly before plowing on. "It's huge, I mean really, I don't think I've ever seen a bed that big. We could both sleep well and barely even know we're both in the bed."

He looks at me skeptically.

"Are you *sure* you're comfortable with that?

I glance quickly at his exposed abs and swallow. "Yep, it'll be fine."

"We should probably head to sleep soon then, since we want to get a head start in the morning. I'll go finish getting ready." He stands, draining the last bit of champagne left in his glass. He emerges moments later in nothing but black boxer briefs.

"Is this, okay? I can put on something else, but I'd really rather not sleep in jeans if you're okay with that." He runs a hand through the hair on the back of his neck.

"Uh huh." I nod dumbly, fully unable to manufacture a coherent thought as my eyes zero in on the tricep muscle bulging from the movement. Why are arms so attractive? I intentionally ignore the *other* attractive parts of his body currently on display.

He moves to sit on the bed, pulling out his phone, and I take my chance and rush to the bathroom to dig through my pile of clothes. Realizing I have nothing that will work as pajamas, I eye Cal's white t-shirt next to my own clothes pile. I unearth my panties from inside my stack of clothes and slide them on, making the snap decision to pull on Cal's shirt.

If I'm gonna do this, I might as well go full throttle. I haven't been with anyone other than Dennis in years, and the attraction is mutual. I should get back on the horse—or under the man—at some point, and I trust Cal. I feel safe with him.

I stare at myself in the mirror and finger comb my hair.

"You got this, Lila. You're hot. He's hot. What's an orgasm between friends?" I ask my reflection.

The one bed trope always works out in the books. How bad could it be in real life? Right? Right. Tons of people were friends with benefits, and it worked out great. I just have to take the leap.

I take one final breath and open the door.

◗ ◗ ◗

Cal is still on his phone, facing the other wall. God, didn't he know I was trying to make an entrance?

I walk around the bed, coming to stand in front of him and slowly he looks up at me, gaze landing first on my bare legs, then catching on the shirt.

"Is that"—he clears his throat—"my shirt?"

"Oh, yeah. Is it okay if I borrow it tonight? None of my clothes would really work to sleep in, and I didn't really want to sleep naked." I force a laugh, but his jaw clenches at the mention of me naked.

I step toward him, reaching up to place one hand on his shoulder. "Cal—"

"Lila, no." My hand slides toward down to his chest. "We don't have to. We can just sleep."

I place one knee on the bed outside his broad thigh. "What if

I want to?" I whisper. I bring my other knee up on the bed until I'm sitting on his lap, straddling his hips. His hands rise to my waist lifting the t-shirt with them, his fingers gripping tightly at my bare skin.

Cal's eyes are molten, reminding me of how they nearly glowed that first night in the bar. I grind down once, and he groans, hands moving toward my hips and pushing me against him. I can feel him growing harder under me, separated only by two thin pieces of fabric.

"Please, Cal," I whisper, my lips grazing his ear. One hand moves to fist in my hair, dragging my lips to his in a searing kiss, the other gripping my ass tightly against him. His tongue sweeps into my mouth eagerly, stroking mine as he grinds against me, swallowing every moan down as if they're water and he's been stranded in the desert.

He kisses me like a man starved, and I've never felt so wanted, so lit on fire by another person. His mouth moves hungrily down my jaw, latching onto a spot below my pulse point that has me whimpering as heat floods my body, my pulse pounding between my legs. I grind down on him to relieve the pressure, and when I feel how hard he is beneath me, a low, swooping sensation in my gut has me clutching him closer.

"Fuck," he groans. "What do you want, love?"

"You," I breathe, moving to push him flat down onto the bed.

With a blazing silver fire in his eyes, he resists. He rises from the bed, bringing me with him and spins to drop me on the bed.

I move to my knees facing him, placing open-mouthed kisses up his abdomen and chest before sucking at a spot on his neck.

His hands are everywhere, running through my hair, along my back, kneading my ass. I sit back on my heels and reach to pull off the shirt, but his hand grabs my wrist.

"Leave it on. Seeing you in my clothes is a fucking religious experience." He surges forward, sealing our lips together once more. He guides me back down to the bed, his body deliciously heavy on my own, and I pull my knees up to bracket his hips, pushing myself up into him.

One of his hands skims underneath my t-shirt, his thumb circling my nipple slowly, rolling it between his thumb and forefinger and bringing it to a sharp peak before moving to the other. He gives the second one a sharp pinch, forcing a heady moan from my mouth, one he greedily swallows. His heat surrounds me, and my body is on fire, the room seeming to tunnel around him. Like my mind can't quite keep up with what my heart and body already know. That I want him.

I reach for the waistband of his boxer briefs, but he pulls out of my reach, pushing up the t-shirt and lowering his mouth to the painfully sharp bud. The room has disappeared around me, because all that exists for me is Cal, and all my needs can now be met with one simple thing.

One long, hard thing.

I whine, and he gives a low chuckle, kissing down my stomach and stopping at the waistband of my thong.

"May I?" He asks, sucking a bruise onto my hip bone.

"Please, yes, God, yes."

He smirks up at me and slides the panties down my legs before standing from the bed. I look up at him confused.

He grabs my ankles and pulls me to the end of the bed, before kneeling slowly as he spreads my thighs, opening me to him. I flush in embarrassment. It's been a while since anyone was really down here and at least a few weeks since my last wax. Even Dennis didn't go down on me much anymore and most of the sex we had was in the dark, clothes half on. Very perfunctory.

"Hey, where'd you go?" he asks, concern coloring his voice.

"What?"

"Where'd you go, Lila? I'm on my knees before you. I'd think that would command your full attention." He nearly growls.

"Sorry," I laugh nervously, "I just—"

"You just what?" He nips at my calf.

"You don't have to. It's okay." I blurt out and try to close my knees.

"Is that what this is? You're embarrassed?" His tongue traces a path up my thigh.

"I'm not embarrassed. I just, I don't know. Dennis didn't . . . I mean, it doesn't really do much for me," I ramble.

"Really? Well, it does something for me. And I don't want to hear another man's name come out of your mouth when I'm between your legs," he growls, his tone in contrast to his fingertips tracing light patterns over my legs.

I flush as hands push my thighs to the bed.

"I've wanted to taste you since that goddamned club." His tongue travels higher, and my breathing hitches. "Lila, will you let me taste you?"

He's kissing along the inside of my thighs, and I'm nearly quivering with anticipation.

I groan, throwing my head back on the duvet.

"Need to hear you, love."

"Yes," I nearly moan. The moment the word leaves my mouth, he's on me. His tongue swiping up my center before circling my clit. His hands reach back around to grab my ass, securing me to his face. His tongue swirls as he sucks my clit into his mouth, and I nearly scream, one hand reaching to grip his hair while the other fists in the comforter.

He hums against me, the vibration sending sparks straight to my core, and I buck up against his face. He bands an arm across my hip bone, locking me in place on the bed, and looks up at me, his pupils blown wide with lust. His licks another broad swipe up my center before thrusting it into me. The strength of his forearm is the only thing that keeps me sane, the heavy weight deliciously grounding in contrast to the stars beginning to pop behind my eyes. His thumb working my clit has my legs starting to shake.

"That's it, love." Two long fingers replace his tongue, and I moan wantonly. His hands are huge, stretching me perfectly. "Come for me," he growls. And as his teeth nip at my clit once more, I go off like a firework, crying out in pleasure. He works me through the orgasm, bringing me back down to earth before removing his fingers slowly.

I shudder, meeting his eyes as he brings his hand to his mouth and sucks his fingers clean.

"Next time, I'll make you clean me off." His voice is full of promise, and I eye his bulging erection, trying to gauge a comparison based on his hand size and swallow.

I reach for him to return the favor or beg him to fuck me into next week, really either one would be okay, but he gives a small shake of his head and reaches for my discarded panties. He hands them to me, coming to lay on the bed behind me.

Once I'm dressed, he pulls me to him, but keeps our cuddling firmly PG.

"You don't want to?" I ask, trying to keep the hurt from my voice.

"I think it's pretty fucking obvious I do."

"Then why?"

"Lila, this isn't going to be something you'll regret tomorrow morning. When I fuck you, I want you to be only thinking of me, and how good I make you feel. Not some asshole who wouldn't even go down on you." His voice is a low growl in my ear.

"Okay," I say quietly.

"Do you need me to prove it to you?" He grips my hip, pulling me flush against his straining cock. "Because I could eat you out all night if it'll show you that I'm in this for more than a quick fuck, but I won't fuck you until you are too."

With my back to him, he can't see my face, and I grin at the words, a warm feeling unrelated to my recent orgasm filling my chest.

"Come on, let's get some sleep," he says after a few moments.

We pull back the covers, sliding under them easily. Cal hesitates for a moment, and calling all my bravery forward, I turn and snuggle into him.

He smiles tentatively, opening his arms and letting my head rest on his shoulder, my hand feeling the heartbeats beneath his muscled chest. I drift off easily, content and warm and safe, for the first time in weeks.

Chapter Twenty-Two

CAL

I wake up warm, too warm. And I can't breathe.

I spit out the mouthful of hair I'd half swallowed and try to catch my bearings.

Lila is sleeping soundly, her leg thrown over mine, and her arm is belted around my waist. I smile to myself, enjoying the feeling of being wrapped in her embrace, even as I replay the events of last night in my mind. Her taste, the little whimpers of pleasure I pulled from her, the way she clenched down on my fingers. I can't help but imagine just how good she would feel milking my cock.

Bloody hell.

I run my free hand over my face, wiping the sleep from my eyes and trying to avoid any semblance of bed head. With horror I realize I'm standing at half-mast. While not uncommon in the morning, Lila's limbs being so close to my cock is raising the flag, so it seems.

I reach for her knee, intending to ease it off my lower half. Just as I make contact, she gives a little groan, and I glance down to her face still lying on my chest. Her eyes flutter open, slowly meeting mine, and she gives a tentative smile.

"Morning sleepyhead," I joke, pushing up into a sitting position and letting her slide off into the middle of the bed.

"Good morning," she yawns, stretching. "What time is it?"

"Uh . . ." I grab my phone from the nightstand and splutter. "It's nearly ten."

She blinks at me in surprise. "I thought we were leaving early?"

"I guess I forgot to set an alarm." Shit. I have two missed calls from Theo, and one unknown number with a voicemail. I listen to it quickly.

"The car is here. They picked it up early this morning and dropped it off."

"Oh good. I guess we should head out then."

"Do you want breakfast first?" I ask. There's something in the gentleman handbook somewhere about feeding a woman breakfast after a night of *escapades*, right?

"Let's just stop for coffee on the road somewhere, I don't really want to risk running into any of the other guests." She shudders.

"Yeah, sounds good to me." I stand and cross to the en suite. "I'll get dressed and then go heat up the car."

I'm nearly ready when I remember the reason that I can't find my shirt is that a half-naked girl is still wearing it in the bed I just left. I step out of the bathroom in just my jeans.

"I, uh, might need my shirt." I say, sheepishly, hand scratching the back of my neck.

"Oh, right." She hops up. "I'll change now then." She scampers around me into the bathroom, snapping the door shut with a click.

I swipe through my messages, one from Mother wishing me a "Happy Thanksgiving or whatever excuse for celebrations Americans are using these days." I chuckle to myself. She never did get over my love of the States.

Lila tosses my shirt to me through a crack in the door, and I have to suppress the urge to try for a peak of exposed skin beyond. She's dressed and back out of the bathroom before I can fully set my mind back to normal.

"Were you going to put it on?" she asks, looking pointedly at the shirt I'm holding.

I flush and tug it on. "Er, I got distracted."

"By what?"

I shrug. "You ready?"

She stares at me with confusion, but lets it drop and heads for the door.

My car is waiting in the small parking lot next to the bed-and-breakfast, and I exhale with relief. Part of me didn't think it'd actually be here, that the address would be wrong or the company would've brought the wrong car or somehow totaled it in transit. But there it sits, no worse for wear than when we'd left the city yesterday other than mud coating the back wheel wells.

As we settle in the car, I'm reminded of the torture on the drive up—trying not to reach over and touch her knee—but it's right there now. And with the physical barriers removed, at least partially, I could do it now.

I hold my breath, and slowly reach my hand over, giving her time to shift positions if she wants.

Touchdown! The announcer screams in my head. I squeeze her knee gently and look over from the road to find her giving me a soft smile. She blushes when I catch her eye, and I grin, shooting her a wink.

We cover the rest of the drive like that, in a much more comfortable silence than the ride up. I'm not exactly sure where it leaves us, but I'll settle for casual touches if that's all she's willing to give me.

🏈 🏈 🏈

I turn down the private drive and glance at Lila as the house comes into view. Her eyes have turned as big as saucers, and I chuckle.

"It is a bit ostentatious, isn't it?" I quip.

"It's enormous. I thought this was just a lake house." She stares up in wonder.

"Well, it is technically on the lake." I point to Lake Superior, visible just over the carriage house.

She blows out a breath and shakes her head. "You guys are both professional athletes, and I know Katie's family is pretty well off but still. For some reason I expected a cabin and some bunkbeds."

I can't help it and burst out laughing.

"Love, we went to private boarding school together. We're all well off." I park the car, ignoring the clench in my chest that she hadn't looked up my net worth already. That she would've still wanted to come even if we were all sharing bunkbeds in a cabin.

I walk around to open her door. "Come on. I'll give you a tour." She's still in some kind of impressed shock but lets me pull her out of the car, following me into the house once I've grabbed our bags from the boot.

As we're walking up the wide staircase through the garden, the front double doors fly open.

"There you are!" Theo shouts down at us. "Took you long enough to get here."

I roll my eyes as he bounds down the stairs, Katie right on his heels to embrace Lila.

"Oi, mate, little help over here?" I call to him, holding up Lila's bag.

"Nah, man, you've got it." He shoots me a wink, before taking her arm and leading her back into the house. God, he's a prick, but at least he's a laugh sometimes. I follow them inside, trailing behind and watching Lila take it all in. She's clearly trying to play it cool, to seem like this is all normal, but Theo likes to show off, and she's the perfect target today.

"Are your folks around?" I ask, intending to say hello.

"They're in Singapore for the month. I think Maggie might drop in though." He shrugs. "You'll be in your usual room, and I put Lila across the hall from you. I grunt in acknowledgement and head up the large main staircase to the room I've stayed in since we were kids.

London was too far to fly home for short breaks during the school year, and while New York would have been closer, being alone with Father wasn't something I ever sought out. Theo invited me once for the Thanksgiving holidays when he realized I was planning to stay at school, and I never looked back. We spent most of that time at this lake house, and it's become something of a home away from home after all these years.

I haven't been back since I was drafted to New York, and I let the memories and nostalgia wash over me as I pace the halls.

My room is unchanged. The dark blue bedspread and pale wooden furniture is so different from my condo in Chicago but comforting all the same.

I drop my bag on the bed, crossing the hall to the room Lila would be staying in for the next couple days. I push open the door and am momentarily caught off guard by the abundance of pink covering most of the room. I set her suitcase just inside the threshold before returning to my own room, deciding a shower and fresh change of clothes might be in order.

A short while later, I'm dressed in fresh clothes and am headed to rejoin the group as Lila comes into view.

"Oh, there you are."

"Miss me already?" I ask, unable to keep the smirk off my face.

"*Theo* misses you already." She laughs. "He was wondering where you got off to. We just finished the tour, and I was going to try to change into some new clothes, but I see you beat me to the idea."

"I usually try not to wear the exact same outfit for longer than 30 hours straight. Though I can definitely see the appeal." I joke and am rewarded with a small giggle.

"Ah, yes, I quite agree," she says in a very bad British accent.

I laugh. "Well enjoy your room, I put your suitcase just inside the door." She opens it, and I can't help but continue. "When you're back down I'll show you *my* favorite parts of the house. Theo most likely skipped the most important ones."

"If I can even find my way back down. I might have to call you just for directions."

"At your service." I give her a small, mock bow. "But seriously, if you do get lost just text me or scream really loudly and one of us will come find you."

"Good to know it's not completely soundproofed then."

"It's soundproofed enough." I say offhandedly, thinking of her small moans last night. She flushes, and steps quickly inside her room.

"See you down there," she says before she closes the door behind her.

I wonder how many more times I have to make her come before I'll be invited in instead of shut out. I run my hand down my face to physically wipe the want from my eyes before making my way down to where I know Theo and Katie will be in the game room.

"So . . ." Katie leers at me the moment I sink onto the couch.

"So what?"

"Your little overnight adventure?" she prods.

"What about it?" I ask as nonchalantly as I can.

She scoffs.

"I know you're going to ask her the second you're alone. Why would I deprive you of that joy?"

Theo snorts and hands me a beer, but Katie just rolls her eyes.

"You care about her, right?" she asks.

"Obviously."

That must be enough for her inquisition because she lets it drop and turns on the TV.

By the time Lila joins us, I'm on my second beer and Katie is fully invested in season one of *Gossip Girl*.

Lila scrunches her nose at the TV and grabs a High Noon from the wet bar. "Blech, season one Chuck." Katie laughs. "At least skip forward a bit."

"Sorry, I'm a goner. I have to watch the entire thing start to finish now."

"Woah," interrupts Theo. We're shooting pool behind the large sectional where Lila now sits with Katie in front of the massive flat screen. "We're not watching all six seasons of *Gossip Girl* this weekend."

Katie's eyes glitter maliciously. "Is that a challenge?" Lila cackles at her friend as the stare down taking place.

"Definitely not." Theo's trying to recover, but the panic in his eyes is giving him away.

"Well, we're already four episodes in."

"It's practically a head start," Lila says as she shrugs her shoulder, grabbing a blanket from the back of the couch and settling in. "And sounds like a perfect holiday weekend."

"Please, no," Theo begs.

"Sorry, babe, you don't choose the CW life, it chooses you." Katie smirks at him, turning up the volume to an unnecessary level and adding subtitles for an extra little punch.

I cough to hide my laugh, and Theo glares at me.

"Maybe we should order some food?" I suggest.

"Pizza?" Lila asks. Her head popping up over the back of the couch. I shrug.

"What do you ladies want?"

"Mushroom!" They both call back in unison. I blanch.

"Is that a joke?"

"Unfortunately, not," Theo sighs.

"They're delicious and good for your brain." Lila pouts playfully at me.

"Love, I literally get hit in the head for a job. I'm not overly worried about brain food," I say, the moniker slipping out before I can think about it.

She rolls her eyes.

"But if mushroom is what you want, mushroom is what you'll get." I ignore the look Katie and Theo exchange and pull out my phone.

Ordering the pizzas takes only minutes, and once they've arrived, Theo and I have no real choice but to pause our second pool game and give in to watching at least one episode of the stupid drama while we eat.

◼ ◼ ◼

I wake up the following morning sitting sideways on the couch with a massive knot in my shoulder, Lila's head in my lap. She's sound asleep even as a season-two episode starts on the TV, thankfully muted at some point in the night.

Theo is nowhere to be found, likely having actually gone up to bed at a reasonable hour, and Katie is snoring under a nest of blankets on the chaise section of the couch. I stretch, trying my best not to jostle Lila too much before moving her carefully off my lap to the couch and standing up. The half empty pizza boxes from last night cover the coffee table, empty cans littering the leftover space. I grab the pizza boxes, tossing them into the large trash can in the kitchen. After a quick check that both girls are still sleeping, I head up to my room to change for a run.

A few miles later, my heartbeat is up, my muscles loose and warm, a sharp contrast to my face which is numb with cold. I leave my AirPods in but strip off my hoodie, leaving me shirtless as I enter the kitchen and grab one of Theo's favorite protein shakes. I shake my head. Personally, I don't like the super weird flavors, preferring a simple chocolate, but I can suck it up today and try strawberry shortcake. I take a sip and grimace.

There's a noise behind me, and I turn to find Lila in the doorway, eyes glazed as she stares at me. I take another long draw of the protein shake, taking in her flushed face as she realizes she's been caught staring. She makes no move to leave, and I prowl toward her slowly, discarding the now empty bottle.

"Good morning," I say, a smirk I can't stop pulling up one half of my mouth.

"Did you work out?" she asks, her voice a bit hoarse, the rasp in it doing strange things to my blood, heating it in a way that should be illegal.

"Just went for a run," I say, my own voice carrying a slightly husky quality now. I take another step closer to her, and she steps back almost involuntarily, her back hitting the door frame. "Had a lot of excess energy to work out." She swallows, her eyes darting down my torso and back up.

"Sure, of course," she murmurs, her eyes glued to my mouth. I place one hand on the doorframe over her head and lean down toward her.

"Do you have some excess energy you need me to work out of you?" My voice drops an octave, and heat blooms in her eyes, her lips parting. Her fingers wind themselves into my hair, dragging my face to hers, and when my lips find hers, I can't help the groan in the back of my throat. My hands find her hips, my fingers sinking into the soft flesh there, even as I pin her between my body and the door frame.

I swallow her moan, grinding into her as her hands roam my naked torso, nails scraping against the muscles still slick with sweat from my run. My index finger traces the waistband of her leggings, slipping just under and running along the top of her thong.

"You know what I'm thankful for this holiday season?" A loud voice interrupts the moment, and we break apart.

Theo is currently sitting at the kitchen island, a shit-eating grin plastered on his face as he sips on another one of his disgusting protein shakes.

"Bedrooms, with closed doors," he continues.

"Fuck off, McClane," I nearly growl at him.

"Seriously, your rooms are literally right across the hall from each other. Can't you please keep whatever this is to *one* of them?"

"It's not anything," Lila says quickly. I still, my body going suddenly cold. Not anything? Really? She must notice my reaction because she continues. "No, wait, Cal. That's not what I meant."

"No, it's fine, I know," I force out. "I'm going to go shower." I step away without meeting her eyes and head for my room.

"Cal, wait," Lila calls, catching up to me.

I pause, turning to her and wait.

"I didn't mean that."

"So, what did you mean?"

"I don't know. That's all I meant. We don't know what this is, and we don't need Theo trying to define it for us."

Unfortunately, that makes sense, but it doesn't fix the chasm in my chest that's been opened. "You're not wrong there, but we're not *nothing*." I admit. "We can take it slow, I'm not in a rush, but we're not nothing."

"We'll just take it one day at a time, okay?" She smiles tentatively up at me, and I can't help that it fucking melts my heart.

"Yeah, Lila. One day at a time." I pull her to me roughly, burying my face into her messy hair. I let go after a moment, pressing my lips to her forehead. Before I can do something stupid like kiss her again, I stride toward my room without a backward glance, shoving aside the hurt blossoming like a bruise beneath my skin.

Chapter Twenty-Three

LILA

I can't stop thinking about that forehead kiss.

It felt like a goodbye.

He's been avoiding me all afternoon, and I can't blame him. I know it was a lie, we're not *nothing*, but I'm scared. I don't want to get hurt, and he's intense, my emotions are intense. It's easier to shut them away and enjoy the hunky athlete than to process everything else in my head.

I've been sitting in the game room trying to read for the past thirty minutes—Katie's *Gossip Girl* marathon abandoned in the fresh light of day—when Maggie's voice calls out from the entryway.

"Sorry I'm late, but I brought donuts!"

I follow the sound of her heels into the kitchen and grab a donut from the Krispy Kreme box on the counter.

"Did you have a good Thanksgiving?" I ask, taking a bite of the glazed goodness.

She shrugs. "It was pretty nice."

"What'd you do?"

"Don't tell Theo. He can get weirdly older-brothery, but I've kind of been seeing someone," she almost whispers, eyes darting to the doorway as if to check for said brother listening around the corner.

I squeal.

"Shhhhh!" She laughs. "I'm not ready to introduce him yet, but I like him a lot, so we spent the evening just the two of us. It was really romantic."

"That sounds so sweet. Can't you give me any more details?"

She shakes her head, giggling as Cal walks into the kitchen, carrying his duffle bag.

"Cal, hi. Donut?" Maggie offers.

"I'm okay, thanks." His eyes don't meet mine, and I feel rush of excitement that followed his entrance into the room vanish.

"Are you leaving?" I ask, trying to keep my voice from giving away the sudden emptiness inside my chest.

"Yeah, the o-line coach just called for an emergency film session tomorrow morning, so I need to head out. Theo can give you a ride back to the city." His expression is guarded, and I don't think he'd lie, but I can't help but feel like he's running away from me.

"Can we talk before you leave, please?" I ask, hoping I don't sound as desperate as I feel.

He gestures for me to follow him from the kitchen.

"What do you want to talk about?" he asks, once we're outside.

"You know what I want to talk about."

He says nothing, putting his bag in the trunk.

"Cal, come on."

"What do you want me to say, Lila?" he bursts out. "I feel like I've made my intentions pretty clear. And I meant what I said, that we could go slow and if you needed time that was okay, but I can't do this back-and-forth thing. You can't throw yourself at me and then say we don't mean anything." I shrink back as his words hit me.

"I'm not trying to do that—"

"I know. I'm not, like, mad at you. But I think you need to make sure you know what you want, and if that's me, great, and if it's not, fine, but you need to figure it out."

I stare at him, unsure what to say to all that.

"I really do have practice," he says after several seconds of silence, his face softening slightly.

I nod. "Okay."

He hesitates, as if unsure whether to hug me, but must decide against it, because he gets in his car and drives away without ever looking back.

* * *

I'm practically catatonic for the rest of the day. Maggie has to ask the same question three times before I finally hear her over the noise in my own head.

"Are you okay?" Katie asks, cornering me after a dinner of Chinese takeout while Maggie and Theo are arguing in the other room over which *Die Hard* is objectively the best. "We never really talked about what happened when you guys got stranded, and you seemed so happy and cuddly I just assumed . . . but then he left."

"I think I fucked up."

"Explain."

"Well, I uh . . ." I start, unsure how to continue. She lets me sit with it, and a few minutes later it comes pouring out of me, every last detail until I'm nearly gasping out his goodbye.

"It'll be okay." She pulls me in for a hug and holds tight.

"I don't know how to fix it," I say, the despair in my voice evident. "I really like him, but I'm scared. What if it gets bad again? Like with Dennis? What if I'm the one who's toxic and ruining it? I'm too old to start over again when it doesn't work out in a year."

She pulls away, her gaze intense. "First of all, don't let your mother get in your head. You're not on anyone's timeline but your own. Second, you're not toxic, that was all Dennis all on his own. And third, why do you think it won't work out?"

"Katie, he's an NFL player. I work in consulting. What can anyone really expect out of us being together?"

"So, you're both busy and successful? Sounds like a power couple to me," she jokes.

"You saw the other women at the game. They're all models or athletes, I clearly don't fit in. And everyone but Cal seems to notice it. Eventually he will too." I shrug.

"News flash. No one actually cares." I blink, shocked, and her voice softens. "Babe, he *likes* you. Does he really seem so shallow that he'd throw you away for no reason?"

"I mean, not yet. But what if I just haven't seen that side of him yet?" I cross my arms, providing a physical barrier between myself and this conversation.

"Don't self-sabotage this by making up his reactions in your head years before they happen. That's crazy, you know that right?" She raises an eyebrow at me, and I feel like I'm losing the point of why I'm upset somewhere. She's twisting my words because there's no way that's actually what I'm doing. Right?

"But—"

"No, it's certifiably insane. I should check you into RUSH this afternoon." She clicks her tongue, and I nearly laugh, coming back up out of my spiral to reality.

"You're probably right," I sigh.

"Can you get that engraved on a plaque?" She teases, grinning at me.

"Oh, shut up." I knock her shoulder.

"Come on, if we're lucky we can sneak the remote back and finish season two of *Gossip Girl*." I laugh, as she grabs two pints of Ben & Jerry's Half Baked from the freezer.

Theo is overruled by three women, and with *Gossip Girl* season two on the big screen, he's pretending to pout in the corner while his eyes are glued to Chuck's every move. I move to sit next to him.

"Is he okay?" I ask tentatively.

His jaw clenches.

"Lila, what do you want from him?"

"What do you mean?"

"What do you want from him? Out of this, whatever it is you've been doing?"

"I uh—" I stammer.

"I think you need to figure that out before you talk to him again."

"That's not fair, Theo."

"Isn't it?" He snaps.

"You know what I've been going through with Dennis and everything. I didn't want to just jump into something."

"But is that something you want? Or are you just along for the ride for now?"

"I care about him."

He takes a deep breath, as if he's praying for patience.

"Look, he's serious about you. So, if you're not serious about him you need to tell him that. Because I can't watch him get dragged over the coals just because you can't make up your mind or won't."

"Okay," I say quietly, sinking back into the couch.

"I think you're good for him, and Katie seems to think he can make you happy if you'd let him try. But you have to try too, ya know?"

"Yeah."

He nods once, and we lapse into silence. I lose myself in the plot as my mind processes in the background.

Maybe I just need to talk to him. Theo's right, it's not fair to him to drag him along if I'm not sure, but why am I not sure? Is Katie right? Am I just self-sabotaging? I think back over the last few weeks, realizing with utter certainty that some of the most fun I've had, the times I've been the happiest and freest, have been with Cal.

I groan. It's too new. I don't know him very well, and these are all feelings I haven't felt in a very long time, if I've ever felt them at all.

Love is stupid. But I want it, and I think I want to try it with Johnathan Callahan Basset, even if he dumps me in six months for a *Sports Illustrated* swimsuit cover model.

〰 〰 〰

We drive back early Saturday, and the following morning I pull on Cal's jersey tentatively—I have it, so I might as well wear it when he plays—and rush to meet Katie. She'd insisted last minute on watching at Cornerside, which was fine by me.

The game against Dallas is largely uneventful but evenly matched. The powerhouse defense manages to hold the Avalanche to only two field goals while we've given up a touchdown. More interesting than two teams who can barely get past their respective forty-yard lines is Katie, completely invested in some hockey talk show playing on one of the other TVs.

"What are you watching?"

"The center forward has a shoulder injury, they're not sure he'll play in the game on Saturday and it's against Detroit." She's worrying her bottom lip, and I can't help but laugh.

She glares at me. "What?"

"Nothing," I gasp out. "You just honestly care about hockey now?"

Her eyes narrow. "So, what if I do?"

"I'm just surprised. After all the shit you've given me about following football, all it took was a brooding hockey player to sway you to the dark side."

She pointedly ignores me, and I laugh.

"Who are you, and what have you done with Katie? I told you we should've come up with a code in grad school, but no. You said, and I quote, 'Lila if someone is impersonating me it should be easy enough to figure out. Who could possibly live up to the impossible standard I set in life, and if I've been abducted, my mother always said she was never worried since I'd be dropped back off in under eight hours.'"

She flushes and elbows me hard in the ribs.

"Okay, okay, I'm sorry. I think it's kind of nice you're getting more into sports. Do I wish it was the sport I already watch and pay attention to? Sure." She rolls her eyes. "But still, it's always fun to have another woman on the team."

She rolls her eyes. "Whatever, just eat your cheese curds."

I pop one into my mouth to appease her and turn back to the game, only for my grin to slide off as I see what's on the screen.

The game, with only three minutes left in the final quarter is running a replay of the last play, before a final pass is thrown. A Hail Mary throw on the fourth down straight into Cal's outstretched hands as he lands in the end zone. The bar explodes around me with cheers, and I scream along with them. Never one for flashy celebrations, he hands the ball to the refs as the crowd goes wild.

The camera pans back to Cal, and I smile.

That's my man.

Well, maybe not yet, but he will be by tonight.

I turn to Katie. "Do you have trench coat I can borrow?"

She eyes me warily. "Am I going to actually want it back afterwards?"

"Uhm, probably not?"

"Ew, fine. You owe me one for Christmas, though."

I hug her as we head out of the bar. "You got it."

"And you have to help me pick out a dress."

I snort. "You've never once actually needed my opinion on clothes, just validation."

"Well, this is different. I want to make a good impression without being *too much*."

"Katie, you're never too much. And if someone told you that you were, give me their address."

"I still want your opinion. Please? It's basically in the best friend handbook, you have to help." She pouts at me until I roll my eyes.

"Going somewhere nice?"

She shrugs.

"Katherine?" I press. "At least tell me who we're making a good impression on?"

"Axel's taking me out, okay? It's our first official date."

"That's the guy you were talking to at Cal's, right?"

"Yup," she accentuates the *p* sound with delight.

"Where's he taking you?"

"I'm not sure." She frowns. "He said it was a surprise."

"We'll find the right thing," I assure her.

⬤ ⬤ ⬤

She's tried on approximately thirty-five dresses by this point, and I'm growing faint with hunger as I lay cross ways on her bed, scrolling social media.

"Can you button me? I think this is the one."

She comes out of her walk-in closet in a black sheath dress that fits her perfectly and turns with her back to me. I do up the two buttons at the top of the neck.

"You're right, this one's perfect."

She twirls in the mirror and checks the time.

"Shit, he's picking me up in twenty minutes. I have to finish getting ready."

"You got this, I have my own man to woo tonight." I waggle my eyebrows at her, and she laughs.

"The jacket's in the hall closet, just make sure you shut the door behind you."

I nod, squeezing her shoulders on my way out of her bedroom.

"And good luck!" she calls out after me.

"You too!"

Chapter Twenty-Four

CAL

I'm staring at my phone as I mindlessly scroll through replays of my game-winning catch earlier, as the documentary on the TV drones on in the background. Somehow it doesn't feel as sweet as it should.

Another text from Lila comes through, and I swipe it away without opening it. I read her first apology text, but until she decides what she wants, I can't talk to her. The back and forth is too much. She hasn't tried to call once, hasn't tried to see me. I need her to take a chance and come to me the way I've been taking a chance on her this whole time.

Theo's face lights up my screen a few minutes later, and I sigh, answering it.

"What?"

"Is that how you always answer the phone?"

"What do you want, Theo?" I ask out of exasperation.

"What are you doing tonight?"

"Nothing."

"You should come out and celebrate the win with us."

The guys got off the plane and all immediately went to the clubs, and I came home.

"Nah, I'm not feeling it tonight."

"So, you're just going to sit at home?"

"Yes. Glad you understand."

I hang up before he can object.

I trudge into my master bath. Maybe another shower will help wash off whatever this melancholy mood is.

I'm finished much too quickly and back on the couch in my favorite grey sweatpants, forgoing a shirt since I'll just end up in bed in another hour anyway.

I turn my attention back to the TV—I found a new episode on grey whales I haven't seen—when there's a knock at my door.

"So help me God, Theo, I'm not going out tonight!" I yell at the door as I stomp over to it.

I throw it open, expecting to see a grinning idiot, and instead see only Lila.

"Hey," she says, breathlessly.

"Hi." My voice is hoarse, my throat dry as I take her in. She's in a long, tan trench coat, belted tightly at the waist, with black stockings covering her legs below the hem.

She's wearing sky high black stilettos. My mouth goes dry as I try to swallow.

"I was going to bring flowers, but Theo said you were allergic, so I baked instead." She holds out a plate I missed, too focused on her legs in the sheer black tights. "They're peanut butter blossoms."

I take the offered dish. "Thanks." My mouth feels parched, and I try in vain to swallow nonexistent saliva.

"So, uhm, I was hoping we could talk?" she asks, her voice more timid than I've ever heard it, and it snaps me out of ogling her legs.

"Of course." I step aside to let her through the door.

I spend a good long time closing the door and locking it behind her, trying to slow my racing heart.

Calm down. You need to talk to her. And she *needs to talk to you. You need answers.*

I turn slowly and move to set the plate of cookies on the counter.

"Congrats on the win today."

I glance up at her, and her eyes are intense, locked on my face. I sigh. "Lila—"

"No, let me." I look at her confused, but she plows on.

"I'm scared. Okay?" She takes a deep breath. "You scare me." That hits me like a punch to the gut.

"What? I don't—" She holds up a hand, and I trail off.

"Not like that, sorry. I actually feel incredibly safe with you. That's part of the problem?" I can feel the surprise coloring my expression. How is that a problem?

"I feel safe with you. But you can hurt me, emotionally I mean. That's why you scare me."

The dawning of understanding must show on my face, because she continues without further explanation.

"Cal, I've been basically alone for a long time. Technically I've been on and off with Dennis, but he's been living in New York full time for a couple years now, and how much of a life can you really build with someone when you live hundreds of miles apart and break up twice a year anyway? Not one worth having." She starts pacing in the kitchen, and I'm frozen, leaning against the countertop with no idea which way this conversation will end up going. I'm more confused than anything, but wasn't I just wishing she would come to me? She's here now, and that's something.

"I was comfortable being alone. I was content to work and be successful, and watch my sister and her husband have kids, to push off my mom's nosy question every holiday and ignore the loud whispering of my aunts whenever I left the room.

She throws her hands in the air as she paces. "I was happy to be Katie's best friend and attend fun parties and meet fancy people who would forget who I was the moment I left to get another drink."

She stops pacing and looks up at me, eyes bright. "But you weren't going to ever be one of those people. And I don't think I can be content with that life anymore." Her chest rises and falls as she takes a shuddering breath.

"Cal, you make me not want to be alone anymore. You make me happy to be doing more. I've felt joy again, not just with you but alone too. It's like I was living in black and white, and you brought color with you, but instead of leaving it dark and grey when you left, I could still see the color, in everything. I don't want to live in grey ever again."

I swallow hard as she draws closer.

"I want this . . . or want to try, at least, if you still want me." Her hand rests lightly on the belt at her waist.

I take her hand, pulling her toward me as my other arm wraps around her crushing her to my bare chest.

I tangle my hand in her hair, holding her to me, and her arms come around my waist to cling to my back, her nails digging into my lats. She smells different today, and I inhale deeply, trying to memorize her new scent. A little bit spicier, it's enticing.

I tug her hair gently, pulling her head back so her face is turned up toward me. I slant my mouth over hers, swallowing the greedy little moans she makes as she opens for me, deepening the kiss. I step forwards slowly, moving her with me until her back hits the island in my kitchen. Her hands come off my skin, and then her jacket hits the floor near my feet. I kiss along her jaw as my hands memorize her skin and lift her easily onto the counter so I can step between her parted thighs. My thumb brushes against a scratchy patch of lace, and I pull back to peer down at her.

My knees buckle as I take her in. Underneath that tan trench coat, she was dressed in nothing but black lingerie.

"Fuck," I breathe as I take in the sheer lace stockings held up by a black lace garter belt to match the bra and thong set she's wearing.

Lila smirks up at me coyly from beneath her lashes.

"Surprise," she says, her voice husky.

I let my head fall forward to rest at the crook of her neck. "Are you trying to kill me?"

She giggles, locking her ankles at my back and forcing me closer. The sound in my throat is part moan and part growl as I reattach my mouth to her throat, more hungrily than before. Her fingers rake my scalp as I press hot, open-mouthed kisses down to the fabric at her chest. I slide my finger slowly under the strap on her shoulder and guide it down, waiting for her to stop me. She arches into me in response. I continue the path, pulling the cup out of the way to suck her nipple. I graze it with my teeth echoing my own need with a guttural sound.

She's hot against me as I grind against her core, even through the two layers of fabric separating us. I trail one hand down along the outside of her thigh and over her knee, sliding it wider before gliding it back up the inside. She bucks against my hand as I cup her, the damp lace adding to the friction. I smirk against her collarbone and ease the scrap of lace to the side.

I tease her opening with my middle finger, circling the entrance and collecting her arousal.

"You're so wet for me, love." I groan and bring my finger up to my mouth. Her pupils are blown wide as I suck her juices from my hand.

"Do you want to taste how sweet you are?"

Something low in my throat escapes as she nods her head, and rather than re-wet my finger, I capture her mouth, instantly deepening the kiss and stroking her tongue with my own. She whines as she tries to pull me flush against her once more.

"Use your words, love."

She gasps, "Please Cal, *please*."

"Please what?" I drag my hand back down circling her clit once. "Please this?"

She whimpers, and I swear to God half my brain turns off, because all I can consciously think about is giving her what she wants, what we both want.

I slide a finger in, heat licking up my spine at how tight and warm she is. I add a second finger moments later, and after only a few minutes circling her clit, I have her wound so tightly her breathing is coming in pants.

"Please," she begs.

"Please what?" I tease again, "Words, love. Remember?"

Her answering moan isn't exactly a response, but the way she reaches for my waistband definitely is.

I capture her wandering hand and intertwine our fingers, keeping them at her side.

"You're going to come like this."

She whimpers again, and I increase my circles, two fingers still pumping in and out in a steady rhythm.

"Can you do that for me?" She shakes her head and I tsk.

"Come on love, be a good girl for me. Come on my hand, and then I'll fuck you so hard you won't be able to remember your own name, because the only one you'll know is the one you're screaming."

And the dirty talk must do it because her walls start to flutter around my fingers. I crook them forward to hit just right and she shatters around me, drenching my hand as I work her through her orgasm.

She sags against me, and I slowly pull out my fingers, gripping her chin with the hand previously holding onto hers. I press the dripping digits into her mouth, and if she's worn out, she doesn't show it because her eyes come alive again as she eagerly sucks them clean, working her tongue over and around them, taking both fully into her mouth and looking up at me through her lashes.

Fucking gorgeous.

I immediately picture how stunning she'd be sucking on something else while looking up at me like that but push it from my mind. Not tonight. Tonight, she's mine, and I want my cum dripping out of her, not swallowed.

I pull my fingers from her mouth and grip her hips, bringing our mouths together once more before lifting her. Her long legs wrap around my waist automatically, making it easier to walk her toward my bedroom, because our first time won't be anywhere but a bed.

I drop her lightly onto the down comforter before crawling over her and bracketing my arms on either side of her face before leaning down to kiss her. This kiss is less urgent now, more exploratory.

I kiss down her jawline and slide my hand under her back. She arches to grant me access as I attempt to open her bra clasp. I fumble for a few moments before it finally comes free. She smirks at me as I pull it free from her arms.

I huff indignantly. "I'm out of practice."

She narrows her eyes as if she doesn't quite believe me, but as I take her nipple in my mouth and roll it between my teeth, she throws her head back against the pillows.

"Not too out of practice then." I smirk against her warm skin, before continuing down her body, nipping everywhere that I can reach and smoothing over the sting with my tongue in the wake, before reaching her panties. I pause, looking up for confirmation. Her eyes meet mine, and it's as if the gold flecks in the brown have turned to flame. She lifts her hips, letting me slide the material down her legs before tossing them to the side.

I kneel in between her legs on the bed, and slowly pump one finger into her, before I reach over to the nightstand to grab a condom.

"You're sure?" I ask. I pray to God she is because if I have to stop now, no amount of cold showers will save me.

"Please." She says it like a prayer, and I tear the wrapper open with my teeth and add a second finger.

I quickly shuck off my sweatpants, thankful she's been too distracted to notice the not-so-insignificant wet spot and roll on the rubber with my free hand.

I line myself up with her entrance and look toward her face, to see her watching the inch of space separating our bodies from each other with such intensity I almost flinch just in case my dick catches fire.

"Look at me," I order, my voice raspy.

Her eyes meet mine, and I sink into her, sheathing myself fully. It's a near heavenly experience to watch her face as she takes all of me, as she stretches to accommodate me. My back stings as her nails find purchase in the skin there. I start to move slowly, flexing my hips just enough to drive some friction between us. Lila's soft moan in response is all the confirmation I need to pick up the pace.

I pull her leg up around my bicep, opening up the angle to thrust deeper into her. The pressure of my long-awaited orgasm builds. How many times had I envisioned this exact scenario? And yet not one of my fantasies came close to the experience of Lila writhing under me, her nails digging into my skin, the flush of her cheeks, the fire in her eyes, and just how perfectly she squeezes my cock inside her.

"Cal, please," she cries, her hand leaving my back to fist into the bedclothes beside her head.

"*Fuck,*" I hiss as her walls tighten around me. I slide her leg up onto my shoulder to free my hand and bring it down between us.

"Oh my God, Cal, *fuck.*" She's babbling a nonsense list of praises and expletives as I circle her swollen clit, trying to get her over the edge once more. "Fuck yes, Cal. Please, please, please. Yes. Don't stop. I'm so close."

"Yes, love, come for me."

A lightbulb flickers in my currently empty brain, dirty talk. It worked last time.

"Come for me Lila, now. In five," I start counting, and her eyes snap open, meeting mine once more.

"Four." The look on her face would make me laugh if I wasn't so caught up in the sex. She's so turned on it almost hurts me to not give into my own release, but part of her looks completely betrayed that I wouldn't let her finish if she can't get there in time. Jokes on her because of course she'd finish, I'd just count again.

"Three." I can feel the fluttering around my cock. *Ten seconds and you can come, hold on to it.*

"Two." Her body writhes under me as her orgasm builds.

"One." I give her one more push over the edge and pinch her swollen clit.

She explodes around me, and a cascade of liquid soaks the bed under us.

Holy fuck.

That does it for me, and I'm following her over the cliff as I fuck her through her orgasm and mine, coming so hard I see stars.

When I'm so sensitive I can't stand it anymore, I pull out and remove the condom. I make quick work of tossing it in the trash in my en suite but grab a towel for the bed and a last-minute thought has me running a washcloth under the tap for Lila as well.

I watch her from the doorway for a few moments, basking in the idea that she's really here in my bed. There's no way it could be a dream, because even in my wildest fantasies, she'd never squirted. She's still lying on the bed, unmoving except for the steady rise and fall of her chest.

I walk back her, wiping her gently with the washcloth before laying the dry towel down on the bed.

She cracks a sleepy smile at me as I ease myself onto the bed next to her, pulling the comforter over us both.

"Will you stay here with me tonight?" I ask, my voice betraying my true emotions.

Lila reaches for me, tucking herself into the space between my arm and my chest.

"Where else would I go?" she mumbles into the side of my torso.

I chuckle. I guess that answers that. I stroke her back as she drifts into sleep, making lazy patterns against her naked skin. Once her breathing has evened out, I relax into the silk sheets, breathing in her scent, and press a kiss to her forehead before I too drift off into sleep.

Chapter Twenty-Five

LILA

W*hy is it so hot?*

I feel like I'm being boiled alive. Even my skin is wet, but instead of sticking to the sheets, I'm pressed up against something hard while silk is draped over me.

I pull the soft material to me, cooling my body and sigh as I sink further into the mattress.

My eyes snap open as the memories from last night flood back. I'm most definitely in Cal's bed. I turn my head slightly to see confirmation from the man still sleeping next to me.

He's always been attractive but seeing how peaceful he looks like this tugs at something in my chest. A flare of heat rises inside me as I trace down his chiseled chest and washboard abs to where the sheet drapes, creating a suspicious-looking tent. My mouth dries remembering all that specific tent pole could do.

I ease myself out of the bed and pad toward the large walk-in closet. I run my hand along the row of suit jackets before I find what I'm looking for. I pull down a white Oxford button-down shirt from the upper row of hangers. I marvel at how clean his closet is as I shrug on the shirt, everything arranged by color, even if it's only neutrals. A few pops of blue and navy stand out as his two team colors over the years.

I leave the first few unbuttoned as I do the buttons of the shirt up quickly. Feeling like I belong in a rom-com movie, I quietly make my way back through Cal's bedroom and into the kitchen.

I find my trench coat in a heap on the floor. I'm definitely going to replace it for Katie, because there's no way I'll be able to return it with a straight face. Even so, I pick it up and drape it over a bar stool at the island and turn back to face the kitchen.

Pancakes are a good start.

I start opening cabinets willy-nilly, trying to find a pan and any semblance of the ingredients needed.

Bingo. The third shelf from the left has a box of protein pancake mix. I grab milk and eggs from the fridge and get to work.

The last of the pancakes are sizzling on the stove when I hear something knock against the counter. I whip around, spatula raised as if in self-defense, only to see Cal leaning against the counter wearing nothing but black boxer briefs. His tousled hair is what every guy at the office imagines they're achieving, but my eyes catch on his face—the smirk playing across his lips and the intensity in his eyes.

"Do you want pancakes?"

"I'm definitely hungry, but I don't think pancakes are very high up on the list."

I deflate at his words. "Oh, uhm sorry about that then. I can clean up—"

"Oh, I'll eat the pancakes," he says, voice rough as he takes slow steps toward me. "It's just not what I want first."

I blink at him, then flush as the realization hits me.

"You're wearing my shirt." He's only a foot away now.

"Is that okay? I—"

He grabs my jaw with one hand, cutting me off before I can

apologize and presses a searing kiss to my mouth, his hand squeezing lightly on the sides of my throat.

My knees buckle, and he catches me wrapping an arm behind my back.

He walks me backward out of the kitchen before guiding me onto his lap as he sinks onto the couch. He releases my throat only to thread his fingers through my hair, fisting his hand at the back of neck. I can't help the whimper that escapes as I grind down onto his very hard cock, realizing the only separation between us is his boxers.

I unbutton another button of my shirt, and he groans, pushing it down off one shoulder and running his tongue along the exposed skin.

Both of his large hands come down to my hips, and I grind against him as he brings one thumb to my clit.

"Fuck, please." I moan, dropping my head back. I slide my hands down his chest, scraping my nails lightly against the toned muscle until I reach his waistband. I ease one hand under the fabric to pull his cock free.

I grind my naked pussy over his hard length, and we groan in unison as I lubricate his cock with my arousal.

I lift myself to position him at my entrance.

"Condom," he rasps.

"I have an IUD." I try to impale myself, but his grip on my hips holds firm as he keeps me above him.

"Are you sure? I'm clean. We get tested every year during training camp."

I pause. I've never actually been tested. He must sense my hesitation, because he continues. "Give me thirty seconds and don't move an inch."

He lifts me off him, gently lowering me to the other cushion before heading for his bedroom. It really is only a few seconds later when he returns, already rolling on the condom.

He pulls me up on my knees before swiping his finger through my folds.

"Good, you're still wet."

"It was only like ten seconds," I laugh. He smirks at me.

"Do you want to ride my face or my cock first?"

I swallow.

"Because you're going to be doing both."

Something in my vocal cords isn't working because I open my mouth to answer, but no sound comes out.

He sits in his recently vacated spot, guiding my leg over his so I'm straddling him again. With one hand on my hip and the other on his cock, he urges me down, sliding along his length until our hips are pushed flush together.

I'm so deliciously full, it nearly makes me emotional. He gives me a moment to adjust, and then he's thrusting up into me, barely giving an ounce of control over the tempo. It's all I can do to cling to his broad shoulders, my head falling forward into the crook of his neck.

"That's it, love. Take my cock. Take all of it." Each word is accompanied by an especially deep thrust, and I whine, biting down on the skin near his neck.

He slows the pace just enough to bring one thumb back to my clit.

"I want you to touch yourself while I fuck you." The hand touching my clit moves to my wrist, dragging it down from his shoulder to the apex of my thighs and the tight bundle of nerves that lays there.

I thumb my clit slowly, making tight circles around the swollen bud. Both of his hands move to my ass, gripping it tightly and spreading my cheeks, before I feel one finger exploring the area in between, spreading my arousal and matching the circles I'm applying to my clit.

I stiffen slightly at the prodding, and his finger stills.

"Do you want me to stop?" he asks, voice gruff.

Do I want him to stop? I can barely keep a coherent thought. I've tried butt stuff with Dennis, but it always hurt, so I never cared for it. Sex with Dennis wasn't nearly as good as it was with Cal last night, and with someone so focused on my pleasure, I trust him to stop if I say it hurts.

"No," I gasp out. He starts slow, circling my hole once more, before one finger teases the opening.

I tense again involuntarily.

"Relax, love." A trail of kisses down my jawline and neck follows his words, and as he sucks on the skin there, I melt into him.

"Keep playing with your clit, but don't come until I say so."

I let out a small whimper but resume my small circles as the pressure builds within me.

"If you come without permission, I'll eat your cunt for so long you won't be able to think straight for days."

His words send me higher, even as his finger slowly enters me from behind. He pumps it in and out in time with the thrusts of his cock, and I swear to God my soul leaves my body.

"You like that?"

"Mhmm," I moan, unable to form actual words at the moment.

He chuckles darkly.

"You like all your holes filled, don't you? You take my cock so well though. Such a good girl taking my fingers in your ass too, aren't you?"

"Yes, *fuck* yes," I pant, still climbing higher.

"Such a good girl for not coming. Beg me, Lila. Beg to come all over my cock with my fingers in your ass."

"Please, Cal, please."

"Please what, love?"

"Please let me come!" I nearly scream it. I'm so fucking close I can taste it.

"Say 'Please let me come all over your cock with your fingers in my ass, sir.'"

If I wasn't already turned on so much that I could power a fucking nuclear power plant, that might have pushed me over the edge.

"Please Cal," I whimper. He smirks at me, adding a second finger to the first and stretching me to the brink of pain and pleasure. "Please let me come on your cock while you finger my ass." He looks at me, waiting. "Sir." I breathe, my face flushing.

"Such a greedy little thing aren't you." He slams up into me before ordering, "Come for me, love."

I detonate with the force of a thousand suns.

● ● ●

The smell of something burning is the first thing I notice when I finally float back to reality post-orgasm.

"Shit, the pancakes." I jump up, nearly falling over immediately since my legs seem to be made of Jell-O, and half run to the stove where the last two pancakes were still cooking before Cal interrupted to introduce me to life changing sex once more.

"Fuck, hang on," he calls from behind me.

I turn off the stove, looking sadly down at the crumbles that used to be pancakes, now resembling charcoal ashes, the ones that did survive the attempt cold and limp on a plate on the counter.

I bite my lip and glance back at Cal who's washing his hands in the sink. "Whoops."

He grins lazily at me. "You can burn everything you ever make, and I won't care if you fuck me like that."

My cheeks flush, recalling why he's washing them so thoroughly. No one has ever talked to me the way he does in bed. I don't know what it says about me that it turns me on so much, but it does.

He must know what I'm thinking, because he comes up behind me and spins me to face him, cupping my face with his hands.

"Did you like what we did?"

I shrug, unsure how to admit my feelings. I remember asking one of my college boyfriends to try spanking and when he seemed aghast at the suggestion, I just never brought it up again.

"Lila," he says seriously, his eyes boring into mine. "If you didn't, you need to tell me."

I shake my head, and he frowns. "No, I did."

"Are you sure?"

I nod.

"It's nothing to be ashamed about. If you enjoyed it, that's literally all that matters."

"Do you still respect me after saying those things?" I whisper, staring at a point over his shoulder.

"Lila, look at me." He waits until I meet his gaze. "Of course, I still respect you. You're one of the most impressive people I know, a little dirty talk during sex won't ever change that."

"Promise?"

"I promise." He kisses my forehead, and I lean into him, his arms circling around me, pulling me into his chest.

"Do you want to go get breakfast? Or do you want to take your second ride of the day on my face?" He grins at me.

I can't help but smile back.

"Maybe food first?"

"You got it. Although I seem to remember you not having any clothes to wear. So, we can order in and kill two birds while we wait for delivery?"

"Deal." I squeal as he picks me up over his shoulder and carries me back to the bedroom.

Chapter Twenty-Six

LILA

I waltz into Cornerside, winking at Ray who's posted at the door, eager to get out of the chilly December air in my minimal clothing while feeling altogether too pleased with myself. My red jersey blazes a path in the patchwork of football fans crowding the space. I had the jersey from an old Halloween costume, and he *is* on my fantasy team, so my reasoning for wearing Travis Kelce's jersey is totally sound.

Cal hasn't been anything but a perfect gentleman since the other morning when he'd altered my brain chemistry with the way he fucked me. I feel like I'm losing my mind thinking about it, and no matter what I do, I can't replicate the orgasm he gave me. The facade of my psyche is cracking, and I need him to lose his composure. I need him just as feral as I am, and even Katie agreed this outfit would be the thing to crack him wide open, even if she laughed at me the entire time I was explaining my plan.

The warmth of success fills me when I catch sight of him at a table with our friends, his eyes bugging out slightly as they rake over my body, noting the oversized red jersey and thigh-high socks. My short bike shorts are hidden beneath, but without belting it, the entire look appears much more risqué than I normally dress. I'd even put my hair in low pigtails, with little red bows to match the jersey to complete the sexy cheerleader look I'm going for. I hesitate for only a moment, before turning toward the bar, giving him a view of the name on my back.

I've just ordered a seltzer when I feel someone at my back, their all too familiar hands on either side of me at the bar, caging me in.

"Really?" he growls in my ear.

I ignore him, staring straight ahead as I collect my drink from the bartender.

I turn to face him, but he doesn't move, effectively putting our faces only a hair's breadth apart.

"Oh, hey Cal." I smirk.

"What are you wearing?"

"I just thought I'd support my fantasy players today." I shrug. "It's not a big deal." I tap his arm, and he drops it from the bar, letting me side-step him as I make my way back to the table where Theo and Katie are already sitting with a large man who looks vaguely familiar. He's as tall as Cal, and if anything, broader through the torso, with dark hair and ice blue eyes that send a shiver down my spine. I vaguely remember him from the fiasco of a party at Cal's a few weeks ago.

"Lila, you made it," calls Katie, waving me over. "You remember Axel?"

I smile at him and hold out my hand. "Of course, I'm Lila." He shakes it.

"So, how did you and Katie meet? Just at Cal's party?" I ask, taking a seat at the large round booth next to Theo, leaving Cal to slide in next to me on the end. He snorts at the mention of *his* party.

"Theo introduced us," Katie babbles happily.

"Speaking of introductions," the devil himself interjects. "I could introduce you to Kelce if you want, Lila. We usually cross paths a couple times a year during promos." He's grinning like he's auditioning for *Alice in Wonderland*. One glance to Cal on my left, and I can barely suppress my own smirk.

"Theo, that'd be *amazing*," I gush. I can almost hear Cal's molars grinding together.

The first half of the game sitting next to Cal is torture. Every brush of our arms sets me aflame, and when he grips my knee under the table during a particularly tense play, a torrent of butterflies erupts in my gut that cause me to entirely miss the pick six scored by the Baltimore.

Finally, I can't take it anymore, and I excuse myself to the restroom down the back hallway. I walk slowly, catching Cal's eye just before I turn the corner. The ladies' room is empty to my relief, and I quickly remove the bike shorts and wait at the sinks, fluffing my hair.

The time ticks by, and I'm losing my confidence. I've almost given up when the door to the bathroom opens and shuts quietly. I glance up, but don't see anyone. A moment later the door slams open.

"What are you playing at?" Cal asks darkly, stalking into the bathroom. I smirk into the mirror, meeting his gaze and adjust one of the bows in my hair.

"I have no idea what you mean, I just wanted to fix my hair."

He flips the deadbolt on the bathroom door and my stomach turns over. He walks toward me with purpose, and I wet my suddenly dry lips, his eyes tracking the movement and darkening to a stormy grey.

He fists the hem of the jersey when he reaches me, spinning me around to face him. "Don't play coy." His voice is raspy, and my knees shake slightly at the tone. I open my mouth to retort when his other hand cups my jaw, his thumb crossing my chin spanning the width of my throat. "You know exactly what you're doing, love." He drops a kiss to my pulse point at the juncture of my neck and collarbone. "Don't you?"

The "no" I mean to say comes out as a sort of keen. One I'd be embarrassed by if this hulking specimen of a man hadn't already coaxed my body into reactions that would have even Katie clutching her pearls. He smirks against my skin, his knee knocking mine to the side to press between my legs.

"It's bad enough that I know you start him in your insane fantasy league over me every week," he mutters, twirling his wrist in the fabric, tightening it across my frame. He pushes his thumb into my hip bone, guiding my body up onto the counter. "But you dance around in his jersey now?" He steps into the space between my legs.

"I'm not—" I start, trying to keep my voice from shaking.

He cuts me off, hand tightening around my throat. Heat floods my core, a swooping in my lower abdomen causing my synapses to misfire momentarily.

"We both know you are." He lets go of the jersey, running a long finger up my center, feeling the dampness that gives me away. He groans in my ear, reattaching his mouth to the space just above my pulse point. His thumb finds my clit, already swollen with desire, and I mew, careening my upper body toward him.

He chuckles darkly. "So wet for me." He slides one finger into me, tearing through a hole in the lace of my thong. "Is this all for me?" His teeth bite into the skin above my collarbone, and I grunt, the only sound I'm capable of making as a second finger joins the first, curling inside me and making me see stars.

"Lila," he purrs darkly, "who's making you feel good like this?"

"You," I pant between strokes of his fingers.

"Right, me. And who does this pretty, little cunt belong to?"

His words cause something to break within me, the headiness overwhelming all my stimulation receptors.

"Lila. Tell me who, or I'll stop." His fingers pause their ministrations but stay inside me, and I whine.

"You, it's all for you," I whine. "Please, Cal, *please*."

"Yes. Me, darling," he purrs, before pulling away.

"Wha—"

"Take it off." I blink at him, disoriented.

"Take off the jersey. *Now*." He growls the last word, and the feral command in his voice has me shrugging out of the jersey, leaving me in a red lace bra and a matching ripped thong.

"Do you want to come, Lila?"

I nod, and he pulls his cock out from his jeans, before spreading the jersey on the floor at his feet.

"Suck."

I drop to my knees on the jersey, sparing a brief moment to be grateful for the thoughtfulness, and reach for him. He catches my hand, holding it above my head as his other hand threads itself through my hair and guides my head toward him.

I take him in my mouth and try to breathe around him even as it nudges the back of my throat. He's thick, and my lips stretch wide, saliva pooling as I work to swallow around him. I try to keep a steady rhythm, swallowing him deep in my throat as his thrusts become more erratic, eventually giving up and letting him fuck my face, just enjoying him coming undone when he finally pulls out of my mouth, pulling my hair back so I'm forced to look up at him. His eyes are wild, pupils blown wild.

"If you don't want me to fuck you, tell me now." I stare back at him and run my nails over his thighs in response. He pulls me up to standing roughly.

He backs me up to the counter and pulls a foil packet from his wallet.

"No," I blurt out. "My test results came back clean." The idea of nothing needing to be between us makes my heart race.

"I'm fine without one if you are." His gaze heats further as he shoves it into his back pocket and lifts one leg into the crook of this elbow, sliding my panties to the side before sinking into me. The exquisite stretch has me crying out before he silences me, slamming his mouth on mine.

"Don't forget where we are," he warns. He gives me a moment

to adjust to the fullness of his cock, before setting a punishing pace. I'm so turned on that I'm close after only a few minutes. Cal must feel me winding up because he brings his thumb to my clit, making tiny circles while whispering praises in my ear.

His nail scrapes the swollen bud, and I shatter around him, his other hand clamping down over my mouth to silence my moans. He fucks me through my orgasm, but as soon as I come back down to reality, he sets my leg back on the floor.

I look at him confused. "Turn around."

He spins me to face the mirror over the sink, pulling my hips back toward him, effectively bending me over the counter. A ripping sound signals the end of my already tattered thong, but he winks at me in the mirror as he stuffs it into the front pocket of his jeans.

"Watch yourself come in the mirror as I fuck you." On the last word he sinks back into me, one hand holding onto my pigtails, the other gripping my hip tightly. The angle of this thrusts hitting the most delicious spot inside me, and my eyes start to close as I give myself over to the pleasure coursing through my body. He releases my hair, his hand wrapping around my throat once more.

"Eyes on my sweetheart, you're going to watch everything I do to you, then you're going to watch yourself come on my cock." I whimper but keep my eyes on his as he slides his hand down my body, kneading my breast and tweaking my nipple through the red lace of my bra before landing once more at the swollen, sensitive bundle of nerves. My walls are fluttering around him, as he continues to pump into me.

"I can feel how close you are, love." He circles my clit with two fingers, and I start the ascend.

"Oh—*Cal!*"

"That's it, love, come for me." That's all it takes. As if my body was waiting for the words, I break apart, slumping over the sink as my body goes limp from my release. His arm bands across my chest, keeping me upright as he follows me over the edge and collapses against me.

We stay joined together for a few moments, breathing hard. After a minute he presses a kiss to my temple and pulls out of me.

I watch him in the mirror, realizing he didn't shed a single item of clothing, while I'm standing naked except for my socks, shoes, and bra in a public bathroom. I grab my shorts and pull them on. He grabs my jersey from the floor, shaking it out and brushing the back where it sat on the floor.

"I should've used my shirt," he apologizes.

I inspect the jersey, and it's not worse for wear, just a little wrinkled where he grabbed it and shrug.

"Next time, just ask me to fuck you." He chuckles as I pull on the jersey, glaring at him.

"That wasn't—" I start, but he steps forward, silencing me with another searing kiss that makes me melt against him.

"We both know what that was." He tucks a loose curl behind my ear and presses a kiss to my forehead.

"Don't clean up. If you're going to wear his jersey, I want you to feel my come dripping out of you while you do it." He turns to the door, pausing to look back at me. "I'll have a fresh drink for you when you're back out."

"And cheese curds," I request, my voice huskier than I intend after his last statement.

He grins. "Coming right up." He flips the lock and eases the door open before slipping out of the bathroom.

I stare at myself in the mirror I just watched myself come in. I'm a little flushed, but other than that don't look much different than before, just slightly mussed as long as I ignore the hickey that's starting to bloom near my collarbone. I adjust the jersey to cover it and tighten up my hair. I don't intentionally clean myself up but do quickly pee just to stave off a UTI and then head back out to the table where a new High Noon is waiting.

I slide into the seat next to Cal, ignoring the smirk Katie shoots me and let him tuck me into his side.

"Cheese curds are on their way," he whispers to me, pressing a light kiss to my temple, and I smile, settling in to enjoy the fourth quarter, having missed most of the third while busy making the mess currently dripping out of me.

⬤ ⬤ ⬤

Three days later, I'm at home reading when my phone buzzes with a package notification. I frown at it. I'm almost positive I haven't ordered anything lately, but I pull on an extra sweater and slip on my clogs to head down to the package room off the lobby.

It's a single small box with no return address, with my name and address written in a flawless, elegant script I'm sure I've seen before but can't place. I carry it back upstairs before tearing it open, beyond curious.

> *Lila,*
>
> *Thought you might like to have a second option for your game day outfits. I hope you'll think of me as much as I'll be thinking of you while you wear it.*
>
> *C*

I smile, pulling the navy blue Avalanche jersey from the box. I turn it over, seeing *Basset* emblazoned on the back above his number with a silver signature near the NFL logo at the hem. Beneath the jersey is a knit hat, complete with silver pompom, and I giggle. A home jersey to match the silver away one. My man just sent me his jersey, and not just any jersey, but a signed one.

I move to hang it in my closet, but pause, an idea taking form in my mind.

I strip out of my loungewear and pull the jersey on. It's a smaller size than my Kelce jersey, leaving significantly more leg on display, and grab my phone from the counter to snap a quick photo in the mirror, capturing both the name on my back and my bare legs. I send it to Cal with a quick "Thanks!" and settle back down to my book.

My phone pings moments later, and I ignore it for a full five minutes before I can't take it anymore and read his reply.

CAL

Glad it got to you.

I huff. Not even a single comment about how good I look in it? Rude. I spiral for a second, wondering if he hadn't enjoyed what happened at the bar as much as I did, before another text pings.

CAL

Please for the love of God, wear pants with it in public. I don't know if I can fight off that many people.

I laugh, it's so him to be both protective and supportive in such a combative combination.

What about when we're not in public?

CAL

Then I'd rather you didn't wear panties either.

Well, I can't afford to have you rip them all off of me.

I'll buy you new ones before I apologize for that.

Don't you think that could get expensive?

Money is no object. Not when it comes to you.
And especially not when it comes to your
fucking golden cunt.

I shiver, the butterflies in my stomach returning with a vengeance.

What if I told you, it wouldn't be an issue tonight?

CAL

Don't do this to me, I'm already hard. Coach is about to give me extra burpees because I've been on my phone.

Do you know how hard it is to do burpees with a hard on?

Sounds tough.

I slip the jersey back on and send him another photo with my hand between my legs, the hem of the jersey just covering anything that would be too problematic.

CAL

Fuck me.

Let me take you to dinner tomorrow.

Are you sure you can wait that long? 😈

I can't in good conscious fuck you the way I want to without giving you a proper date first.

The butterflies rejoice.

Dinner it is.

CAL

I'll pick you up at 7. Wear something nice.

Sounds good.

Something NOT red.

I laugh. I have a feeling red will be a new trigger color for him. I think through my closet for a minute, landing on the perfect dress.

How about navy?

CAL

Perfect.

Sorry gtg

I put my phone down and hang up the jersey, trying to keep the smile off my face as I refocus my attention on my book. I fail miserably and instead daydream about tomorrow evening.

Chapter Twenty-Seven

CAL

I'm grateful Coach pushes us hard today, because otherwise I'm not sure how I'd release the amount of nervous energy I've built up anticipating tonight with Lila.

I'd wanted to take her out since that first night at the club. It was electric, making me feel alive in a way I've only heard about during wedding vows. But even with a false start or two, we've finally got enough momentum to be moving in the right direction. The sex alone—I look up at the ceiling of the training facility and count to ten to get ahead of the rush of blood already flowing south.

"My man," a voice calls as a hand claps me on the shoulder. I pull out one AirPod to see Theo and DeVonte Matthews, another wide receiver, looming over me with matching grins.

I raise an eyebrow at them. "Did you need the machine?" It's unlikely given there are two other empty fly machines within thirty feet of me, but with superstitions being what they are at this point in the season, I don't bother pointing it out.

"Nah, man," Matthews says, "McClain was telling me about your date tonight, and we agree it's about time."

I stare at Theo incredulously. "Excuse me?"

DeVonte blinks confused. "She's hot, I was just trying to hype you up a bit."

My jaw ticks at the way he boils Lila down to just some hot girl, and not the accomplished, smart, down-to-earth, funny woman I know her to be. "Yeah," I grind out. "We're going out."

His smile is back, and I'm treated to another shoulder smack. "Congrats, hope it goes well, man."

I soften a bit at his sincere tone. "Thanks."

"Alright, well I'm gonna hit legs." He wanders off toward the squat machines on the other side of the weight room as I glare at Theo.

"What?" He holds up his hands in mock surrender.

"You know what," I snap. "How did you even find out?"

"Katie," we say in unison. I roll my eyes.

"Where are you taking her?"

"Chicago Cut." The steakhouse was one of the first places I went when I first moved here, and the relationship I've built with the staff makes it the perfect place where I know I can get a river-side table and the best cuts.

"Are you sure she eats meat?"

What? She definitely ate some of the charcuterie on the beach, right? And when we had dinner at that blasted bed-and-breakfast, she ordered meat right?

"I think so?" The panic definitely bleeds through, and Theo laughs.

"I'm just kidding. She definitely eats meat." I level him with a flat gaze that has made three-hundred-pound linemen swallow.

"Lighten up, Basset. I'm just trying to loosen you up."

"I'm fine," I grunt.

"Right." He rolls his eyes.

I put my AirPod back in, seething as I do another set of flies.

He taps my arm again when I've finished, and I sigh, removing it again.

"Yes?" I say with a touch of exasperation.

"I really do hope it goes well. She's good for you."

"Yeah, me too."

He finally walks away to finish his own workout, leaving me in peace, if slightly more nervous about dinner altogether.

● ● ●

My heart is pounding more than it did during my NFL debut as I stare at myself in the full-length mirror. I've changed three times, the other two suits strewn over my bed, but I think this is it. Charcoal grey with sapphire cufflinks, a gift from my grandfather on my eighteenth birthday, and a white button-down. I tried six different ties, but ultimately all of them make me look like I'm going to a business meeting, and while I want to make a good impression, I'd prefer if the night was anything but professional.

There's a text from Lila when I check my phone.

LILA

Black or red?

Black

We talked about this.

Oh, I'm still wearing the navy dress…

Fuck me. Now I'll be picturing whatever she's wearing under her dress, regardless of how great it looks on her, all night.

It doesn't matter if we've already slept together. Regardless of how amazing it was—and it was incredible—this is basically our first date. I can't even count the picnic since Theo and Katie came along. Lila's quickly become one of my favorite people to be around, and I want her to have a nice time tonight.

I take a deep breath as I slide into the seat of my Mercedes,

245

inhaling the comforting scent of leather and my overly expensive cologne. It always seemed a little frivolous, but it was a gift, and Lila complemented it once, so it was the perfect opportunity to wear it. We're not going very far, the restaurant is honestly within walking distance from both our apartments, but something about tonight just feels like I should pick her up the old-fashioned way, even if parking valet will be entirely too expensive. It's not like I can't afford to splurge a bit.

The car rumbles to life beneath me, and I can't help the grin that breaks out over my face. What can I say? I'm just a man, and fast cars are basically built into our DNA. I screech out of the parking garage, covering the three blocks between our condos quickly, and pull up in front of her building. I hesitate, wanting to meet her at her door but not exactly wanting to get towed.

I flip the hazard lights on, and just when I've opened my door, I see Lila walking out toward me.

"You look gorgeous." I manage over the dry lump in my throat, because wow she really does. A soft dark blue material clings to one shoulder, draping lightly over her torso before flowing over her hips like water and landing just above her knees. Gold heels wrapping up her calf, highlighting her long legs and glistening in the light of the streetlights.

"Thanks, you don't look so bad yourself." She winks at me and moves toward the door.

"I got it." I walk quickly to her side of the car, sweeping down to kiss her cheek before opening the door for her. She smiles up at me as she gracefully seats herself in the low bucket seat.

"So, where are we going?" she asks, once I'm settled back in my own seat.

"Chicago Cut."

"Oh, I've never actually been there. I've heard such amazing things over the years, though."

"It was one of the first places I went to when I moved to the city."

"I'm excited to try it." She smiles over at me, and I notice the hem of her dress has ridden up, exposing a few inches of her thigh. I war with myself to touch her, ultimately dropping my hand on her thigh just below the hem.

Her breath catches, and I fight to hold back the smirk that graces my face. It's nice to know that I'm not the only one affected by this tension.

"How's work been going? You signed that big client, right?" I ask.

She brightens, filling the silence the rest of the short ride with explanations of the client and her coworkers.

"I applied for a promotion, actually. They're opening a new division specifically to cater to the newer tech and social media companies. And since I have more experience with tech clients, I talked it over with a few of my mentors, and I put my name in for the partner role."

"Lila, that's amazing."

"The best part is, I could take a few of my current clients over to that division, so I wouldn't be starting from scratch. And there are a couple other partners who have clients who would be better suited to the new TSM group, so they'll all be coming over too. It'll be busy, but I think I'm up for the challenge." She grins at me.

"Of course you are. You can do anything."

"You really think that?"

"Honestly? Yeah, I do. You're so capable, it makes me feel inadequate sometimes." I laugh, but she frowns. "But that's my problem to deal with. And the way to alleviate it is to better myself or just be content to cheer you on from the sidelines as you kick ass and make a difference in the world, and I just run around playing with footballs all day." She rolls her eyes, but the frown is gone so I've succeeded in something at least. "Tell me more about the clients you'll be working with."

She continues chatting even as I pull up to the valet and hand over the keys. I could listen to this woman talk about grass growing and would still never want her to stop.

"Mr. Basset," Leroy calls out as we enter. The manager really values being on a first-name basis—or in this case, last name—with his regulars. I respect it.

"Leroy." I shake his offered hand. "Good to see to see you again."

"And who is this lovely lady with you tonight?"

"This is Lila," I turn to her, "Lila, this is Leroy the manager here."

"Oh, *the* Lila?"

She raises her eyebrows at me.

"Oh, don't worry. He's only said good things, though he was awfully nervous about this date tonight. Must have called three different times to make sure we had everything set up right."

He winks at her, and the sound of her laugh warms something in my gut.

"It was only once," I mutter, which only causes more laughter, and I can't help but grin down at her.

"Well, we better get you seated before the embarrassment sets in." He leads us through the other tables to the very back of the restaurant where a table sits looking out over the Chicago River, a vase of pink peonies on the table and a bottle of champagne chilling in the ice bucket.

"Cal, it's beautiful." The awe in her eyes fills some well of hope inside me. Leroy pulls out her chair for her, leaving me to my own devices on my side of the table, before he pops the champagne and fills our glasses.

"Ricky will be your server this evening." At his words a young man appears at his side, holding a water carafe and menus. "Please let either of us or any of the staff know if you need anything at all."

Ricky fills our water glasses before handing us each a menu.

"Thanks, Ricky," Lila smiles at him as she takes the menu.

I nod as he hands me mine.

"Leroy seems nice."

I snort. "He has never once been that nice to me when it's just me. Or even when I've brought Theo. It's all you."

"You know I would've gone out with you to a Portillo's drive thru. You didn't have to put in all this work."

"Love, it's because I know you would that I *want* to put in the work. You deserve nice dates, and someone to spoil you. And I want to do that. Besides, if we go to Portillo's, we have to get the cake and it's not exactly car friendly."

She laughs, but the soft smile it fades to is enough of a response.

"So, what's good here?" She opens the menu, color staining the apples of her cheeks.

"Well to be completely transparent, I've only had steaks, but they've all been pretty good."

"Steak it is." She laughs again, and the fluttering in my gut is back.

We place our orders with Ricky and return to another bout of somewhat tense silence.

"I—"

"What—"

We start at the same time. Lila gives a nervous giggle.

"You first," I say, taking a large sip of the champagne.

"Is it supposed to be this awkward?"

"Have you ever been on a first date that isn't a little bit awkward?"

"I guess not." She shrugs. "Although, given that we've already slept together, and have been friends for a bit, I thought it'd be easier."

"You already know I like you. And you like me?" I end the last thought in a question, but she just nods in confirmation. "So, there's no weird question there, but maybe we just focus on getting to know each other a little better? Or not even worry about it and just hang out, but over good food."

"Yeah, that sounds like a good plan." She smiles. "Just promise not to tell Katie I was nervous, she'll tease me forever about it."

"Only if you promise not to tell Theo that I really did call the restaurant three times." I wink, and she laughs again.

"Deal." We toast our glasses together, draining them.

"I know I ordered the champagne ahead of time, but do you want to get a red?

"Definitely, maybe a Cab?"

I make eye contact with Ricky who's been watching at the end of the room, and he saunters over.

"What can I get for you?"

"Can we do the Paso Robles Cab please?"

"Of course. Two glasses or the bottle?"

I flick my eyes to Lila. "The bottle."

"*Hey*," she whisper-scolds me. "I could just do a glass."

"Yeah." I roll my eyes. "But you *wanted* the bottle."

"Fine," she huffs. "It's unfair you already know me so well."

"I pay attention," I say, and she blushes. "We should go to Napa."

"Have you been before?" she asks.

"Yeah, a few times. One of my dad's big clients owns a few vineyards out that way so we'd try to go every few years."

"What does your dad do? I haven't heard you really mention your family much."

The warm butterflies I was feeling promptly still, leaving a cold lead weight in their place.

"I don't really talk about them if I can avoid it."

Her gaze is intense on mine, urging me on.

"I'm sure you know by now that I was born in England. My mum is still over there along with the rest of my extended family. My dad brought me over to the States when I was five when he expanded his firm and opened a New York office. I eventually ended up at an upstate boarding school where I met Theo and Katie." I shrug, not quite meeting her gaze. "Then I went to Yale and ended up in the NFL."

She blinks at me.

"Are you serious?"

"What?" I frown at her.

"That's it?"

"Erm, what more is there?"

"Cal, come on."

"If you want to know something else, I'll tell you. But I don't know what you're asking." I cross my arms over my chest and gaze at her, unsure what more she wants from me.

"I asked what your dad did, and you not only didn't tell me but summarized your entire life in three sentences, not one of them told me anything about how you *felt* about any of it."

"I don't really know what to say. It all happened so long ago. And I live here now, I'm out with you. I can tell you how I feel about that."

She flashes a brief grin. "Yes, please do. But first, what does your dad do that he moved his firm here when you were little?"

"He runs a consulting firm. So, a little of this, a little of that really." I take a deep breath. "I'm supposed to take over for him. Or I was."

"Was?"

"He's not exactly a fan of the whole football thing. Especially *American* football."

"Ah. That has to be tough."

"Yeah, well, I think moving to Chicago might have been the last straw. At least when I was with the Cosmos, he could pretend it was only a hobby."

She snorts. "A hobby of playing professional football. He should really go on ESPN. They'd get a kick out of him."

I grin wryly. "He'd love that, I'm sure."

"How does your mom feel about you playing?"

"If she paid enough attention to notice, I'm sure she'd think it was horribly uncouth, but all that really gets across is that I still live in America and don't visit her nearly enough to be paraded about her friends and all their daughters."

"Wow, I thought I had a rough family."

I shrug. "It is what it is. I like playing football, but it can't be forever."

"Yeah?"

"I'm already feeling it in my body significantly more than I did five years ago. The hits hurt more, the recovery takes longer. I might be stronger, even faster, but I'm still older. There's a reason the average retirement age is twenty-eight, and I blew by that pretty fast."

"Bone-in ribeye for you, sir," Ricky interrupts as he sets down my plate in front of me before handing Lila hers. "And a Delmonico for the lady. Anything else I can get you?"

"I think we're okay." Lila smiles at him.

He leaves, taking some of the heaviness of the prior conversation with him. The steaks are delicious, and we pass the rest of the meal in lighter, companionable conversation.

● ● ●

I unlock my apartment door, holding it open for Lila.

"Hey, thanks."

"For what? You took me out."

"No one's really ever asked how I feel about everything. Or asked about my family at all. Even my friends from boarding school, their families are all just as messed up. It kinda makes it all feel normal."

She laces our fingers together. "Of course. I want to be a safe place for you to land when you need to. We can take care of each other, Cal. It doesn't all have to just be you."

I tug her into my chest and thread my free hand into her hair as my sinuses burn. We stand in silence for what could be hours, Lila just letting me hold her as long as I need to. Eventually, I loosen my grip, and she raises her eyes to meet mine before rising onto her toes to press a chaste kiss to my mouth. I meet her with fervor, surging forward to deepen the kiss, even as I walk her backwards toward my bedroom, intending to see what I chose black for earlier this afternoon.

Chapter Twenty-Eight

LILA

I wake with anticipation, my anxiety spiking when I see the gold dress hanging on my closet door. Tonight is the annual Avalanche Christmas gala and after our date the other night as we were lying in bed in post-orgasm bliss, Cal invited me to go with him.

Katie, who unhelpfully isn't going, helped me find the perfect dress, a soft gold number that just toes the line between sexy and elegant. Cal's picking me up tonight at five and I took the day off, so I have all day to spend getting ready and stressing about meeting the entirety of the Avalanche staff and team along with a number of wealthy other notable Chicagoans. Colten's covering a meeting this morning with Dover Industries, and I know I'm going to have to put in at least a couple hours this weekend to catch up, but it'll be worth it.

I'd given up the idea that I would be doing my own hair and booked a blowout at Drybar this afternoon, so at least my hair is taken care of, and even if my makeup looks less polished, I'll still be okay for any of the photos that will inevitably be taken and posted online.

I stare at my ceiling and sigh in disbelief that this is my life.

I can't believe that I was living in a state of such unhappiness and trepidation every day, but everything is finally going well. My job couldn't be better, unless I finally get that promotion. Even pottery is going well. I've been able to consistently go, and have made a few pieces I'm really proud of, including hand-building a realistic ceramic football for Cal. Cal himself is amazing. We've only been able to go out one other time since our official first date, but we make time to at least see each other most evenings, even if all he has the energy for after practice is a single episode of *Love Island* before he falls asleep on the couch. He's slotted himself in my life so seamlessly it's almost like he's always been there. Or at least that there's always been a hole waiting there, that up until meeting him had only been half full, like trying to shove a circle block through a square hole. It went through, but it wasn't right. I just had to find my square block.

I groan, a stupid smile on my face, and roll out of bed. If I'm not working today, I might as well do something productive until I have my hair appointment, and I am very behind on my Christmas shopping.

After a quick shower, I'm dressed and headed out the door and down to Michigan Avenue—the perfect place to get all my shopping done if I'm on a tight timeline.

Katie is always easy, but that's the bonus of knowing someone for so long. I even find gifts for my family with ease, choosing several more outfits for baby Gregory than I had planned but how anyone can withstand those teeny tiny clothes I'll never know. I even found an absolutely horrible argyle pattern hat that I know Theo would love.

Though I'm laden with bags when I return home, I'm still missing a gift for the one person I desperately want to find something for. I'm at a loss of ideas for Cal. I'm hoping that when I find the right thing it'll speak to me in the moment. I have the piece of pottery, but it feels wrong to just give him something handmade, regardless of the amount of time and energy I've spent smoothing the clay and molding the laces just so. But each store I went into, I found everything but a perfect gift.

Hours later, I'm ready and standing in front of my full-length mirror, when there's a knock at the door. The flutters are back as I open it to reveal Cal, looking better than any one person has a right to, dressed in a black tux with gold details that match my dress perfectly.

"You are breathtaking." He steps into my condo, pressing a kiss to my temple.

"You clean up pretty nice yourself," I joke, my mouth drier than I'm used to.

"Are you ready to go? Or do you need a few minutes? I know I'm a little early."

I check the clock on the stove.

4:58 p.m.

"You're two minutes early, but I suppose I can be ready."

"I don't mind waiting," he rushes out.

"No, it's fine, I really just need to put on my shoes, and I'm ready to go.

"Are you wearing heels?"

"I was thinking about it. Why?"

"Just wear something you can dance in." He grins.

"Dancing?"

"Nothing crazy, but I've heard they always get a good band. And if you'd do me the honor"—he gives a mock bow offering his hand—"of having a dance, madam?"

I playfully shove his arm away.

"Of course I'll dance with you." I turn to grab a pair of heels I pray are more comfortable than they look, before glancing over my shoulder. "If you play your cards right." I wink, and his eyes darken as they take in the low open back of my dress.

His shoes click across the floor, and his hands grip my hips from behind.

"I'll play whatever cards you tell me to." His hot breath ghosts my ear, and I shiver involuntarily.

I finish slipping my shoes on, leaning into him for balance. He holds me steady, a solid presence behind me, and when I finish, I turn to face him placing both hands on his well-defined chest.

"That's what I like to hear." I kiss him softly, dragging my teeth against his lower lip before stepping away. He growls at the loss of touch.

"Come on." I laugh. "Don't we need to leave?"

He checks his watch. "Yes, unfortunately. The car is ready downstairs."

I pull out a vintage fur coat I borrowed from Katie for the occasion with promises that it wouldn't meet the fate of the last coat I borrowed and slip it on. It doesn't quite close, but it still completes the look. So many people wear coats open anyway, no one will notice it's a size too small. Okay two sizes.

A large black SUV is waiting in front of my building, and to my surprise Cal opens the back door for me.

He must notice my expression because he answers my unasked question. "I didn't want to worry about how much I drank and then driving back so I just got a car for the night."

"Oh, good thinking." I step up into the car before Cal shuts the door and slides in on the other side.

The Field Museum isn't a far drive, but it takes nearly twenty minutes with the number of cars lining up around the circular drive. This is what I imagine walking the red carpet must feel like. Everyone is dressed to the nines and stepping out of luxury cars. There's even the occasional camera flash as a particularly well-known athlete poses with his date.

My breathing comes faster, and the car feels hot all of a sudden. They're all so small, like model thin. Hell, most of them probably are models.

"Hey, Lila." Cal shakes my shoulder. "Are you okay?"

"I—I'm not sure."

"Deep breaths. It's okay." We inch closer to the front of the queue of waiting cars.

"I don't think I should come in with you."

"Why not?"

"I'm just not feeling well."

"Lila." He tilts my head up with one finger, meeting my gaze with his own. "If you're actually sick, we can go back."

"You don't need to come. You shouldn't miss your party."

"I'm not done, love." He puts one finger over my lips. "If you're actually sick, *we* can go back, and of course I'd come with you. You're more important than some stupid holiday party. But, if you're feeling nervous or scared or anxious, don't be. I *want* to be here with you. You look incredible. No, you *are* incredible, and I want to introduce you to my friends and teammates because you're important to me, and it's important to me that they know that."

The tension drains out of my shoulders, and I slouch back against the seat.

"Okay."

"Okay what? Are we going back home?"

"No," I say quietly.

"That's my girl." He slides an arm behind my back and squeezes my shoulders. "You can do this."

I take a deep breath. "I can do this." I smile at him.

"Perfect timing." I blink and look out the window. We'd made it to the front of the line during my little panic attack, and the fear is back in force.

"Come on. Don't let it get to you." He slips out of the car and opens my door for me. "Let's go."

"Basset! Basset, over here!"

"Who's the girl, Basset?"

"That's her from the game!"

Shouts fill the air as soon as we step onto the stairs. Cal loops his arm around my waist, and his touch is grounding. I smile at the crowd, flashes nearly blinding me, as he leads me up the stairs and into the museum before checking our coats at the table in the foyer.

The main room is filled with round tables, like a large holiday wedding. A couple hundred people are milling about between the tables and spilling out into the cocktail area where a large grazing table is set up down the middle, parallel to a bar carrying everything from McCallan to Coors Light.

"Want something to drink?"

I nod my head.

"Lila," a familiar voice calls out.

I turn my head to see Theo beelining straight for us.

"Can you wait here with her while I get us drinks?" Cal asks him.

"Oh, sure man, I can introduce her around."

Cal scowls at that. "She's *my* date McClane."

Theo rolls his eyes before shooting me a wink. "What do you say, Lila? Wanna ditch the grumpy one and get out of here?" His eyebrows waggle suggestively, and I burst out laughing.

"Where is *your* date, Theo?" I ask, pointedly.

He shrugs. "I'm flying solo tonight."

"Right, I'll be back in a few then." Cal heads to the bar, leaving Theo and I alone.

"So, looks like you made your decision then?" he asks in a low voice.

"Yeah." I smile after Cal's muscular back disappearing into the crowd. "Yeah, I did."

"Well good, I think you work well together."

"Thanks, Theo."

"Theo! Good to see you again." A dark-haired beauty appears in front of us, throwing herself into his very much not waiting arms, knocking my shoulder in the process.

"Oh, I'm sorry," she says, turning to me. Her voice is annoyingly breathy. "I didn't see you there, and I just had to say hi to Theo. I'm Cynthia," she simpers.

"No problem," I mutter, rubbing my shoulder. Her elbows are bony, and it kind of hurt.

"Is this your date?" she asks, turning her body to block me from their conversation.

"No, just a friend," I answer for him.

"Oh, I see." Her expression warms slightly. "And how do you know each other?"

Theo opens his mouth to respond, but I cut him off. "We have some mutual friends."

Just then another girl joins us, this one a blonde so platinum they could make jewelry out of it. "Theo, you remember Stephanie, right?" Cynthia introduces the blonde.

"How could I forget?" He kisses her knuckles, and the girl giggles.

"I'm sorry," she says to me, though she doesn't sound at all apologetic. "I didn't catch your name." She looks down her nose at me, and I fight the instinct to scoff.

"It's Lila."

"Pleasure." The irritation bubbles in my gut, and I grimace at her. Where did Cal go? Surely our drinks can't have taken that long.

"Oh Cal, you didn't need to bring us drinks," Cynthia says, and I turn to see him coming up behind me, holding two glasses of wine.

"Don't worry, I didn't." He smiles at them, but it doesn't quite reach his eyes. "Here you are, love." He hands me one of the drinks, his smile warming as he looks down at me. "When Theo said he'd introduce you around, I'm a bit surprised this was the first group he thought of."

"I didn't exactly seek them out," Theo defends himself.

I place one hand through Cal's arm and both girls clock the

possessive gesture. "We were just getting to know each other, weren't we, ladies?"

"Of course, "Cynthia says. "Well, we should make the rounds."

"Good seeing you both," Stephanie says. "And lovely to meet you, Lila."

They walk away arm in arm. "Well, they're nice," I comment dryly.

"Vultures," huffs Theo. "The lot of them." He nods his head at a cluster of young women, all dressed with more than a little skin showing, each more beautiful than the last.

"Who are they? It doesn't look like they're here with anyone specifically."

"Some are local models, some are the daughters of notable Chicago families or big football names," Cal explains. "Some are just in it for the status, some for the money, but very few actually want a real relationship or at least not one that exists outside social media. Most don't even particularly care about the player for more than the amount of play time they get."

"That's nearly predatory. If it were the other way around, they wouldn't be allowed in." The heat from the car rising again, although for a different reason now.

"Most of us know better, but some of the rookies have a tough time the first year or two in the league. Though so many of them come from big football schools it really isn't much different than some of the groupies in college these days."

"It's just a game. How is it this big of a deal?" I say, exasperation coloring my tone.

Cal and Theo gape at me.

"Oh come on. I obviously love watching games as much as the next person, but the obsession surrounding the players is a little insane. At the end of the day it's just your job, and it *is* just a game."

"You know that *game* is what we do for a living?" Theo asks.

"Well yeah, but—"

"That it's a billion-dollar industry?"

"Yes, but—"

"I know what you mean, it's just not something anyone usually says to professional players."

"Oh," I flush with embarrassment.

"Especially not to players they're dating," Cal teases.

"Oh, shut up." I bump him with my hip. "Let's go find a table." I nod toward the mass of people moving toward the main dining room doors.

"Are you sitting with us?" I ask Theo.

He shrugs good-naturedly. "Yeah, might as well."

Being on Cal's arm is surreal as we enter the main dining room. I've never attended an event like this without being a last minute plus-one, courtesy of Katie. I can feel eyes on us as we wind our way through the crowded tables and force myself to stand a little taller, leaning into the touch of Cal's palm ghosting across my lower back as he guides me through the tables.

We're sitting down when Cynthia and Stephanie stand from a few tables over, flanking none other than Victoria Winston. Her ice blue eyes are locked on Cal, casually lounging in the chair next to me in deep conversation with Theo. Something about Kansas City and their playoff strategy. An uneasy feeling twists in my gut as I turn back to watch them whisper. Victoria must sense my gaze, as her eyes flick to mine, a smirk pulling up at the corner of her mouth.

I suck in a quick breath and choke on it, my mouth completely dry.

"Lila, love, are you okay?" Cal asks, breaking off his conversation with Theo.

I nod, coughing into my elbow as delicately as I can.

"Here do you want water?" He hands me my water glass, and I gulp it greedily.

"Sorry," I say, setting down the now half-empty glass. "I'm not sure what happened."

I glance quickly toward the other table but find the three women nowhere to be found.

"As long as you're okay." He frowns, giving me a once over, when an elderly woman walks slowly to the small platform on one end of the room.

"Who is that?"

"She's the owner of the Avalanche." Theo mutters, the hall going quiet as she steps up to a podium.

I blink in surprise. I didn't realize the owner was a woman. If I didn't have two reasons sitting next to me to cheer for my home team, I have one more now.

"Welcome, everyone, to the Chicago Avalanche Annual Holiday Party," she begins. Her remarks are brief and festive, congratulating the players and coaching staff on a successful season so far. The playoffs are in their grasp, it's not time to let up now. It's time to give it their all. She receives a standing ovation and once everyone has returned to their seats, an army of servers appears, trays loaded with bread baskets and salads.

After an incredible meal fit for NFL linemen, I'm completely stuffed and feeling more than a little uncomfortable from the combination of too much good food and a few too many glasses of wine.

"I'll be back," I say, standing as I look around for a ladies' room. I spot it just outside the main doors and give Cal's shoulder a light squeeze.

"We'll be out by the bar." He smiles up at me.

"I'll find you."

After using the facilities, I spot the gleam of his silver blonde hair in the corner of the room and carefully make my way through the crowd.

I'm only a few feet away when I catch the voices, my footsteps freezing in their tracks.

"So, is this why you haven't bothered to text me back?" a cool, female voice asks.

Cal replies calmly, "I told you I was seeing her. We were never exclusive anyway, don't pretend this is anything more than a hit to your ego that someone didn't choose you."

The woman scoffs.

"Come on, Tori. You don't want to be with me, anyway, so why are you making this a thing?"

"Does your father know about her?"

"I'm sure he's been informed. We haven't been keeping our relationship a secret."

"So, they haven't met then."

"Of course they haven't met, do you think I'm daft?"

"Sometimes." Cal chuckles, and my heart clenches.

I take one step to the side to see a stunning brunette give him a disappointed look. Victoria Winston is somehow more beautiful in person than the photos make her look, and I feel suddenly out of place watching them together.

"It's always complicated with him, you know that." His voice is filled with despair, and a bolt of confusion hits me.

"You can't have a real relationship hiding from your father, Johnathan."

"Don't call me that."

"Oh, Johnny boy." I swear I can hear Cal's teeth grind together from several feet away as she pats his arm condescendingly. "When this blows up, you can still call me. You know he at least approves of *someone*." She steps around him, eyes widening as she sees me a moment later, before her lips pull in some complicated smirk dripping with pity.

I pull myself straighter and roll my neck to join Cal now standing alone, looking morosely into his drink.

His eyes light when he catches sight of me, and I force my lips to smile.

"Hey, I was wondering where you went."

"Just got a bit lost on my way back from the bathroom."

He laces once hand with mine, frowning slightly at how tense my muscles are.

"Do you want another drink? I can introduce you to some of the other players." There's an offer in his eyes. A silent plea to stay. "I believe I promised you a dance." He smiles and my heart cracks.

I want to do nothing more than dance with him.

But I can't. Not after what I just heard.

"I'm feeling a bit tired honestly."

"Oh," I want to take it back from the way the light in his eyes dim. "We can head out, no problem."

"You don't have to, this is your party after all, I can just grab an Uber home."

He scoffs, looking mildly offended. "If we're leaving, we're leaving together."

"If you're sure, I just don't want to drag you away from the fun."

"I'll call the driver and meet you by the coat check."

I nod, and his lips brush my cheek before he steps away, pulling his phone out.

I steady myself with a breath before turning to leave a party I was once so excited to attend.

"Are you okay?" Cal asks, when I've been silent for nearly the entire ride home, sitting huddled toward the door and away from him.

"I'm just tired. I can feel a headache coming on." It's not entirely a lie. The conversation that keeps cycling through my head would make anyone's head pound.

"Can I do anything?"

"No, I just need to go to bed." I turn to him and smile. "Thank you for a nice night."

He grins at me, some of that charm melting back into his features.

"Do you want to come over to my place? We can just sleep if you're not feeling well."

"Sorry, Cal, I really just want to go home to my own bed."

"Right, yes of course."

I twist my face, so his goodnight kiss lands on my cheek, ignoring his confusion as I push open my door, trying to get inside as quickly as I can to the safety of my apartment.

"Lila," he pleads. "Talk to me. Something is clearly upsetting you. What did I do?"

I step toward my building, only a few feet away now.

"You didn't do anything, Cal. I just had another piece of the puzzle that is you fall into place tonight, and I'm not sure our lives really fit together as well as I thought they did."

"What are you talking about?"

"I heard your conversation in the bar."

His face goes white.

"I think you maybe have some things to figure out this time."

I step inside the door quickly, counting the click of my heels against the flooring.

After I pass the front desk, I chance a single glance over my shoulder, and he's still rooted to the spot where I left him.

Chapter Twenty-Nine

CAL

"Fuck!" I yell, kicking the back tire of the car.

The passenger window rolls down. "Sir, if you damage the vehicle I'll have to file a report."

"Right, sorry." I mutter. "You can go. I'll walk home."

"You sure? I have another thirty on the clock."

"Yeah." I pull out a couple twenties from my wallet and drop them through the open window. "Happy Christmas."

I shove my hands unceremoniously into my pockets and set off down the city street, taking care to avoid the small salt piles scattered along the sidewalk.

I can't deny Tori's last few comments hit me with some confusion. She's never liked to share her toys, even as kid. Theo and I were on the receiving end of that ire more than I can count when we would pretend her dolls were the villains for our action figure heroes. But it was more than that tonight and targeted to hurt Lila.

My hands clench, because she's not wrong about one thing.

I've been avoiding my father for weeks now. But that ends now.

I can't protect her from my family forever. Lila deserves to have all the pieces of the puzzle before she decides if she can love me.

He answers on the first ring.

"Johnathan."

"Hello, Father."

The knock on my door jolts me from my wallowing.

"I can't pretend I wasn't expecting it," I mutter to myself as I pause my Taylor Swift *Heartbreak* playlist. I've been listening to it for most of the morning as I worked through my backlog of emails. Nothing spurs productivity like wanting to avoid negative feelings.

I run my fingers through my hair and quickly clean under my eyes with a tissue before heading to the door.

I open the door to Cal holding a bouquet of white peonies.

"Hey."

I stare at him.

"Uhm, these are for you." He hands me the flowers.

"Thanks."

He stands there, looking uncertain.

"Can I come in?"

I open the door wider, and turn back into my condo, finding a vase to put the flowers in.

"I wanted to talk about what you overheard."

"Okay." I honestly can't think of anything I'd rather talk about less, but we probably should discuss it.

"I'm not on great terms with my father."

Well, that's not where I thought this was going. I had found rock bottom last night in my spiral and had fully convinced myself our next conversation was going to be him ending things to be with Victoria Winston.

He takes a deep breath, holding eye contact before continuing. "I'm not keeping you from him. You're not a dirty little secret for me. If anything, it's the other way around."

"But how does *she* know him?" I burst out.

"Tori?"

I snort. "Of course you call her Tori."

He shoots me a look of disbelief. "I've known her since before grade school. Our parents are friends, and we grew up together. When she moved to the States full time to pursue modeling, we reconnected. As *friends.*" He clarifies the last part at my raised eyebrow.

"It definitely sounded like a friendly little chat I heard."

"We never officially dated or anything like that. It was always mutually beneficial to be seen together, and that was it. I mean, we fooled around a bit, but it was always just casual."

I huff and cross my arms. He pulls my wrist from the cross of my arms, pulling me toward him gently.

"I've never felt for her the way I feel for you." He kisses my palm, then the inside of my wrist, eyes locked on me, even as my breath quickens.

"She is nothing but an old friend to me. And one I don't need to see anymore if she's going to talk about you or about us like that."

"Are you sure?"

"Lila, you are *the only* one I want to be with." He places my hand over his bulky shoulder as his hands find my waist, leaning into me. "Please," he begs, his breath caressing my neck.

Heat floods my system as I arch into his touch. But one single warning bell rings in my mind.

"Wait."

He freezes instantly, pulling back to look at my face.

"I want to know *you*, Cal. That includes knowing about your family. I was upset not just because one of the most gorgeous women I've ever seen—she literally gets paid for being pretty—made it entirely too obvious she wanted you, but because I realized that I don't really know you, and she knows you better."

"You might not know my entire life story, but you do know me. You know who I am, possibly better than anyone else does."

I shake my head. "I *want* to know your life story." Doesn't he get it? "Don't you want to know mine?" I can't quite keep the hurt from my voice.

"Lila, I want to know every single thing about you. I want to know what you eat for breakfast every morning, so I can see what you like to start your day with. I want to know what your favorite show to watch as a child was, so I know what comforts you. I want to know what lip gloss you wear so that I never have to go a day without tasting you. I want to know what shampoo you use so I can smell your hair when I sleep." He presses a kiss to my forehead, one cheek, then the other, before ghosting one across my lips. "I want to know *everything*. I just don't always know how to ask, and I didn't want to push you."

"This relationship won't work if you're scared to talk to me." I frown, realizing a bit of a pattern. One I have had too much of a role in creating in the first place.

"I know. Do you want to meet my father?"

I hesitate and nod. "Would it be better to meet your mom first if your father is going to hate me that much?" I try to tease, but the humor falls flat.

"Well since she's in England, it poses a bit of a problem."

"Oh right. Yes, I think I should."

"I was hoping you'd say that." He grins at me.

"Why?" I ask, suddenly unsure.

"Because we're having Christmas dinner with him."

I gape. "Excuse me?"

"I thought it was time to introduce you, so I called him on the way home after I dropped you off from the party."

"What if I had said no?"

"Well then I'd cancel." He shrugs.

"You already had that planned before you got here?"

"Of course." The open affection on his face combined with his thumb slowly rubbing circles in my hip is too much, and I surge forward to kiss him.

"I'm sorry," I whisper against his mouth. "I know I overreacted last night. I just—well I have a lot of insecurities about not being good enough, and I heard in real time how I might fall short of your expectations. I don't want to disappoint you or your family."

"Love, you won't disappoint me. But you should know one more thing about my father before you meet him."

I look up at him, waiting.

"He controls my trust until I turn thirty-five. Because of it, he feels he gets a say in my life, especially about how I'm 'carrying on the family legacy.'"

"Trust?"

"Yeah, my family's what you might call old money."

"You're a professional athlete," I say, confused. "Why do you need a trust?"

"I don't really. But he could take all of it, the way the wording is set up. And I'd like to have something to leave for my own legacy, whenever that is." He sighs. "Besides, I actually don't keep any of my salary from the Avalanche. It goes straight to charity."

"Cal, please tell me you don't actually donate millions of dollars a year to some whale conservancy." I fake exasperation, and he scowls at me.

"Not all of it. Most goes toward research grants back at Yale, or local scholarship programs both here and in New York." I can't help but laugh.

"You're incredible, you know that?"

He kisses me. "Just let me be incredible for you," he says, pressing his mouth to mine once more.

His arms tighten around my waist, pulling me flush against him. His head slants, deepening the kiss as his tongue sweeps in, tangling with mine. I sink my fingers into his hair, the platinum strands silky beneath my hands.

"Bed," I breathe as he kisses down my jaw. He lifts me and walks toward my bedroom, his hands beneath my upper thighs as my legs wrap around him automatically. I have a moment of panic as I think back to what state I left my bedroom in this morning. It doesn't matter how many times my mother yelled at us to make our beds every morning, it didn't stick. When his mouth reaches the juncture of my neck and shoulder any worry melts away because nothing could possibly matter as much as having his hands on me. I tug at his collar, and he breaks away, settling my feet back on the floor to pull his sweatshirt up over his head before tossing it on the floor and peeling my own hoodie from my body. We crash back together, and when his fingers tease my nipple through my tank top, I'm grateful I didn't bother to put on a bra today. He pinches it, and I gasp.

The next thing I know, I'm against the wall, Cal pressing into me as his hands grip my ass, grinding me down on his thigh. I can't help the moan that escapes me. The pleasure builds low in my gut as I drag myself along his muscled leg, my leggings creating a barrier from the friction I so desperately need.

"Yes, love. Take what you need from me."

"Can't—leggings. Off." The headiness of my words doesn't hit me until I hear his chuckle.

He tilts my head up to meet his eyes, darkened with lust. "No, I think you can come like this."

I whimper, and he squeezes the sides of my neck, a challenge in his gaze. The heat in my body rises as the lightheadedness takes over. He pulls the waistband of my leggings taught, increasing the friction, and I'm rising higher. So close I can almost taste it.

"Cal," I moan. "Please. I'm close."

"I know, love." He grins wickedly down at me. "Eyes on me, I want to watch."

My eyes meet his, and the hunger in them drives me onward, spiraling even higher to the precipice.

"Come for me, Lila."

And I free fall into my orgasm. He doesn't give me a second to come down before he picks me up dropping me in the middle of my bed and peeling my soaked leggings off me.

I glance at his jeans and see a wet spot on his thigh.

"Your jeans—"

"Don't fucking care. That was one of the hottest things I've ever seen and if I don't taste you right now, I'm going to lose my mind." He kneels at the foot of my bed, and drags me nearly to the edge, throwing a leg over each shoulder and taking one long swipe of this tongue over my center and up to my clit.

We groan in unison, and he wraps one arm around my hips, pinning me to the bed before he devours me like I'm his last meal on death row. With a combination of long drags of his tongue and small circles around my clit, it doesn't take long until the pressure is building once more, and I fist my hand in his hair.

He smiles against my skin before his teeth drag across my clit, forcing a cry from my mouth before he pushes his tongue into me.

"Fuck, Cal."

"I love the way you taste," he growls.

His tongue thrusts into me, and if I cared, the combined sounds of my moans and heavy breathing and the wet slurping sounds from Cal would be nearly obscene.

"One more Lila, and then I'll fuck you like the good girl you are."

Two fingers replace his tongue, and when they curl up into me, I crash into yet another orgasm.

He stands from his place on the floor, his eyes feral as he licks his fingers clean, before climbing over me, guiding his cock to my entrance.

One glance at me to check that I'm ready, and he pushes in to the hilt.

I gasp, but he gives me a second to adjust, though it's only one before he's moving within me. There's nothing slow or tender about the way he's fucking me, but it's not just for pleasure either. There's something in his eyes, locked onto mine, that I can't place. I grip his shoulders tighter, moving one hand to cup his cheek. He wraps my hand in his before pinning it to the bed above my head, and lowering his mouth to mine, his tongue stroking mine in tandem to his cock. I can taste myself on his mouth, and it's hot as hell.

I grip him to me, relishing in his weight pressing me into the mattress.

"Fuck," he groans, when I scratch my nails along his back. His thrusts turn faster, more disjointed until he stutters to a stop. He kisses me once more, before kissing my temple and leaning his forehead to mine. I swallow my disappointment that it's over.

"Sorry, love. I wasn't planning for it to be over that fast." His sheepish grin is answer enough.

I laugh. "I'll take it as a compliment."

"You should." He kisses my forehead again, and something in my chest melts. "But that doesn't mean it's over." He eases out of me slowly. "Do you have a toy you like to use?"

The melty feeling promptly freezes.

"Uhm, that's okay," I say, embarrassed, and try to roll out from under him.

"No."

"Excuse me?" My face is heating for an entirely new reason now.

"Let me rephrase. Do you want me to make you come using your favorite toy or my hands?"

"You don't have to, I'm fine."

"Don't do this to me, love. Let me get you off again." He nuzzles my neck, planting kisses along my collar bone.

"Bedside drawer," I gasp out.

The grin he gives me is sinful before he leans over to the small drawer, removing not just one, but two hot pink silicone toys,

"Tsk tsk tsk. I think we can do better than this." He holds up the dildo.

"What do you mean? It gets the job done."

He holds it next to his own member. While they might be a similar length, Cal is definitely thicker.

I snort. "Well, you won't ever feel inadequate at least."

He lines up the toy, and pushes it in slowly, holding eye contact.

"I'm going to fuck my cum back into you." I whimper as he holds up the second toy, turning it on, a subtle humming filling the space, and holds it to my clit.

My body jerks at the touch.

"Be a good girl and stay still for me, love."

The intensity of the vibrations nearly sets me on fire. I've gone solo using these two toys plenty of times, but just being able to feel the pleasure without the added ache in my forearms of doing it myself is something I've decided every woman should experience once.

Cal twists the dildo as he pumps it in and out, and I shoot off like a rocket, shuddering around the silicone as he fucks me through my orgasm, switching up the tempo so instead of coming down I stay high, the pressure already wound.

"One more I think, since I couldn't do it on my own today."

He turns on the dildo vibration, angling it to hit my g-spot.

"Oh God, Cal," I call out. I'm right on the edge, and as he

turns up the vibration another notch on my egg, I see white, my muscles locking up as I have what might be the best orgasm of my life.

When I finally come down, Cal is in my bathroom, cleaning the toys. It's all I can do to roll over, feeling entirely worn out, but in the best way, and I know I'm going to be deliciously sore in a few hours.

"How are you feeling?" He smirks at me from the doorway to my en suite.

"Good." I smile sleepily at him.

"Just good?"

"Hmm, maybe a little better than just good."

"Are you hungry?"

"Not yet, but I didn't eat lunch so . . ."

"I'll order something." He grabs his phone from his jeans, still on the floor by my bed. "Chipotle, okay?"

I nod. And the conversation from earlier comes flooding back.

"So, Christmas Dinner with your dad?"

"Yes, if that's acceptable?" He looks up from his phone, standing at the edge of my bed.

"Yeah. I guess you should meet my family too then. Right?"

"Only if you want us to meet. I know it's not always the easiest with them. But if you want me to, I'd be more than happy to meet them."

"I'll call my mom." I sigh. "I guess this means we're getting serious, huh?" I joke.

"Lila, I've never been more serious about something." He leans over, pressing his mouth to mine slowly, sweetly.

The look in his eyes is overwhelming, and I glance away not quite ready to think about what that means.

I burrow myself into the blankets on my bed, and he moves to sit next to me, pulling me against him.

"Sleep, love. I'll be here when you wake up."

I smile, and the last thing I see before I drift off are his eyes looking down at me with something suspiciously like love in them.

Chapter Thirty-One

LILA

I take a deep breath, straightening my spine as I stare at my childhood home. Cal comes around the car and wraps one strong arm around my waist.

"You okay?"

"Yes." His eyes narrow a fraction. "Okay, no." His face softens, his arm tightening around me. "But we're here, and there's nothing left to do but get through it."

"I'll be right here with you," he promises. "And we can leave whenever you want."

"You don't have an early practice tomorrow or anything do you?" He laughs at the hope in my voice.

"I have some film to watch if you need an excuse."

I grin up at him, and he presses his mouth to mine softly. "Come on, Lila. Let's face the music."

I frown, and open my mouth to respond, but he steps forward up the front path, pulling me with him.

The front door opens to meet us, my mom dressed in her best 'I didn't try too hard, but I'm still better than you' attire.

"Lila," she croons. "And you must be the boyfriend." She turns her blinding smile on Cal.

"I'm Cal." He holds out the red flowers he brought for her. "Thanks for having me today."

"Oh, you're too sweet," she exclaims, taking the flowers and looping her arm through his to pull him into the house, leaving me figuratively and physically out in the cold on the front stoop.

I steel myself for the second time in as many minutes and step inside, closing the door behind me, trying to shake the feeling that I'm locking myself in a den of hungry lions.

"Cal, do you want something to drink?" My mother's voice floats through the hall from the kitchen, bringing with it the scent of baked ham, sweet potatoes, apple pie. My mouth waters, and I follow them.

"Just one," he says as I round the corner to find her pressing a glass of white wine into his hand.

"Lila, you know where everything is right?" She nods at the fridge.

"Do you have a red open?" Cal asks, his eyes flicking to me before smiling at my mother with his stupid charming smile.

"Oh, of course." She takes the glass from him. "Alex, do you want this Chardonnay?" My brother-in-law appears a moment later and takes the glass, now abandoned on the kitchen island. He eyes it for all of a second before shrugging and taking a large gulp.

"Hey, Alex." I smile at him.

"How's it going, Lila?" He nods.

"How's Kayla?"

"She's good." He runs a hand through his hair. "She's just uncomfortable all the time."

"Well, that's to be expected." I laugh.

"I honestly don't know what's worse, the idea that once the baby comes I won't get any sleep or knowing that until the baby comes I won't get any sleep because my wife can't get comfortable and constantly reminds me it's my fault."

I pat his arm sympathetically. "Well, I'm sure once little Greg gets here, all of it will be worth it."

He takes another large drink of wine. "Yeah, I'm sure you're right."

"Lila." Cal's voice gets my attention. "Did you want red?"

I nod and can't help but smile when I realize he only requested red for me.

My mom rolls her eyes, but grabs a second glass from the cabinet, filling them both before handing one to me.

"I didn't realize you liked red. I would've gotten another bottle."

I shrug. "I've always preferred it."

She huffs and strides from the room.

"I'm Alex, Kayla's husband," Alex says, holding a hand out to Cal.

"Great to meet you." He shakes his hand. "I'm Cal, Lila's boyfriend."

"You look really familiar. Have we met before?" He frowns, looking Cal up and down.

Cal looks to me. "Uh, I don't think so."

"I didn't exactly tell them what you do," I say sheepishly.

The realization hits him. "Ah, I erm, play for the Avalanche."

"No fucking way." Alex's mouth drops open in shock.

"Yeah, I was just traded from the Cosmos this season."

"You're the new tight end." His voice takes on an excited pitch. "Basset, right?"

"That's me."

"Can you sign my hat? I think I have it in the car."

"Alex," I scold.

"No, it's fine. Sure, man. Whatever you want."

His face lights up like a kid on Christmas.

"This is the best. Thanks, dude." He hugs Cal, who manages to not look too weirded out by the sudden affection.

"Consider part of your gift playoff tickets in a few weeks."

"No way."

"I was going to suggest it later after dinner, but Lila thought it'd be weird."

I roll my eyes. It's still weird, but whatever, as long as they're both happy.

"I can't wait to tell Kayla. I'm going to an Avalanche playoff game."

"Let's maybe just ease into it, okay? I want to get to know Lila's parents outside of the whole football thing, yeah?"

"Got it." He nods solemnly.

"Come on, boys." I nod toward the living room, where my parents and Kayla are waiting.

"It's so nice of you to come for dinner, Cal." My mom gushes. "We just couldn't believe our Lila was bringing someone home, could we, Terry?" Dad just grunts, eyes glued to the mystery novel in his lap. "Even Dennis never made it out to visit us much, but we know how important work is to him."

Cal stiffens slightly from where he sits next to me on the loveseat in the living room.

"It was important to me to meet Lila's family." He smiles at me, his hand squeezing my knee and the physical contact floods me with warmth.

"Well, isn't that sweet." Her saccharine smile hurts my teeth.

"You have a lovely home," he says glancing around the large living area filled with seasonal greenery and splashes of crimson.

"It's not much, but it's home. We raised both our girls here. Where is your family from?" Her question is more pointed than it needs to be, but I let it slide.

"I was born in England actually."

"Oh?" Her eyes narrow. "You don't have much of an accent."

"Only on certain words, I'm told." He grins, winking at me. "I moved to America in primary school. My mother still lives there full time as does most of my extended family."

"And your father?" My teeth grind together, but Cal's fingers tap my leg, and I work to release the tension from my jaw.

"He's back and forth. That's why I moved to the States actually. He opened a New York branch and brought me with him."

"It must've been difficult going back and forth all the time," my dad says, finally putting his book down.

Cal shrugs. "I was in boarding school, so I only went home during the breaks anyway."

"I could never send my child to boarding school." Kayla sounds horrified as she clutches her belly.

His jaw ticks, and I place my hand over his. "It's pretty common in our family circles, so whether in New York or Geneva, I was going anyway."

"Geneva? Switzerland?" Alex asks.

He nods.

"Who are your parents?" Dad asks.

"Uhm—"

"Dad, is that a new book?" I break in, and his eyes light up.

"I think you'd really like this one actually, Lila. It's about—"

"Terry, we're trying to get to know our guest, not start a book club," Mom interrupts.

He sighs, shooting me an apologetic look from across the room.

"So how did you two meet?" Kayla asks.

"Katie introduced us actually," I respond. Mom rolls her eyes. She's never been a fan of my best friend.

"That's nice. So many of my single friends are stuck on dating apps these days."

I cringe and smile up at Cal, squeezing his hand. "Yeah, we got lucky." His face softens and he flips his hand to thread our fingers together.

"So, what is it you do, Cal?" Dad asks, and I frown at him. There's no need for the macho 'Can you take care of my daughter' routine.

"I actually play for the Avalanche."

Mom's eyebrows disappear into her bangs.

Dad blinks in surprise. "What? I think I must've misheard you."

"You didn't," Alex says excitedly. I roll me eyes. "He's the new tight end, John Basset." Dad takes in Cal with his eyes, hungrily, and he shifts with unease next to me.

"It's really not—"

"Lila," my mother interrupts me, her tone sharp.

"What?" I snap.

"Can I speak to you?" she hisses. "In *private*?"

I stand slowly, darting a look at Cal before following her back into the kitchen.

"What are you thinking?"

"About what?" I ask, confused.

"You've been with Dennis for years, and all of a sudden, you bring by some other guy with only a few days' notice? And an athlete?"

"I'm sorry for the short notice, Dennis and I broke up weeks ago, and Cal and I—it's just right, you know?"

"That's all fine, I'm sure he looks great in a suit, but what are you going to do when he gets bored and some girl throws herself at him after an away game? And how will he take care of you? If he's even remotely age appropriate, he only has another year or two left of playing."

"Mom, he cares about me—"

"You can't honestly think that a *football player* is a good fit for the life you want to live."

"He's a great fit for *my* life. Because it's *mine*, not yours."

"What's his plan after he blows out his knee and can't play anymore?"

I'm speechless, I didn't exactly expect her to approve, but this is extreme, even for her.

"Is he saving? Did he even graduate with a real degree? You can't expect to have a life with someone like that."

"I'm sure he's fine," I snap. "And he went to Yale, so I'm sure he'll be okay after he retires if he wants to get a normal job."

She snorts. "What was so wrong with Dennis? Even if you didn't want to settle down with him, don't you think you overcorrected a bit? You can't honestly expect an NFL player to be serious about you, can you? What can you even offer him that he can't get better from someone else?"

Anger rises in my chest, delayed only by my shock. "He respects me. And I care about him. If you can't accept that, I think we should leave."

"I just can't believe you brought your rebound home for Christmas Eve, it's just so irresponsible. I expected better from you, Lila." I see her mouth moving but I can't hear anything else, a buzzing filling my head.

"That's it. I'm done."

I hear those words as though through a distant tunnel, but they feel right. The weight off my chest is instantaneous.

"Excuse me, young lady, we are not done here." Her voice is shrill, cutting through the tunnel of sound, but it doesn't penetrate the layer of ice that's solidified around me.

"You might not be." I stare straight at her. "But I am."

I stride back through the living room, Cal looking up with concern.

"We're leaving." He stands, offering a nod to my dad.

"It was nice meeting you all. Merry Christmas," he says to my dad, who shakes his hand with a sigh.

Kayla hugs me at the door. "Merry Christmas, Lila." I give her a sad smile.

"I'll come visit before the baby comes, I promise." I whisper, ignoring the stinging behind my eyes.

Cal opens the front door for me, brushing his lips against my temple as his hand comes to rest against my lower back and we walk back to his car.

We reach the passenger side, and he stops to stand behind me as he opens my door for me.

"Not here," he murmurs into my hair.

"Wh—what?" I chatter, and I realize I'm shaking.

"Don't let them see you break." He lifts my chin up, so our eyes meet, the stormy grey filled with emotion. I nod, and slide into the leather seat, keeping my hair pulled forward to hide my face from the window.

We ride in silence except for the passing of cars on the Kennedy Expressway.

"Are you okay?" he asks.

"Not really." I take a deep, shuddering sigh, my whole chest expanding. "Did you hear it?"

"Some of it," he says shortly.

"You have to know I don't think any of those things."

"I know, Lila." He drops his hand from the gear shift to my knee and squeezes gently."

"So, we're okay?"

"We're okay." I smile, feeling lighter than I have all day.

Chapter Thirty-Two

CAL

Lila's been quiet this morning, whether she's mourning her family on Christmas day or just tired, I can't tell. She's still lying in bed, curled up with her phone as I make us breakfast. I hear her soft footfalls from behind me as I flip the omelets in the pan on the stove.

"You're up," I say, without turning around. "I was going to bring you breakfast. Omelet okay? Or I can do something else."

She doesn't answer, and I glance over my shoulder and freeze. She's standing there, silent tears streaming down her face, wrapped in the fluffy blanket from my mother. I'm so thankful I have it right now. I flick off the stove and stride to her, pulling her into my arms. She nearly collapses against me.

"What is it, love?"

"She didn't text."

"What? Who didn't text?"

She sniffs, pulling back to look up at me. "My mom always texts me on Christmas morning if I haven't been able to be home. First thing in the morning, and always by nine when they do presents. It's 10:15. She didn't text."

"I'm sorry." I can't think of anything else helpful to say, when all I want to do is yell at her mother.

"I shouldn't even be upset. I'm the one who left."

"You're her child, Lila. She signed up to love and care for you. You don't owe her a damn thing."

"You really think so?"

I nod, wiping her tears from her cheeks with my thumb and pressing a soft kiss to her forehead.

"I know so."

She steps back out of my arms, wiping her own face. "I think I just needed to cry about it for a bit. I'm going to shower and try to de-puff my face before we have to get ready to meet your dad."

I shrug. "Do you want breakfast? I can have it ready for you when you're out."

"Yes, please."

I turn back to the stove as she disappears into her bedroom and sigh as I realize I forgot to take the skillet off the stove, and what was once my omelet is now smoking and burned. I scrape it into the trash and crack three fresh eggs into a bowl to start anew.

● ● ●

"Ready?" I ask as we pull up to the steakhouse valet in downtown Chicago, where my father made a reservation for today.

"As ready as I can be." She smiles at me, the trace of her earlier breakdown gone from her face.

I take a shaky breath and put the car in park.

"Are *you* ready?" she asks, placing her hand on my thigh.

"I think so." I kiss her quickly, and open my door, glaring at her through the windshield when she reaches for her own door handle.

"You should know better than that," I tease when I open the passenger door for her a moment later. She rolls her eyes, but I'm able to admire the way her ass is accentuated by her dark green sweater dress and heeled booties as she walks away. I lick my lips as she looks over her shoulder, her gaze heating as she meets mine. I wink at her and smirk as I see one of the other ladies eyeing her Christmas present from earlier with envy—a black mini Kelly bag she eyed on her laptop one night. One phone call to Mother, and the Hermés employee couldn't wrap up the bag fast enough.

She nearly cried all over again when she opened it after breakfast, though out of the gifts, I got the better end of the deal. What's a few thousand dollars compared to the time and effort Lila spent on the ceramic football woven with the blues and greys of both teams in my NFL career and Yale. The best part is yet to come though, when she's taking me to the studio for a private lesson next week.

We step to the hostess together, my hand ghosting her lower back. "It should be three under Basset," I tell her.

"Ah, yes, the other member of your party has already been seated. If you'll just follow me."

I check my watch and scowl. We're five minutes early to the reservation, but that won't matter if he's already here. If he's here and seated, we're late.

"What's wrong?" Lila hisses at me. I shake my head.

"Johnathan," a deep voice booms out, and I force myself not to cringe at his overly posh British accent.

"Hello, Father." I shake his hand as he stands from his place at a corner table overlooking the city. "This is Lila."

"It's lovely to meet you." She beams up at him, offering her hand.

"Yes, so nice of you to finally introduce us." He ignores her hand, sitting back down, and I grit my teeth. Already, we're off to *such* a wonderful start with him playing the part of overgrown aristocrat instead of loving father. It makes me glad I've lost most of my own accent.

"Let me get your chair," I murmur to Lila, pulling it out and waiting for her to sit before I take my own place across from my father.

"I was starting to get worried you weren't coming," he muses, not taking his eyes off the wine list in front of him.

"I thought the reservation was for six." Lila says before I can jump in.

"So it was." His smile drips with condescension, and she straightens in her seat, her eyes dropping to the menu in front of her.

"A nice Chardonnay to start with, I think," he tells the waiter as he approaches the table. "And we'll do the '95 Cabernet for dinner, finishing off with a sherry." His eyes turn to us. "Assuming that is acceptable, and you don't need a Moscato or something of that nature?"

"That sounds fine, Father," I say my molars clenching so hard I make a mental note to see a dentist first thing in the new year.

"I haven't been here before," Lila says pleasantly. "Do you recommend anything, Mr. Basset?"

"Well as they are a steakhouse, I'd likely recommend one of those."

She forces a laugh and closes her menu.

"Son," he says, turning to me, "I see you're doing well in your *game* this year, but I do hope they're leaving you time to spend on some of the more important aspects of your life."

"Well, seeing as it is my job, I can't say they much care about what else I do so long as it doesn't reflect poorly on the team." I take a sip of my water to calm myself.

"Did you see the papers I couriered over yesterday? I was hoping we could discuss them tonight." He glances at Lila. "Even if we do have company."

"I haven't seen them, no. We spent the day yesterday with Lila's family, celebrating Christmas Eve."

He huffs, swirling his wine. "I see."

"Did you think I asked you to have dinner to talk about the company?"

He shifts uncomfortably, and I pin him with a glare.

"I suppose we can enjoy a meal for the holiday."

"Thank you." I reach for Lila's knee, squeezing it briefly.

The next hour actually passes surprisingly well. Our food comes, and it passes even my father's strict inspection, the wine leaving little to complain about as well. Our conversation, while stilted and not what one would call *pleasant*, is polite at least. By the time our chocolate mousse arrives, my bladder is screaming, and as much as I wish to never leave Lila alone with my father, I have to head toward the bathroom.

"Please excuse me, I'll be right back." I stand, nodding at my father, and drop a kiss to Lila's temple.

When I return only a few minutes later, Lila is gone, and my father looks a little too pleased with himself. My heart sinks.

"What did you do?" I bite out.

"I only had a frank conversation with her about your future together." He shrugs. "She's the one who chose to leave."

I drag my hand down my face and fight the urge to hit him with it.

"What did you say to her *exactly*?"

"I find I can't quite remember the specifics. Son, did you know her father used to work as an electrician?" He scoffs. "These aren't our kind of people. Now, if you want a girlfriend to play with, I can understand that. I know Victoria has shown interest in the past, and her parents—"

"Stop," I interrupt. "Have you spoken to Tori recently?" The conversation from the other night flooding back.

"Victoria, Johnathan. Honestly nicknames are so uncouth.

And I believe we had lunch a few weeks ago when she was in New York for a Dior show."

I grind my teeth together.

"You set her up to say those things to Lila at the gala, didn't you?"

"I have no idea what you're speaking of. We simply discussed her future. It's awfully bright, you know. You two would make a wonderful family together." He smiles at me, and it's so genuine I feel sick. "I just want what's best for you, Johnathan."

My vision starts to waver, tinging with red. "You can't possibly mean that." I laugh because what the actual *fuck*.

He looks stricken. "Of course, that's all I've ever wanted. You're my son."

"I wish I wasn't." I scoff.

"Now wait a minute, you will not speak to me that way."

"I mean it, Father. If this is what being your son means, I don't want it. I love that woman, and I enjoy playing football. And I'm damn good at it, because in case you haven't noticed, the NFL doesn't have that many players."

"That's nice. Of course you're good at it. You're a Basset. We're good at everything."

"Evidently not."

"Excuse me?"

"Mother—"

"My relationship with your mother is none of your business. We are both perfectly content with the lives we lead. And your mother agrees with me. It's time you stop playing around with your game and learn how to run Basset Holdings. We have a legacy to uphold."

"I don't want your fucking company!" I roar, and several tables turn to stare. "I don't want to run a company, I want to enjoy my life, something you never stopped to do. I want to fall in love. I want to travel, where I see more than just the inside of board rooms in the financial district. I want to have a *life*." I'm heaving, but I can taste the freedom on the other side of this conversation. "I love Lila. I want her in my life, permanently. That is assuming she'll even still want me after you butted your nose in."

I take one deep breath and continue. "She's funny and smart and beautiful and probably would have loved to talk about work with you since she works in consulting too, but you wouldn't even give her a chance, because you decided from the beginning that she wasn't good enough. Which is a complete lie. If anything, we're not good enough for her." I shake my head. "I'm done." I back away slowly and pull out my phone, opening the email I drafted after the Christmas Gala and hitting send. "If you want to hold my trust, fine. All it will do is reduce the charitable contributions in the Basset name.

His phone vibrates on the table and his eyes flick to it, widening in surprise.

"Don't call." I turn on my heel and stride from the restaurant.

I nearly jump when I see Lila leaning against the passenger side of my Mercedes, quickening my strides until I wrap my arms around her tightly.

"You didn't run."

"I didn't run," she breathes into my neck.

Chapter Thirty-Three

LILA

I stare at my phone, the conversation I just had echoing in my ears.

A job. Or at least a verbal offer.

From Basset Holdings.

Cal's getting dressed to travel for an away game tomorrow when I find him in his room.

"Your dad called." His eyebrows shoot up, and he pauses to stare at me.

"Sorry I think I just hallucinated. What?"

I let out a nervous laugh. "Your dad called me. And I answered because I didn't recognize the number and thought it might be a client."

Cal pinches his nose as a breath hisses between his teeth. "Tell me he didn't. This has to be a joke."

"It's not a joke." I open the email and hand over my phone. "We talked for a few minutes and then he offered me a job."

His head snaps up, his eyes wild as they meet mine.

"Excuse me?"

"He offered me a job.

"Is he serious? He just expects to give you a job and have this whole mess go away? You already have a job."

"Yes, I'm aware." His hands clench. "He apologized."

He laughs.

"I'm serious." His blink is all it takes to realize he's never apologized to Cal.

"It wasn't exactly the most genuine thing ever. It seemed very clear my value was tied to my success." I shrug. "Not exactly the loving relationship to have with your father-in-law." His eyes widen, and I freeze.

"I didn't mean it like that, obviously we're not like getting married or anything. I mean not right now, like I'm not expecting anything soon. It's still early, but I think it's going well, right? Although I guess you also need to agree, but—"

"Lila, it's fine. What else did he say?" he asks, cutting off my panicked rambling.

"He said after the email you sent him at dinner that he decided to look into me further, since he assumed I was just some cleat-chasing gold digger. So, feel free to explain what you sent him." I raise my eyebrow and cross my arms.

He has the decency to look sheepish. "I just sent him your LinkedIn profile with one of the deals you closed in Austin. That's it, I swear. I know he respects power and competence, and you're good at your job. I just wanted him to respect you because whether or not I agree with how he values people, you'd be someone he values. Not that I don't find you valuable, obviously."

I roll my eyes.

"Yeah, that explains it." I drop my arms. "Well, he basically apologized for not knowing who he was talking to and offered me a job at his company. Said, he could 'use someone like me,' and that he'd send an official offer via email, but if I was serious about you, if *we* were serious, that he wouldn't take no for an answer and would do what was necessary to make it work."

"He can't do that." Cal's eyes heat with anger.

"It's okay, I think it might be a good thing," I soothe, but the fire in his eyes doesn't dissipate.

"Did he say anything else about our relationship?" he spits out.

"Uhm, not really. It was honestly mostly about the company and how with my tech background, I could bring in a new market to the firm. It sounded like he might actually appreciate the work I could bring."

He doesn't look convinced. "But 'he wouldn't take no for an answer' if we were serious?"

"I think he might have been kidding."

"He wasn't," he says darkly.

I frown. "What do you mean?"

"My father doesn't joke. It's just a way to control me and our relationship, and he's doing it through you."

"I don't know that that's fair—" I start, hurt clouding my words.

"You don't know him, Lila." He checks his watch and gathers his stuff for the game quickly. "I have to go, I'll miss the bus."

"Okay." I let him press a kiss to my temple.

"Just promise you won't accept it."

My brow furrows. "Cal, that's not—"

"At least don't do anything until we can talk about it when I'm back, okay?"

I nod, and he heads out the door, my feelings completely turned upside down.

●■● ●■● ●■●

I'm at the studio, letting my mind process in the background as I work on a new matcha bowl for Katie when my phone starts vibrating with a call from James. I quickly wipe my hands off on a towel and answer breathlessly. My gut is twisted in knots knowing there's only one reason my boss would be calling right now.

I deserve this promotion, and he knows it.

"Hello? This is Lila," I answer.

"Hey Lila, got a minute?"

"Sure. Do I need my laptop?" I don't have it with me, but I can make do on my phone for anything small.

"No, nothing like that."

"Okay. What can I help you with?" It's Saturday, and he normally keeps calls to weekdays, even if business hours are a bit questionable. It has to be about the job.

"It's about the new partner role." I pull the phone from my ear and do a silent happy dance.

"Oh great, any update on the candidate selection?" We haven't even had interviews yet, so I should probably not jump to conclusions.

"I wanted you to hear it from me." He sighs and my heart drops like an anchor. "They're going with a junior partner out of Seattle, so it'll be a lateral move for him."

"Oh, okay." My voice sounds brittle, even to my own ears. "Thanks for telling me."

"Lila, I'm sorry. I wanted it to work out, but you're still very young. Keep putting in the hours and you'll get there."

"Of course. No worries. Thanks, James."

"I think they'll be announcing on Monday."

"Great, thanks for the heads up."

Click.

I stare at my screen, willing myself not to cry. Because of course it couldn't be an easy decision to stay and turn down the offer from Basset Holdings.

I take my seat at the wheel once more, and willfully choose to ignore my problems until this bowl is finished.

◆ ◆ ◆

On Sunday, I'm trying and failing to pay attention to my book, my eyes flicking to the blank TV. I war with myself for another few minutes before giving up and turning it on. The playoffs start next week, and just because I'm annoyed at him doesn't mean I don't want him to do well.

I find the Avalanche game and frown. They're down by seven in the third quarter. They might have locked in a spot in the play-offs already, but if Pittsburgh has taught anyone anything, it's that getting a spot doesn't mean you can win a game in the post-season. I want it for him so badly. Want it for the city, sure, but mostly I want it for him.

Theo makes a catch for a first down, and I cheer, my book officially lying abandoned on the couch next to me.

The rest of the quarter plays out with no change to the score. My eyes find Cal every time our offense is on the field, but he doesn't play much of a role in any of the downs. He blocks and makes runs, but not one catch to account for, and I can't tell for sure, but he looks a bit sluggish.

The fourth quarter starts off without a hitch, both teams driving down the field but not putting anything on the scoreboard until the Avalanche connects a long pass to one of the other receivers on the team—Matthews I think—and we're within field goal range. With only three minutes left on the clock, this is likely our last chance to come back from behind, and we have to do it slowly so New York can't score again.

The first pass goes wide out of bounds, and the second down only gains two yards after a false start from Cal that has me gnawing my lip. Third down conversions haven't been our strong suit this year, and we need to connect the pass to move forward.

They break, and time slows down as the center hikes the ball. Cal takes off running and turns, the pass headed straight for him.

"Come on!" I yell, urging him from hundreds of miles away to make the catch.

He doesn't.

The ball slips from his hands, hitting the ground as the safety hits him hard from behind. I gasp at the contact and don't breathe until he gets up. It's slow, and he immediately goes to the sidelines as special teams comes out to make the final field goal attempt.

The camera finds his face, the announcers commenting on his game play today, musing about trade possibilities. If I open Twitter, I'll see thousands of gym class all-stars calling him all sorts of things I don't need to see right now. He won't have his phone on him, but I pull up our text thread, silent since he left for New York yesterday.

> Can you call me when you're back home?

I pace my living room, even though I know he won't have his phone for at least an hour. And then they need to fly back from New York.

New York sets up in victory formation as they run down the clock and the game is over. Twenty-eight to twenty-four, and we've lost.

Chapter Thirty-Four

CAL

The away crowd is booing, and it doesn't take a genius to know it's directed at me. If I hadn't gotten a penalty and then dropped that catch, we might still be in the game. Might have even won if we went for two.

But I did. Becker made the kick, so at least got the points for the differential, but it didn't win us the game. And whether it's just an incomplete or a fumble, I know that I could've had it, and I quite literally dropped the fucking ball.

I'll be the first to admit that my head has been all kinds of fucked up since dinner with my father, but having twenty thousand fans yelling how terrible you are at your job isn't exactly boosting my mood.

"Hey, Basset!" Coach yells, waving me over to him.

"Yeah?" I ask once I jog over from the bench where I've been wallowing.

"You good? I've seen you make that catch eighty times in practice."

I grit my teeth and nod.

"Right." He claps my shoulder. "Don't let it get to you. Better now than next week, yeah?" He grins, and I force a smile before heading back to my bench.

The final whistle blows, and I follow the team into the locker room, not bothering to shake hands with any other players today. I stride quickly to my locker, slamming my helmet to the ground at the base of my chair.

"Fuck!" I yell, smacking my hand against the top wooden panel.

"Basset, media room," a booming voice calls out from the entry way.

I glare at Stacy, the media coordinator. She stares blankly at me until I shove myself off my locker and follow her to the post-game media frenzy, trying—and probably failing—not to outwardly sulk.

The Cosmos's quarterback is just finishing up, laughing with the reporters as he basks in his win. I scowl, but school my features when Stacy glowers at me. She gives me approximately thirty seconds before ushering me into the chair at the front of the room.

"Tough break, John," a reporter for *Sports Illustrated* says from the front row. I shrug, staring blankly at a fixed point on the wall above the camera line. He clears this throat. "So, we're doing the question thing again?" My eyes drop to him and the corner of my mouth tugs up in a smirk.

Stacy rolls her eyes, but I'm here, so I can't get fined.

The reporter clears his throat loudly. "Do you think you could've caught that pass?"

I sigh. "Hypothetically? Yes. But as you all know there are a thousand different micro-causes that impact each play. The wind —and no I'm not saying I didn't catch the ball because of the wind—but the wind, the glare from the sun, my run, the angle of the pass, the defense position. So yes, theoretically, if Blaze were to throw the exact same pass from the exact same place and I was in the same place, I could catch it."

He grumbles something I don't hear, and I scan the crowd of reporters for the next question.

The rest of the press session is brutal, each reporter asking a variation of the same question. Why couldn't I make that catch with the game on the line? Did I crack under the pressure? Do I think I'll be able to hold up to the pressure of the playoffs? After my allocated thirty minutes, I'm exhausted. The adrenaline from the game is rapidly wearing off as the sweat evaporates, leaving my body coated in a salty film I'm dying to wash off.

"That's all Basset has time for, folks," Stacy calls out after what feels like an eternity. I stand abruptly and am out the door before she can even thank the reporters. Most of the team has made it in the locker room, and I stride through the men in various stages of undress to my locker, smacking the side of it before resting my forehead against the panel at the top.

"Cal," a low voice scolds from behind me. It's Blaze, and I don't bother turning around.

"What?" I bite out.

"It's not your fault. That throw wasn't perfect, and neither was the catch. It's not on your head." His hand grips my shoulder in what I assume he thinks is a comforting gesture.

"I've been off all week. The throw was fine, and you know it."

He shrugs. "I don't. There's no way to know, and you're the only one who was out there catching the ball. Only you know for sure."

"Is this supposed to be motivational?"

"I'm not the best with this shit, okay? That's why I leave the captaining to Thompson over there." He nods toward our Center who makes one hell of a captain, having been on the team for almost a decade.

I roll my eyes.

He smacks my shoulder once more and drops his hand. "Seriously. Coach won't say it because it's bad for morale, but every single player in this room and every fan outside knows this game

302

didn't really matter. We weren't going to get the first seed anyway, but we have a playoff spot. Some teams would've rested their starters today."

I laugh but it's icy.

"Shake off whatever's bothering you and bring your A-game next week, yeah? No one will care you didn't catch the ball today."

I nod. "Easier said than done, but I know. I'll figure it out."

"Is it the new girl? If you want to talk . . ."

I snort. "I'm not about to talk girls with you Meadows." I smack him on the shoulder. "No offense, but you can't keep one happy enough to stick around longer than a few weeks."

He flushes, a glance behind him before he says, "Oh please. If I wanted them to stick around, they'd *stick around*."

"Gross."

"Anyways, I meant that McClane would talk to you."

Theo's head pops up from a few lockers over. "Don't start shit you can't finish Meadows," he calls over, and I can't help but grin at Blaze's exasperated look.

"I'm gonna shower. You two figure out whatever this is." I glance between them meaningfully and Blaze hits me with a glove.

"Fuck off."

I head toward the showers to wash off the sweat and shame that's lessening by the minute amongst my teammates. Not one of them is treating me like I lost them the game. A few have patted my back and offered a word of encouragement or condolences, but most have completely moved on from the play amidst the playoffs coming up.

I'm changed and waiting on Theo to head out to the bus when I finally decide to check my phone. It was my least favorite thing to do whenever we lost a game, knowing that I'd have no one's notification waiting but a slew of media tags on what I should've done differently. But that was before Lila. I don't know exactly where we stand right now, though. I didn't leave in the best headspace, so I have no idea what may or may not be waiting for me when I turn it back on.

The green message icon pops up, and my stomach plummets when I see her message across my screen.

> Can you call me when you're back home?

I debate asking her what she wants to talk about, but instead, I look around for Theo, who's still in the shower, and hit call.

"Hey," she answers on the second ring.

"Hey, love." The moniker slips out, and I kick myself, knowing I'm likely on thin ice, if any ice at all.

"You're home fast, the game just ended an hour ago."

"I'm still in New York, but I didn't want to wait."

"Oh."

"Sorry, I just saw your text and wasn't sure if you were okay. It's really good to hear your voice after that game." I'm rambling and promptly shut up before I say something incredibly stupid.

"No, it's fine. I just wanted to talk."

"Okay. About anything in particular?" My heart's thudding, and the room feels warmer than it did a minute ago. If I don't get through this conversation soon, I'm going to need another shower.

"I wanted to talk about us and about the job. You probably figured that out already, but it can wait. Are you doing okay after the game? I know how hard you are on yourself."

"Lila, please," I beg. I really can't take much more of the back and forth, and talking about my missed pass is the last thing I want to do.

"I'm sorry, I'm not trying to drag this out. I was hoping you'd be home, or we could at least talk in person, can you come over after you get back? It'd be, what, another couple hours at most?"

"Yeah, I can come over. But please don't make me wait if

you're just going to break up with me officially. It's been a hell of a day, and I'd rather just know now."

"Cal, I'm not breaking up with you. But I do think we need to talk some stuff through."

"Alright, I can live with that."

"I'll have dinner ready when you get here. Pasta, okay?"

"Pasta sounds great." I can't keep the grin off my face. She's not breaking up with me.

"What's got you so smiley?" Theo asks as I hang up, toweling his hair dry with another wrapped around his waist.

"Lila called."

"Good news then?"

I shrug.

"Nice. Well, you're good together, I'm glad you're making it work even with all the shit from your dad."

I grunt, less happy now that Theo knows for some reason.

"Hurry up, would you? Most of the team is already on the bus."

"And the other half is still in the showers, calm your ass down." He throws the towel at me, and I bat it away into one of the chairs.

I read a few news articles on my phone while I wait for Theo. Ever since I was traded, we've boarded the buses and planes together. I think he started it to make me feel included with the new team, but now it's just a habit. And it doesn't matter how comfortable the bus is or how short the ride, it will always be cramped to a professional football player. At least anyone other than kickers.

I throw myself into a window seat, shoving my bag under the seat in front of me where a dozing lineman spreads out over the double seat, and Theo takes the seat next to me.

"You know it's kinda creepy how happy you look after losing."

I snort. "You know it has nothing to do with the loss." Being reminded of it does sober me slightly, but nothing can quite dim the lightness in my chest lingering from Lila's call.

"I bet you'd make that catch now," he says, voice low.

I huff out a breath. "Yeah, you're probably right." I turn my head toward the last two guys from special teams as they cross the parking lot.

"Hey." He hits my shoulder lightly, and I turn back to him. "Better now than next week. Shake it off."

🏈 🏈 🏈

I practically leap off the plane the moment the doors are open, nearly sprinting to my car and letting it roar to life around me.

Making a snap decision, I stop at a Jewel and emerge minutes later with three different bouquets of roses and a more-than-half-way-decent bottle of red. I should really do something nicer with the flowers, but it's the thought that counts right?

> I'm on my way.

LILA
> I'll start dinner.

I smile, and buckle my seat belt, intent on breaking at least three rules of the road in the next twenty minutes.

I'm giving the sauce a final taste when there's a loud knock at my door. I give the pot one last stir before opening the door to find Cal, dressed in grey joggers and an Avalanche hoodie. In one hand he's holding a huge bouquet of red, pink, and white roses, and in the other a bottle of wine.

My heart stutters as I take him in, his hair slightly messy from where it likely dried on the flight here, one corner of his mouth pulled up into something that fits somewhere between a smirk and a true smile.

"Hey," I say, slightly breathless.

"Hello, love." He bends to brush his lips to my cheek.

I open the door wider, inviting him in, and he sets the bottle of wine on the kitchen island.

"Do you have a vase?"

I snort, remembering the six vases I came home with after sorting through the ones good enough to gift as Christmas presents.

He quirks an eyebrow, and I shake my head, pulling out a large white and pink vase from the cabinet.

"Did you make this?"

"Yep, it didn't make the cut for Christmas gifts this year, so it lives with me until I find a place to donate it." I turn back to the stove and start plating up our dinner.

"Seriously? It's amazing."

I shrug. "How hungry are you?"

"I skipped dinner on the plane."

"Alright," I answer, a lilting rise in my voice as I try not to laugh, doubling his portion and setting it in front of what's become his place at my kitchen island over the last several weeks.

He sets down the vase on the center of the island, now full of the roses he brought.

"I thought these would brighten up your condo." He smiles, and I realize that, while they look lovely, nothing brightens up the space quite like he does when he smiles like that. No barriers, just raw joy emanating from him, and I can't help but grin back.

"Thanks. They're lovely."

He presses a kiss to my temple, his hand brushing my hip as he steps around me to take his seat.

"This looks amazing. Seriously, so much better than whatever the rest of the team ate."

I laugh. "Thanks. Wine?" I pull out a corkscrew and start on the bottle he brought. He nods, scooping up a forkful of the chicken Alfredo.

He groans as I'm pouring the wine, nearly making me spill the blood red liquid all over my quartz countertop. "Lila, this is incredible."

"It's just Alfredo sauce. It's my grandmother's recipe." I place both wine glasses down and sit to take a bite of my own pasta. He's right, it's damn good.

"I'm so glad I skipped dinner for this." He's nearly finished with his plate, and I'd be concerned if he hadn't just played three hours of football.

"I can make it whenever you want. Though, you might want to try some of the other recipes before you pick a favorite.

According to legend, her chicken piccata got her an extra carat on her ring." He laughs, and I can't help but join in.

I'm halfway through my own plate when he speaks again.

"So, you said you wanted to talk."

I push my plate away, my appetite suddenly nonexistent as my stomach twists itself into knots. "Yeah, I did."

I take a deep breath and pull out my phone, clicking through my email to find what I'm looking for. "Here, I want to show you the official offer letter."

He looks down at the phone and reads the words I've memorized over the last few days.

Ms. Summers,

Please see the offer attached. As mentioned, we can discuss details at your earliest convenience once you've had time to review the entire package. I look forward to your call.

Sincerely,
William Basset
CEO of Basset Holdings

"Open the offer." He clicks on the attachment in the email, and silence follows.

"This is . . ."

"I know."

"Do you even want the job?"

"It's a good offer. If it wasn't your father offering it, I would've accepted already." I laugh at the irony. "A fifty percent pay bump is enticing on its own, but he's offering partner. I didn't get the promotion, by the way. They offered it to someone else—some guy based out of Seattle, if you can believe it. I found out yesterday after you left. So, it might be a sign it's time to move on anyway."

He frowns. "If we weren't together, would you take it?"

"Like if we broke up? Or if I'd never met you?"

He frowns. "For the sake of argument, both."

"If we broke up, I don't think so. I'd want a clean break, I think, and working for your dad wouldn't be clean." I gnaw on my bottom lip, his eyes tracking the movement. "If we'd never met? Yes, I would."

"So, what's stopping you now?"

"Aside from knowing how he treats people generally?" My laugh is harsh. "He's still your dad. You have a lot to work through, the two of you, if you want to have any type of relationship. Not to mention what if we *do* break up? I'll have to quit. I don't know if I can have my career tied up in a relationship."

He frowns. "Let me handle the relationship with my dad. If you want the job, I'll figure it out. Hell, it might get better if he feels someone's there to carry on his legacy."

I wait for him to address the slightly more prudent point in my argument, but he doesn't.

"You clearly don't want me to work for your dad. And I don't have to decide right now."

"Then don't decide yet." He shrugs.

"It's that simple to you?"

"Is it not to you?"

"I don't know." My heart falls. I'm not sure what I expected, not necessarily a promise of undying love, but some small part of me was maybe hoping for a declaration that we wouldn't break up so there was no reason to worry. I should've known that Cal would be a realist. And it's a real possibility. We haven't known each other that long, and sometimes love isn't the most important thing.

"Lila, what is it?" He turns on the barstool, his knee knocking mine as he pulls me toward him by my empty hand.

"Nothing." I shrug and glance up to meet his gaze. "No. Not nothing. I want some reassurance, I guess. My last relationship was going nowhere, and while that was partially my fault, I don't want us to go nowhere. But I also don't want to put my career on the back burner."

"You want a promise you know I can't make. If it was up to me, there wouldn't be a question, but it's not just up to me. There's two of us in this relationship." I meet his eyes, knowing he can see through the hurt I can't possibly hide, no matter how hard I'm trying to reason myself out of it.

"Lila Summers, I love you. You're exactly right for me in ways I didn't know could be possible. When I met you, it was like I didn't need to make space for you in my life because the space was already there, waiting for you to fill it. I didn't even realize it was a part of me until you came in with your tequila shots and your reality TV shows." It's so similar to how I feel about him I want to cry, my body not fully capable of containing the emotion rising within me.

"Ask me again. Ask me who I play for, because it's you. You're it for me. So, if you want me to say I don't want to break up, this is me saying it. I don't want to break up. I want you, however you'll have me, for as long as you want me."

He swipes his thumb under my cheek, wiping away the tears I didn't even realize were falling.

I step between his parted thighs, setting my wine glass down to wrap both arms around his shoulders. "I love you too, Cal." I lean in and he meets me halfway, our lips pressing together in something more resembling a chemical reaction than a kiss. It fizzes as the heat works its way up through my body, beginning at the tips of my toes as I rise onto them, up through my legs and hips, pulsing in my core. It floods my chest—not just heat and lust, but love and comfort too—as it flows down my arms and into my fingertips. I grip his hair, slanting my mouth over his.

He edges his mouth down my jawline, one hand tangling in my hair as he tugs my head back to give him room to move to my neck. I groan as his teeth nip at my pulse point. He stands, his other hand palming my ass as he presses against me, the hard length of his cock pressing into me so perfectly outlined by his grey joggers. I run my hand up his shaft through the pants, and he hisses, his breath ghosting the shell of my ear.

I step back, lacing my fingers with his, and tug him toward my bedroom.

His hoodie is the first thing to go. He pulls it, along with his shirt, over his head in one yank. My mouth is suddenly dry as I take in his chiseled chest and his stormy grey eyes blown wide with lust. He reaches down and peels off my own sweatshirt. He swallows when he takes in my naked torso. His rough palm skates across my skin, up my hip to cup my breast, kneading it gently.

"Beautiful," he whispers, leaning in to press a kiss to my mouth. I flush under his gaze, his words, his touch. It's all too much and my body temperature rises at least five degrees.

He eases me back onto my bed, his hands moving to the waistband of my leggings, a question in his eyes. I life my hips for him, and he peels them down my legs, bringing my panties with them and leaving me bare before him.

"You're fucking gorgeous, love." His gaze drags over my skin, burning wherever it touches, and I feel as if I'm going to burst into flame if he doesn't touch me.

"Please," I nearly beg and reach for his own waistband.

He grabs my hands, holding both wrists in one of his own.

"I don't want this to be fast. I want to show you how much I love you. How much I love your body, your mind, your soul." He punctuates each part of me with a kiss, one to my sternum, one to my left inner thigh, the other to my right, as he settles himself between them.

"Please Cal, let me just feel you." He smirks and takes one long lick from my center to my clit. "No, I *need* to feel you." I cry. I'm begging, and I don't care, even as a keening whine escapes me. I need *him*, not just to come but to join together, as completely as possible.

He stops immediately. "Lila, what's wrong?" His eyes are frantic running over me in concern instead of lust, checking to see if I'm hurt.

"Please, you. I need you." I repeat, and when the concern in his face doesn't ebb, I lift my legs, shoving his joggers down with my feet.

"Are you sure? I can make sure you're wet—"

I silence him with my mouth, surging up to kiss him as my hands thread through is hair, pulling our bodies flush. I reach down to guide him where I need him, but he moves first. Keeping his mouth securely locked to mine, slipping two fingers inside me.

"Fuck," he breathes, pulling back and dropping his head to my collarbone, before replacing them with his cock as he sheaths himself inside me in a single thrust. I moan, and my eyes sting as a piece of me comes together once more. He was right earlier.

"Love, what's wrong?" His thumb sweeps across my swollen mouth, and I shake my head.

"Did I hurt you? You felt ready."

"No," I choke out. "I—you feel like coming home. And I missed you." A tear spills over, and he kisses it away and then starts to move.

The heat from earlier is nothing compared to what I'm feeling now. My senses are overwhelmed, and I can do nothing but cling to Cal, trusting him to get us both where we need to go. I open my eyes, not even realizing I was squeezing them shut to see him watching me. He laces his fingers with mine holding my hand up by my head as the other braces his weight.

He slides his arm under my leg, pressing it open against his shoulder as he slides deeper and keeping his eyes locked to mine says, "I love you."

He snaps his hips faster and that's all it takes before I'm spiraling into oblivion, crying his name. He must've finished right after I did, because as I float back to the bed, coming down from my high, he's stilled inside me, his weight heavy between my thighs and breathing heavily.

I pull his head to mine, whispering, "I love you." He kisses me then, full of promise and affection.

As I fall asleep, with his body curled around mine, I realize that this man is mine.

And I'm never letting him go.

Chapter Thirty-Six

CAL

The wild card round goes as well as anyone could hope. We claim a two-touchdown lead in the first half led by Theo and manage to hang on through to the final few minutes, celebrating the win with thousands of fans surrounding us, all excited for our first appearance in the playoffs in years.

While I didn't score today, it's night and day from last week when they were booing me off the field, and knowing Lila is up in a box supporting me is the cherry on top. As a tight end we don't get a lot of the glory; doing our job well could mean very few receiving yards and even fewer touchdowns, but with the rise of the rest of my cohort in the media, my jersey sales have done nothing but rise. Post-game, some players have stuck around to sign autographs for fans, and I hear my name being called by a little boy who can't be older than four or five.

I step up to the edge of the stands where he's leaning over, his dad holding him and grinning at me.

"Mr. Basset, can you sign my jersey?" he asks.

"Sure, buddy. What's your name?"

"Jeremiah."

"Well, it's great to meet you, Jeremiah, I'm Cal." His eyes are wide with wonder, and I try not to laugh.

"Have you been an Avalanche fan long?"

He nods solemnly. "My whole life." I chuckle as I sign the jersey for him.

"Wow, I think you might deserve something a little more than just a signature then." I wink at him and wave over one of the media coordinators, standing off to the side with some press.

"Hey," I whisper, just in case I can't deliver, "can we get them two tickets to the next round?"

She scrolls her phone and makes a note before nodding. "Yep, no problem at all."

I turn back to the boy. "How would you like to go to the next game in Green Bay?" He lights up, bouncing up and down, while his dad seems frozen in shock.

"Do you have an email where we can send the tickets?" I ask the dad, who nods and rattles it off to the media coordinator, who in turn types it into her phone.

"You'll get the tickets via email within a few days," she says, leaving me with the pair.

"Thank you," the man says earnestly, and I nod.

"Have fun and go Avalanche."

I jog over to join my teammates starting to make their way back to the locker room.

"Rookie move, Basset." Meadows smirks at me, clapping my shoulder.

"What do you mean?" I frown.

"Giving playoff tickets to a kid. A kid you don't even know." He shakes his head. "My mother would kill me if I gave away her tickets."

I shrug. "My mother's in England. She probably doesn't even know we made the playoffs." He gives me a horrified look. "What do you want me to say?" I laugh. "Lila's really the only one who I want there."

A chorus of *oooooo*s greet this statement, and I shove at Blaze.

"Mate, you can make fun all you want. At the end of the day, she's the only one I need."

"She must give a mean blow—"

Wilson, the rookie corner, doesn't finish his sentence before I shove him into a wall, holding him there by his jersey against the stone tunnel.

"Finish that thought," I growl. "I fucking dare you."

"Not cool, man," Blaze scolds. "Apologize to Basset. That's his girl, not some random jersey chaser."

The rookie holds his hands up in surrender. "Sorry." I grip his jersey tighter. "I'm sorry, really. It won't happen again."

I grunt in agreement. "Better not," I warn and drop him, striding off to the locker room, my good mood from winning the game gone in an instant.

I stand under the shower head, willing my heart rate to level even as I look forward to the celebration that will inevitably follow our win throughout the city. I want to win as much as the next guy, but a small piece of me—or maybe not so small, after all —longs to disappear into anonymity. But my girl is out there waiting.

"Hey, love," I say after finding her waiting with some of the other families and chatting with Blaze's mom. I press a kiss to her temple as she hugs me.

"Congrats on the win." She smiles up at me. "One step closer."

"Well don't you two make a handsome couple," Anita Meadows says.

"Thanks, it's all Lila." I smirk, and she laughs. "Good to see you, Mrs. Meadows."

"I won't keep you kids but behave yourselves. We still have three more games to win." She gives me a stern look over her glasses which have slid down her nose.

"Yes, ma'am." I turn back to Lila. "Ready?"

She nods. "Let's get out of here."

"You know you'll need a new jersey for when we play next week."

"I was hoping you'd say that." She grins up at me. "I've been told I look great in white."

I think my brain short circuits for a second as a short scene plays through my head like a reel of film: Lila wearing white surrounded by faceless people as she walks down the aisle.

"Cal?" Her question breaks through, and I blink at her.

"Erm." I clear my throat. "Yeah?"

"Are you okay?"

"Yep, why wouldn't I be?" I start walking toward my car, Lila following in my wake.

"You kinda froze up back there, are you sure?"

I spin around, cradling her face in my hands and kiss her. As she moves to deepen the kiss, I pull away. "I love you."

"I love you too," she mumbles. "What was that for?"

"I hadn't told you today. Now I'm good, great even."

● ● ●

It's bitterly cold out as I stretch with the rest of the team. The Green Bay stadium in the winter is anything but forgiving, and I'm grateful I've played for both New York and Chicago rather than somewhere in the south.

No amount of stretching can warm up your muscles when it's four degrees out, but here we all stand, putting on this little show rather than curled up in our puffer jackets on the sideline or, better yet, back in the locker room with heat and walls to keep the wind out.

"Alright, numbers!" yells out one of the offensive coaches. "Let's go!" He calls after we're a bit slow on the jog over to the corner of the field.

"One," calls Blaze, as the throws the ball to Theo.

"Two," yells Theo, tossing the ball to another wide receiver.

I step up as the next receiver takes off after them.

"Five," I shout after catching the ball. Turning to throw it to one of the second-string running backs.

"What was that throw, Basset?" Coach calls, and I grind my teeth. I'm not a quarterback, even in high school when some of the other receivers played QB or stepped up for a game or two. I don't get paid to throw the ball, and it's better for all parties.

We run through the drill twice more, and each pass I throw is a perfect spiral, landing in the hands of the running back behind me easily as he runs down the field. Coach only nods at me, dismissing me to where the offensive line is warming up with their footwork drills, and I sigh. At least the movement will help keep me warm.

Soon enough we're headed back into the locker room, the heat bringing forth more than one audible groan from the team, earning those who couldn't close their mouths rightful ribbing from the rest of us.

"Alright, guys," Thompson starts. "This is the biggest game we've played this season. Against one of our biggest competitors, and on their home turf." He looks at each of us in turn, but no one breaks the silence. There's a rumor of his retirement after this season, and while I'm not as close with him as most, I can recognize what a great leader he's been for this team. I want him to get a ring before he calls it quits.

"It's not going to be easy. But the win wouldn't feel as good if it was. And I truly believe we're the better team. We *can* win, but it will take all of us, playing our best, giving it our all. Leave everything out on the field, fellas, because when has the cold ever stopped an avalanche?"

"Never!" I shout in unison with the rest of my teammates, familiar now with the call and response cadence of Thompson's speeches.

"Whose game is this to win?"

"Ours!"

"Let's fucking get it done!"

We cheer, whoops and hollers that can likely be heard all the way back to the city of Chicago.

When we run out onto the field less than an hour later, we're greeted with shouts of support and boos alike from opposite sides of the stands. That's the benefit of having the division playoff game teams as close in geography as Green Bay and Chicago. The oldest rivalry in the NFL, and the winner moves onto the NFC championship game against Dallas, who's on their first winning streak in years.

My eyes flick up to the boxes, knowing Lila's up there with Maggie and Katie. I count to where she should be and wink.

We win the coin toss and start with the ball, Theo making a few truly spectacular catches at the end of the first drive, and we're only left with a field goal before the ball turns over. On fourth and one, we leave everyone guessing when we go for it, scraping by with a first down and putting us in the red zone.

The rest of the offense watches from the sideline, willing our defense to hold the line. But after three downs, Dallas manages to convert and bring the football through to the end zone, pulling ahead by four points when the extra point sails through the goalpost.

"Let's bring it back," Blaze says, when we huddle at the twenty after getting the ball. I move to my place at the end of the line and wait for Blaze's shout before taking off toward my target, the current leader in sacks this year.

Theo makes the catch, and we gain another fifteen yards.

"Fuck yes." We slam our helmets together as the team congratulates him quickly, already setting up for the next play even as the crowd screams around us. Wilson picks up another five yards, and I nod at him. Being a rookie is tough; being a rookie during a playoff game is make-or-break tough.

The next ball is mine, and I take it seven more yards before

I'm pulled down by the fullback. I shake it off as we move down the field once more. Something twinges in my shoulder as I roll it out after the hit, but I ignore it, setting up with the linemen.

Another two plays, and we're within field goal range once more. One pass to Theo and Blaze is able to carry it home for the touchdown, and we're up on top once more.

We hold Green Bay to their one touchdown plus-one more field goal until half time, while we score once more putting us up by seven going into the second half. We all jog to the locker room, desperate for the warmth and short respite from the wind.

I set in front of my locker, feeling a strange urge to check my phone. Normally I turn it off during games, so I'm not even tempted to check. I don't need any distractions—or the fine that comes with it—that can ruin the second half, but I slip it out of its cubby, turning my body to hide it from the rest of the team and coaching staff that have just entered behind us players.

There are several dozen notifications, but one stands out.

LILA

Care for a little bet on the game?

You know we can't bet on our own games...

What do you have in mind?

If you win, you can fuck me in your jersey.

I cough, shifting in my seat as my uniform pants get uncomfortably tight.

I think you've got yourself a deal.

LILA

I have a second condition for you . . .

I swallow, my throat suddenly dry and take a swig of the Gatorade I grabbed on the way in.

oh yeah?

LILA

If you score

if I score?

?????

I want you to fuck my mouth until my mascara is running down my face.

I'm definitely hard now. Fuck.

Deal.

I have to go.

Fuck I love you.

LILA

love you too (kissy face emoji)

I clench my thigh muscles through the entire pep talk, barely hearing a word throughout the entire half-time break.

"Blaze," I call as we start to head back out onto the field.

"What's up?"

"I need to score."

He snorts. "Yeah, sure."

"No." I grip his arm. "Meadows, listen to me. I need to score."

"You have some kind of bet going on?" He lowers his voice.

"Not the kind you should be worried about."

"You know three guys already got booted from the league this year alone when they bet on games. You can't do this, man."

I chuckle. "No, I promise, it's nothing like that. No money is involved."

He stares at me hard, and I sigh. "It's just between me and Lila."

He snorts. "Ah, it's a sex thing."

"Can you just"—I rub my forehead—"not? Please?"

"I'll see if there's anything in the playbook that works with the OC. We'll try to get you laid no problem, Basset." He laughs and turns to catch up with the offensive coordinator on his way out of the tunnel.

I'm definitely going to regret telling him. But knowing what will be waiting for me when I get home? I'd do it again in a heartbeat.

Chapter Thirty-Seven

CAL

G reen Bay starts with the ball this half, and I've never been so restless to be sitting on the sidelines while the defense is on the field. We hold the line, and within minutes I'm back on the field.

I spit on my gloves, rubbing them together to keep my hands warm. If I drop the ball today, I won't forgive myself. Lila would never withhold sex just because I lost a game or didn't score, but it's so much sweeter if I earn it like this. And even if we didn't have our little bet going, I want a ring.

Theo makes the first catch, putting him at over a hundred receiving yards so far this game, something I only know because they flash it on the screen behind his headshot. We near the end zone but can't finish, although I do end up with a few more rushing yards to add to my post-season stats. Becker, our kicker steps up with special teams as we swap places on the field, and every person in the stadium holds their breath as he attempts a field goal at fifty-three yards, a career record for him by eight yards.

It's just shy, hitting the crossbar with a *DING* that echoes across the stadium right before a roar starts from the home side of the field.

We hold them off in their next drive attempt, keeping our lead going into the fourth.

"Alright, we have one maybe two more drives in this game. We don't want to go into OT," Thompson hypes us up as we huddle in time-out. "Let's get it done this drive. Make it a two-score game." We break, each of us determined to do our part for the game.

The ball finds its way to my hands first, and I get the first down, feeling pleased with myself, even with over half a field left to go. Theo takes it another five, Blaze runs the last five himself, and we're on the other side of the field, closer to our final goal.

"Hail Mary, they won't expect it." Blaze says quietly. I frown, I need to block, to give him time in the pocket, but if we get it, we might have time for another drive.

He hikes the ball, dropping back as we hold the line, giving him time to find the receivers sprinting down the field. He throws, and we all watch as it flies through the air, headed straight for Matthews with only a single man covering.

That single cornerback knows what he's doing though, because just as our receiver stretches his arms out to snag the ball, the CB snatches it out of the air, bringing it down in a roll for an interception.

Blaze hangs his head.

"Hey, shake it off. We'll have at least one more drive now. And that was a beautiful ball." I tell him, Thompson nodding along with me.

He shrugs, moving off to sit with the QB coach at the end of the bench.

Our defense is cold and tired. They've been playing with the best of them against a veteran quarterback and a wicked-fast running game. No one can blame them when they miss one of the Green Bay receivers sneaking past and bringing it in for a touchdown.

The extra point is good, and once more we're fully tied up—in the fourth quarter with three minutes counting down on the clock.

Green Bay calls a time-out, likely to throw us off our game, but we use the time game planning.

"McClane, you've been hot tonight. But you're getting double teamed almost every play. If you can get open, it's yours but you have to get open."

"Got it." Theo's face is hard with determination.

"Basset, I know you want a touchdown. Get open and make it happen, and I'll get you the ball." I nod. "We'll play you as a third receiver this drive. If there's a blitz the runners can play short pass. We need to move the ball."

The timer is counting down and we need to move back out on the field before we get penalized for delay of game.

"Avalanche on three."

"One, Two ,Three, Avalanche!" we shout in unison, taking our places along the line of scrimmage, ready to end this game on our terms.

We move slowly and methodically down the field, with short, quick passes guaranteed to connect and gain yards. Our three minutes slowly ticks by, and we're barely in field goal range when we hit the dreaded last two minutes of non-stop play.

We make it to the red zone with thirty seconds left on the clock. I take off as soon as we're set and Blaze has the ball. The receivers spread out as the lineman fight to protect the pocket, even as Blaze dodges the defensive tackle who slipped through.

I have space and look back to Blaze, who sees it too and the ball soars toward me the same moment the fullback changes direction.

I jump, and the world slows down around me. My fingers lock around the ball, pulling it from the air as I tuck it into my chest, landing on one foot then the other. As I pivot to start my run, I see, with horror, the two-man coverage that had been on Theo moments ago, both with a new target in mind. *Me.*

I lock eyes with Theo who drops back and to the outside as I continue forward, and as you can only do with someone you've known since childhood, I understand what he's suggesting.

I close my eyes for a fraction of a second, still letting the world move at a glacial pace around me and say goodbye to winning my bet as I secure the ball in my right hand, orienting my fingers along the laces, something I usually don't bother with. The stadium is silent around me, and I can hear my heartbeat ticking along.

As my eyes open, the world resumes a normal pace, catching up with me, and I let the ball fly parallel and back half a yard to the outside of the field where Theo now moves alone, with a free lane to run. And run he does.

All the way into the end zone.

The sound roars back to life around me as my teammates converge.

"You fucking dog!" Blaze screams at me as he hugs me from behind. "I thought you couldn't throw."

I laugh and pull myself free. "I can't really, not like you. But I have thrown a football before Meadows."

He cocks his head, listening to the radio communication in his helmet.

"We're going for two."

I glance at him shocked. I know the statistics, but stats aren't people. People don't make rational decisions. It's a much safer bet to go for the extra point and give us another shot in overtime than to risk everything on a final conversion.

But I'm not the coach, so I line up with the rest of the offense on the two-yard line.

Blaze drops back into the pocket, and I find a spot in the end zone, only one defenseman following me to my back corner. I box him out as the ball comes straight toward me—toward my knees more accurately—and I dive forward scooping it out of the air and twisting to land on my back. The ball is securely cradled to my chest leaving no room for a challenge or possibility of a flag.

I lay there, trying to catch my breath and it takes me a minute to realize we won.

We're going to the NFC Championship. And I had the final catch.

The game-winning catch.

A smile creeps onto my face of its own accord because it knows what I know. I think that will count as a score.

Theo stands above me, offering me a hand up and I take it. There's a camera right there, capturing the whole moment, and before I let my team congratulate me, I hold the ball up with one hand and point to where Lila sits. Blaze catches my eye as he jogs over to us and winks, and then the team converges, and I can't see anything but white jerseys and blue helmets. As if I would want to.

I get a media request which I barely sit still through, though the questions are much more positive than my last appearance.

"I really owe my performance today to my girlfriend," I announce. "She's my biggest supporter and without her I wouldn't have played like I did today." They love that. When my time is up, I rush through my shower and open my phone to see a few texts from Lila.

LILA

A win is a win.

I'm not sure that should really count as scoring, but since it was the game winning play AND you got the two-point conversion, I guess I don't mind.

I smile. How did I get so fucking lucky with this woman. I make quick work of booking a room for the night. There's no way

I'm waiting until I get home to see her, and we can ride back together in the morning.

> Room 314 at the Hyatt. You're on the reservation.

> I want you on your knees in nothing but my jersey when I get there.

I'm see her response as I'm getting dressed and wish I hadn't.

LILA

Yes sir.

My cock strains against the towel, and I pray no one is paying too close attention. I dress quickly and tell coach I'm not taking the plane home tonight. The Uber crawls along amidst the traffic away from the stadium until finally I see the hotel a few blocks away.

I hurry through the lobby and straight to the room.

> Coming up now.

There's still no response as I step off the elevator and move to unlock the door with my phone key.

"Lila?" I call out into the dark hotel room. There's no response, but there's music playing from where the bed must be further in. It's a corner room, and I can't see the bed from the door.

I drop my bag in the entryway, throwing off my coat. My hands pause on my belt before sliding the strap back into the loops. I kick off my shoes, my foot catching in a piece of fabric, and I have to catch myself against the wall, swearing. I snatch the scrap of offending lace and steady myself on the wall again for an entirely different reason.

Her fucking *panties*.

I fist them and feel the dampness still there, and my knees buckle. I bring my fist to my mouth to muffle my groan, and her scent fills my nose, the sweet musk hardening my cock painfully against my zipper. I inhale deeply and drop my fist, still clutching the panties. If Lila wants to play, I can fucking play.

I round the corner and stop stock still. Lila is reclined on the bedspread against the pillows. Her long legs bare, one knee bent enticingly and my jersey pooling around her hips. Her hair is loose around her face like a halo—my own personal angel, designed to bring me to my knees.

"I got your present," I say with a smirk, holding up the panties dangling off one finger.

"I thought you wanted me in nothing but your jersey." She lets her knee fall open, exposing a strip of pink flesh peeking out from beneath the hem of the jersey.

"I thought I also told you to be on your knees."

She smirks. "I've been thinking about that. You didn't really score, did you? I'm not sure it counts."

I'm not sure what the sound that comes out of my mouth is, but it takes me by surprise, though Lila's eyes darken with need.

I crook one finger toward me. "Come here."

She pushes up on her knees and crawls across the bed toward me, her bare ass swaying in the air. She waits at the end of the bed, her pupils blown wide with lust.

I lean forward, wrapping my hand around her throat and bringing my lips to her ear. "On. Your. Knees." I let my teeth graze the shell of her ear and squeeze my thumb and middle fingers against her pulse points. She swallows and slides off the bed, kneeling in front of me between my legs.

She leans into my hand, pressing it harder into her neck, and I slip my thumb around to cradle her cheek instead. She pouts, and I smirk down at her.

"You'll want all the air you can take right now, love." Her mouth drops open in surprise. "Take it out."

Her eyes drop to the tent in my jeans as she reaches up, slowly undoing my belt and dragging down my zipper. With my free hand I shove them down, kicking out of them leaving me standing in my boxers. She reaches in with one hand, pulling my weeping cock out, and I hiss as she squeezes it once. My hand moves from her cheek to her hair, and I tighten my grasp at the back of her neck.

"A deal is a deal, wouldn't you say?"

"Yes, sir." My dick twitches, and she smirks as she takes it in her hand. I grip the base, tapping it against her mouth, and she opens voluntarily her pink tongue poking out to lick the wetness off the crown.

"You know what we agreed on. Beg for it."

"Please fuck my mouth, Cal." I give her a moment to breathe and then give her what she wants, sliding deep into her wet, hot mouth until the head of my cock nudges the back of her throat and she gags.

I still, waiting for her to adjust, to breathe around me, and when she swallows, I groan at the constriction. But I need more.

I ease out slowly, pumping back in, savoring the feel of her mouth on me, her tongue as it swirls around the underside of my shaft.

"Fuck," I moan, my release building much too quickly for the amount of time she's actually been sucking me off. I tilt her head back, opening her throat and thrust forward faster, as she braces her hands on my thighs, letting me take what I need.

"Taking it so well. You love this, don't you? Getting your throat fucked?" She whimpers, her thighs rubbing together. "You can touch yourself, love."

She parts her knees, one hand leaving my leg to trail between her own as she circles her clit slowly. The vibration from her hum of pleasure rockets through me, building at the base of my spine, and I tighten my grip in her hair even further.

"Swallow for me like a good girl, yeah?" Her eyes meet mine, her free hand moving to cup my balls, and it doesn't take anything more before my release is spiraling through me, my spend shooting down her throat.

She swallows every drop, sucking me dry as she massages my balls. When I pull out, she licks her lips, and I swear I'm ready to go again, though my body didn't quite get the message as it begins to soften post-orgasm.

"Your turn," I say, pulling her to standing.

"Hang on." She puts a hand to my chest halting my move to kiss her.

"Love, I don't care," I laugh, attempting to find her mouth once more. Tasting my seed on her mouth isn't the worst thing I've ever done, and I'd rather kiss her than not.

"No, it's not that, I just want to talk to you before I forget."

I pull back with a sigh. "Seriously? Right now?" I motion between us."

"Well, you're on hold for a few minutes anyway." Her eyes flick toward my now flaccid dick.

"I can do other things you know," I deadpan.

"Yes," she mocks, patting my cheek twice. "And you're very good at them too."

I frown. "Your orgasms all were real, so I'd say yeah I'm pretty good."

"Seriously, Cal. I want to talk to you before we finish celebrating."

"So celebrating isn't off the table entirely tonight?"

"Cal," she starts.

"Okay, okay." I hold my hands up in surrender. "What do you want to talk about?" I pull up my boxer briefs and cross to the bed to sit down.

"You remember where we left the conversation about the job?"

Well, that's a great way to kill my mood. "Yes, vividly."

"I think I want to take it," she nearly whispers.

"You can't be serious."

"Do you really think it's that bad of an idea?"

Yes. No. I don't know. "Why do you want to take it?" I ask instead.

"I know it's more money, but that's not the main reason." I raise my eyebrows for her to continue. "I'd be basically running the division, and he wants to open a Chicago office, so it might be a lot of travel at first, but within the year, I'd be almost entirely full-time here."

"And you're interested in running a division?" I ask.

"Yeah, it's the equivalent of making partner, *and* what I was hoping to do with the promotion I got passed up for. And I could hand pick my team, build my own client profile, take on problems that are exciting and matter. I wouldn't be stuck in tech just because I'm actually young enough to know what Instagram is."

"It's going to take time to build the team and your client book."

"I know, but I think it'll be worth it. It's everything I've been looking for in my career. It's just attached to your father."

I suppress a sneer. "I can find a way to live with it if it's what you really want."

"I think we should talk about what it means for us."

My heart sinks, and it must show on my face because Lila immediately follows up with a reassurance. "Not like a 'I can't date you because I work for your dad,' but maybe just a mutual understanding that this is real? Because I don't think I can take it if we're not serious about this." She laughs bitterly. "I'm actually pretty sure he'd fire me on the spot if we broke up."

"Hey, you're definitely qualified for the job, it's not a handout."

"I know I'm qualified, but that doesn't mean there aren't a hundred other people waiting to take my place the moment the chance to prove myself is ripped away. It's about opportunity, not ability."

"I think you know how I feel about you at this point."

She glances up at me through her lashes. "Maybe, but it wouldn't hurt to have a bit more confirmation before I hit accept." Her cheeky grin gives her away.

I roll my eyes and pull her to me. "I love you." I shrug. "You're it for me. I don't see a life where you aren't right there with me. Where you go, I'll follow, even if it's to the ends of the earth."

"You're hot when you're confessing your love for me."

"Yeah?" I quirk an eyebrow at her. "That's what does it for you?"

She laughs. "It helps."

"If you want the job, take it. I don't have any plans to not be with you, so if you're sure this is what you want"—I motion between us—"don't let it stop you from taking everything else you want. I'll be here behind you for support every step of the way. We're a team."

"You don't feel like I'm taking your place at the family company, right? I know you never wanted the job, but it was always there with your name on it."

"You're the better pick for it. But no, even if you didn't take it, I wouldn't want it. I like playing football, and when it's time to retire, I'll find something else to do." I kiss her forehead, cradling her into my chest.

"You're sure?"

"One hundred percent. Maybe I'll become a full-time whale watcher and give tours."

She laughs but sits up and looks me squarely in the eye. "I'm taking the job."

"You know what this means right?"

"What?" Her face freezes in panic, and I laugh.

"We now have two things to celebrate." I yank her down and roll on top of her, pinning her to the bed with my hips.

"I guess we do." She smirks.

I work my hand between us and groan. "You're still soaked."

"Some of us didn't get to cum earlier," she pouts.

"Pardon me, ma'am. I'll rectify that immediately." She's wet enough, and I slide in easily, and this time, it feels like the last puzzle piece snapping into place.

The next couple weeks pass by in a blur of color and happiness as the Avalanche dominate Dallas in the NFC Championship, Katie and I screaming with delight in her apartment as we watch them play at the AT&T stadium in Texas, her dirty martini slopping down my back as she leaps into my open arms for a hug.

As we head into Super Bowl weekend to face off against Baltimore, I can tell the stress of it all is starting to weigh on Cal. But every time I bring it up, he brushes it off, saying he's just nervous, and hasn't played this far into post-season in his career.

He's getting ready to fly out to Tampa, where this year's game will be held when he holds up four tickets for me.

"For Sunday?" I ask.

"Yeah, I'm assuming you'll bring Katie, but I wanted to offer the other two since I know my parents won't come. You can invite your family if you want." He's providing a peace offering if I want to use it, and I love him more for it.

"I think I'd like to invite my dad." Even if I never speak to my mother again, I wouldn't want to lose my relationship with him. Cal nods, a knowing smile on his lips.

"Sounds good." He shrugs. "You don't have to, you can raffle them off for charity if you want, but I managed to get four so they're yours, however you want to use them. You're my family."

My heart swells, and I launch myself at him from where I sit on the couch. He drops the shoes he's packing to catch me and laughs.

"What's that for?" he asks, folding me into his chest as he drops a kiss to the top of my head.

"I just really like you."

"You only really like me?" he teases.

"Love and like are different. I can love you and not like you. Actually, I think that's pretty common, just look at both our families." He scoffs. "And you can obviously like someone and not love them. But to love someone as much as I love you and genuinely like who you are is pretty special, I think."

He pulls back to meet my gaze. "I think so too." He pressed a chaste kiss to my mouth. "And I really like you too."

I want to squeal. Something about this man just makes me want to be the absolute cringiest possible version of a 2000s romcom, and I can't stand it. But I also love it.

"Finish packing, I have some calls to make."

He grins, picking up the shoes. "Tell Katie I said hi."

● ● ●

"I can't go."

"What?" I ask, stunned and sure that I misheard her from the other end of the line.

"I'm sorry," Katie continues, "but I can't go to the Superbowl. I need to go to LA this weekend."

"Are you joking?"

"I wish I was." Her voice is quiet over the phone, like I'm on speaker and she's only half paying attention.

"Is everything okay? I know we haven't spent much time together lately, but we can do a girls' night next week as soon as I'm back from Tampa."

"Yeah, I'm good. That sounds nice. I could use a martini night." She sounds exhausted, and my stomach sinks with guilt for not knowing why.

"Consider it on the calendar." I force a laugh. "What's in LA?"

There's a pause on the other end of the line, and I wait it out. "My mom needs me, but it's okay. At least flights out there will be cheap with everyone flying east."

Kevin pokes his head into my office. "Lila, Colton's waiting in conference room B."

I nod at him, standing and grabbing my laptop from its docking station.

"What's wrong with your mom Katie?"

"It's nothing I can't handle, I promise."

I sigh. "But you know you don't have to, right? Not on your own."

"Yeah, I know."

"Okay." I nod at Kevin who's waving at me through the window to my office. "I have to go. But call me if you need me. I'll see you when I'm back."

"Bye babe." She hangs up, and I frown down at my phone. I haven't been the best friend in the last few weeks, so overwhelmed with Cal and our budding relationship, the playoffs, and getting ready to start my new job.

I see Sadie at her desk and make a quick detour. Colton can wait three more minutes.

"Hey, are you busy this weekend?"

She grins up at me. "Oh yes, actually. Our band got booked for two weddings back-to-back. Isn't it awesome?"

"Sadie, that's great," I say and mean it, even if she's unavailable to come to Tampa.

"I know, right?" She shakes her head in disbelief. "Oh, while you're here," she drops her voice to a whisper, and I lean in. "I put together a list of clients we might want to consider taking with us. I think I might have found a loophole in the non-compete."

Sadie had been my first hire for the Chicago branch of Basset Holdings; Kevin was second. Clearly it was the right move.

"You're incredible. Can you send it to Kevin so he can get the paperwork started?"

"Yup, will do." I smile, my heels click-clacking against the hardwood flooring as I make my way down the hall.

"What's up with you?" Colton asks lightly as I enter the glass conference room.

I shrug, an idea taking shape in my mind. The offer is out of my mouth before I can think about the consequences. "Hey, do you want to come to the Super Bowl?"

His mouth drops open for a full five seconds. I know because I count them.

"Are you serious?" He glances around wildly. "Am I being punked?"

I roll my eyes. "That show hasn't aired in years."

He narrows his eyes at me.

"Yes, I'm serious. Katie can't go, and Sadie's busy, so I have an extra ticket."

"Oh my god, you *are* serious."

"Do you want to come or not?" I snap.

"Of course I want to come. I'd do your paperwork for a month to come."

"This is probably a good time to tell you I'm resigning. So, you'll be doing it anyway, at least for the clients who don't follow me, but good to know."

It's a full seven seconds this time, and I smirk, waiting for the words to process in his mind.

"You're leaving?"

"Yup." I accentuate the *p* sound, smacking my lips together.

"Well damn, and here I was starting to enjoy working with you."

I grin, because he's grown on me too.

"So, the Super Bowl?"

"Abso-fucking-lutely. I'll book my flight right now."

True to his word our meeting starts approximately ten minutes later after he's secured a ticket for the following afternoon to Florida.

"Let me get this straight." Cal says in a flat tone. "You're bringing the guy you used to not be able to stand, instead of Katie, or literally anyone else, to the biggest game of my career."

I cringe, grateful he can't see me through the phone. "He's not been so bad lately. And Katie can't go, she has to fly to LA, and it kinda slipped out."

"Fine," he says with a sigh. "I said they were your tickets. I'm not going to be annoyed at how you use them."

"I know, it was kind of an accident. But it'll be fun," I say with false cheer as I gnaw on my bottom lip.

I swear I can hear his eyes rolling.

"I think he'll get along well with my dad and Alex."

His voice softens. "I'm proud of you for inviting them."

"Thanks," I say quietly. I'm a bit proud of myself too honestly. "They're both so excited."

"I can't wait to see you tomorrow, Tampa kind of sucks." I can hear laughter in the background and smile, because even with his teammates and friends, my man misses me.

"I'll be there soon. And I'll be there to meet you on the field after you win the Super Bowl."

"Don't jinx it."

I laugh. "The jinx can't hurt you when you've got the talent."

"I have to go. We're watching film all day today. Love you."

"Love you too."

⬤ ⬤ ⬤

The heat is nearly unbearable as I step out of the airport in Tampa the day before the Super Bowl.

"Wow, I thought I'd at least be fine with a hoodie. It's February," Alex complains, stripping his Avalanche sweatshirt off in favor of an Avalanche t-shirt underneath.

"You really went full out, didn't you?" I mutter.

"Hey, it's a lifestyle."

"I'd think you'd be more decked out in gear yourself since you're dating a player," challenges my dad, wearing a matching hoodie to the one Alex just took off. He removes his glasses, foggy with humidity and wipes them clean.

"I can't believe you got matching sweatshirts." I roll my eyes.

"We offered to get you one too," Alex defends himself, and I laugh.

"Katie would kill me if I was on national TV in a hoodie." He shrugs in response as my dad flags down a cab.

"Kayla didn't text you at all while we were in the air, did she?" he asks, nervously looking at his phone.

"No, why?"

"What if the baby comes early?"

I roll my eyes, but my dad responds before I can.

"Son, if she was that close to making me a grandpa, neither of us would be here right now." He claps his son-in-law on the shoulder. "Now get in, I'm sure Lila has some event to get ready for tonight." He winks at me over the roof of the car as I slide into the backseat, leaving my suitcase for them to heft into the trunk.

● ● ●

I'm nearly ready for my first official girlfriend-of-the-player event —as long as you don't count the gala, which I'm not. It's not an officially sponsored event, but Maggie texted me this morning and asked to meet up, so we'll at least grab some drinks and maybe meet some of the other players' plus-ones.

I'm just putting on a final dab of perfume when she's knocking on my hotel door.

"Coming," I call out, hopping on one foot as I tug the zipper up my bootie.

I throw open the door to find not Maggie but Cal, in an extremely poor attempt at a disguise: sunglasses and a baseball hat pulled low over his forehead.

I burst out laughing, and his eyes narrow. "What are you wearing?"

"I didn't want to get followed," he mumbles, pushing past me into my room.

"What are you, a superhero?" He pouts at me, and I sober myself. "Are you allowed to be here?"

"Good to see you too."

"Oh, shut up." I hug him, and he presses his mouth to mine before I pull away, yanking the Yankees cap off his head. "Of course I'm happy to see you. But I thought you had to stay with the team."

"Yeah, we're supposed to for security. No one's allowed into the training facility, the field, or the hotel if they're not staff or players. Even the press has to do their interviews in an off-site pop-up."

I stare at him, attempting to determine a point in that sentence but not finding a single one.

"They unofficially gave us a few hours before dinner to see our families, since we won't see them before the game."

"Oh, that was nice of them." I press another kiss to his lips. "I *am* glad you're here, I just wasn't expecting you."

His eyes skim my outfit. "Are you going somewhere?"

"I was going to meet Maggie for drinks in about twenty minutes. I think we're going out with some of the other partners of the team."

"That sounds fun. I'm glad you're getting to know some of them. Maggie's great, she was a few years behind us in school but always a good laugh."

"Yeah, I wonder if they'll want to push back drinks if the other players also got a chance to sneak away."

"I'm not sure many of them did."

"Really? You're playing in the Super Bowl tomorrow and some of them didn't want to see their wives?" I flush. "Not that I'm your wife or anything."

"I know what you mean. But security is tight, and a lot of the guys are more recognizable than me, I'm not sure the Marvel disguise would work for everyone."

I laugh. "Yeah, probably not."

"There are people lining the streets of the hotel we're staying in, screaming, and there's so many you can't even understand what they're trying to say. It's kind of a lot," he mutters. "Where are you meeting Maggie?"

"The lobby, she's staying across the street."

"I'll walk you down then."

"Hang on," I say, as he heads for the door. "I still have fifteen minutes if you want to just relax for a minute."

His mouth quirks up at the side, before he flops down on the king-sized bed. "Come lay with me."

I pull off my booties and lay carefully down beside him, pulling my curled hair out of the way before he loops an arm around my waist.

"Are you ready?" I ask.

"For tomorrow?" I nod.

"I don't know," he admits.

"What do you mean?"

"At some level, it's just another game. Fans will fill the stadium, they'll cheer, the winner will celebrate, the loser will go home." He pauses, and his chest expands behind me as he takes a deep breath. "On another level, it's *the* game. The biggest football game in the world, with millions of people watching. So many people want tickets that the *starting* price is thousands of dollars. If we win, I get a diamond ring that's basically priceless, and I'll forever be a Super Bowl winner."

He takes a deep breath. "If we lose, it'll be one of the most devastating losses of my career, which is crazy because that meant we had to be the best in the conference to even get here in the first place."

I brush my hand through his hair, and my heart clenches at his vulnerability.

"I've been watching film of old games, and almost every single game you can pinpoint the single play that made or broke the team. Sometimes it's an interception or even a pick-six. Sometimes it's a one-handed jump catch into the end zone. Sometimes it's as simple as a lineman moving three inches before the snap. It's not just the better team that wins. The game is decided by several tiny moves that add up to the biggest win of a season." He closes his eyes and pulls me close, burrowing his face in my shoulder.

"Everyone wants to have the once-in-a-lifetime catch for the winning touchdown, but so many more are the cause of a holding penalty or a false start on third down, costing the time of the entire drive. I don't want to be that guy."

His voice is rough toward the end, and I can sense the true fear coursing through him.

"You won't be."

"But what if I am?" It's too earnest to not be the reason he's here.

"Okay, what if you are?"

"What happens if I'm traded? Or the entire city turns against me?"

"Well even if the entire Chicagoland area decided they hated you, you'd still have me. And I think Katie and Theo would agree with me, and that makes three of us in your corner."

"What if they trade me?"

"We'll figure it out, Cal."

"You love Chicago, though. I can't ask you to move."

"First of all, you're not. You still play for the Avalanche. Secondly, I didn't say I'd move. There are players who live full-time in the offseason somewhere else. You could get an apartment in the new city and live permanently in Chicago." He opens his mouth to object, and I hold up a finger to silence him. "And thirdly, I do love Chicago. I loved growing up near the city, and I love being downtown as an adult." I pause and pull away to force him to look at me. "But I love *you* more. We would figure it out, okay? And you won't be playing forever so if we have to move to Texas or North Carolina or something for a few years while you play out your contract before we move back, we can talk about it."

I smirk ."Just please not New York, I hate New York."

He chuckles and presses a kiss to my forehead.

"I love you."

"Mmm," I hum.

We lay there for the rest of the time we have in a comfortable silence, just enjoying each other's company. When it's time, Cal helps me zip up my booties and dons his hat before ushering me out to the hotel lobby.

B *EEEP. BEEEP. BEEEP.*

I groan, turning off the alarm blaring from my phone, though the cadence continues through the pounding of my head. I roll out of bed, nearly falling to the floor when my feet get tangled in the sheet, but I finally make it to the bathroom.

It's not a pretty sight. I have drool crusted on my cheek, uneven, worn-off pink lip stain across my mouth, and smudged eyeliner that Ke$ha would be proud of. At least my curls from last night are still intact, even if it's in a boho beachy, Serena from *Gossip Girl* way.

I'll need to seriously step up my game if I'm going to keep up with the other women, even though most of them have the advantage of being in their mid-twenties, so they're still able to process a hangover in one day, which helps.

Drunk me gave me a bit of a head start last night though, setting out a bottle of ibuprofen and another of Pedialyte right beside my water cup on the dresser. I take the pills and drink the entire glass of water before refilling it and drinking another half.

I let the water in the shower heat up as I order breakfast from room service, having missed the outrageous complimentary stations this morning in favor of sleep.

I step out, feeling not amazing but still much better with a clean face and a reduced headache as the ibuprofen kicks in. I settle on a navy sweat set since I have several hours before game time, and sit on my bed, towel wrapped around my head, scrolling through my missed notifications as I wait for my food.

MAGGIE

Hope you're feeling okay this morning, I knew those last two drinks were a mistake.

If I don't hear from you by one, I'm coming to get you.

I check the clock and it's barely eleven, but I text her anyway.

I'm alive, don't worry.

Her response is instantaneous.

MAGGIE

Oh great. How ya feeling?

Hungover

But fine, just showered and ordered food.

The knock at my door speaks to the arrival of said food.

I grab the tray from the server, handing him a ten-dollar bill, and open the lids on the dishes to reveal a bowl of fruit and wheat toast. I take a piece of toast and go through the rest of my messages, sending an extra to Cal for good luck since they start warm-ups in only a couple hours.

I savor the iced coffee, feeling more refreshed by the minute.

DAD

Want to meet for lunch? Just us. There's a diner with good Yelp reviews a few blocks over.

> Yeah, I need like an hour though. I just got out of the shower.

> I'll meet you in the lobby.

Fifty-five minutes later, I'm sitting in the hotel lobby, my hair dry and straight down my back with my face mostly bare save for sunscreen, dressed in jean shorts and an Avalanche T-shirt. I probably won't get recognized, but if I do, I should wear something team oriented.

Dad steps off the elevator wearing a vintage Avalanche tee and smiles as he sees me waiting for him.

"Ready?"

I stand. "Yep. Did you get settled in okay last night?"

"Oh yeah. Alex is still worried about Kayla, but he caught sight of some players on the news out and about so he's spending the day camping out by the training facility until it's time to head over to the field."

I roll my eyes as he holds the door open for me.

"I wanted to have lunch just the two of us anyway though."

"Oh?"

"Yeah."

He's silent for a moment as if he's choosing the exact right words.

"I wanted to talk about Christmas."

I feel the burn of my coffee in the back of my throat.

"No, Dad. I don't want to—"

"I want to apologize."

I blink at him shocked. "What?"

"I want to apologize. What your mom said was out of line, but I won't apologize for her. You two have your own relationship, you can work it out if you want to." He takes a deep breath through his nose, closing his eyes for the duration of the inhale and when he opens them to meet mine, they're lined with silver.

"But you're *my* daughter Lila. You made me a father. You're one of the most important people in the world through my eyes, and I'm supposed to protect you. I failed."

"Dad, you didn't—" My voice comes out choked, and I have to stop to clear my throat.

"I did. You were hurt, right there in front of me, and I did nothing. Hell, I even likely contributed, and I'm sorry."

"I love you, Dad."

"I love you too, Lila, and I hope you can forgive me for the role I played."

"Of course I forgive you." I lean forward and wrap my arms around his middle.

He ruffles my hair like he used to, and we head into the small diner together, my heart lighter than it's been in years.

The diner is everything I'd hoped for, with beer-battered fries and flavor-filled smash burgers. A comfortable sense of déjà vu comes over me as my dad chats happily about the new book he's been reading, an epic science fiction world he found at the library last weekend.

Alex meets us in the lobby once we're back, his face pink and voice hoarse from cheering with the crowd.

"Did you see anyone?" my dad asks, shaking his head.

"Just some of the staff, but no players."

"They're kind of intentionally hiding," I say, pressing the button for the elevators.

"Why?"

I roll my eyes at his absolutely devastated face.

"Are you kidding? It's annoying and hugely invasive to wait outside the facility like that."

"But we're just cheering them on."

"Half of you are. The other half are jeering."

"Well, but it's important," he argues, confused.

I hold the doors open as they ding for my floor. "It's really not. I know it's exciting, but at the end of the day it's just a game."

I step out of the elevator, ignoring his flabbergasted expression.

"See you at 4:30." Dad says as the elevator doors close, and I nod.

◉ ◉ ◉

My mascara keeps clumping, and I swear to God I'm going to lose it. But if I cry, I'll ruin the rest of my makeup too—the painstaking blending that went into a daytime smokey eye courtesy of several year-old Jaclyn Hill tutorials. I cannot cry today.

This is Cal's day. He's playing in the fucking Super Bowl, and my only job is to cheer him on. That, and hopefully not look like a drowned raccoon on the Jumbotron or in front of millions of people watching at home.

I take a deep breath and clean off the wand with micellar water, wiping it dry and brush out the lashes clumped together. It's not professionally done, but it's passable and that's really the goal at this point. Maybe I can just wear sunglasses the whole time, and no one will notice.

It's 4:30 on the dot when I leave my hotel room, dressed in a one-of-a-kind dress I bought from an Etsy shop. It's made from one of Cal's jerseys pieced together and paired with my trusted leather booties. My dad and Alex are waiting in the lobby for me, both wearing Avalanche jerseys.

"Ready?" I ask, my heels clicking on the marble floor.

They stand, and together we walk toward the stadium, funneling in with the hundreds of others going early to the game to see warm-ups.

We circle the stadium to find our private entry and find Colton waiting at the door. I scan our tickets, the stadium employees directing us up to the suite level and toward our box.

We're the first to arrive, which I'm immediately grateful for when Alex squeals at the spread of food available.

"Alex, don't be such a boy," I scold, rolling my eyes but I can't keep the smirk off my face.

"Lila, I know you've been in and out of suites all season. But I've never been in a box. And this is the *Super Bowl!* I'm not just excited, I'm fucking *pumped*."

I open my mouth to reply and just sigh, pouring myself a drink from the shelf of liquor along the back wall. He's right, it is exciting.

I settle into a seat in the front row and search the field of players below for number eighty-five, a strange feeling washing over me as he runs drills with the other players.

"You know if you fog up the glass drooling over your man the rest of us won't be able to see," Alex jokes as he takes the seat next to me, his plate piled high with chicken fingers. I snatch one from the top and bite into it.

"Hey," he protests.

"I'm the reason you're here," I sing-song back at him. My dad chuckles as he sits down on Alex's other side.

"How's Kayla?" I ask, polishing off the tender.

"She's good. She and your mom took a walk today up to the park and back, but no contractions or anything yet."

"You know she's only thirty-six weeks, right? She's not like ready to pop any minute."

"The doctor said it could be anytime now," he says defensively.

"If that baby is anything like his mother, he'll be too stubborn to come out before both his parents are solidly in the same state, don't worry," Dad says, effectively ending the argument before it could begin.

The suite door opens, and Maggie's platinum blonde head pops in.

"Lila?"

"Down here," I call, standing and waving her over.

"Oh, thank God. Soldier Field is so much easier to figure out."

"You can't possibly mean that. Have you ever tried to leave an event with thirty-thousand people all trying to make it through the one tunnel under Lake Shore Drive?"

She snorts. "Fair enough. What are you drinking?"

I nod to the bar. "Whatever you want."

She makes us both a drink and plops down on the other side of me, handing me a cup with a chocolate chip cookie balanced on the top. Colton slides into a seat behind us, his own plate filled with food from the buffet.

"Do you see him anywhere?" she asks, scanning the field.

I point to Theo, standing near Cal in the end zone.

"Hmm." She purses her lips but doesn't say anything, almost as if it wasn't her brother she was looking for.

I narrow my eyes at her, but drop it for now, turning back as the players start another round of stretches.

Over the next hour, the suite fills with other players' families. Blaze's mother sits next to Maggie, an act that, for whatever reason, has Maggie looking terrified.

The players return to their locker rooms as the stadium begins to fill up and celebrity after celebrity flashes up on the Jumbotron. I stifle a laugh at the outfits that some of the social media influencers are wearing.

Maggie slaps my arm when I snort at one Instagram model wearing head-to-toe denim like she's Britney Spears circa 2001. But as iconic as Britney is, it was still hard to pull off on her.

"Stop, at least she didn't make her boyfriend match."

"What are you girls laughing at?" Mrs. Meadows asks.

"Nothing, just caught the giggles." Maggie sobers instantly.

"Can I get you another drink?" I ask, gesturing to Mrs. Meadows's nearly empty glass of white wine.

"Please." She hands me her glass, before turning to Maggie. "Now tell me about you, sweetie. A pretty young thing like you must have a vibrant life."

I laugh as I head to refill her wine, chatting with some of the other family members now packing the box full with excited energy.

"Hey," Colton says, pulling me to the side on my way back to my seat.

"What?"

"Thanks for inviting me. I know we haven't always been on great terms."

I level him with a look.

"Okay, I know I was kind of a dick to you for a long time. So, I appreciate the olive branch, and I know you're leaving the firm, but if you ever need anything." He holds out his hand, and I roll my eyes, pulling him in for a hug.

"Just don't be a dick to any of the other women in the office, and we'll call it even."

He grimaces. "Deal."

"And let me know if James passes you up for another promotion. We might have room for one more." He grins at me.

"Deal," he echoes.

I get back to my seat right as the team runs out onto the field, the crowd cheering wildly and me right along with them as I spot Cal in the middle of the pack.

The national anthem is sung by an up-and-coming country artist named Bryan Campbell. Baltimore wins the coin toss, and the clock starts its first countdown of the night.

The box erupts in cheers when our defense holds them to only a single field goal on the first drive of the game.

"They have one of the best quarterbacks in the league," my dad says knowingly. "Cutting off their momentum early on is key if we want a win tonight."

I can only nod as the offense takes the field, Cal lining up at the far side.

Theo has the first catch for the Avalanche, a near-perfect pass from Blaze that picks up an easy six yards. The rest of the drive doesn't go as well since we can't make it within field goal range, giving Baltimore the ball back. They make quick work of their next opportunity, scoring off a beautiful thirty-yard pass straight into the end zone and leaving us in a ten-point deficit in only the first quarter.

The energy on the field matches the energy in the box when the offense jogs back onto the field. Tension lines the players' faces as the Jumbotron zooms in on Blaze and a few of the key players, Cal included.

They manage to make it within field-goal range this time, bringing us within one score as the first quarter comes to a close.

"Damn," Alex says quietly checking his phone.

"They'll get it back. It's only one score behind."

"No, that's not it."

"Kayla?" My head snaps up at him.

"No, sorry, it's just the guys. We have a squares bet going on."

I roll my eyes, focusing back on the game in front of me as Baltimore drives down the field once more, their running back nearly unstoppable against our linebackers. They get another field goal, bringing us back to a two-score game.

Theo makes a superb one-handed catch to start the next drive off, immediately gaining the first down. Cal makes a great block on the next play, letting the running back through a gap and gaining us another four yards.

"Yes!" I cheer, as they set up along the line for the next down, moving methodically down the field and into field-goal range.

Cal snags the ball out of the air on second down, bringing us into the red zone. I swear the entire box holds its breath as Theo brings in the catch, both sets of toes touching the ground before he falls out of bounds. Maggie screams as her brother gets his first Super Bowl touchdown, and I join in while the Jumbotron moves from his celebration to our box.

Baltimore gets the ball back and drives down the field, bringing in another touchdown, and with only thirty seconds on the clock yet, we only get one down and a Hail Mary that goes wide before halftime is called.

While we might still be down by ten points, everyone is excited for the halftime show, which is featuring a popular K-pop boy band that must have been the choice of one of the commissioners' granddaughters. Regardless of who chose the group, they bring the energy, and the crowd sings along to their most popular hit, "Game Day," which spent entirely too long on the radio last summer.

We start with the ball going into the second half, and they come out on fire, moving down the field as a trained unit with Blaze sliding into the end zone like he was built for it.

"Praise the Lord!" Mrs. Meadows shouts clutching a rosary I didn't even realize she was wearing, as Maggie's cheers echo the loudest throughout the box.

Our defense comes out strong too, forcing a field goal once again but keeping it within a one-score game in the second half. The third quarter passes quickly with neither team able to get anything on the scoreboard.

We start with the ball going into the fourth quarter. Fifteen minutes, and the Super Bowl will be over. Well fifteen football minutes, so more like an hour.

We use seven of those precious minutes on our first drive but can't convert the third down at the thirty-yard line.

We'll likely only get one more drive, and it won't be very long, but Chicago's coach calls a time-out. After thirty seconds, instead of sending in special teams, the offense takes the field again, going for fourth and three in the most important game of their careers. Theo snatches it out of the air but is hit mid-air and knocked out of bounds.

The yellow flag is thrown, and fans are screaming at the dirty hit as he slowly gets to his feet, cringing, only to go straight to the sidelines. A receiver I don't recognize comes on the field as Baltimore takes a penalty, giving us the first down.

I grip Maggie's hand. "He's okay, he'll be okay." She only nods, her eyes glued to the front of the blue medical tent.

The new receiver makes the catch, tying the game up. Once more, special teams stays on the sidelines as we choose to go for two. I groan, hiding my face in my hands, while peeking through my fingers as the ball sails through the air and onto the ground.

"Why would they go for two? We were already tied," my dad grumbles.

Baltimore takes the ball back with seven minutes left. We all watch with bated breath as they slowly work their way down the field, intentionally taking up as much time as possible on each drive, nearly running out the clock each down so we can't get the ball back.

Every Chicago fan is screaming their support for our defense as time and time again Baltimore gets their first downs. My stomach sinks like a lead weight when they finally make it to field goal range, nearly at the final two-minute mark. They keep lining up, because why would they chance a field goal further than they need to.

They call a time-out once they reach the twenty-five, their coach and quarterback nearly yelling at each other on the sidelines, and it doesn't take a genius to understand why when their special teams unit jogs onto the field. Their kicker bounces on his toes.

"We won't have enough time," Alex says tightly.

I can't tear my eyes from the field as the kick is good, bringing Baltimore back in the lead by a measly three points.

"One more Hail Mary throw. Blaze can do it."

Theo limps onto the field, throwing a towel at the trainer on his way and sending the other receiver off the field.

"Can he do that?" Maggie asks.

"Uhm, well, I think he just did." I nearly laugh as the entire coaching staff crosses their arms in disapproval, though they leave him on the field.

The ball finds a second receiver first, then the running back. It looks like we might have a chance, even as we hit the final two minutes.

I don't even notice I'm standing until Mrs. Meadows yanks me back.

"Sit. We're all nervous, but you don't need your face pressed against the glass."

I sit on the very edge of my seat, my knee bouncing as I keep one eye on the game clock and one on the play happening on the field below me. Cal makes a fantastic catch, gaining another twelve yards before he's pulled down.

We're down to less than a minute with thirty yards to go until we're in field goal range, and that's just for a tie. Blaze sends a long pass, which flies wide past the second receiver, still held up with the cornerback tailing him.

We only have time for one, maybe two more quick plays with a lot of yards to cover. I hold my breath and squeeze Maggie's hand.

Blaze goes for a short pass this time, straight to the running back, who's brought down quickly. They line up for potentially the last time, Blaze sending it long to where Theo's waiting hands should be, but the Baltimore cornerback gets there first, snatching the ball from just in front of Theo and bringing it down.

The cheer from the Baltimore end of the field is deafening, even as their offense takes the field, lining up in victory formation.

I have eyes only for one player, who is currently making his way down to the end of the bench on our sideline, finding an empty spot toward the end and hanging his head.

My heart hurts for him, especially as the cheers for Baltimore swell to a decibel yet unknown to humankind when the purple confetti rains down on the field.

Cal gets up after only a few moments, congratulating his

opponents, the new Super Bowl champions, and then helping Theo off the field and onto the cart which takes them out of sight into the locker room.

"I need to see him." I stand, as if I can run right this second.

A field employee opens the door just then to announce we can wait here or follow him to the family waiting area downstairs. I bolt toward him, dragging Maggie behind me, our hands still clasped together.

I don't realize we have an entourage following us until Colton calls for us to slow down.

We only need to wait a few minutes before the players start trickling into the room, many un-showered and still in their uniforms. Several reporters follow us into the room, which feels more than a little predatory.

Theo is the first one out, clutching at his ribs. Maggie rushes him but stops short as she sees the pain etched across his face.

"Shouldn't you be getting medical attention somewhere?" she asks, smacking his free arm.

"Well, maybe if you'd stop hitting me." He glances around at the small group of us,—his sister, my brother and dad, Colton, and Mrs. Meadows.

"Blaze will be out soon I think, he had to talk to Coach first." He tells the older woman.

"Thank you."

His eyes take on a strange glint when he takes in Colton. "I don't think we've met, how did you get down here?"

"I—uh." Colton looks at me for help.

I laugh. "Katie couldn't make it, so I invited Colton. Colton Varga, Theo McClane."

"How'd you like the game?"

"You played great. That hit looked bad."

Theo shrugs. "Want to see the bruise?"

Before anyone can answer, he lifts his shirt, flashing his

impressive set of abdominal muscles one side of his ribs already covered in a molted purple bruise.

"Ouch." I wince. "Hey, did you see Cal in there?"

"He should've been right behind me." He turns toward the doors, and I peer around him.

I spot a blonde head and beeline for Cal. He catches me as I throw myself into him.

"I love you, you played so well," I whisper to him, clutching him to me.

His answering sigh doesn't instill much confidence.

"Basset," one of the reporters starts, and I turn to them with murder in my eyes. "Uhm, I'll wait over here for you, shall I?" He laughs nervously but backs up several paces.

I turn us so his back is to the room, reporter included.

"Are you okay?"

"Lila," his voice cracks. "We just lost the Super Bowl."

"I know. But it's not your fault."

"You sure you still want me?" He laughs nervously, but I know it's not really a joke to him.

"I'm not going anywhere, Cal. I'm right here."

He takes a deep breath, hugging me tightly, before pulling back and turning to face the reporter, lacing our fingers tightly together.

"Tough game out there, Basset."

He waits silently for a question.

"Do you think you could've made that catch?"

"I don't know."

"Do you think McClane could've made that catch if he wasn't injured?"

"I don't know."

"Well at least tell me what's next for you."

"Tonight? I'm going to spend some time with my girl." He looks down at me and smiles. "And then we'll get back to work. And we'll be back."

CAL

One Year Later

We're down one point with minutes to go, and Coach calls for a two-point conversion.

Blaze looks at me. "Ready?"

"Today? Definitely."

"Two, forty-three, mission five!" he yells as Thompson, our center, hikes the ball.

I take off, and time slows down, the sound of the crowd muting to a dull whine. I'm sprinting to the far corner of the end zone and leap up to catch the pass, stretching to get both toes in the paint. The sound in the stadium comes back with a vengeance as our score rises by two, and we're back in the lead with forty seconds of the Super Bowl left.

The defense miraculously holds, and the crowd is screaming even louder than before.

We turn as one team toward the scoreboard.

PITTSBURGH: 21 — CHICAGO: 22

The announcers voice, barely heard above the roar of the stadium, proclaims, "The Chicago Avalanche win their first Super Bowl of the millennia!"

I take in the win, my teammates around me doing the same as the confetti rains down in blue and silver. The overwhelming elation is nothing to what it'll be in a few minutes though.

"Hey, Coach," I call, jogging toward him. "I think you have something of mine?" He pulls a small velvet box from his pocket and passes it over.

"Congratulations, man. Go get her." He pulls me into a hug, slapping my back twice before releasing me with a shove toward the tunnel where the friends and family of the team are pouring onto the field. I pop open the box, taking in the large cushion cut diamond before snapping it shut and eyeing the tunnel the families will be funneling through any moment.

I spot her, golden hair flying wild in the wind, surrounded by both her parents and mine. Her mom smiles wide as she holds her grandson and waves his little hand at me. My mother is beaming, unperturbed for the first time by being surrounded by Americans, holding hands with my father, who can barely contain the smirk that threatens to become a full-on grin. Lila's bundled up in a vintage Avalanche jacket and a hat with my number knit into the side, radiating joy.

It's time to get my girl.

ACKNOWLEDGMENTS

I have so many people to thank for this book, but first to myself. You freaking did it?!

First, to one of my best friends in this world, and fellow author, Hannah Danielle. I couldn't have done this without you. Your support and help along the way has made it possible to bring The False Start into the world and I'm so grateful to have you by my side in this adventure. Love you <3

To my dad, for proofreading the book and not judging the spice and providing fun marketing tools along the way, you're the dad every girl should grow up with but only we got to. Thanks for loving me always.

To Sam, my biggest cheerleader and future assistant, your support and excitement has kept me going on even the days I can't spell my own title correctly. I look forward to returning the favor soon ;)

To my Beta Readers: Natalie, Tori, Lauren, Jana, Sara, TC, Liv, Maddie, Natalie, and Anne, thank you for reading the roughest of drafts and not completely tearing it to shreds. I'm grateful for every bit of feedback and it has helped make a book I'm quite proud of.

For my real life coworkers, thank you for letting your favorite personality hire do something even more outside the box than usual and being some of my loudest cheerleaders along the way.

And to you, my readers. Thank you for making this dream a reality. I appreciate each and every one of you, and hope both sides of your pillow are always cold.

ABOUT THE AUTHOR

Lillian Lyle is an indie romance author living in Chicago. She's a lover of sports and romance and prefers to fall into a good book rather than for a mediocre man on Hinge. When she's not nose to the keyboard in a local coffee shop — or hiding her AO3 tags from the public view — she's slaving away in an excel spreadsheet for her day job.